Villains Valiant
The Fight For Survival

Peter A.R. Surtees

Grosvenor House
Publishing Limited

The right of Peter A.R. Surtees to be identified as the author of this
work has been asserted in accordance with Section 78
of the Copyright, Designs and Patents Act 1988

This book is published by
Grosvenor House Publishing Ltd
Link House
140 The Broadway, Tolworth, Surrey, KT6 7HT.
www.grosvenorhousepublishing.co.uk

This book is a work of fiction. Any resemblance to
people or events, past or present, is purely coincidental.

A CIP record for this book
is available from the British Library

ISBN 978-1-83975-969-7

Acknowledgements

To John West and Alan Harris, journalists with *The Coventry Telegraph*, who encouraged me to continue with my writing.

To Steve Chaplin. I'd like to thank for his advice and expert knowledge on coal mining procedures, particularly the workings at the coal face.

To Bedworth, "The Town That Never Forgets", where I wrote this book and drew inspiration for one of its characters.

Dedications

Firstly, I'd like to dedicate this book to my grandfather, Johnathon Copson, coal miner and soldier, who lost his life bravely fighting for his country on the Somme in 1916.

Secondly, to coal miners, past and present everywhere, who've risked their lives toiling underground in the cold and darkness, to give us warmth and light.

Thirdly, to our beloved grandson, Toby, who brought life, love and laughter to us all, but sadly is no longer with us. Rest well, dear Tobes, we all love and miss you very much, and will never forget you.

Finally, to our much-loved daughter Helen, who although no longer with us here on earth, will remain in our hearts forever.

Prologue

Although a book of fiction, events which occurred in the Korean War and the war in French Indochina have been included, to blend in with our story and the part its characters played in it.

Events written about the struggles in Southern Africa, although fictitious, have a certain resemblance to actual events which happened in that troubled and unsettled part of the continent.

The London Gang Wars were another feature brought into our story by the author although seeming very harsh and brutal, similar occurrences did transpire in real life.

The training and general life of recruits in the French Foreign Legion, although harsh and austere, was, in actual fact, the norm during that part of the century – the 1950s. In reality, some may claim Legion life was much tougher than that portrayed in this book.

The retreat from Na San in northern Vietnam was an actual event, and most incidents described by the author actually happened. He has used the actual siege, and subsequent withdrawal, to set in motion a chain of events which bring danger and realism to the plot.

The brutal conditions and horrific events in the Viet Minh prisons were no exaggeration of the general practices experienced by the hapless prisoners at the hands of their cruel tormentors. In fact, once more, some ex-prisoners might describe them as worse.

Death cannot be taken lightly, and the author, whilst realising this, has done his best to inject a little humour – mostly dark – to soften the blow and make the story more palatable to the reader.

The four main characters in this story had a dark past, and if justice was to be served, they needed some kind of punishment or retribution to pay for their iniquities. However, the fair-minded reader, after reading of their privation and adversity, might agree they'd suffered enough for their transgressions, and deserved deliverance, as opposed to retribution. However, the author has left this deliberation entirely in the hands of the readers, who after reading this inspiring story of evasion, capture and escape, may draw their own conclusions.

It may be a little confusing with the names and new identities given when joining the Legion, but to avoid confusion, the author has kept the characters' first names very similar to their real ones. Example; Jorge instead of George, and Frank and Eddie instead of Franco and Eduardo. Paddy remained the same.

The story begins well into the late 1970s, but reverts back to the early part of the century, and the beginning of the real adventure, and how and why these four comrades in arms came to be together. I really hope you enjoy this fine book... I know I did!

Preface

Whilst traveling home to England on the overnight train from Berne in Switzerland to Gare de Lyon in Paris, I shared my compartment with three legionnaires who were returning to Paris after a short furlough.

I'd been living for three months in Yverdon with a Swiss family, on an exchange programme organised with my school. I was there to improve my French, whilst my opposite number lived with my family to improve his English.

Being fluent in French at that time, after speaking it solely for three months, I was able to converse freely with my travelling companions. Their stories of adventure and romance filled me with excitement, to an extent that, on arriving in Paris, all I wished to do was enrol in the Legion.

Unfortunately – or, on reflection, most fortunately – I'd just had my fourteenth birthday in Switzerland, which made me much too young to have even been considered as a recruit. As I watched these "three musketeers" disappear along the platform, I knew one day I'd write some of the stories they told me of their exploits and wild adventures, but, through later years, I realised the yarns they spun were only to excite the imagination of a vulnerable teenager.

After reading books and taking a great interest in the operations of the Legion, the last thing on my mind was to even think of joining up. The life was hard and gruelling with death and injury lurking around each foreign battlefield, fighting wars for France, and dying in the process.

However, it didn't deter me from writing about the Legion, and, this being my second novel on the subject, will hopefully lead to penning just one more.

Table of Chapters

Introduction   xv

Chapter 1.   Invasion by Stealth.   1

Chapter 2.   The Setup.   12

Chapter 3.   The Rehearsal.   27

Chapter 4.   The Hit.   38

Chapter 5.   Cry Havoc!   49

Chapter 6.   The President is Dead...Long Live the President!   57

Chapter 7.   The Hunt is On.   66

Chapter 8.   Closing In.   76

Chapter 9.   Devastating News.   90

Chapter 10.   A Flight to Remember.   102

Chapter 11.   The Birth of a Dynasty.   115

Chapter 12.   Gang Warfare.   120

Chapter 13.   Execution Dock.   131

Chapter 14.   Honour Thy Father.   135

Chapter 15.   First Blood.   141

Chapter 16.   Marseille.   154

Chapter 17.   Café Caligula.   166

Chapter 18.   Femmes Fatale   177

Chapter 19.   The French Foreign Legion.   190

Chapter 20.   The Miner from Bedworth.   203

Chapter 21. The Argyll and Southern Highlanders. 211

Chapter 22 Action in Korea. 218

Chapter 23. Mrs Agnes Tweedsmuir. 229

Chapter 24. A Fall from Grace. 241

Chapter 25. An Incident on the Road to Colchester. 261

Chapter 26. The Crossing. 277

Chapter 27. Intense Training Begins. 291

Chapter 28. Talk of Desertion. 308

Chapter 29. The Parachute Regiment. 323

Chapter 30. Na San, French Indo China. 329

Chapter 31. Descent into Hell. 335

Chapter 32. Abandoned! 346

Chapter 33. Surrender or Fight On. 369

Chapter 34. The Suicide Squad. 380

Chapter 35. Camp Chao Mung. 389

Chapter 36. Heads Will Roll! 401

Chapter 37. Should We Stay, or Should We Go? 409

Chapter 38. Raise High the Black Flag my Children. 418

Chapter 39. Breakout. 433

Chapter 40. Remember the Alamo! 444

Chapter 41. In Sight of the Promised Land. 455

Chapter 42. An Unexpected Confrontation. 462

Chapter 43. Back on the Run. 481

Chapter 44. The Diamond Mine. 499

Chapter 45. Yet More Surprises. 511

Introduction

The People's Republic of Zuberi is a landlocked country in Central Africa. Originally a protectorate of Great Britain known as Stanlasia – named after the famous British explorer, Sir Henry Morton Stanley – it later became an independent nation and called itself Equantania. Although its new name implied equality for all, Equatania was anything but what its name inferred. The population was 92% Black, with 5% Arab or Asian, and the remaining 3% white European. As most of the businesses and important governmental positions were held by the white minority, this naturally caused much resentment to most Black African citizens.

The economy couldn't have been better; being rich and fertile, cereals including wheat and maize were grown in abundance. Tobacco, coffee and cotton were also grown, and together with the mineral deposits mined there, they created a highly lucrative export industry. Amongst the chromite, copper, nickel and iron ore, were such valuable deposits as gold, platinum and even diamonds, which added to the county's wealth.

Unemployment was virtually unknown, and those who couldn't work, for health reasons, benefited greatly from a generous welfare system, similarly based on that of Great Britain's. The government, although all white, were very fair with everyone, and treated transgressions by the Black majority with fairness and humanity; no death penalty existed, and prisons were quite humane – again, like those in the UK.

Living in such a utopia, one would assume everyone would be happy and content, as most of their envious neighbours never enjoyed a lifestyle anything like those fortunate to live in Equatania. Naturally, there were residents from bordering countries who wished to settle there, but borders were strong, and immigration laws very strict. This kept most of the undesirables out, except for those who could contribute something useful to the community. There were, however, those who did manage to avoid the border restrictions, and succeeded to infiltrate the country. These infiltrators were anything but an asset to this rich country and did their best to sow seeds of discontent and revolution. Their argument was that, as most of its residents were Black, why were all the governmental positions held by whites? Apart from this, the mines and farms were all controlled by the whites, with very few Blacks holding positions of authority. In many ways, this was true and could be described as grossly unfair. It could also be construed as racial, because the ruling minority made it patently obvious that, no, or very few, Blacks could be included in the running of their country. As the racial inequality gave the whites more privileges than the Black majority, the agitators made it known this was their country, and the whites being invaders, had no right to be there.

What both sides of this argument failed to recognise were each other's rights to rule or even be there. The Blacks insisted Africa was for Black Africans, and they had every right to rule, or at least have a say in its administration, which, in some ways, could be correct. The whites, on the other hand, maintained it was they who developed the mines, the agriculture and its economic structure, with, of course, the help and cooperation of the Black majority. There was no giving way by either side, except that the white minority had the whip hand, and controlled the armed forces as well as the police and judiciary.

It would have been much better for everyone involved if the ruling whites at least gave most people a say, or indeed a bigger share in their country's riches. As it was, although the Blacks of Equatania were all employed and relatively better off than their neighbours, they never lived in such fine houses, or took part in events the Europeans kept mainly for themselves. Of course, there was much resentment, and this began to boil over – helped by the overzealous actions and stirrings-up of the infiltrators. Various organisations sprang up, with huge outdoor meetings held, as well as mass demonstrations ending in violence.

If only the ruling whites had seen the writing on the wall and given way to some of the demands from their fellow countrymen – who just happened to be Black. Had they read their history well, and took a lesson from pre-revolutionary France in 1789, they would have seen what organised and disorganised mobs were capable of.

The various Black African dissenting groups soon swelled into much larger organisations, forming themselves into strong and determined political parties. There was much violence, and as the army and police force were predominately white, they came down heavily on the Black opposition. Other African countries saw this as an unfair attack on citizens' rights and sided with their Black brothers. Armed groups were formed, and numbers swelled into many thousands, demanding equal rights with the ruling minority. There were some clever and ambitious leaders amongst the Blacks, who could see a great opportunity on the horizon. They knew, although violence and killing helped their cause, the white majority were beginning to suffer. The only way for them to gain the confidence and cooperation from the world's leaders, was to insist on elections being held; these would decide who the majority wished to govern them.

Reluctantly, the ruling administration agreed to hold elections, if only to appease the new political parties and other African leaders. The outcome of these elections could not have been foreseen, otherwise it's doubtful they would have been held. The mistake that Equatania made when they became independent from Britain was to lose the protection of its military forces. It was doubtful, however, if the British government would have stepped in to assist, as they realised this confrontation could escalate into a huge conflagration. Britain had enough problems of their own at that time and didn't wish for any more overseas engagements.

Abuchi Abimbola, the self-styled leader of the main Populist Party of Free Africa (PPFA) took complete control of the government by winning 120 of the 130 seats. The remaining ten went to those of smaller parties. He didn't really wish to win all the seats – he could, had he wished – as he wanted to demonstrate democracy won the day, even if, in reality, it was won by intimidation with the threat of brute force and violence.

The ruling white minority were aghast at this result and weren't anticipating being in such a catastrophic situation. They were in effect booted out of government, and at a loss of what to do next. Leaders of the army and police force were completely impotent, as this election was won by democratic means, and the whole of Africa and, indeed, the rest of the world was looking on. Had they failed to recognise this result, and put up an armed resistance, it was quite possible foreign armies would have been involved in upholding what, to them, was a fully legal and democratic election.

Abimbola and his thugs just couldn't wait to take control; they informed the outgoing administration that a friendly and peaceful transfer of power would be preferable to an acrimonious or uncooperative exchange. Slowly and thoroughly, the changeover took place. There were some heated exchanges between those coming in and those going out, but both sides made concessions, and agreed that it had to be done with the minimum of animosity and violence.

Within a month, the new regime had just about taken over, not just the administration, but the economy and the armed forces. The country's name changed from

Equatania to The Republic of Zuberi, a name chosen by its new president. The predominately white army and police force was now mainly Black, with just one or two exceptions – made solely for appearances. Important positions in mines, factories, police, army and governmental positions were now all Black - as well as being associates of their president, Abuchi Abimbola. Much worse was to come later, when white farmers and landowners were relieved of their lands, farms and businesses, which were given over to their workers, who, in turn, argued and fought over who should have what. Many white farmers refused to hand over farms that had been in their families for generations; this resulted in many farmers being savagely murdered as well as dispossessed. Abimbola had numbers on his side; the whites were outnumbered by almost a hundred to one. Faithful Black servants and workers who stood by their employers suffered also and were badly beaten up for going against their government's declaration.

The whole country soon descended into chaos, and it was only by brute force involving savage beatings and murder that normality – of a kind – was restored. All the decent people of all races soon left rather than remain and face possible beatings or death at the hands of these out-of-control thugs. Many faithful workers who didn't have the time or resources to leave their country, ended up in prison and faced torture at the hands of the president's barbaric thugs. Many decent men, women and children died at the hands of these savages.

There were some mine owners and industrialists who *did* see the writing on the wall, and realised if the opposition won the elections, their mines and businesses would take the form of a type of nationalisation, similar to what happened in Communist countries. Realising this, valuable assets such as gold and diamonds from their respective mines were gradually smuggled out of the country to one of their friendlier neighbours. Owners of some of the smaller banks did the same, and others followed suit. Anything of real value was moved to other locations away from the greedy hands of the PPFA party leaders. Those financial assets belonging to the country that couldn't be moved in time were soon swallowed up by building huge ornate palaces to house the president, his wives, the families of his many supporters and hangers-on.

For a short time, most of the population were happy, as there was a token sharing out of some of the country's wealth. Houses owned by the previous administration soon became occupied by party members and government officials. Problems arose when various municipal workers needed paying. These were the people who kept the country clean and in working condition. Garbage collectors, road repairers, gas, electric and waterworks employees all needed paying, but there was no money left to pay them. Mine workers never got paid because the whole export structure of their industries had broken down. Before long, the whole country had fallen into complete disorder.

Abimbola's answer to this shortage of cash was to print more. He ordered the mint to print new bills of all denominations depicting his portrait. The problem this time was no other country would accept these new notes. Whenever funds became short, they merely printed more, so that eventually hyperinflation occurred... On a huge scale.

Observers in the West were monitoring the events in The Republic of Zuberi, and very concerned that where there was chaos, countries such as China or Russia might interfere and gradually infiltrate. To overcome this, leaders of America, Europe and Britain met to discuss an aid package, before China or Russia could step in. This was acceptable to the PPFA and, as a bonus, some neighbouring countries agreed to send fortnightly shipments of food to help feed the starving population. The cash that came into the country from Europe and America was not used in the maintenance of Zuberi's infrastructure, or even to get the deserted mines and other industries back working; this cash was spent on arms, more sumptuous palaces and gifts to the high-up members of the political party. Fleets of cars were bought and lavished on Abimbola's cronies to keep them sweet, and so maintain his position as president.

Everyone was happy except for the ordinary working population. Most of these resorted to living in tin shacks and other make-do forms of shelter. The Zuberi dollars they were paid, soon had less value than the paper they were printed on. Hyperinflation continued and goods in shops became scarcer than ever. Food banks were set up to feed the poor. Huge queues formed outside stores, only to discover that, by the time most people got to the end of them, they'd sold out!

It was decided that to cure this shortage problem, there would be a massive share-out of the food that arrived in

Zuberi from its generous neighbours. To quell the discontent, and let the population see and become familiar with their president, it was decided *he* would distribute the free food fortnightly. The place chosen for this was the huge sports stadium on the edge of the capital city. This gesture worked wonders, and the hungry masses were fed... From the hands of their generous president. Generous he may have seemed, but the hungry masses were only given a half of what was intended for them; the remainder was sold to unscrupulous traders, who then resold it to the public for whom it was intended, at highly inflated prices.

Apart from the rich countries who were monitoring Zuberi, there existed in America a very mysterious organisation with many rich and powerful members, whose wealth came from most dubious sources. Their money was acquired from gambling, prostitution, drugs, illegal arms shipments, robberies, highly suspect deals on the stock markets – in fact anything that could be acquired by fair means or foul and wasn't declared to the tax authorities. They needed outlets and investments for the vast sums of cash they couldn't spend legally and were always looking for ways and means to launder their ill-gotten gains.

Our story begins around the late 1970s in the USA. One of the administrators of this organisation – which in fact was run by the Mafia – who'd been watching the events in Zuberi, hatched out a very complex and ambitious plan of how to gain control of the country, and all its untapped riches. It was just ripe for a massive influx of the organisation's investors and their vast amounts of money. With the consent of the other members, the administrator began to buy up many of the extremely cheap shares of companies which had not been nationalised and amassed a sizeable portfolio. He had to do this in such a way that his actions didn't attract too much attention, otherwise Zuberi's officials might become suspicious. The mines and agricultural industries had now become stagnant through lack of investment. Only the gold and diamond mines were operating, although at less than full strength. The bounty from these mines was not used to help the county's failed economy; instead, vast quantities of gold and diamonds ended up in the hands of Abimbola and his army of hangers-on. They were, in fact, plundering the natural wealth of this now destitute country.

The head of this investment organisation, Carl Ryan, could have approached Abimbola with a proposition to invest heavily in his country and get the mines and industries working again. He decided against this, as, quite simply, the man could not be trusted; besides, he had a huge private army and an unscrupulous police force to back him up.

A general meeting of the International Investment Corporation (IIC) was convened, with the organisation's senior investors discussing which course they should take. They'd already invested millions of dollars into the country, with no visible returns likely for the near future. That money was as stagnant as the mines and companies it was invested in. However, being major shareholders, they *did* hold title to these mines and industries. They had the choice of having to sit and wait for a change of regime to occur or make that change happen themselves.

The meeting was held at one of the company's many hotels, where food and drink – especially drink – were laid on in the huge conference room. The doors were locked, and armed men stood guard outside with instructions not to let anyone near the room. Ryan opened the meeting and outlined the agenda, after which he asked for suggestions. All sorts of ideas were bandied about, some serious, some verging on the ridiculous, and others quite outrageous, but workable. Some called for a complete pull-out from the country and claw their investments back. Others suggested doing a deal with the president – which had previously been considered but later rejected. One very quiet and serious member of the 'firm', who had until now said nothing, stood up and asked for silence, as he had something important to suggest. After much bickering, moaning and groaning, this man was given what he asked for... Silence.

"I've been sitting here for almost two hours listening to you guys going on and on about this, that and the other, but until now I haven't heard one sensible suggestion." He paused for a reaction, and soon got one.

"What do you suggest, big mouth? Do we get an army and go and invade the fucking place?!" This was met with an uproar of laughter and banging on the tables by the rowdy and inebriated members, as they waited for the quiet man's reply.

"You know, mister, that's the most sensible suggestion I've heard since I've been sat here listening to you guys; you've taken the words right out of my mouth. You are correct, we invade the fucking place, but not with a huge army, we do it slowly and surely, bit by bit." The laughter stopped suddenly as the audience absorbed what this man had suggested.

"So, give us your plan, what are your suggestions on how to invade a country without the people who run it knowing?" called out a rather plump, balding man, chewing on a huge cigar.

"If you guys are as educated as you think you are," said the speaker, waiting for a reaction but getting none, "you'll have heard of the wooden horse of Troy."

"I've had a few nags like that at the races, cost me lots of dough; these weren't wooden, at the speed they ran you'd think they were made of cast iron... Ha ha ha," interrupted one of those in the audience.

Much laughter followed the humorous remark, prompting the chairman to call for order. Luke Rosen, the man making the sensible suggestions began to lose his cool. "I'm wasting my time with you guys, you just don't have a fucking clue; I'm off, I've had enough of you silly fuckers, that's it!" he called out. "Open those doors and let me out of here!"

"No, no, hang on, Luke, let's hear what you've got to say, ignore these stupid bastards and their stupid remarks!" called out the fraught chairman.

"If I have any more stupid remarks, I'm off; you either listen and discuss what I've got to say, or just forget it!" This did the trick – everyone at the meeting sat up and listened to what Luke had to say, and at the end of his speech, they took a vote and agreed to his most audacious plan; the invasion, by stealth, of the Republic of Zuberi.

Chapter 1

Invasion by Stealth

Luke Rosen's plan to invade Zuberi wasn't as outrageous as first appeared. The International Investment Corporation had more money than the country's entire economy. The only way to run it successfully, along with utilising all its resources, was to own it. They'd already got a toehold there and had lots of men on the ground. The need now would be to introduce greater numbers by stealth, and get the opposition party on their side, with the promise of money and power – though not too much. Friendships were made and associations developed with the right people. This went on under the noses of the dreaded secret police and their army of informers, The IIC was adept at buying loyalties, and equally as ruthless in getting rid of anyone who crossed them or stood in their way. The organisation relished the idea of having their own country, meaning they could invest vast amounts of dirty money into something legitimate for a change.

The metaphoric wooden horse was the infiltration of dozens of the company's trusted men, who'd recruit locals as workers in the copper or iron mines, keeping them on standby for the day they could depose the current regime. How they did this was amazing; the secret police had spies everywhere and had no idea what was going on. If they encountered any of these hateful and detested spies, with a chance their plan would be discovered, these informers simply disappeared. There were many wild animals in that country who were always very hungry. If it was thought Abimbola and his henchmen were cruel and heartless, IIC and its associates were much worse. They would stop at nothing to achieve their aims.

The main problem confronting the IIC was how would they get rid of Abimbola? He rarely showed his face in public and spent most of his time in lavishly furnished palaces, living the life of a Roman emperor. Meetings were held and all suggestions listened to, until they finally came up with a suggestion from Rosen – 'Ruthless Rosen'. "We zap the bastard… That's what we'll do, we'll shoot the fucker!" The meeting was more serious now with so much at stake, and silly suggestions were not entertained in any circumstances. All they had to decide was where, when and who would assassinate the president of Zuberi. For this job an 'agent' was brought in, one who had worked for the organisation on several occasions and was 100% trustworthy. The agent chosen for the job was Diego Delgado – DD to his chums – an American of Spanish origin. After he was fully briefed and given the requirements, a price for the job was agreed, allowing him the opportunity to engage two of the best hitmen in the business. The men chosen were brothers, Franco and Eduardo Capuano, born in England, whose grandfather was Sicilian, but mother and father both English. Senior members of the IIC relished the Sicilian connection, as their founder members in the Cosa Nostra hailed from that part of Italy. Both brothers changed their names to Frank and Eddie Best when they joined the French Foreign Legion. According to Delgado, they were the best in the business, fully dependable and therefore worthy of the highest price for doing this job; one million dollars!

DD and the brothers had good contact with each other, and either party was always on hand if their services were needed. Most of the 'jobs' the boys undertook were arranged by DD, and the agreement between the trio was to split their fee three ways. Each party took a quarter of the agreed 'service fee', leaving the remaining quarter for travelling expenses, hotels, purchase of guns, ammunition, vehicles and anything else needed to expedite the job in hand. If there was any money left from the expenses contingency, this was divided three ways also, giving each party a third share of the proceeds.

Although DD never took part in any of the 'hits', he did have to negotiate with some very dangerous and ruthless individuals to arrange the payment – half before the job was done, then the other half on completion. The system worked well between the three, and there were rarely disagreements. Although he acted as an agent, organising 'hits' for the underworld, DD was also an agent for theatre acts, mainly singers and bands. Another of his legitimate roles was as an impresario, arranging concerts and outdoor gatherings, sometimes for charities. This gave him credibility, as well as legality, making it easy for him to travel the globe booking acts as well as arranging assassinations on behalf of certain underworld clients. The business was run from a small office in New York, where he, along with a staff of two, kept things going. This office was where he could be contacted by his clients, legitimate and otherwise; at present he was anxious to contact the brothers to discuss the job he'd just taken on. Usually, if the brothers had no work, they would call his office in New York weekly to see if there was anything available. This weekend was no exception, as one of the brothers gave him a courtesy call, enquiring about the availability of any decent vacancies that needed filling – their way of finding out if there was a 'job' available.

DD had no way of contacting the boys apart from this, as they moved about frequently. Being on the wanted list in half a dozen countries made this necessary. Now they were laying low in Sicily. Having a Sicilian grandfather meant they had relatives in that beautiful but mysterious island off the western coast of Italy. Known for the birthplace of one of the three main Mafia organisations in that region, the Cosa Nostra, which was very active at that time. The Capuano brothers had dealings with the 'mob', but never joined them, preferring to work on their own. It was a rarity for the Mafia in allowing independent operators to work in their territory, but, as the brothers did a few 'favours' for them, and had an interesting history which proved their reliability, they were left to their own devices. It would have been suicide to act against the 'mob', and those stupid enough to do so always ended up dead – suffering a brutal death in the process. The two boys were very popular with the Mafia bosses, as their grandfather had been generations ago. Blood and family went a long way in that part of the world; knowing when to keep one's mouth shut ensured staying alive and healthy. If they had a job to do in any Mafia territory, they always cleared it with the bosses of the relevant organisations that operated there, before they went about their 'business'.

When DD received a call from the brothers, he immediately arranged a meeting with the boys in Pretoria, South Africa. They were not too surprised at this venue, as most meeting places he arranged were always in the strangest settings. Immediately, flights were booked after deciding which of the many passports they should use. Kissing goodbye to their aunt, in whose house they'd been staying, and after giving her a huge amount of cash, they advised her it could be a week or two before they'd return – or even *if* they'd return. After stepping off the plane at Pretoria Airport, they found the temperature much higher than in Sicily, from where they'd just come. They'd spent time in Africa on previous occasions and knew what to expect. After clearing passport and immigration controls, it wasn't long before they were met by their agent and helped with their baggage to a waiting taxi.

"You boys haven't changed since the last time we met, when was it, almost six months ago?" said the small balding man as he reacquainted himself with the brothers.

"Sorry I can't say the same for you, my friend," joked Frank, "you've got fatter and lost more of your hair."

"If you had the stress and worry that I have, you'd lose some of that beautiful black hair, and you'd look like me," replied the chubby, balding agent.

Rooms were booked by DD at a swanky four-star hotel in the middle of Pretoria, and soon after checking in, the brothers showered and changed. Their agent was waiting for them in the foyer; together they found a discreet table in the lounge and ordered three ice-cold beers. Before beginning with the proposition they'd come to hear from DD, they got most of the irrelevant small talk out of the way, finally getting down to business.

"Why bring us all the way out here to listen to your proposal," asked Frank, "when we could have had a meeting somewhere a little nicer in a more familiar setting?"

"Because I want to kill two birds with one stone," came DD's reply. He went on to say, "The location of the job I have for you is not too far away, so holding the briefing here would save a lot of time and trouble."

"What makes you assume we'll agree to do the job?" asked Eddie.

"If I mention the sum one million dollars, will that answer your question?" There was a gasp, and then a short silence as the two brothers took in the size of the fee mentioned.

"Money always talks, so, in that case, carry on, we are now very interested," came the brother's eager response.

The waiter came to the table and asked if they needed more drinks, after which they drained their glasses, ordered three more and gave the empties to the smartly dressed waiter.

"Okay, as soon as those drinks arrive, I'll get down to brass tacks and fill you boys in with the bones of the job, after which we can all get together and put some flesh on those bones." Waiting until the waiter disappeared after delivering the beers, DD went into dialogue and gave the brothers the low down on what the job entailed.

"I can see where you are coming from, my friend, but this job needs much thought and planning; how long have we got?" asked Frank who was the most practical of the two brothers. Eddie, by contrast, was a little more daring, and it was he who was the better shot, so he concentrated on doing the 'business' leaving the brainwork to his older brother.

There was only a year between them, but the physical difference was greater. Frank was the taller of the two with well-coiffured straight black hair. Eddie was a little shorter, with unkempt curly dark brown hair. Both boys were loved by the ladies, and between them had many successes with the fairer sex. The brothers were inseparable since childhood, and each agreed that if they had to, they'd stop a bullet for their sibling; during their experiences, this was put to the test on several occasions.

Diego Delgado thought highly of his partners, having a great rapport with the pair. The three trusted each other and could always be depended upon to go that extra mile if needed. Having the initial or nickname DD was quite appropriate for the Spanish American, as he had an uncanny resemblance to the film actor Danny De Vito. He even spoke like him with his New York accent and was often asked for his autograph.

With the proposition, and full explanation of the conditions and consequences of this job out of the way, the three men, being very tired after their separate journeys, decided to turn in as they had a big job ahead of them in the morning. It was decided at the meeting to hire a car and make the 150-mile journey to Zuberi. They needed to take a good look at the stadium where the president handed out the free food to his starving subjects, as well as choose an ideal spot to assassinate him… Earning them a million dollars for doing the job.

With a sumptuous breakfast in their stomachs, and a fresh change of clothes, they hired a car from a dealer recommended by the hotel. Ensuring it was filled with fuel, and carried a road map, they headed for the border some 100 miles away, that took just under two hours to reach. Upon arrival, they joined a queue of other vehicles wishing to cross into Zuberi. A very large, stony-faced guard approached the car and asked for their passports, which Frank had ready. After slowly turning each page of the passport over, the guard looked at the three men sitting in the hired car, then motioned them to an area where other vehicles were being checked over.

"Get out of the vehicle and wait here," ordered the guard as he pointed to a vacant parking space.

"I don't like this at all," said DD. "That guy was giving us some strange looks."

"Relax," replied Frank, "he's only doing his job... The miserable-faced fucker."

Keeping out of the sun, the three sat under a tree and waited to be checked over by the zealous border guards. After a fifteen-minute wait, two different guards approached holding their passports. The senior of the two had a good look at the trio sitting in the shade and told them to follow him to an office.

"Sit down, gentlemen, please," requested the well-spoken officer, who was obviously a higher rank than the other guards who were on duty at the crossing. "I've looked at your passports and can see from reading them you are all Americans."

"That's correct, sir," answered DD to the officer. The others nodded in agreement.

"I'm interested in the purpose of your visit to our country?" DD smiled at the officer, then, reaching in his pocket, produced a business card and handed to him. After reading it, the officer gave a surprised look and asked DD to explain.

"Well, sir, as you can see from my business card, I am an impresario and agent for lots of show business people – you know, pop stars and the like." The officer became interested, motioning the small, balding American to continue. "My associates here, along with myself, are looking for a stadium big enough to hold a pop concert in aid of the poor and homeless people of Africa, especially the children. The last time we held one in England, we raised millions of dollars in a venue called 'Music Aid'. Much of this money went to South America, but this time we want the money to come here – Africa."

After considering what DD had just told him, the officer replied, "Well, you will not find many poor starving people in our country, but we would be interested in raising money to help those less well off than ourselves."

The three men looked at each other; Eddie responded by saying, "We didn't imply that, sir, and we are not particularly wishing to hold a concert here, but wherever it is held will bring lots of money into that country and do wonders for their economy."

The officer thought for a while, wondering if what he said had put these three promotors off holding a pop concert in his country. "If I may suggest, you might wish to visit our Freedom City Stadium, which isn't too far from here, and on the outskirts of our capital," he suggested enthusiastically.

"Well, that does sound great!" replied DD just as enthusiastically. "How far away is it and how do we get there?" Relieved that he hadn't put them off, the officer wrote instructions on how to find the stadium as well as a short letter to the manager, instructing him to give full assistance to the bearers. "That is most helpful of you, and thank you very much for all you have done for us...

By the way, what is your name so that I can mention you should we decide to hold our venue there."

Feeling very pleased with himself, the officer added his name to the letter and spelled it out so the others would pronounce it correctly. If any accolades were to be given, he wanted to make sure it was known he was the officer who recommended the Freedom City Stadium to the three Americans. Escorting them personally through the checkpoint, he watched as their vehicle slowly disappeared, feeling very pleased with himself.

"What a fucking jerk that guy was, did you hear him, 'there are no starving and homeless people in our country!' Who's he trying to kid?" sneered DD, imitating the officer's African accent.

"Well, I thought he was a very nice man," replied Frank jokingly.

"Me too!" shouted Eddie from the rear seat. "A veritable gentleman, unlike someone I could mention!"

Chapter 2

The Set-up

The three 'impresarios' were well on the way to the Freedom City Stadium near the outskirts of the capital city, which bore the same name. They had quite a job driving on the bumpy potholed roads, which did nothing for the suspension of their hire car, or indeed for their aching limbs.

"Boy oh boy, what a shit heap this place is, it's like putting the clock back a hundred years. Lousy roads and no real signposts to speak of; just look at the place, filthy and dirty!" remarked DD as they drove along the pothole-ridden highway.

"They don't need any signposts as there's hardly any other roads, and this one goes straight to the main town... Or city, as they like to call it. I wonder what it's like there!" replied Frank.

"Well, I, for one, can't wait to get there," called out Eddie, "this bumpy road has just about shaken every bone in my body!"

By now, the trio were becoming hungry and very thirsty, as the temperature was in the thirties. They were on the lookout for somewhere to grab a quick snack, and especially a beer or two. There were roadside vendors dotted around, but nothing that appealed to them. Suddenly, Eddie gave a shout as he spotted a roadside diner. "That place looks okay, and reasonably hygienic," he called out, "at least we'll be able to have a sit down in there." They pulled up and parked alongside the other vehicles and made their way into the diner. Eddie was correct, it did look reasonably clean and hygienic; all they had to do was choose what to eat.

As usual, it was left to DD to do the talking, so he wandered up to the counter, looked at the menu and placed an order. "Well, there ain't much of a choice, boys, so I ordered the dish of the day, or, should I say, the dish of every day, and three bottles of the local brew." The others agreed to go along with their agent's choice, and it wasn't long before the 'plat de jour' was delivered to their table, accompanied by three bottles of the local beer.

As it turned out, the meal of stewed meat and veg, together with a half loaf of bread, went down well with the hungry trio. After finding the beer was up to their taste, they ordered three more. "Don't drink too many of these beers, guys, we don't know how strong they brew it here!" warned Frank.

"So, I expect it's me who has to settle the check, is it, boys?" asked a cynical DD.

"I'm afraid it is," replied Eddie. "You're the one with the money, and, besides, you are responsible for the expenses, not us... We just do the assassinations." At this response, they all laughed, and the boys got ready to leave.

"Do you accept American Express?" asked DD as he sauntered up to the counter.

"I'm afraid not!" replied the assistant rather apologetically.

"Well, we ain't got none of your local currency, neither do we have any South African rands, or whatever they call 'em, do you accept US dollars?" The assistant took advice from a superior and confirmed they accept American dollars. "Okay, let's do the business, how much do we owe you?" The assistant handed DD the bill as he reached for his wallet. "What the fuck's this, seventeen and a half million dollars, are you having a fucking joke?!" retorted DD, in language as colourful as the Hawaiian style shirts he wore.

"No, sir, that's the amount you owe for your meal... There are three of you so it's for the three meals."

"I know you have an inflation problem here, but this is ridiculous!" blurted out the chubby American as he was trying to come to terms with what the three meals had cost them.

"You did say that you wanted to pay in US dollars, did you not, sir?" DD just nodded. "Right, sir, that will be twelve dollars and fifty cents... please, sir," replied the assistant after making a calculation of the conversion rate.

Still trying to come to terms with what he was being charged, DD changed his attitude completely. "Did you say twelve and a half bucks?"

"Yes, sir, I did," replied the slightly exasperated assistant.

"Okay, have you got change for twenty dollars?" Once more the assistant took advice from his supervisor, who immediately disappeared into the back office and reappeared a few minutes later with huge bundles of cash. "Okay, how much of this do I take for my change?" asked DD.

"All of it, sir, that money is your change out of the twenty-dollar note that you gave me."

"What?!" replied a completely incredulous DD upon being confronted with the huge bundles of cash. "I can't take any more of this, come on guys, we're out of here... Keep that Mickey Mouse money as a tip, I ain't got no use for it!" he called out to the assistant; with that, they all left the diner, laughing their heads off.

"You look and sound more like Danny De Vito each time we see you!" remarked Eddie to a laughing DD.

"That guy's an Italian American, I'm a Spanish American," replied a slightly indignant DD. "Besides, I've got more hair than him, and I'm definitely better looking!"

"We won't argue with that, my friend, but you could be taken for twin brothers." DD just laughed, throwing his head back in a nonchalant manner.

It wasn't long after leaving the roadside diner that they saw signs to Freedom City; as they neared the main road into the city, signs for the stadium appeared. Following the road signs, they soon arrived outside the huge stadium which appeared to look quite shabby and run-down. Few vehicles were in the huge car park, so they had no problem parking up near the entrance.

"Can I help you?" called out a voice from the doorway.

"Yes, sure you can," replied DD, "we're looking for the manager of the stadium."

"You just happen to be talking to him... Yes, it's me," replied the tall, well-dressed man who had come outside for a smoke. "What business do you have with me?"

DD then went into his usual routine about being a promotor and impresario, as well as their search for a venue to hold a huge pop concert. Flashing his business card along with the letter from the officer at the border, the stadium manager invited them into his office. Strangely enough, it was very cool inside but stuffy, as the air-conditioning unit needed servicing. It was cooling the air, but not taking all the stale air away. Frank noticed this and mentioned it to Eddie.

"This all seems quite a bit of a surprise to me, gentlemen," he said as he invited the three men to sit down, "but if I must say, a very nice surprise!"

"There ain't nothing definite now, sir, we are just checking these places out. When we choose a venue, we must get it okayed by the sponsors, as well as finding out if some of the big names will be available at that specific date," explained DD to the enthusiastic manager.

"You mention big names... Anyone in particular?" he asked, enthusiastically. DD quickly had to think up a few familiar names to impress him.

"Er, let me see now, er, Bob Dylan, Elton John, oh yes, then there's Rod Stewart who says he might come; Dolly Parton expressed an interest too."

"Can I get you gentlemen some refreshment or something?" asked the manager to his three important guests. "We can discuss this in more detail... Bob Dylan, Elton John, wow, such big names."

Eddie and Frank looked at each other, wondering if their impresario friend hadn't 'overcooked' it a little, especially mentioning those particular names. DD thought the same, when he saw the manager go into raptures at the thought of having such famous show-business people performing at his stadium.

"Now look here, fella, don't you get too darned excited, cos nothing's been finalized yet, and what I'm telling you is in complete confidence... So don't breathe a word to no one else, savvy?"

"Of course, of course, this is just between us, but I'd love to be able to tell my wife, and perhaps my children."

DD was getting a little worried that he'd indeed overdone it by mentioning those names, so he had to try and play it down a little. "Like I said before, you tell no one, not even your good lady, and them kids of yours... Especially them kids."

"I won't breathe a word," whispered the manager, holding his finger to his lips.

The three men had to put into perspective the *true* reason for their visit, namely, to arrange the assassination of the country's president. After they'd had the welcome refreshments served by one of the manager's staff, DD asked to look around outside. Wandering around in the huge stadium, Eddie and Frank were looking for an ideal, if not perfect, spot in which to position their sniper gun, which hadn't been delivered to them yet; that was DD's job. Pointing over to three blocks of apartments or, rather, tenement blocks, Eddie asked his brother what he thought. Straining his eyes in the strong sunlight, he asked Frank how far away they were.

"Not more than 700 yards or so, perhaps even less," replied Frank, rubbing his slightly dazzled eyes.

Looking at his wristwatch and noticing the time, Eddie remarked, after looking at the apartments ahead of him, "That's great, at this time of day the sun will be behind us, so we'll be in shadow; we should get a good shot from there if we locate a good spot. On the roof of that middle block looks okay to me."

If they were able to acquire the rifle that they asked for, the 700- to 600-yard distance would be fine. "If DD can supply us with the Remington M40, it has 800 yards killing range. We should be well into its capacity, although we'll need to have it for at least a day to enable us to calibrate it and make a few practice shots out in the wilds somewhere," he advised his brother.

"You can't get an accurate estimate of the distance by looking directly at it, we really need to look at the apartment block and the stadium sideways." They walked outside the stadium and calculated a more accurate distance and agreed on a 650-yard killing range.

"What we need to do now is look at the middle one of the three blocks and select a base. I reckon we'll have to set up on the roof and get the feel of the place. This is going to be a very important 'hit' and we don't want anything to go wrong," Frank assured his brother.

Whilst this was going on, DD was busy keeping the manager happy, giving him a load of twaddle about the venues he'd set up, along with the names of some famous performers. Telling the gullible manager he was friends with Frank Sinatra and Dean Martin seemed to impress him, but once more, the fat, balding, little American did tend to elaborate slightly; a less gullible person could pick holes in his tales of fantasy, and possibly ruin the whole exercise... Resulting in the team being apprehended, and the plot revealed.

After assessing the killing range for the 'hit', the brothers re-joined the other two men who were standing in a shady spot under the seating area of the stadium.

"It's just as well you didn't decide to come here this Saturday," said the manager.

"Why?" asked a curious Frank.

"Hey, that's the day our president is coming to distribute food parcels for some of our country's poor and hungry people!" The three men gave each other a surprised look; in three days, their target would be standing where they were now.

"How often does he do this? asked DD.

"Each fortnight as a rule, but it does vary as our president is a very busy man, and he spends much of his time with affairs of state, as well as the smooth running of our country."

Once more, the three men gave each other a puzzled look, realising that three days would be insufficient for them to make all the arrangements, as they would need a good working plan, taking at least a week to formulate.

"It won't affect your plans though, gentlemen, please carry on with your arrangements. I can assure you that we'll give you as much cooperation as possible; please take my card which you can use to contact me should you wish for further information," said the manager as he handed DD his business card.

"Remember, this is top secret, if you blab it out to anyone, the whole deal will be off... Savvy?" The manager nodded his head and held his finger to his mouth once more. They waved goodbye to their host, as DD copied his mouth and finger gesture, indicating secrecy.

"Before we hit the road back, I'd just like to take a peek at those apartments and see how easy it is getting onto the roof of the middle one," Eddie mentioned to the others.

After driving around to the apartment blocks, the brothers walked into the middle one, and searched for the elevator. The whole place stunk of stale cooking and sewerage; the drains must have been in a terrible state. There was a lot of shouting and bellowing going on, as well as music being played very loudly. The elevator was out of order, so they had to climb twelve flights of stairs in the six-story building, to reach the roof access. Finally, they made it to the roof space through a locked door which opened easily with the help their lock-picking tool; a small item they always carried. After having a good wander around and choosing a suitable spot to mount the sniper rifle, the brothers agreed with their choice, relocked the door, and slipped away down the stairway, joining DD waiting across the road.

"We need to gas up this jalopy, then we'll head back to civilisation; I can't wait to get away from this stinking shithole!" called out DD to the brothers. After filling up their car, and paying with a credit card, the three conspirators decided not to stay the night at a hotel in town, and instead made their way back to South Africa, and civilisation, as DD made clear.

The drive back to Pretoria was quite uneventful but resulted in the trio arriving at the hotel slightly late.

They popped into the bar for a nightcap, after which they decided to get their heads down and have a good sleep.

"Goodnight, boys, see you in the morning," whispered DD so as not to disturb any of the sleeping guests.

"Sleep well, we'll have a good chat in the morning after breakfast," replied Frank, giving a wide yawn. Eddie signalled the same to their agent as they all turned in, hoping for a good night's sleep.

The three men were late going down to breakfast, and the waitresses were starting to clear the tables in the dining room to prepare for lunch. DD's usual chat lines soon persuaded the staff to bring them some breakfast, which they took to a secluded corner in the lounge. After finishing their meal and pouring the coffee, they sat back and decided to go over the previous day's events. DD began proceedings by asking the boys what they thought so far and had they any ideas on how to get started. Frank was the first to reply.

"I've given this matter quite a bit of thought, especially on the drive back last night. There's much that needs discussing, so now's the time; just let me run the plan by you both and we can iron out the details later."

Frank went on to divulge his plan for this very important and dangerous assassination job. The plan was to hire a medium-sized panel van – which had to be white – and have plastic adhesive signs made up and printed, enabling them to change the appearance of it when needed.

"I suggest you have printed on the sign, 'Air Conditioning Maintenance Engineers', with a false telephone number and address underneath it. Have two made up that will be easy to peel off when we need to."

"Carry on, Frank, I'm becoming very interested," replied DD as he poured himself another coffee from the almost empty pot. Turning around to get the attention of a waiter, holding the pot in the air, he ordered a fresh one and continued listening intently to Frank's suggestion.

"If we are going to pose as air con engineers, can I suggest we get hold of a couple of air con units; say a brand new one, and one that's been used, to look as if we are replacing it," suggested Eddie, "that way, in case we are stopped by a nosey cop, we'll look as if we are on a job."

"Bloody good thinking, bruv; we can also include some piping and other bits of gear to make us look like legit engineers. Great stuff, let's carry on," added his big brother, a little more excited now. "Those pieces of pipe will also help to hide the rifle, which is something else to sort out."

"I'm on to that, boys; when I go Stateside tomorrow I'll get one delivered to the hotel – car park, of course – from somewhere here in South Africa. The guy I deal with has contacts all over the world, and he's never let me down yet!" stressed DD.

"Make sure you get the one I asked for, Remington M40 sniper rifle, along with a full box of ammunition so that we can practice here somewhere in the wilds," reminded Eddie. "I'll need to calibrate the scope, assuming the killing range will be about 650 yards."

DD didn't understand the technical jargon very well, but he always managed to come up with the goods. "Anything else you'll need, boys? I'll be away for three or four days; that should give me time to get the sign made up and printed whilst I'm there." The boys thought for a while but couldn't think of anything else they needed from the States. "So, what will you two guys be doing while I'm away sourcing gear for this very tricky job, lounging around the pool all day in-between pulling a couple of the local beauties, I'll bet?"

"Not a chance!" replied Frank quite adamantly. "Not whilst we are on the job, we can do without any distractions of the female type; there'll be plenty of time for that when we've finished this operation, and, by the way, let me have that calling card the arena manager gave you, it'll come in handy for what I've got planned next."

"What'll that be?" asked the little American inquisitively.

"This job is more dangerous than we thought previously, much more, in fact. We must get it right first time; we'll need a rehearsal, as well as an exit strategy should something go wrong," replied Frank to DD's question.

"What can go wrong, you've got this job sewn up, and, besides, you pair are the best in the business, that's why

I chose you, and that's why the syndicate gave me the job; you've got my full confidence!"

Eddie answered DD's question by telling him that to fail to prepare, will result in preparing to fail. "All chances of failure must be factored into the plan, and in the unlikely event something bad does happen, a contingency plan put into operation might just save our skins."

On hearing this, DD became concerned and a little nervous, but the brothers reassured him all would turn out fine if they planned wisely. Frank came up with the final part of the plan, which gave more confidence to their agent and helped put his mind at rest.

"The manager at the arena told us that this weekend was when the president arrives to give away food parcels to the needy. The next time it happens will be in about two weeks. What my brother and me intend is to drive back to the arena in our hire car and take a look at just exactly what occurs when the president goes into his routine. We want to be up on the roof to observe the proceedings; looking out for any flaws we might encounter when we decide to 'knock him off'." The others were listening intently to Frank, as he enlightened them with the final part of his plan.

"So where will you stay when you are down there waiting for the show to begin?" asked a curious DD.

"Last time we were there, I noticed a few deserted farms with outbuildings that could hide our vehicle if need be.

We'll sort out one of these to 'hole up' in should anything go wrong. Being on the road in a conspicuous vehicle could be dangerous, so I'm gonna sort out a bolthole for us. See what I mean, have all of your bets covered; is that okay with you, bruv?" Eddie just nodded in agreement, and with no more questions, the little meeting in the hotel bar came to an end.

During this impromptu meeting between the three plotters, two men sitting on the far side of the hotel lounge had been taking an interest in the conversation. Although they were out of earshot, they did their best to listen to what was going on, but fortunately never heard any content of the conversation. Being quite observant, Frank noticed them watching, and became mindful of their appearances, intending to follow his suspicions through later. He never alerted the others, as he didn't wish to let those watching know they'd been noticed.

Chapter 3

The Rehearsal

Diego booked his flight back to the States shortly after his meeting with the brothers. There was a lot to discuss with the bosses of the organisation who'd hired him for the 'disposal job', as they called it. They were paying out a million dollars for the services of the two brother assassins and were anxious to discover how much progress had been made, as well as ensuring their investment was in safe hands – those of Diego Delgado.

DD always insisted on half of the contract fee up front, as he needed some of this money for expenses and such. He had to pay for a vehicle as well as the contents needed to ensure their stratagem would look and seem convincing. A weapon had to be ordered and delivered to their hotel in Pretoria from an arms dealer in South Africa; this would not come cheap. His two accomplices in this planned assassination would need spending money. To appear legitimate and run a *bona fide* show business agency in New York, staff had to be employed and paid wages.

There was also the question of the adhesive sign needed for the van they'd have to hire, or even buy, for this job.

Expenses were mounting up, and DD had to ask Carl Ryan, the boss of International Investment Corporation, for this money.

"Well, how's these two brothers working out, are they any good?" asked Ryan.

"At present, Mr Ryan, they are doing well; they've done jobs for me before and never let me down," replied DD.

"That's good to hear, I say, really good to hear," repeated Ryan to a slightly humbled DD.

"There's a lot riding on this caper, y'know, an awful lot; not just money but lives, men's lives," he stressed, twirling the huge cigar around in his mouth, as he emphasised the importance of this job to the chubby, balding man in front of him, who was listening to every word and agreeing, persistently nodding his head.

"Like I said, Mr Ryan, these two guys are very dependable and perfectionists in their business; very professional and precise, sir."

"Good, good, that's really good to hear; now what can I do for you? You haven't come here just to have a chat with me, I'm darned sure of it." The nervous agent was dreading the next part of their conversation, when he had to ask for a cash advance to pay for his ever-mounting expenses.

"If you could see yourself clear to advancing me two hundred and fifty thousand dollars, I'd be very grateful to you, sir," asked the nervous agent.

"What do you want that much for?" yelled Ryan. "I don't mind laying out my cash, but I need to see what it's being spent on." DD then had to give a list of the items he'd need, as well as paying certain people, including his office staff and the two brothers. "If I advance this much, I want a complete breakdown of where it's gone and who's had it; do you understand?"

"Yes, sir, I'll do that, of course, I'll do it right away."

"I've got people I have to answer to, so I'll need some proof to show them if they ask; okay?" DD simply nodded his head in agreement and wondered how difficult it would be to obtain the balance of their agreed pay-out when the job was done.

"Nothing had better go wrong, you hear; our company's got a lot riding on this, and many people's lives depend on a successful outcome; understand?" reminded Ryan.

"Yes, sir, I understand fully."

After receiving his grudgingly paid deposit for doing this particularly complicated job, DD was wishing he'd turned it down. He was dreading the consequences if anything *did* go wrong.

Back in South Africa, the brothers were planning another sortie into Zuberi to take a good look at the man they were being paid a huge sum of money to kill. They knew he'd be at the stadium on Saturday. Deciding to take the hire car and drive to Musina, on the border with Zuberi, they'd size the situation up, and take a chance crossing through, and drive directly to the stadium.

The border crossing wasn't as busy as envisaged. They'd been there a couple of days ago and were questioned about the purpose of their journey. This time they were given a cursory glance by the border guards and waved straight on.

"Thank Christ for that!" said Frank, who was driving. "I didn't fancy being interrogated again, as long as we have an uneventful drive to the stadium, I'll be quite happy." Eddie, who was half-asleep, simply yawned and nodded in agreement.

It wasn't long before they reached their destination, as they'd become familiar with the area. Wide awake now, Eddie suggested they should look around to find a place to spend the night before inspecting the apartments where they intended to mount their rifle and take stock of any peculiarities which could occur.

"We want a straight in-and-out with this job," Eddie advised his brother, "once we've done the business – shooting the president – we need to make a quick and clean getaway, with nothing to slow us down; capisco?

"Si, si," replied Frank, speaking as they often did in the language of their grandfather "There are lots of deserted farmsteads around this area, we must pick one not too far away that hasn't been burnt down, and has a barn where we can hide the van after we've done the biz."

"If everything goes to plan, we shouldn't really need to hide, as the announcement of the president's death will be the signal for the rebellion to commence," said Frank.

"Look, bruv, it's not the police and bodyguards I'm concerned about, it's the guys who are supposed to be on our side. I just do not trust any of 'em!"

Frank responded to his brother's misgivings by agreeing with him, and added he had serious doubts about the job, wishing they'd never taken it on. "Look, bruv, it's not just a simple job that we're used to, y'know, bang bang, then fuck off as quick as we can with no comebacks; this is a bigger kettle o' fish; we are kicking off a revolution, where lots of people are gonna get killed because of what we do. If things go wrong, we are in the middle of it. Even if things go to plan, we still don't know if this organisation in the States might want to get rid of *us,* as we are evidence of their conspiracy in this caper."

"You definitely ain't wrong, bruv, I'm all for giving DD a shout and calling the whole thing off... It stinks to me," replied an unhappy Eddie.

"For now, we'll go along with the set-up as planned. Who knows, it might not seem too bad after we do a dress rehearsal. So, let's just carry on for now."

After airing their doubts and misgivings about the job, the brothers went in search of a deserted farmstead where they could 'hole-up' for the time being and have a place to hide when the job was done.

Searching for a homestead that hadn't been completely burned to the ground, as had happened with many others around that area, they were pleased to discover one which had a barn. Apart from that, it had a huge door, enabling them to hide their vehicle. The farmhouse, to which it was connected, would give them shelter for a couple of days until the heat died down. They decided to spend the night there and pay a visit to the apartment block the next day, where the assassination would take place in a fortnight's time. The following day, being Saturday, would enable them to study the man they were going to kill, when he put in his fortnightly appearance at the stadium to distribute food to the needy.

After a reasonable night's sleep in the hire car, it was decided to drive to the stadium, park up and then walk to where the apartment blocks were situated. The whole area was busy as those wishing to grab a hold of the free food parcels were all trying to get to the front of a disorderly queue.

"If you lot don't get in line and stop pushing and shoving, the distribution will be called off; there's to be no disorderliness, did you lot hear that, no bad behaviour!" called out a soldier who was trying – without success – to get the unruly mob into some kind of order.

As his pleas were ignored, another half dozen soldiers arrived with long canes, and took great delight in beating sections of the crowd into submission. Their crowd management skills left much to be desired, or, in fact, were non-existent. After taking a few whacks from the soldier's heavy canes, the queue took on some semblance of order. Brute force triumphed over friendly persuasion.

After witnessing this brutal example of maintaining some semblance of order, the brothers decided to inspect the apartment block they'd selected for the hit. They had to climb twelve flights of stairs once more, and after a little puffing and panting, arrived at the top floor. It was here the door leading to the roof was situated, and after picking the lock and locking it again, left them at ease to wander around, familiarizing themselves with the surroundings.

"This looks a good spot to mount the rifle," said Eddie, pointing to a clear view of the position on the sports field where the president would appear shortly. "Once he arrives, we'll get a good idea of the angle, distance and timing for our killing shot. I want to get a perfect idea of conditions, as well as what we may have to contend with in the event of any contingences we may have to deal with." Frank nodded in agreement; he was not actually going to squeeze the trigger, but act as a spotter, or lookout, should anything unexpected appear on the scene.

After the two assassins had familiarised themselves with the surroundings, they sat in wait for the 'guest of honour' to appear. He was never on time and delighted in making the crowd wait for his highly anticipated appearance. "What makes me very curious is the complete lack of security here. One would assume as the president is about to appear, and make himself a possible target for an assassin, the area where we are now would be awash with security; but not a sign of any; very strange indeed." observed Frank, as being a lookout, he was always mindful of these issues.

"One would have thought having a couple of security men placed more or less where we are would be in order, as this spot is ideal for taking a shot at the man they are supposed to be guarding," replied Eddie. "It's just as well that they are not too fussy about security, as it'll certainly make our job much easier."

After waiting a further half hour, things began to stir below in the stadium. A cavalcade of fancy limousines appeared, complete with an entourage of press and security men. Once through the huge gates, the vehicles began to disgorge its passengers... Except one. When everything had been readied and made secure, the man himself made his theatrical entrance, amid a cacophony of cheering and flag-waving – all provided and orchestrated by part of the entourage. The television cameras could roll once the cheering and flag-waving had begun, and it was time for the president to do what he was there for; distribute food parcels to the needy.

Once he'd given out a couple of dozen or so of parcels, two of his attendants took over, followed by two more. There was much food to distribute, and they had to get the job done so as not to keep their president from his other duties. It was a colourful and entertaining spectacle the two watchers on the roof of the apartment block witnessed, but their main purpose was to calculate the feasibility and timing for what they had planned. They noticed the president left early and quietly, entrusting the food distribution to members of his entourage; but the time he spent there – albeit a short amount – gave the brothers enough time to make their plans.

Within a couple of hours, the whole ceremony was over, and the stadium slowly emptied its huge crowd of people; some were lucky and received a food parcel, others were not. However, the whole show was over now, and would be repeated in two weeks. When the crowd dispersed, the brothers made their way down the twelve flights of stairs after locking the door leading to the roof behind them. There were people milling about in the street, as well as some bargaining going on from those lucky enough to leave with a parcel. The food it contained was resold to the highest bidder, or those not lucky enough to receive a parcel.

"Come on, bruv, let's drive up to the deserted farm and settle down for the night; we've seen enough to give us a good idea of how to carry out the 'hit'," suggested Frank. "We can open up the hamper the hotel prepared for us; let's hope they put more than a couple of beers in it cos I'm absolutely dying of thirst!" Eddie, deep in thought, agreed to Frank's suggestion as they made their way to their vehicle and drove to the farmhouse where they'd spend the night.

After dining on what the hotel had prepared for them, as well as sinking down a couple of warm beers, the brothers had a little discussion and turned in for the night. They never had much sleep, so they decided to start early and stop for breakfast once they crossed the border into South Africa.

"We'll do the same in a fortnight; drive straight to the farm and lay low until the ruckus has died down. We won't surface until everywhere is quiet; with a change of regime, we won't know if those in charge will be friendly or not; it's not worth taking any chances. Once DD comes up with our money, that'll be us finished; and for a long time because these jobs are becoming harder, and I wish we could get out of the game and do something less perilous," said Frank.

"What do you mean by something less perilous?" asked Eddie.

"Oh, I don't know, perhaps a steeplejack or possibly a lion tamer; anything would be safer than being a hitman," replied Frank jokingly.

"Since we left the old country – England – we've had more than a few dangerous jobs, coming out on top and earning good money; the problem is, we spent most of it living the life of a pop star or Premier League footballer. If we'd saved our money we could have retired early and done away with all this," reminisced Eddie with some regret.

"We worked hard for our money and enjoyed it whilst we had it. If you've got money and you don't spend it, you're no better off than someone who's skint," mused Frank rather philosophically. "We'll get the pay-out from this job and do a disappearing act. Three hundred grand plus apiece will soon have us back in shape, straining at the leash for our next job."

Arriving at the border crossing and passing through was relatively easy, except for the guards on the SA side who wanted to see their passports and ask a few questions. Making their way to a diner, both men tucked into a good breakfast with lots of coffee, after which they continued their journey to Pretoria where they had a meeting with their agent, DD.

Chapter 4

The Hit

During the time DD was busy in the States making arrangements, the brothers took delivery of the sniper rifle ordered by him from a South African arms dealer. It was delivered in plenty of time for them to take it out into the wilds and practice shooting and calibrating the scope at the same time. A small handgun accompanied the rifle, as an occasion could arise when it would be needed. There was also the problem of the men who seemed to be listening to their conversation back at the hotel. Frank informed his brother about his suspicions, and seeing these men at breakfast one morning, approached them quite diplomatically asking if there was anything he could do for them. The men were a little surprised at being approached this way, but it turned out they thought DD was in fact Danny DeVito. They were going to ask for his autograph, and even have their picture taken with him. Just as well DD was in the States at the time, as knowing him, he'd have gone along with the ruse, pretending to be the great man himself. Fortunately, the men in question left the hotel before DD returned.

The big day loomed ever closer. All preparations the team had made were about to be put to the test.

Comparable to thespians on the opening night of a new play, the brothers were a little nervous about how their performance would go. Although they never had to learn any lines, they did have a script – or plan of action, in their case – which had to be adhered to. If for one moment they believed their plan would go wrong, it was very unlikely they'd have gone ahead with it. Confidence was key now, and to dither or falter would not only put the plan at risk but could cost them their lives. Frank and Eddie were heading for the front line, whereas DD would be out of harm's way back in Pretoria; they reminded him at every juncture of this, just in case he thought that he had the hardest part of the job.

The three men ate a hearty breakfast together as they went through their plans. Mobile phones never existed in that period and contacting one another was at times very difficult. They agreed on the need to have some contact arrangement should anything go wrong, in which case they decided to use the agent's call centre in New York to accept and pass on messages.

After breakfast, they drove off in the hire car and the van they were using to pose as air conditioning engineers. Choosing a lonely spot, they came together to check the van had everything necessary, such as the air con units, pipework, both plastic and copper, as well as the most important piece of equipment, the sniper rifle – well-hidden and camouflaged amongst the rest of the gear. Included in the van's equipment were a couple of blankets along with food and drinks, as they intended spending the night at the deserted farmstead. This was an opportunity to fix adhesive signs to each side of the van, with the simple wording 'Air Conditioning and Heating Engineers of Pretoria' printed on each side, along with a bogus phone number... Which hopefully wouldn't be used by anyone. A tool bag containing tools was amongst the equipment, but the main purpose for this was to hide a small handgun and the cartridges for the rifle. Eddie insisted he'd only need one shot to complete the job. A small canvas cushion filled with sand, which they'd use to steady the rifle barrel, was amongst the mixture of what, on first inspection, would look like everyday tools service engineers might use in their business.

"Can you think of anything we've missed?" asked a concerned Eddie. The others inspected the contents of the van once more, and whilst looking at each other, told Eddie they couldn't think of anything. With the brief inspection over, it was time to wish each other good luck and go their different ways. The three men shook hands, and after a brief spell of reflection on the last couple of weeks, climbed into their vehicles and drove off. DD went back to Pretoria to await news of the developments, whilst the brothers made their way to the border crossing at Musina, and, from there, directly to the sports stadium.

Making their way through the border on the South African side was quite easy, allowing them to continue through to the Zuberi checkpoint with relative ease. As anticipated, because they were in a commercial vehicle, they were challenged by the Zuberi border officials. Apart from wanting to know the reason for their journey, they asked to inspect the contents of the vehicle. This situation was a little fraught for the brothers, as, if the hidden rifle was found, it would take much explaining as to why it was there. They had a readymade excuse – that it was to ward off any wild animals they were confronted with on route to their destination. Thankfully, these guards weren't as thorough as they could have been, and after a quick look into the rear compartment of the van, they gave the signal to proceed through the customs check – much to the relief of the brothers who simply remained cool and calm during the inspection.

Well and truly on their way, the boys relaxed, as part one of their plan was over, now they could concentrate on part two. The drive to the stadium went without incident or further checks by roadside police; these were most prominent because of tomorrow's visit by the president. The brothers drove directly to the deserted farmstead in preparation for the big day, which loomed closer by the hour. As they passed the stadium, crowds of hopeful recipients of the food parcels began to queue for the next day's visit of their president, who'd distribute them.

Reaching the farmstead, they hid the vehicle out of sight and spent their time in the empty house going over the next day's plans for the 'hit'. Their main weapon, the sniper rifle, was checked over to make sure every working part was in order. They'd already had a few practice shots after receiving it near to a deserted quarry in Pretoria; there they calibrated the scope. The ammunition, 7.62 by 5mm. cartridges, were inspected one by one, although hopefully only a single shot would be needed to complete the job. Both being light sleepers and having experienced bunking down in strange places during their Legion days, it was decided not to have a watch system, but to get as much sleep as they could, and be reasonably fresh and alert for the next day's important event.

Neither of the brothers had a good night's sleep as there was too much on their minds. The possibility of things going wrong, and other unforeseen circumstances had to be dealt with... In their heads. The biscuits and water they'd brought with them were very welcome at breakfast time, and hopefully would keep them nourished for most of the day – they had no idea of where they would eat after the 'job' was completed, but at that time it was inconsequential.

"Okay, bruv, this is it, the big one, are you ready for it?" asked Frank as he splashed some of their precious water on his face.

"You bet, let's get and do it," replied Eddie, rubbing his eyes and stretching out his arms. "I'm really looking forward to this job, it's been a very long time coming; I'm just hoping that we are not out of practice." With that, they made their way to the barn where the vehicle was parked, and after checking it over, drove towards the stadium and their date with death.

Parking the van across the road from the middle of the three apartment buildings, Eddie opened the rear door and took the bundle of plastic and copper tubing out, lifting it onto his shoulder. Being very careful not to slide the hidden weapon out of the centre, he waited whilst his brother locked the van doors. The assassins walked slowly and purposefully across the road to the building's entrance. People were milling around here and there, but none of them took any notice of a couple of workmen about to engage in their business.

The lift was still out of order, so the twelve flights of stairs in the six-story building had to be climbed once more to reach the roof space, from where they would mount their sniper rifle. "Phew, those bloody stairs really knacker me up," complained Frank, who'd taken the load off his brother's shoulders halfway up the stairway. "I just hope coming back down will be a lot quicker and easier."

"It'll definitely be bloody quicker!" replied Eddie. "Quicker than you bloody well think, I can assure you!" Frank just responded with a little smile.

On reaching the top of the sixth floor, they headed towards the locked door which led to the roof, only to find it unlocked. "What the fuck's going on here!" called out a surprised Eddie as he was about to place his lock picking tool into the slot in the door. "Someone's left the bloody door open, it's supposed to be locked at all times for security and safety."

"Anything goes in these places, bruv, I suppose we're lucky to find a door that's still on its hinges; who knows!" responded Frank.

"I know that, but we don't want any kids, or anyone else up here whilst we are in the middle of a very important job," Eddie replied with a snide grin.

Their questions were soon answered, as voices were heard coming from the position on the flat roof where they'd decided to mount the rifle previously. Believing them to be security guards, they were about to make a dash for the door but were prevented from doing so when a man in overalls appeared behind them.

"What are you two doing up here?" he asked. Being used to thinking quickly, and trying to act unconcerned, Frank explained that they were about to carry out some maintenance work on the air conditioning units.

"Well carry on," replied the workman, "as long as you keep out of our way; we're up here to repair the leaks in the roof."

Once again thinking quickly, Frank responded after sniffing the air, "From the smell, I'd say you're using hot bitumastic; that stuff gets down my throat and makes me feel ill; I reckon we'll move to one of the other buildings until you've finished here." After hearing Frank's reply, the workman shrugged his shoulders and told them to suit themselves.

"Okay then," chipped in Eddie, "we'll leave you to it and come back after you've finished." With that, they headed slowly towards the door and made their way back down the stairs to the entrance of the building.

"Well, that's fucked us up," said Frank, clearly showing his disappointment, "well and truly fucked up!"

As they reached the van, Eddie replied to his brother's annoyance, "Not necessarily, brother, we'll just have to use one of the other two buildings."

"Which one do you suggest?" asked Frank a little less annoyed now. After walking up and down taking a good look at the other two apartment blocks, Eddie pointed to another of the three buildings, and suggested they try the one to the right, nearer the road but, nevertheless, just as good, strategically.

"We really need to go up and take a look," suggested Frank.

"We don't have the time for an inspection, we've wasted too much time already; the president might be on his way right now, and besides, the lazy bastard only stays for about half an hour," explained Eddie. With both men in agreement, they decided to pick up the equipment and give it a try. If the new position on the roof was unsuitable, the job would be called off – costing them their share of a million dollars.

Once again, the two men crossed the road leading to the entrance of the other apartment building. It was the same layout as the previous one they'd chosen, except it had a fully functioning elevator – much to the joy of the brothers. "Thank the Lord for small mercies," said Frank, "at least we don't have to carry these bloody pipes all the way up those bloody stairs." Eddie smiled and nodded in agreement. Reaching the top floor, they made their way to the door leading out on the roof, which was soon unlocked, and after entering, locked up again to keep unwanted visitors out.

The layout was the same, so they made their way to the spot that would give Eddie the best shot at their target. Quickly sliding the rifle out of the bundle of tubes, and careful not to disturb the telescopic sight, they set it up on an air con unit ensuring Eddie had a comfortable 'prone' position. This entailed the sniper lying flat on his tummy, with his left elbow supporting the rifle barrel, with the butt pressed hard against his shoulder whilst both legs were spread apart. The cushion filled with sand was placed under the end of the rifle barrel, preventing any wobble. Obviously, he couldn't maintain this stance for long, so after making sure he was able to get back into position quickly, and checked the magazine held the five cartridges, Eddie stood up for a while to exercise his arms and fingers, taking deep breaths and exhaling slowly to reduce his heartbeat. Frank's job was to act as' spotter', always on the lookout with his small telescope. He'd keep the intended target in view, and anything or anybody out of the sniper's vision.

Suddenly, Frank noticed a lot of activity below in the stadium, indicating the arrival of the president. The huge vehicles containing the sacks of rice, flour, dried fruit, boxes of tinned fruit and vegetables and all manner of different food items were already in position. A small platform, big enough to accommodate the president and his aides, was in position, surrounded by members of the security squad. The huge gates of the stadium opened, and in drove two huge limousines. A half-dozen men in dark suits jumped out and made their way to the vehicle behind and opened its door. A huge cheer rang out as the president emerged from his limousine, dressed smartly in a military uniform, festooned with a multitude of medals. Waving to the onlookers, he signalled to the security guards to let the people outside come in and receive their free food allowance. As usual, there was plenty of pushing and shoving, but this was kept in check by the ferocity of the security men, who lashed out at the unruly ones in the crowd with their long canes.

"Get in line and in some order, or you won't get anything!" bellowed the guards. This threat didn't stop the pushing and shoving, so the brutal security men simply waded into the crowd, hitting out at them with their huge canes. Realising they wouldn't receive anything until order was maintained, the crowd eventually settled down in anticipation of receiving some food.

As this was going on, up on the roof of the apartment block, Eddie was busily zooming in on his target. His aim wasn't helped by the commotion below, but he soon realised this could be used to his advantage. After eventually 'dropping' the president, his security guards would find it difficult to see or hear where the shot came from. Signalling to his brother he was about to take the shot, Eddie slid back the bolt of his rifle, sending a cartridge into the chamber, and made ready to fire. Slowly and intently, he moved the rifle around, following the movements of his target. Once his objective appeared in the cross hairs of the scope, he maintained that position. Knowing he wouldn't have long to take the shot, he exhaled very slowly; keeping perfectly still, he squeezed the trigger, sending a bullet directly to the head of his target, bringing instant death to President Abimbola.

Those people below in the stadium couldn't believe what they'd witnessed. One minute the president was getting ready to distribute the food boxes, then suddenly he collapsed with his skull shattered, covering those nearest to him with blood, brain and bone fragments. It was surreal and took the onlookers a little time to realise what happened; when they did, all hell broke loose. People flattened themselves on the ground, others dived for cover under the food-laden vehicles; others ran to the gates trying to get away, believing more shots would follow. At that moment, no one knew where the shot *did* come from.

Up on the roof, the two brothers – happy with the outcome – quickly prepared their getaway. With the rifle quickly tucked away, covered by the plastic tubes – they left the copper ones on the roof as they were too heavy – they unlocked the door and headed directly for the lift. Catching his breath, Frank congratulated Eddie on a fine job; he'd witnessed the shot through his telescope. "Brilliant shot, bruv, I watched as his blood and brains splattered those standing close by; I doubt they'll be able to bring him back to life after that!"

"Let's bloody hope not, we don't want to go through this again, not even for another million dollars!" responded Eddie with grim determination. "Let's get the fuck out o' here, I've had enough killing for one day!"

Chapter 5

Cry Havoc!

The lift swiftly took the brothers to the ground floor, close to the entrance. Luckily, it didn't have to stop to let anyone else on, so there was no dialogue between them and anyone else; but that was about to change.

Hastily making their way to the entrance, they were accosted by a group of people preventing them from leaving the building. "That your van out there?" asked a huge man blocking the door.

"If you mean the vehicle across the road, yes, you are correct; what's your problem?" replied Frank.

"Our problem is we've been waiting over a month to get our air con repaired, and we ain't seen no one 'til now!" came a reply from one of the group.

"Sorry about that, but we are only contracted to service the appliances on the roof; we can, if you wish, take a booking to do yours at a later date. Now, if you don't mind, we are in a bit of a hurry as we have to be elsewhere, and we are late for an appointment," explained Eddie, who was in a rush to get away, as from the noise outside, it seemed the situation was getting out of hand.

"That's no good to us, we want our air con fixing now; understand?!" shouted the spokesman of the little group. The brothers became more impatient at this unwelcome and unforeseen holdup. They simply wanted to get away as quickly as possible; developments at the stadium were becoming chaotic.

"Okay, we'll look at your air con, but can't promise to fix it today as we're late for our next job," explained Frank to the persistent group. Taking his tool bag with him, he asked the whereabouts of the non-functioning unit, after telling Eddie – who was carrying the bundle holding the rifle – to take it to the van and wait for him there. Fortunately, the apartment where he had to inspect the air con unit was on the ground floor. After being shown where it was situated, Frank took a couple of tools from his bag and began to inspect the unit that was causing the trouble. If there was anything in the world, he knew absolutely nothing about, it was air conditioning. Trying to look as professional as he could, realising these people wouldn't take no for an answer, he declared the unit was defunct, and irreparable; but help was at hand.

"We have a new unit in our van; if you come across the road and carry it in, we'll install it when we've finished our next job, and have it working for you before this evening; how about that?" promised Frank.

"Seems okay to us, how will we pay for it?" asked one of the group.

"Don't you worry about it; we'll sort something out, don't worry!" assured Frank.

By now, the situation at the stadium had worsened, and bands of people came rushing by carrying boxes of food they'd taken from the vehicles in the stadium. They were being chased by police and guards, waving their huge canes and issuing threats to bring the parcels back or face the consequences.

Hastily, the brothers slid the new air con unit from the van to the waiting tenants, again assuring them they'd return within a couple of hours to install it, and have it working before the day was out. This promise seemed to satisfy the men, and they were only too happy to receive the new unit regardless of anything else.

Whilst this little incident was occurring, the situation in the arena had gone from bad to worse, becoming more riotous as the day went on. Seeing the president's head almost blown off before their eyes took a while to accept. As soon as the waiting crowd realised their country was without its figurehead of law and order, they began to take the law into their own hands. There was a massive surge towards the food items on the trucks, and instead of waiting in a line to have it distributed in an orderly fashion, there was a mad rush, which developed into a free-for-all to grab as much as they could. Trying to keep some semblance of order, the police and guards waded into the crowd with their clubs and canes again and again. Tired of being bullied and beaten by the thuggish guards, the long-suffering and hungry people decided to fight back. Unfortunately for the police and army personnel, they found themselves outnumbered, so they resorted to using their firearms on the crowd. Instead of restoring order, this action only made it worse. When the crowd saw their friends and neighbours being beaten and shot by the overzealous guards, they decided enough was enough, inciting them to rebel and rise up. After grabbing their weapons and clubs, the crowd turned on their oppressors and gave them some of their own medicine… Tenfold.

The word got back to the authorities that reinforcements were needed; resulting in more police and soldiers being swiftly dispatched to the stadium. Seeing their comrades getting shot and beaten caused the soldier's behaviour to become more brutal, wading into the crowd using clubs, batons *and* guns this time. The crowd swelled as they began to take their revenge on the army, who, despite being reinforced, were greatly outnumbered. Dead bodies piled up, many of which were police and army. Old grudges were being settled as the crowd beat their attackers with brutality unseen there for many years. As word got around to nearby residents of a massacre in progress, they turned up with knives, clubs and machetes to dispense some of their own justice.

The events happening at the sports stadium provided a welcome distraction for the brothers. With so much disruption and turmoil taking place, instead of identifying those responsible for the president's death, the security guards were more concerned with saving their own skins. The dead president was picked up, unceremoniously shoved into his limousine, and driven away from the rabid crowd, who were now releasing years of pent-up anger against those whom they saw as their oppressors. More police and army personnel arrived, only to be confronted with an inordinate number of crazed townsfolk, all hungry for blood and revenge.

After supplying the residents of the apartment with a new air con unit, and the promise of a prompt installation that same evening, the brothers, now unimpeded, were able to continue with their getaway. Valuable time was lost because of these unforeseen circumstances, but it was now possible to head for the deserted farmstead, where they'd remain until things became quieter... Easier said than done! As they managed to escape the turmoil and slaughter at the stadium, believing their way would now be clear, their brief feeling of elation soon changed to despair. Blocking the road ahead was a police car, with its two occupants pointing guns at them.

"Where you guys come from and where you heading?" called out one of the officers.

Being completely caught by surprise, Frank answered a little croakily, "We're heading up north, Officer, well away from the commotion back there."

"What you got in the back of your vehicle?" asked the other officer, believing it to be loaded with contraband stolen from the stadium frenzy.

"I'll open the door for you, Officer, if you give me a minute," called out Eddie, who was not sure what to do next. The taller of the two policemen walked over to the van and tried to open the door; finding it locked, he told the brothers to unlock it so he could inspect its contents.

"Oh, fuck it," uttered Frank in despair, "I left the tool bag in the back with the handgun inside, the bloody rifle's in there too amongst those pipes. If that nosy copper pokes around inside, we are well and truly fucked!"

"Calm down, bruv, take your time, we aren't done for yet," replied Eddie in an attempt to calm his brother. "Just let me handle it." Eddie got out of the van and headed for the rear doors, intending to open them for the suspicious police officer. His idea was to climb into the back and drag out the tool bag containing the handgun and use it on the unsuspecting police officers.

"It's a lovely day today, Officer; very warm too!" said Eddie to the watching policeman, trying to make a conversation.

"Just open up the fucking door, will you, and shut up about the fucking weather!"

Eddie was most surprised at his attitude, but realised these men were there for a purpose, namely checking vehicles for food boxes stolen from the stadium. Thinking it wiser to keep quiet, Eddie opened the van doors only to be pushed out of the way by the anxious officer. "What's in that bag?" questioned the impatient policeman.

"Tools, sir," replied Eddie.

"Open it up!" ordered the policeman, signalling Eddie to where the bag was situated.

This is it, copper, I'll teach you to be fucking nosey, he thought to himself as he fumbled around for the hidden gun. Releasing the safety catch whilst taking it out, he slipped it in his pocket, holding it firmly ready to shoot. Eddie called out to his brother in Italian, stating his intentions, causing Frank to get out of the vehicle and head towards the other policeman.

During this operation, the brothers were beset with unforeseen and unwelcome setbacks. At first, the incident on the roof of the first building they'd chosen, causing them to use the apartment next to it. There was the hold up by the irate residents demanding their air con be repaired straightway, and now the roadblock by two suspicious and overenthusiastic police officers. Having to shoot these two men would be comparatively easy for two experienced killers, but it would throw up even more problems in hiding their bodies, as well as dumping the police car somewhere. More and more complications for the two. But just as the god of misfortune had been visiting them, it was now time for the god of fortune to pay a visit to the pair. This visit came in the form of a message on the police car radio, instructing the two cops to get themselves down to the stadium immediately, as their services were needed. Still with his hands on the gun, Eddie waited for the policeman's reaction to the message. As the cop ordered Eddie to empty out the contents of the bag onto the floor, he suddenly realised the bullets were still inside. Whilst complying with the impatient police officer's order, Eddie waited his chance, and kicked the box of cartridges underneath the van, just as the officer turned to his head for a second. After having a quick look at the bag contents and peering inside the van to make sure there weren't any boxes of contraband food hidden there, he gave Eddie a sneer and returned swiftly to the police car, driving off with blue lights flashing and sirens blaring.

"That was too bloody close for comfort," called out Eddie as he took the gun from his pocket, clicking on the safety catch once more. "I really thought we were gonna have to kill those two coppers."

"Well, it would have been them or us!" replied Frank with a sigh of relief. "We'd better get our arses into gear, and drive to that bloody hideout before we have any more nasty surprises."

With that, two very relieved brothers drove off to the location selected to lie low until the commotion had died down; away from the chaos and havoc they'd caused.

Chapter 6

The President is Dead...
Long Live the President!

Some eighty or so miles away from where this commotion was taking place, in a palace not dissimilar to the Roman Villa Jovis on the Isle of Capri, an elderly gentleman was enjoying the company of a dozen or so naked girls sprawled around a gigantic and sumptuous swimming pool. As the 'old lecher', Emperor Tiberius, had enjoyed such entertainment at his palace a couple of millennia ago, this gentleman emulated his hero's activities similarly. Champagne flowed freely, and small sachets of cocaine were offered to anyone who wanted to take the drug. A select few of his entourage had been invited to the orgy and were busily enjoying what was on offer... Especially the naked women. Whatever happened at a Roman orgy was replicated here – except for the sniffing of cocaine.

The huge ornate doors to the pool area suddenly burst open and in rushed a very excited and agitated member of the household. "President, you must come quickly, something terrible has occurred at the stadium, someone shot and killed Kambo whilst he was standing in for you!"

The ageing man, now in a near stupor, hardly stirred on hearing this devastating news, and the highly agitated aide had to repeat the message once more. "My president, you are needed at the capital to give advice on the situation there and put your people's minds at rest... Everyone believes you are dead!" Still no reaction from the drunken and drugged up president.

Getting no reaction at all, the aide left the scene of the orgy and returned with a body of men in military uniform. Confronted by what they saw put them in a quandary. They knew the president used a stand-in for his fortnightly distribution ceremony, but it wasn't because he feared assassination, it was because he had more important things to attend to – namely drug-fuelled orgies with lots of beautiful naked women.

None of his closest associates cared or complained about the use of a stand-in now and then, as a chosen few were sometimes invited to participate in one of these orgies. On seeing the state of their president, and the possibility he would not be in a presentable condition to appear on state television to disclaim the rumours of his death, threw up a huge dilemma for his retinue of advisers... And a difficult problem to solve. The longer the news of his apparent death was believed by the citizen of Zuberi, the greater the chance of the uprising becoming permanent, with the opposition taking charge of the country. This would not do, as many people in the president's huge retinue would lose their lucrative lifestyle, or even worse, be slaughtered by the rebellious mob who were becoming more violent by the hour. Someone had to restore law and order.

General Jawara, one of the senior advisors of the president, realised he was the only one capable of taking over and sorting out this very dangerous situation. "Okay, everyone, clear the area and just leave the president here with us!" were the orders barked out to those involved this setting of drunkenness and debauchery. "Get yourselves away, and not one word of what has occurred here... UNDERSTAND?" he called out threateningly. The drunken revellers fully understood, knowing those who were the slightest bit indiscreet about their president's unsavoury activities ran the risk of never being seen again. Fear reigned in this country, especially amongst those members of the administration who said or did anything detrimental against its president.

An emergency meeting was called by the president's senior advisors. In all, there were around a dozen of these top-ranking men, each of whom had a department to officiate. Their main concern was to sober up the president and make him presentable to appear on the state television. Showing his face nationally and making a statement would help refute claims that he'd been assassinated. It would be extremely tricky explaining why the president had a stand-in to perform the distribution ceremony, instead of the man himself. This was just one of the questions that needed an answer to satisfy any queries that could arise from those people curious enough – or brave enough – to ask.

"We must get the old lecher sobered up enough for him to make an appearance in front of the cameras," ordered the general. "We'll have to spin a story about him being too unwell to perform his duties at the stadium; also, why he used that bloody stand-in instead."

"At least when he does make an appearance, he'll be in such a drugged-up state, those watching won't need much convincing of his illness, and hopefully believe he really *is* sick," suggested an adviser.

Whilst the debate on what to do to about the president's absence from his duties went on, an adviser and associate of the general was deep in thought. Sidling up to Jawara, he motioned the general to one side, suggesting they have a little chat away from the others. "What's so important to bring me away from this very important meeting? If you have anything to say, do it in front of everyone, instead of nudging and winking as if we are trying to cook up something by ourselves," was the general's angry response to Hagos, the associate and advisor.

"General, when you hear my plan, you'll agree the suggestion I'm about to make is not for everyone's ears; in fact, the less people who hear it the better," muttered Hagos in reply to the general's sharp reaction.

"Okay, let's hear it, and make it bloody quick, if those others over there see us talking together on our own, they'll think we are plotting something together we don't want them to know about."

"My general, that is exactly what I intend to suggest; this is the chance you have been waiting for, and there'll never be another, please believe me and listen to what I have to say!" pleaded the devious Hagos.

Meanwhile, almost eighty miles away, in the vicinity of the stadium, where death and destruction on a large scale was in progress, the brothers, Frank and Eddie, now back at the deserted farmstead, were in somewhat of a predicament, partly of their own making. Their planning for this operation was so precise and carrying out the assassination of their subject worked perfectly. However, no contingency was made to extricate them from a tricky situation should anything go wrong, and lots did go wrong, which they hadn't foreseen.

The operation of taking over and installing a new ruler of their choice into an African country required, firstly, the brothers to get rid of its ruling leader. Once they'd done the job they were paid to do – and quite handsomely – their part was over. All they wished to do was get back home and enjoy the fruits of their labour. The final part of their plan was not going well, and unfortunately for them, seemed as if it would get worse. They had no interest in what happened after they'd assassinated the president, and assumed leaving the scene of their crime would be comparatively easy. The drive to the border at Pretoria wouldn't take long, and even if it was closed on the Zuberi side, there were ways and means to cross with relative ease.

This wouldn't happen now, as the country had descended into a state of looting, rioting and killing. None of the roads would be safe to use, as gangs of looters and rioters, as well as the police and army, would be patrolling them, looking for plunder and plunderers. The brothers had been in worse situations, and always managed to extricate themselves from them, coming out comparatively unscathed; apart from their time served in the Foreign Legion.

After hiding the van and keeping their arms in readiness should they be attacked, the brothers sat down and took stock of their seemingly hopeless situation. "We've made a right fuck-up here, brother," said Eddie to his brother, who was scanning the outside dirt road for any signs of activity.

"We sure have; we definitely never planned on this. By now we should have been well out of here, but we can't go anywhere; give me a look at that map while you take over as lookout." Eddie picked up the map and handed it to his brother, taking his turn as lookout.

"I'm getting damn hungry now, I can't remember the last time we ate," said Eddie as he opened the map and spread it on a large table, which, being too heavy to lift by previous looters, was simply left where it stood.

Scanning the map, Frank placed his finger on their whereabouts, and traced a road that would lead them well away from the city to a point where they could cross the border. As it didn't seem to be a main thoroughfare, the chances were that it might not be patrolled by police or army; in fact, it could be deserted. After looking at his brother's suggested crossing point, Eddie remarked, as the terrain looked steep and rocky, it would be unsuitable to cross – except for ex-legionnaires, who'd find it relatively easy.

"The country bordering here isn't South Africa, but one of those small French protectorates. It's about a quarter of the size of Zuberi and could be our best chance," remarked Frank after studying the map.

"How far is it to the border?" asked Eddie.

After making a few calculations, Frank guessed it to be around forty miles or so. However, he did emphasize that the road seemed to have a lot of twists and turns on the map, indicating it could be quite hilly – mountainous, in fact. Rather than remain where they were, the idea of taking this route seemed preferable than the possibility of being discovered, resulting in fighting it out with the military. It didn't take long for the brothers to make their decision – one which they both agreed on. So, the die was cast, they would head out towards the border, taking the rough but seemingly safer mountain road; the sooner they began their journey, the better.

Meanwhile at the palace, everything possible was being done to sober up its drugged and inebriated president. Doctors were summoned to do whatever they could to make him as presentable as possible for an appearance on television, and discredit rumours of his apparent assassination. The official responsible for this hasty but necessary procedure, General Jawara, was having his ears bent by one of his associates, Jomari Hagos. He listened impatiently to what this devious individual had to say, and, after a little thought, called for two of the guards to attend immediately. Hagos couldn't understand why Jawara hadn't given him an answer to what he believed was a brilliant but underhanded suggestion. When two soldiers appeared and were given an order from General Hagos, he soon realised he'd overstepped his position as adviser to his superior.

"Put this traitor in irons and throw him in one of the cells. He'll have a fair trial tomorrow but select a firing squad in preparation for his execution, because he *will* be found guilty of treason; make no mistake!"

Poor Hagos couldn't believe what was happening, as only ten minutes previously he was giving advice to General Jawara on how to become the leader of the country instead of President Abimbola, whom everyone had assumed was dead. He now faced death by firing squad, although there were more barbaric methods of execution in this country – being shot was much preferable to being stoned, drowned, or thrown to wild animals. His legs turned to jelly, trembling uncontrollably, as the soldiers dragged him away.

"General, what was all that about, what has poor Jomari done to warrant such treatment?" asked one of the surprised officials.

"I'll tell you all what that slimy traitor suggested, shall I? After which you can decide for yourselves what treatment he deserves," answered Jawara. The general went on to describe in detail what their associate had suggested. Hagos, after taking the general to one side, suggested he should take advantage of this opportunity by killing their president – as he was already thought to be dead. Arrangements could be made for him to rule the country instead, by installing himself as its new president. The most abhorrent and repulsive part of the plan was to kill everyone who knew the president was alive and dispose of their bodies. After taking over the army and police, he could then do what was necessary to put down the revolt, in such a brutal manner, no one would dare to oppose him. After hearing this much of Hagos' suggestion, General Jawara was in no mood to take part in any plan to become the country's leader; he was happy with his present position and didn't wish for a change. Having a slimy individual like Hagos as a co-conspirator in this coup, was more than he could contemplate, so he ordered his execution without delay. His primary intention at present was to try and get the country back into some semblance of order. In doing so, he'd need to be ruthless and punish any transgressors taking part in this revolt and come down on them harshly. Hopefully, by being ruthless, it would set an example to others who even thought of joining the rebellion. First, he would have to get a sobered-up president to the capital, show his face on television and quash the rumours of his assassination.

Chapter 7

The Hunt is on

After the president signed the execution warrant for the traitor Hagos, General Jawara ordered those relevant to board the president's private plane. This had previously been made ready for the comparatively short flight to the country's capital. Instructions were given regarding the traitor's death by firing squad, and it was set for the following morning. Disposal of the body was left to the officer in charge.

Phone calls were made to officials in the capital in readiness for television and radio broadcasts; these would take place shortly after the president's arrival. Calls had also been made to the country's head of security, Englishman, James Strickland, or 'Sticky', as he was known. Strickland was a no-nonsense man who learned his profession in the British Army as a military policeman, and later became a member of the Security Service. Having fallen out with his superiors in that branch of the army, he offered his services to one of the new African nations. He was later accepted as the national security chief of Zuberi, with the rank of colonel.

Strickland was a like a dog with a bone. Once given a task, he'd use his given powers to see the job through to the end; often resulting in the deaths or torture of those he was tasked with hunting down and bringing to justice – Zuberi justice. His orders at present were to track down the men involved in the assassination of Kambo, the stand-in for the president. This he intended to do, and there would be no rest for him or his team until they achieved the task given.

His first port of call was the stadium where the assassination took place. Whilst wandering around, he imagined being the assassin, looking for the ideal spot in which to take a perfect shot at his intended victim. Turning around back and forth, his eyes rested on the three apartment blocks. He selected three groups of men and told them to search each block and ask the residents if anything unusual had taken place recently. The three groups set off, and it wasn't long before they reported back; indeed, there was unusual activity at two of the buildings around that specific time. One report came in about a group of men repairing the roof on the centre block; another was the repair and installation of air conditioning equipment at a different building.

"Return to these buildings and get a description from the men who were working on the roof; I'll come over and assist in the questioning," ordered the security chief. It wasn't long before the security team had a vivid description of the air con repairers, and, more importantly, their vehicle. These seemed likelier to have mounted a sniper rifle aimed at the president's stand-in at the stadium. He ruled out the roof repairers simply because they were still there, repairing another roof.

"Concentrate on the two men in a van, that's an ideal place to hide a rifle as well as other equipment they'd need. Make it top priority!" he called out. "We need to nail these two bastards before they leave the country; unless they already have!"

Strickland, still thinking like an assassin, tried to figure their next move after they'd left the apartment blocks. His suspicions were aroused when a report came through from some patrolmen who'd encountered two men in a vehicle of the same description. The patrolmen were summoned to the stadium and questioned by Strickland and his team. They gave a full description of the vehicle, and an account of their search of the van.

"And you never saw any sign of a rifle or other weapons inside the vehicle?" shouted Strickland excitedly.

"No, sir, we examined the contents of a small bag they had and were about to examine the inside of the vehicle, when a call came over the radio, requesting our presence at the stadium," replied one of the officers a little sheepishly.

"That call possibly saved your lives; it's for sure that if you *had* managed to search inside the vehicle and found the weapon, you'd both have been dead before you hit the ground" responded the security chief, a little more excited now, as he believed they were getting closer to their quarry.

"Which direction were they heading before you intercepted them?" enquired Strickland.

"North!" called out the patrolmen in unison. "North towards the deserted farmsteads."

"Good work, gentlemen," said Strickland, praising up the two patrolmen, "I think we have them now, I wonder if they can feel my warm breath on their necks, because they really need to be concerned now, or, should I say, frightened." The security chief was talking as if he'd already apprehended the brothers and seemed to be in a celebratory mood.

"Right, listen up, you guys," Strickland called out to his men, "I want every farmstead or deserted building north of here to be given a thorough search; leave no stone unturned; a bonus will be paid to the first search team to find these men. I want them both alive; a little gentle questioning will give me the names of those involved in this assassination. We've got 'em good and proper now, there's nowhere for them to hide." More men were called out from the base outside the city to assist in the search. At that moment, things were looking bad for the brothers.

Anyone with a television set or radio was urged to tune in to the State Broadcasting Station (SBS) as a special announcement was about to be made. More of the population had newly acquired TV sets now, because of the looting in the city and townships around Zuberi. These new viewers were hastily arranging makeshift antennae out of wire coat hangers and the like to tune into this special announcement. Loudspeaker vans patrolled the townships, giving out the time the transmission would begin. With plenty of time to spare amongst the residents and subjects of Zuberi, a carnival atmosphere developed. Food and drink were brought onto the streets – mostly stolen from the liquor stores during the riots – and those who could, placed themselves in front of a TV screen. Almost everyone knew of the assassination, and assumed their president was dead. This news gave people hope for a change of leadership, and, indeed, a change of fortune for the hard done by and oppressed population of this mineral-rich African republic. What would this special broadcast reveal? A new president, perhaps; one who would be more in touch with their country's needs. Whatever the announcement, it could be no worse than what they had to contend with at present.

At their hideout, a good distance from the stadium, the brothers decided on their next move. Whilst preparing for the 40-mile journey across some rough terrain, Frank wondered about the weather they'd encounter. If it snowed during their journey through the mountains, their crossing into the French protectorate would be most difficult indeed.

"I hope it's nothing like the crossing into Andorra from France, climbing the Pyrenees," stressed Frank.

"I bloody hope not!" replied his brother. "We aren't exactly equipped for mountain climbing... I bet it'll be bloody cold!"

The clothes they wore at present were simple lightweight jackets and trousers, not enough to keep them warm for what could be a very cold journey through a mountain pass. Eddie looked around at what was at their disposal, and suddenly had a great idea. "Those two blankets we brought to keep us warm during our first night here could come in very useful."

"Enlighten me," replied Frank.

Eddie spread both blankets on the floor, and with his knife made a huge slit in one, big enough to get his head through. After pulling it over his head, he measured down to where his hands were, then made two more slits, so enabling him to pass both arms through the blanket. "Voila!" he called out. "I've just made a poncho; tell me what you think, brother!"

"Bravo!" replied Frank. "Now make me one!"

With their ponchos sorted out, they looked around to see what else they'd need for the hazardous crossing at the border. Unfortunately, there wasn't anything else to carry with them except for water. No hats or warm gloves – simply what they wore on arrival.

"Okay, let's make the best of what we *do* have and give it a go; besides, it may not be as cold as we're imaging it to be," said Frank after resigning himself to the fact they might be ill-equipped for their journey. After one last perusal of their map, they checked around the farmhouse and set off on their journey to the border, which would take them to the old French colony of Rougemont.

The weather was warm as they left the farmstead, with around three hours of daylight left. The drive didn't take as long as anticipated, and no other vehicles were encountered on the deserted road, which had now changed into a rocky and dusty track.

"I wonder if this track has been used before," said Frank.

"Not for a long time, I'll bet," replied his brother as he examined it for signs of vehicle use.

"In that case, I wonder why," replied Frank. "Too bloody dangerous, I'll bet."

After removing anything of use from their van, including the rifle, they decided to ditch it as the road ahead wasn't wide enough for a vehicle. They selected a suitable spot, released the handbrake, and pushed it over a steep embankment to the rocky ground some 40 or 50 feet below. Luckily, when coming to rest, it positioned itself amongst some dense undergrowth, appearing almost invisible from above.

The road ahead changed into a track, and then a single pathway through the mountainous terrain. The light was fading, and they really needed to get a move on before darkness set in; spending the night on a mountain pass in the cold and darkness would have many hazards to contend with.

The brothers were about halfway through the steep mountain pass when they decided to rest up as they couldn't see any further ahead. Luckily for the pair, the weather remained calm, apart from being extremely cold. Congratulating his brother for hastily making two ponchos out of the blankets, Frank moved close to Eddie as they huddled together to keep warm.

A couple of hours previously, Strickland took a call from a search party who'd found evidence of a deserted farmstead being previously occupied, but now deserted. There were signs of fresh tyre tracks, as well as other indications someone had recently been there.

"Don't disturb those bloody tyre tracks!" shouted Strickland to the officer making the report. "Try to ascertain which way they are heading; I'll be there as soon as possible with the tracker. I've got a funny feeling we're about to nail these villains. It won't be long before we have them in our grasp!" Feeling very confident, the security chief, along with the local tracker, later confirmed the tracks to be about an hour old. This meant their prey was just one hour ahead of them.

Anxious to discover which route the assassins had taken, Strickland opened out a map of the region. There were four main routes heading north out of Zuberi, and one road petered out into a track leading to the mountain pass. Carefully studying these routes, 'Old Sticky' became a little excited at the thought of apprehending his quarry so soon. "Where does this mountain pass lead to?" he asked the tracker, who was busily studying the map.

"Rougemont!" he replied. "It's the old French colony which became independent about twenty years ago."

"What do you know about it? I've heard of it, obviously, as it's so close to us but have never had the need or desire to go there," continued Sticky.

"Not much, it's a country about the size of Andorra in the Pyrenees, between Spain and France. It's mainly tourists who visit, as its very picturesque; being a tax-free state also makes a visit there most desirable," replied the tracker.

Going over in his head what the tracker had just told him, the security chief became exhilarated. He gave orders to his men that four teams would patrol the four main routes out of the country, whilst he, along with two men and the tracker, would look at the mountain pass. Once more, his sixth sense gave him signals which needed following up.

After giving his men their orders, along with his small team, they drove in the direction leading to the mountain pass. On arrival, the light was fading fast as night began to fall, but not before the sharp-eyed tracker caught a glimpse of something white in the valley below, protruding from the undergrowth. After clambering down to investigate, the tracker shouted up that it was probably the van used by the killers. Seeing an old air con unit inside, as well as other bits and pieces, confirmed it.

"Well done, my man, we are almost there; we have them now!" exclaimed Strickland as he congratulated the tracker on his discovery. "My instincts were correct; I feel I know these people, as I'm beginning to think like them."

"What are they going to do next, sir?" asked one of the other men.

"Well, as it's dark, except for that welcome moonglow, I'd say they'll bivouac down on the pass somewhere and wait for daybreak before they carry on – which is what we'll do."

Climbing back into the car, the four men settled down for the night, starting the engine to warm up the car's heater. "This'll keep us warm through the night, men, settle down and get some rest, we have a little climbing to do come daybreak."

Halfway along the mountain track, and only about an hour ahead of their pursuers, the brothers were anything but warm and comfortable, huddling together to ward off the night-time chill that descended upon them suddenly.

Chapter 8

Closing In

It was a half hour before sunup, and just light enough to find one's way on the steep and winding mountain path. Hopefully, this would eventually lead the brothers to the shelter and safety of another country. Having had not much sleep and still feeling tired, they decided, despite this, to continue their journey as it now seemed safe to do so. The sun slowly appeared from the east, and its welcome and warming rays began to thaw out the half-frozen bodies of this intrepid pair.

"I'm bloody sure I've got frostbite," said Eddie as he he'd lost all feeling in one of his feet.

"Nar, that's just bad blood circulation; once you get moving it'll soon start to flow again," replied his brother reassuringly.

"What I'd give now for a mug of steaming hot coffee," said Eddie wishfully.

"With a generous helping of brandy in it to warm us up," agreed Frank.

They'd reached the highest point in the steep, rocky, and narrow path that led to Rougemont. This tiny country, previously a part of France, had become a self-ruling state, administered by a democratic government. Its economy relied on the tourist trade, but there were also one or two mines and various types of farming operations. For currency, they adopted the South African rand, as the neighbouring country was friendly and helpful to them; unlike their other neighbour, Zuberi, that was, in fact, an unfriendly dictatorship.

Reaching the highest point and now in descent, the sight of a small township in the far distance came into view; this did much to warm their spirits – but not as much as a steaming hot cup of coffee would have.

Stopping for a while, they had to decide what to do with the sniper rifle they'd taken turns carrying. "We can't exactly walk into a township carrying a bloody sniper rifle, can we?" exclaimed Eddie. "People will think we're about to invade the bloody place." Frank just laughed and suggested they throw it down below somewhere; after decommissioning it. This delicate procedure entailed smashing it against some rocks, before jettisoning the parts as far as they could down to the valley below. With that out of the way, they agreed to retain the handgun, as it was much easier to conceal.

They were almost on the outskirts of the little township, similar in size to an English village. Thankfully, as small as it was, it had the obligatory French boulangerie which one could always find in villages and hamlets the length and breadth of France. This legacy dated back to the Napoleonic era, when the emperor decreed that all towns, villages, and cities in France should have its own boulangerie or bakery, to ensure the French people wouldn't starve. The aroma of freshly baked bread gently wafted in the cool morning air, reaching the nostrils of the brothers, who'd forgotten the last time they'd eaten.

"I wonder what currency they take here; all notices are in French, so I hope it's not French francs," uttered Eddie as the doorbell clanged after entering the adjoining shop.

"*Bonjour, messieurs, que voulez-vous?*"

Replying to the proprietor in French, Eddie asked for two large, filled baguettes and asked if coffee was available."

"*Non, monsieur, je suis vraiment désole.*"

After being told coffee was unavailable, the brothers sat outside and tucked into their ham and cheese baguettes. "Boy, would I love a coffee right now, brother," uttered Eddie wishfully. Their wish was about to come true, when they were joined on the long bench seat by the local policeman, Sergeant Renard. Continuing the conversation in French, the cheerful police officer politely bade them good day and asked how they'd arrived at the village.

"We walked, sir; we have no transport, so we came on foot," replied Frank.

"I guessed that" continued the officer, "there are only two ways to get to my village, and I know it wasn't by road, as my gendarmerie faces the only road through our village, and I would have seen you."

"So, the only other way to arrive here is by way of the mountain pass?" enquired Frank.

"Correct, sir, that's the only other way," replied the officer. Eddie tried to change the conversation by asking where they could buy a couple of mugs of fresh coffee. "We have only one bar here, but that doesn't open until lunchtime."

"We'll have died of thirst by then," joked Eddie.

"I tell you what, gentlemen, how about being my guests, and join me in some fresh coffee at the gendarmerie; I'm about ready for one myself, and, if I'm not mistaken, you two are long overdue," suggested the police officer. The brothers looked at each other in such a way they didn't know what to make of this sudden – but welcome – offer from a kind and friendly police officer. Accepting the offer, they followed him to his small, but compact, police station, or gendarmerie, as it's known in French.

"Lambs to the slaughter, would you say, brother?" muttered Eddie.

"Not really, it'll be his funeral, not ours, if he tries any funny stuff," replied Frank speaking in Italian.

Colonel Strickland and his three colleagues had spent a reasonably comfortable night in their vehicle, warming up the interior with intermittent blasts from the car's heating system. There was ample room to stretch their legs, so, in all, when they did wake, they felt relatively refreshed – unlike the brothers they were pursuing, who had a terrible time sleeping outside halfway along the mountain pass.

The dilemma Strickland had to face and act upon was should he command more men to join him and the other three, now that they seemed very close to making an arrest? He didn't wish to bring too much attention to themselves, as until now they believed the brothers to be unaware of their closeness to them. If the brothers did spot them, and being in possession of a sniper rifle, there was a chance of being picked off, one by one. Apart from that, if they entered Rougemont with a company of armed men, it could be construed as an act of aggression, and cause an international backlash from the surrounding countries.

Convinced he'd acted correctly, it was now time to continue the hunt, and eventual apprehension of the two killers. The tracker took the lead, walking with his head down and slowly looking around for signs of recent activity. It wasn't long before he had the scent of those they were following. The tracks were no more than twelve hours old and *had* to belong to their quarry as no one else had passed them previously. After pointing this out to Strickland, the security chief asked how far ahead they were.

"It's hard to say at the moment, but when we reach the spot where they spent the night, I'll have a better idea, because they would have continued their trek at the same time as us – daybreak," replied the tracker, stroking his stubbly chin.

"Okay, men, get a move on, I can feel we're getting closer by the minute; it won't be long before we slap the handcuffs on 'em. By the way, did anyone bother to bring any?" In answer to this question, the others just shrugged their shoulders, indicating that, indeed, they hadn't bothered to bring handcuffs as they relied on someone else to do it. Seeing their shrugs, Old Sticky just growled and carried on with the hunt.

After about a couple of hours from setting off, the tracker came upon where he believed the brothers had spent the night. There was evidence of the stones and soil on the path being disturbed, as well as the spot where the brothers had peed not long ago, as it was still wet. This discovery cheered Old Sticky up immensely, and to celebrate, he peed in the same spot and urged the others to do the same, as from now on, there would be no time to waste on such matters, being so close to making a capture.

The pleasant aroma of freshly brewed coffee emanated from Sergeant Renard's coffee machine, filling the tiny office of his police station where he was 'entertaining' his two guests.

"My God, I just love that bloody smell; along with freshly baked bread, there's nothing to beat it," remarked Eddie.

"I love the smell of freshly peeled fruit, oranges in particular," agreed Frank. "What about you, Sergeant, what aroma turns you on?"

The sergeant looked in the air, and squeezing his lips together answered, "Fresh, mountain air, just as we have here in our lovely country, there's nothing to beat it!

The three men seemed to be getting on quite well, but this was possibly a disarming ploy which could catch the brothers off guard.

"Oh yes, gentlemen," muttered the sergeant, "I never asked to see your passports; assuming you have them with you!"

"No problem," replied Frank as he poked into their handbag and produced two passports.

"Ah, I see you are Americans?" said the police officer, after examining their passports and expecting an answer.

"Correct!" replied Eddie.

"I did wonder where that strange French accent came from; where did you learn French?" he asked. The brothers could hardly tell their inquisitive host they were all compelled to learn French in the Foreign Legion, and they were both wanted by the French authorities for certain crimes committed there; so, Frank opted for Canada as the country where they both learnt French. "Ah, that explains the pronouncement of your vowels, you are in fact speaking French Canadian, am I correct?" responded the sergeant whilst making a statement but expecting an answer to a disguised question.

This was beginning to get a little tedious for the brothers, which prompted Frank to poke around his bag and position the handgun in readiness, should it be needed. "Are you alone here, monsieur?" asked Frank.

"Why do you ask?" replied the sergeant.

"Just wondering, that's all," Frank replied, looking at Eddie and indicating they may have to go into action soon.

"In answer to your question, yes, I am the only police officer here as only one is needed. We have a church, a bar, a garage... Of a kind, as well as one or two stores, including the boulangerie. We rarely have trouble, but should I need assistance, I only have to pick up the phone or use my police radio and it'll arrive very quickly," stressed the police officer.

Police Sergeant Paul Renard served with the Paris Constabulary. He'd put in many years' service and rose to the rank of sergeant later in his career. During a bank robbery in Paris, he was hit by a bullet from one of the robbers, which almost cost him his life. After making a full recovery, rather than retire early and lose some of his pension, he was offered the job of local policeman of a small village situated in the old French colony of Rougemont. Although independent now, its government still relied on France for protection, so allowed France to station certain military personnel as well as provide a police force. He took this job, as being divorced and with no children, he'd only himself to be responsible for. After serving almost ten years as local bobby, he had just two more years to do, before retiring on a very lucrative police pension; plus, good service and injury bonuses. All he wished to do was to serve these last years in peace and quiet and retire in full health to enjoy what life as a civilian had to offer. He was in somewhat of a predicament now, as the two men entering his country claiming to be trekkers, were about to spoil his plans.

Sergeant Renard encountered trekkers many times living in a mountainous area, and he knew all trekkers wore the appropriate clothes and footwear. Most carried a stick to help support their legs and maintain balance on mountain tracks; almost all carried rucksacks with ample food, water, and maps inside. The two men in his office had none of these, and insisted they were simply out doing a trek. The astute police officer knew instinctively when someone was lying, and his two guests were doing plenty of that.

It was obvious these were the men being hunted for the assassination of the president of Zuberi. He had notices sent to him and was warned to be on the lookout for anyone strange entering the country from the pass. Frank and Eddie fitted this description, but Renard's problem now was what to do about it.

"Some more coffee, perhaps, gentlemen?" offered the policeman.

"If there is any, yes please!" answered Frank.

This strange scenario had all the ingredients of a 'Mexican standoff'. Both parties were putting on an act, and it was left to one of them to put their cards on the table. If the sergeant tried to apprehend the two men, it would end with him coming off worse. There were two of them, and most likely they'd be carrying a weapon, he thought. If he allowed them to continue their journey unmolested, and his superiors found out later, he would lose his job and his pension. Which was more important, his life or his pension? No contest!

It was Frank who decided to end the stalemate when he asked, "Sergeant, shall we cease playing this childish game and come to some sort of arrangement?"

"What do you mean, monsieur?" asked the sergeant, pretending to be surprised.

"We don't want trouble and neither do you, so let's stop pussyfooting around and get down to an agreement." The policeman dropped his act and agreed with Frank that, indeed, there was a problem here which needed sorting out.

"All we wish for is to catch a plane and get out of your country, without leaving any dead bodies behind, so let's make a deal," suggested Eddie.

The sergeant looked at his watch and advised the brothers to get to the bus station immediately and catch the coach into town. Gilbert the driver, and mechanic, always left at 10am and returned three hours later. "It's almost time, so I urge you to hurry," implored the sergeant.

"Oh yes!" replied Eddie. "And whilst we are on our way, you'll phone for reinforcements to intercept us at the airport!"

"No, no, that will not be the case, you have my word I'll not call for assistance until you are well away from here; I promise!" insisted the policeman.

Frank thought for a moment and suggested instead of relying on the sergeant's word of honour, they lock him in his cell, hide the key, and rip out the phone and decommission the police radio. "It's either that or we kill you," said Frank menacingly, "make your choice."

Poor Sergeant Renard, what a choice. Reluctantly he gave the cell door keys, along with his gun, to Frank, walked inside and sat down, resigning himself to the fact he had been outwitted by the brothers, but at least he was alive, and hopefully his superiors wouldn't think he was guilty of colluding with the assassins whilst making their escape.

Strickland and his team had come to the end of their trek along the mountain pass and could see plainly where the village was situated; hopefully harbouring the wanted men. Poor Old Sticky, this journey had been a little too much for him, so he ordered the men to rest for a while before continuing to the village. "We're almost there now, so ten minutes or so rest won't make much difference." He began to remove his shoes and socks to give his feet a well-earned massage but discovered blisters had appeared owing of the lack of appropriate footwear or sensible socks. His colleague's feet fared no better, causing them to remove their footwear and massage their tired and blistered feet. It was only the tracker, being used to climbing and walking on rough terrain and dressing accordingly, who never had a problem with his feet. Unfortunately for the three men who removed their footwear, they found it extremely difficult to put their shoes back on because their feet had swollen. The ten-minute break they'd anticipated, lasted much longer – a good half hour, in fact.

With the police sergeant locked away in his cell, the phone ripped from the wall and the radio smashed, the brothers headed for the bus station, which was, in fact, an old barn doubling up as taxi rank, repair shop and transport office. As there was no sign of the motor coach which ferried people to town, the boys began to think they'd missed it. Walking around the rear of the barn, they spotted what appeared to be a coach inside.

"Monsieur, are we in time for the bus into town?"

A rather plump, bearded man in greasy overalls, apparently servicing the vehicle, slowly brought his head up from the engine compartment and replied, whilst staring at the two strangers, "This old heap's going nowhere at present, not until I've stripped it down and replaced the cylinder head gasket."

"How long will that take?" asked Frank.

"All bloody day, I imagine. I'll then have to go into town to get new parts; that's assuming they're in stock," replied the mechanic with a sigh.

"What about the taxi?" asked Eddie.

The mechanic pointed to a rusty old heap at the rear of the barn, replying, "That's it, but it's waiting for repairs at the moment, I can't get the bloody spares!"

"How can we get to the town? We need to get to the airport!" exclaimed Frank impatiently.

"Hard luck, it's no concern of mine," answered the mechanic disconcertedly.

Eddie began to get annoyed with the intransigence of this man and was close to losing his patience. "It *is* your concern, you ignorant halfwit, if *you* are bus driver, taxi driver and mechanic all rolled into one; lose that fucking attitude or I'll ram that monkey wrench you're holding right up your fat arse!"

"Eddie, calm down and watch your language, this is getting us nowhere!" Frank apologised to the mechanic and enquired if there was any other mode of transport which would get them to the city.

"Nope, just my bus and taxi," Gilbert lied. In fact, the police sergeant kept a Land Rover in a garage at the rear of the police station, but he didn't wish these two men to know that. Frank took a wad of notes from his pocket, and waved them at Gilbert, whose eyes almost popped out at the sight of so much cash. "Well, er, let me think now; for the right price I could get you to town." Then, again looking at the wad of notes in Frank's hand, he continued, "But it will cost you."

Frank peeled several notes from the wad and handed them to Gilbert, enquiring if that would be enough.

"That'll do, monsieur, more than ample," the mechanic replied, whilst snatching the cash from Frank's hand and squeezing it into the pocket of his greasy overalls. Ambling over to the rusting Renault saloon, apparently out of commission, he gave the engine a few turns with the crank handle, and after much coughing and spluttering, it burst into life. Huge clouds of black smoke spewed from the exhaust, but eventually the tired old engine began ticking over – to a degree. Gilbert called out to his waiting passengers, "Come on, hop in, be quick about it, I've got a business to run!"

The brothers jumped into the rear seat, as Gilbert manoeuvred the rusting heap out of the barn and on to the road outside, whilst constantly revving the engine. Hearing a strange noise coming from the engine, Eddie remarked, "What's that funny knocking sound?"

"Oh, don't worry your pretty heads; we are only firing on three cylinders instead of the four, as we should be. There's a burnt-out exhaust valve giving us the trouble, but this old heap should get there; it's getting back's gonna be the problem." So, with a chug chug, bang bang, followed by puffs of black smoke, they were safely on their way to the town, and hopefully, later, the airport.

Chapter 9

Devastating News

After security chief Strickland and his tracking team of three had rested their tired and blistered feet, they limped the final few hundred yards to the village. The sun was higher, and the warmth of its rays was felt by the weary pursuers.

Arriving at the centre, they were amazed by the lack of facilities. Discovering the one and only bar, and finding it wouldn't open for another half hour, did nothing to raise their spirits. Spotting the gendarmerie, Strickland thought it wise to make a visit and explain their presence; after all, they'd entered another country and formalities had to be observed. Seeing the gendarmerie door was open, and entering inside, Strickland was shocked to see a police officer sitting in the prison cell. At first, he couldn't believe what he saw, but, after further observation, noticed the cell door was locked and secured. Being curious, he asked the occupant whether this was an exercise, or had he been locked inside purposely.

Fortunately, Old Sticky was reasonably fluent in French, which was just as well, as Sergeant Renard's grasp of the

English language was anything *but* fluent. Swiftly spotting the ripped-out phone and broken radio, and discovering the absence of the cell door keys, Old Sticky grasped the situation perfectly with his sharp eye and even sharper wit. "Unless I'm mistaken, Sergeant, you've had a visit from the two men we are trying to apprehend."

Playing dumb, Sergeant Reynard asked, "Now who would they be, monsieur?"

"Let's not play silly games now, my friend, we both know who we are talking about; you are not in any position to play dumb, are you?" After giving it some thought, Renard agreed with Strickland, but explained he was ordered into his cell at gunpoint and had no idea where the two who locked him up were at present. Both men agreed on the identities of those being pursued, and the crime they'd committed, namely the assassination of President Abimbola. After searching for the cell door keys, but without success, Old Sticky discovered a bunch of car keys. "What are these?" he asked.

"The keys to my Land Rover," Renard replied.

After explaining about the vehicle situation in the village, and his Land Rover being the only vehicle available, Strickland asked the sergeant where the two men who locked him up were heading. After being informed they were heading for the town, Sticky asked to borrow the Land Rover, with the promise of informing the authorities about the sergeant's demise as soon as they arrived in town – which he had no intention of doing.

"I have no choice, monsieur, they took the only set of cell door keys with them, and you now have the keys to my vehicle – what else can I do?"

It was about time for the bar to open, and the others pleaded with their chief to allow them to pay a visit. Realising his men had neither eaten or drank anything since early morning, he agreed on a half hour break for something to eat and drink. Finding a payphone in the bar, Strickland, now brimming with confidence of an early capture, rang his superior officer in Zuberi to give him the good news. He prematurely, and foolishly, informed General Jawara there would be an arrest very soon – possibly within the hour.

Gilbert the mechanic had managed to coax the old Renault 'taxi' to the town centre. It was beginning to overheat, so after he'd dropped the boys off in town, he chugged over to the filling station to replenish the radiator with water, and check the engine over. After the quick service, the old Renault, driven by an even older Gilbert, slowly made its way out of town, back to the village, blowing out puffs of smoke and misfiring in the painfully slow process.

The brothers, by contrast, were feeling elated – civilisation at last! The first stop in this newly found haven was a barber shop where they had a haircut and shave. Their next call was to a men's outfitters to buy new clothes; something more appropriate for a couple of sightseers, of whom there were lots about; they blended in quite well. Getting rid of their scruffy, dirty clothes was next on the list, as well as the tools and handguns carried in their bag. Their remaining possessions were carried in the bag, along with biscuits to eat during the flight. With these necessary measures complete, a decent lunch was next on the list. Oblivious to the fact they were being pursued and were only about an hour ahead of their pursuers, the brothers were also unaware the 'mission' they'd planned so meticulously was a failure.

The consequences of this failure would plunge them into more danger. Not only were the Security Services led by Strickland hot on their tails, but once their paymasters in New York found out they'd failed to kill the right man, and caused complete havoc in Zuberi, they too would be after their blood. There was also the down payment given to their agent, Diego Delgado, which would have to be returned... With interest. Unfortunately, Frank and Eddie were unaware of the gambling habits of their agent, DD; the down payment he'd been given by the Mob was used to settle his gambling debts.

Had the brothers been aware of these events, instead of being in the happy and elated mood they were at present, they'd be pulling out all the stops to get away from there, far enough from the clutches of Strickland and his bloodhounds. Even worse were the far-reaching tentacles of the International Investment Corporation, the thinly disguised Mafia organisation, which was to be feared even more.

Suitably refreshed with the aid of a couple of cold beers and a sandwich or two, Strickland and his team climbed aboard the sergeant's Land Rover. The tracker, who was driving, pointed out they were low on fuel and needed to find a filling station. After driving about four miles, they came upon a broken-down Renault saloon, with steam hissing from the radiator, and a plump man in greasy overalls with his head under the bonnet. Feeling charitable, Strickland ordered his driver to stop and ask if assistance was needed. Extricating his head from under the car bonnet and seeing Sergeant Renard's Land Rover being driven by strangers, Gilbert became suspicious.

"Is there a filling station nearby?" called out the tracker. Gilbert told him there wasn't, and the only place to obtain fuel was in town. "Have you any to sell us?" continued the tracker.

"Sorry, I'm repairing this car for a customer, and as far as I can see, he hasn't a spare can either," replied Gilbert.

"Okay, thanks for your trouble, we'll head into town." The tracker revved the engine and headed off in the direction of the main town.

Gilbert was left worrying about the welfare his friend, Sergeant Renard, and decided to head directly to the village to make sure he was okay. He knew he wouldn't lend his vehicle to anyone he didn't know, and Gilbert certainly didn't know the occupants driving away in his beloved Land Rover. Realising it was about three or four miles to the village, and with the hot sun bearing down on him, the ageing mechanic decided to ditch his Renault, and began the long walk back.

Arriving in the town centre, after carefully and slowly driving their vehicle to save fuel, Strickland told the driver to pull over to the filling station, situated across the road. It was his intention, after filling up, to drive to the airport and resume their search for the men they were hunting. Little did he know, they were just a stone's throw away from them, across the road, finishing their lunch in an Italian restaurant. Fully refreshed now, Frank and Eddie came out of the restaurant and took a taxi to the airport.

About twenty minutes later, they were looking at the arrivals board for the availability of flights. The brothers were disappointed, but not surprised, to discover only domestic flights left from this relatively small airport; short haul flights of no more than 1000 miles or so.

After taking a long look at the destinations board, they enquired at one of the check-ins for a flight to the USA. The nearest airport to offer any long-haul flights was Luanda in Angola. They arrived at Pretoria airport from Europe, but South Africa was the last place they would head for, as the security services would certainly wish to interview them… So that was out. Luanda in Angola was around 700 miles away. Being a safer option for them, they bought two one-way tickets for the relatively short flight of around three to four hours.

"Your flight leaves in one hour, gentlemen, and you'll need to be in the departure lounge ready for take-off in about 40 minutes. This gave the boys time to visit the bar and have a couple of pre-flight drinks; neither of them relished the thought of flying as they both hated it, having good reason to. A couple of drinks beforehand always settled their nerves.

At the petrol station in the centre of town, Strickland and his team had finished filling up their vehicle and were about to make their way to the airport. A policeman, spotting Sergeant Renard's distinctive looking Land Rover, and believing his friend and colleague would be driving, was surprised to see four strangers sitting inside. Walking over to them to enquire why they were driving the sergeant's vehicle, Strickland, who was now behind the wheel, assured the officer that Sergeant Renard had given them permission to borrow it for a visit to the airport, where they had to meet someone.

Not believing this paltry excuse, the police officer ordered them out of the vehicle. As they were getting out, the astute officer noticed a gun protruding from the shoulder holster of one of the security men, which Strickland spotted too. "I can explain this, Officer, if you'll give me a chance!" exclaimed Strickland. The police officer, feeling a little uncomfortable and realising they may all be armed, called for back-up on his radio.

"Everybody, put your hands in the air, and don't make a move, I have reinforcements on the way, and we don't want matters to escalate... So, hands up!"

This officer looked nervous, and Strickland realised they could easily overpower him if they wished, but thought it pointless starting a shooting match in the town centre. It wasn't long before two police cars turned up, and swiftly disarmed the security men amongst the protestations from Strickland.

"How did you take control of this vehicle, and where is its owner?" barked a more assertive officer. Strickland tried to explain, but instead, realised the situation was hopeless, so he surrendered. All four men were bundled into the two police vehicles and driven to the gendarmerie. Meanwhile, one of the police officers tried to contact Sergeant Renard on his radio, and being unsuccessful, decided to take a colleague with him and drive to the village in search of their fellow officer.

About a mile and half from the village, after passing the broken-down Renault, the police officers came across the easily recognisable Gilbert lying on the grass by the roadside... He was merely exhausted. They helped him into the police car and tried to find out what was going on. After arriving at the gendarmerie in the village and finding Sergeant Renard locked in his cell, everything was explained to them. With the sergeant's explanation of what happened to his Land Rover, all became clear to the two officers.

"Them two blokes I dropped off in town told me they were heading for the airport," said Gilbert, trying to clarify what was going on.

"Okay, in that case we'll alert the airport authorities with their description, and once apprehended, we'll get to the bottom of this!"

A little before these revelations were made public, the brothers were on their second cognac, congratulating themselves on their apparent success. Draining his glass and assuring Frank they had time for just one more, Eddie ambled up to the bar. Whilst waiting to be served, he casually glanced at the television, fixed to the wall. The picture of a man speaking on the TV seemed familiar to him – indeed, he'd seen that same face in the scope of his sniper rifle; it was the picture of the man they'd come to assassinate. The sound was off, and Eddie, although being French spoken, had difficulty reading the subtitles on the screen, displayed in French.

"Could you turn the sound up please," he asked the barman, "I can understand better if I *hear* what that man's saying." As he waited for the barman to turn up the sound, he called Frank over to have a listen. "This'll amuse you, it's the guy we shot the other day, they've brought him back from the dead." The two brothers started laughing out loud; but after the sound was turned up and they could hear what the speaker was saying in English, the smiles drained from their faces.

"What the fuck's going on?" said Frank. "This guy is supposed to be the president, and he's dead... Unless they have a bloody good double standing in for him!"

"Either that, or the guy we killed *was* the double, standing in for the president!"

"Just be quiet and listen to what's being said," interrupted Eddie, "there's something wrong here, I can smell a rat. If it's what I'm thinking, we've been stitched up, and we have killed the wrong fuckin' man!"

In fact, it *was* President Abuchi Abimbola in person, being televised addressing the nation. He went on to explain, because of overworking whilst running the affairs of the nation, he suffered a slight heart attack, and asked his friend – who *just* happened to look like him – if he'd take his place and distribute food to the hungry people of Zuberi. "Unfortunately, whilst helping an old friend, by doing a great service our country and its loyal subjects, he was cruelly murdered by agents of a foreign country; those being the USA and Great Britain. God must have ordained that I should be spared by giving me that heart attack, otherwise I would not be here today." The president spoke to his countrymen and followers as a Sunday priest would, addressing his flock during a sermon. He then went on, "My efficient Security Service now have the instigators of this plot to overthrow me almost under arrest. They will have a fair trial and *if* found guilty, punished accordingly."

The crowd was listening intently to what their hard-working and indefatigable president had to say. They'd become mesmerised by his speech, and were feeling sorry about the looting, robbing and destruction to property they were guilty of – although not sorry enough to return the TV sets and other goods they'd stolen during the riots. Hearing the next part of the speech elated most of them and gave them hope for their future. The president went on to promise everything was going to change from that day on.

"Together with my government, we will nationalise all the mines, factories, and farms to create employment for everyone, giving wealth and prosperity for all.

We will expel from our country all foreigners who wish us harm and take over their businesses." He went on and on, making promises he knew would not be kept, but by doing so, gave the people of Zuberi hope, and the promise of wealth and prosperity. Hopefully they'd cease the rioting along with the unrest and settle down to enjoy what the future had to deliver.

"What a load of fucking crap and drivel," remarked Eddie, "this old bastard and his henchmen have no intention of doing anything that will benefit the people of Zuberi. They follow him like sheep; in a month or two, they'll be back to square one, begging in the streets." But it was what came next from the president's glib mouth that really worried the brothers, something they had to be concerned about and not take lightly.

"Today, I have received a report from my chief of security, now in Rougemont; they are only minutes away from making a capture." Sticky's claim had been exaggerated somewhat. "The two assassins who murdered my great friend and benefactor of our country are within reach of being apprehended as I speak!" This news caused the mesmerised crowd to jump up and down in glee, cheering their president for the good work he was doing, making their country safe once more.

The look on the brothers' faces was one of shock, horror, and disbelief after hearing this news. Not knowing what to believe from this leader, who was renowned for his dishonesty in making false claims, threw the pair into disarray. In fact, this time what the president said was completely true, the brothers were literally minutes away from being apprehended, though not by Abimbola's men, but officers of the Rougemont police.

The call had been put out to the airport authorities to be on the lookout for two rather shabby-looking men, sporting a week's growth of beard and dishevelled appearances. Fortunately, this description didn't fit the brothers, although an hour or so beforehand, it would have.

The pair quickly downed their drinks and made a swift but dignified retreat from the bar and into the departure lounge, just hoping their flight would not be delayed. As they walked through the concourse on the way to the departure gate, waiting to have their passport and tickets checked, they were just able to hear the sirens from two police cars screeching to a halt outside.

"Departures for Luanda Airport will leave very shortly, please have your passports and tickets ready for inspection," came the instruction from the airport loudspeaker. As the boys passed swiftly through and made their way across the tarmac to the waiting plane, the relief felt by the brothers was indescribable. Hopefully this flight would carry them to safety and sanctuary... Or possibly not!

Chapter 10

A Flight to Remember

The brothers were a little surprised to see a small aeroplane waiting on the tarmac. Much smaller than those they were used to whilst flying around the world. It wasn't exactly tiny, thirty or so seats was its maximum capacity, but much less than the huge airliners they'd become familiar with. However, if it flew them to their destination in safety, all well and good.

The boys were further surprised when they saw the pilot of this aircraft. He wasn't young, or even middle aged; Frank put his age down to around sixty years old, although this could have been a slight exaggeration.

"How old must pilots be before they reach retirement?" asked Eddie.

"Whatever age it is, I'd say this old fella is way past it!" answered Frank sarcastically.

Two ladies in the queue ahead of the boys suddenly turned around when they heard Frank's sarcastic remark aimed at the apparently aging pilot. "Captain Jomo

Hagos is an extremely capable pilot, and a gentleman. We've flown with him on countless occasions, and he has never given us reason to doubt his capability and proficiency as a pilot," assured one of the irate ladies.

"I'm very sorry, madam, if my remark has upset you; please accept my apologies," responded Frank, not wishing to make an enemy of his fellow passengers.

"Your apologies are accepted, young man; we'll say no more about it, but please remember that we are in the capable hands of one of the best pilots this airline has." Frank just smiled and carried on his conversation with Eddie.

As they neared the end of the queue and were about to climb the steps to the aircraft, the man who they'd been talking about stepped out to greet them… In a somewhat old-fashioned manner. "Good day, gentlemen, welcome aboard my aircraft, and can I wish you a safe and memorable flight."

"That will be up to you, Captain," quipped Eddie as he stepped on the first rung of the ladder leading to the open door of the aircraft.

Another greeting was given by the sole member of the cabin crew, Anne Maria, an attractive lady in her early thirties. "Welcome, gentlemen, please show your tickets and I'll take you to your seats." Eddie gave this lovely air hostess a knowing wink and a smile whilst thanking her; after which she led them to the rear of the plane where the last two seats and the galley were situated.

Meals were not served on this flight, only sandwiches, tea, coffee, and soft drinks.

Once settled down in their seats, Eddie asked Anne Maria the whereabouts of the co-pilot, and was puzzled when she replied that small domestic planes with less than thirty passengers didn't require one. This explanation satisfied Eddie but left him feeling puzzled, as his belief was all passenger planes, no matter what the seating capacity, required two pilots. However, after conferring with his brother, they both accepted the air hostess' explanation and didn't wish to make an issue of it.

With everyone aboard, the passenger steps taken away and door slammed shut, the order to fasten seat belts appeared on the overhead gantry. After starting the engines, the pilot waited for instructions from the flight controller. Having received them, he taxied the plane gently to his allotted position, awaited instructions, and made ready for the take-off. Once in the air, after completing a perfect take-off, the seatbelt sign appeared, advising them to be unfastened. Captain Jomo came on the intercom, and once again wished everyone a happy flight. He went on to advise his passengers that, if they wished, they could lay back and relax or maybe sleep. Tea, coffee, or soft drinks would be served later by Anne Maria, as well as freshly made sandwiches. Captain Jomo then went on to report, "The weather forecast is good; however, we may feel a little turbulence later in the flight, but don't worry, I've flown this route hundreds of times, and have never come across anything I couldn't handle."

Frank and Eddie looked at each other, and felt assured the man they'd belittled previously was turning out to be quite the capable pilot as the lady in the queue described.

"Well, at least we're away from that shitstorm we caused back there. It was a close call and could have turned out badly for us. We'll have to rethink our plans when we arrive at Luanda airport and decide where we are going next," remarked Frank.

"It's for sure we can't go to the USA, as we don't know what sort of welcome we'll receive. We can't go to Sicily, as the Cosa Nostra will wish to *talk* to us. France is out as we're wanted there, as well as in the UK. North Africa is most definitely off the menu as are most big countries with warrants out for our arrest," stressed Eddie. "We've been naughty boys in the past, and I'm afraid it's all beginning to catch up with us."

"What about Switzerland? We have most of our money in a Zurich bank, and they are very discreet. We can rent a chalet up in one of the remote mountain villages and ride out the storm in relative comfort. It'll be much better than sitting in a prison cell... Or worse," suggested Frank. The brothers settled down to decide which course they would take whilst falling into a gentle slumber.

Approximately halfway through the four-hour flight, Captain Jomo made a habit of switching on the flight control system, usually known as the autopilot. He suffered from cramp on occasions, and found a walk up and down the aisle – whilst having a chat with his passengers – helped alleviate this. The autopilot could be set at different modes; the heading, altitude, and speed, as well as a weather contingency setting, which Jomo hardly used as he was never away from the controls for long periods.

With autopilot on, and disconnecting himself from the communications, Jomo stood up, stretched his legs, had a long yawn, and slid open the cabin door. At times, passengers on previous flights were a little alarmed to see their pilot nonchalantly walking amongst them, but their concerns were swiftly alleviated by Jomo's description of how the automatic flight control system functioned.

"Good day, once more," greeted the cheerful pilot, "if anyone has questions to ask, or is concerned in any way, please let me know and I'll do my best to answer them and put your minds at rest. We are more than halfway through our flight, and due to land at Luanda airport in good time, so, everybody, please sit back and relax."

This exercising of his cramped legs routine not only improved the aging pilot's stiffness in his limbs, but gave him a chance to speak to passengers and relieve them of any concerns. Many people were still afraid of flying, and needed lots of assurance before or, indeed, during the flight to put their minds at rest. This flight was no exception, and the captain did his best to calm the nerves of *some* of his anxious passengers.

Captain Jomo had finished his leg stretching routine, as well as his public relations exercise, and took a cup of coffee from the galley. This he intended to take to his cabin and enjoy whilst sitting in the pilot's seat. Suddenly, the aircraft lurched sharply to the left, causing him to spill coffee over Eddie who screamed out in pain. The plane swiftly corrected itself, but this sudden unexpected turbulence caused another sharper twist to the left, resulting in the cabin door sliding shut.

Anne Maria was busy trying to sponge the hot coffee from Eddie's clothes and soothe the scalding he'd sustained. Reaching into the first aid chest, she managed to find an anti-burn cream which she applied to Eddie's wound, easing the pain instantly; thankfully the scalding was not too serious.

Captain Jomo rushed to the cabin, hoping to regain the controls, but discovered the door wouldn't slide open. The excessive impact had caused it to come off the sliding rail between the bottom of the door and the cabin floor; it became jammed... Very tightly. "Don't panic, please, we have a slight problem, but one we can easily sort out!" assured the captain. Passengers *were* beginning to panic, and this wasn't helped by hearing the sudden scream from Eddie, after having hot coffee accidently spilt on him. Whilst examining the cause of the door's failure to open, Captain Jomo – who, by now, was beginning to panic himself – called out to the airhostess to bring a knife from the galley with which to prise the door open.

"We only have a bread knife and butter spreader that I use to make sandwiches, Captain... Will they do?"

"Yes, er, yes, the bread knife will do, bring it here quickly!" shouted the harassed pilot.

After snapping the breadknife in two by inserting it under the jammed door and trying to prise it open, the perplexed pilot rubbed his bearded chin in the hope of finding inspiration to solve this tricky problem – which was worsening by the minute.

Passengers were beginning to panic even more now and screamed out. "We're gonna crash, we're all gonna die!" screeched a frightened passenger.

"The plane's losing height, we'll hit the ground any minute," called out another.

"There's a mountain range in the distance, we'll hit it if we don't gain height!" shouted a man whilst looking out of the window towards a ridge of mountains in the far distance.

Two priests, on their way to a conference in Luanda, tried to give comfort to the frightened passengers. However, after looking out of the window and noticing how low the plane was becoming, one priest, Father Michael, began to panic himself, and started praying, urging others to do the same. His form of prayer was akin to a priest giving the last rites to everyone, including himself! Hearing a priest behaving in such a manner, and appearing very frightened, resulted in the worried passengers taking to their knees on the floor of the aircraft, and praying with great intensity and purpose... Even the irreligious amongst them.

"Father Michael, please quieten down, you are frightening everyone," whispered the other priest, "our job is to comfort people, not frighten the bloody life out of them!"

Whilst all this was happening, Captain Jomo had tried just about everything he could to get the jammed door to move but was less successful than before. He made an appeal for everyone to settle down as the situation was in hand. Whilst peering out of the window and seeing how much height the plane had lost, as well as the proximity of the mountain range, he called out to the male passengers for help. One or two answered his call, but most had their arms wrapped around their loved ones, comforting and shielding them against the inevitable impact; others were on their knees praying.

Incredibly, as all hell was breaking loose, Frank was fast asleep, but was suddenly wakened by the screaming and shouting. As he stirred and peered out of the window, he noticed the ground was nearer than before. This led him to believe they were losing height in order to land. Standing up and seeing the shenanigans at the front of the plane, he called out to his brother, who was nursing his recent scalding, "What the fuck's going on down there?! Women and men screaming, priests praying, the pilot shouting for help... Just what's the matter?!"

"I reckon we'd better get to the front and see if we can help, otherwise there's going to be a disaster happening very soon," stressed Eddie.

With that, both men rushed to the front and were quickly put in the picture by the extremely frightened pilot.

"We need a crowbar or large screwdriver to shove under the door and prise it upwards onto the rail so we can slide it back again. I must get to those controls. The shuddering and shaking of the aircraft has done something to the autopilot's control system. We keep losing height and suddenly regain it to the pre-set altitude. For some unknown reason, the plane drops again only to repeat the process. Luckily, we've managed to avoid that mountain range, but if we encounter another, we'll be in big trouble," explained Captain Hagos.

"How bloody ironic," uttered Eddie, "we've just dumped the very tools that could get that door open; a crowbar and screwdriver. What do you suggest, brother?"

Bending down to look at the bottom of the sliding door, Frank suddenly jumped up, shouting triumphantly, "Eureka! I've got it!" He motioned to Eddie the position he wanted him to adopt, which was to put both arms under his armpits and grab his shoulders. This position would enable him to give support for what he intended doing next. Once in that position, Frank told him to brace himself ready for what was to happen. "Lean back and support me whilst I give the bottom of that door a good kick; we need to somehow get it back on the rail to slide it open," instructed Frank to his brother. After three or four kicks from Frank's heavy boots, the door became dislodged from the pillar. The problem was however, it wouldn't slide on its rail.

Pandemonium had set in behind them, with the incessant screaming, shouting and loud praying. This chaos and turmoil did little to help the brothers' efforts in releasing the door, which was jammed rock solid. Captain Jomo simply stood back, helpless and dismayed as he looked on at the futile attempts to un-jam the immovable cabin door. Taking a small breather, Frank instructed his brother to hold on to him even harder as he was going to make one last attempt to kick the bottom of the door in... But sadly, to no avail.

"Instead of supporting you, let's both kick that bloody door together; the double impact might move the stubborn bastard!" suggested Eddie, who was fast becoming annoyed from the racket behind him. "Listen everyone... Just shut the fuck up... We're trying to save everyone's lives here... Just give us a bloody chance, will you!" That seemed to work, as most of the screaming died down.

Now, both brothers stood side by side with one arm each over the other's shoulder. Eddie's right arm wrapped around Frank's right shoulder; Frank did the same with his left arm. With the brothers now tightly linked together, they agreed to stand on the left foot, and use their right foot to batter the door... In unison. Despite his recent scalding, Eddie grabbed his brother as tightly as he could, rubbing his wound against Frank.

"Okay, after three... Ready?" called out Frank. "One, two, THREE!" Their heavy boots hit the door at the same time, causing it to shudder. "Again!" called out Frank. "Boot the bastard again; imagine you are hitting the face of that bastard of an NCO who got us put on fatigues back in the Legion!"

That did it. Eddie kicked the jammed-up door with such intensity it jumped off the rails and swung into the cabin, pivoting on the upper rail. "That's it, keep kicking, it's come free!" called out Frank. "Now hold it!" he shouted. "Take a running shoulder to it and push the bastard into the cabin!" This they managed to do, by barging into the door and causing it to come free and land inside the cabin next to the pilot's seat.

Seeing this, Captain Jomo lost no time clambering into the cabin and dragging the battered door away from the pilot's seat. He quickly took his position in front of the controls, and released the autopilot, reverting to manual control of the aircraft. It had become dangerously low by now, and the speedy action of the experienced pilot forced the plane to swiftly regain height, thus taking it out of danger. Once the normal operating altitude and course were reset, Captain Jomo let out a huge sigh of relief. Eddie and Frank removed the remains of the door out of the cabin into the plane's gangway and were greeted by tumultuous cheers from the relieved passengers, many of whom believed that day was to be their last.

Of course, the priests tried to take credit for the apparent miracle, by claiming their prayers had given the brothers the strength and ingenuity to save them all from what could have been certain death. Whether the distraught passengers believed there was any truth in this or not, it didn't prevent them from waving their arms in the air, hugging and squeezing each other in pure relief and delight. Normality was almost restored to the aircraft and its passengers, but this shocking experience would be with them for many years to come. In fact, there were those amongst them who would never fly again because of this terrible event.

When the passengers were back in their seats, with sanity and reason restored, the captain announced it wouldn't be long before they landed at Luanda airport. He apologised for the events which had taken place and hoped it would not put anyone off flying again. Captain Jomo then gave thanks to Eddie and Frank for their quick action in averting a tragedy; although he still claimed that the situation was under control, and things weren't as bad as they seemed. This remark led to more than one or two derogatory comments from the passengers.

"If you hadn't left your place at the controls of the aircraft, this frightening experience wouldn't have happened!" called out one man.

This was followed by, "Your bloody stupidity almost had us all killed. If it wasn't for those two brave men, we wouldn't be here now. You're a bloody disgrace, you should retire before you kill somebody!"

These vicious remarks upset Captain Jomo greatly, and he began to wonder if, indeed, he should retire, before a real disaster occurred owing to his age and creaking bones. However, he made a perfect landing at Luanda airport, but only a few loyal passengers shook his hand or wished him all the best. On the other hand, many of them gathered around the brothers, thanking them, and patting them on their backs in appreciation for what they believed to be decisive action in the nick of time, resulting in saving their lives.

As they walked towards passport control and baggage retrieval, they hurried through, not wanting to speak to police or reporters who'd got wind of the near disaster. Out in the airport concourse, they scanned the arrivals board for a flight which would take them to Switzerland. Lufthansa could fly them to Frankfurt, where they'd take a flight to Geneva. Once there, they would feel safe again... But only for a short while.

Chapter 11

The Birth of a Dynasty

Stephano, the swarthy looking Italian sailor, couldn't take his eyes off the pretty young lady whilst she served customers at the dockside café. He'd eaten breakfast there many times yet didn't have the nerve to engage in a conversation with her.

"Linda!" called out the café owner. "When you've finished serving that customer, there are tables that need clearing and wiping down!"

"Okay, Dad, as soon as I can, but I've only one pair of hands!" she replied to her father.

Stephano, still watching her, hoped she'd come to his table and clear it, then the opportunity would arise for him to chat with her; but as his table was still occupied, she didn't bother; so, the wishful diner lost another opportunity.

The constant glaring at his daughter by Stephano didn't go unnoticed by her father. Being very protective of her, he was suspicious of any man who tried to 'chat her up'.

The year was 1909 and certain procedures had to be observed if a young man wished to meet up with a young lady. Being Italian – Sicilian born – and not speaking English very well, made it difficult to converse with either the young lady or even her father.

Stephano could easily have eaten breakfast on his ship without paying for it. After being at sea for a few weeks and finally docking, he simply wished to get away from his shipmates and have some time on his own. He turned down the offer to go out on a binge with them; usually a pub crawl culminating in a 'cherchez la femme' exercise, where they'd end up in a local brothel or pay a prostitute for her services.

Back in the café and finally plucking up courage, he decided not to attempt to speak with the girl, but to her father. He knew the language was going to be a problem, but nevertheless, gave it a try. After approaching Linda's father – who at the time was extremely busy – the young sailor attempted to ask if he might 'pay court' to his daughter. Her dad didn't really understand what was spoken by the nervous sailor, so he told him to 'be off', and stop pestering him or ogling his daughter.

When Linda saw Stephano scurry out of the door after being told off by her dad, she asked what the fuss was about. "That bloody foreign sailor's asking if he can go out with you, that's what it's all about!" he shouted back at his curious daughter. "The bloody cheek of the man; what's 'e thinking of?"

"Perhaps he thinks I'm for sale or perhaps you're a pimp," Linda replied to her father with a little chuckle.

"Well, 'ed better not come in 'ere again, or I'll give 'im what bloody for!"

Most men would have given up after being told off as he'd been, but not the plucky Sicilian. He returned to the café the next day but chose a time much quieter than his previous visit. Carrying a huge bag with cigarettes and tobacco inside, as well as a huge bunch of flowers, Stephano entered the café and walked slowly up to the man who'd only the day before told him not to come back.

Linda's dad was taking a break after a busy morning, as well as having a well-earned smoke. Whilst scanning the local newspaper, he saw Stephano approaching, and was about to give him his marching orders. Outdone by the Sicilian, he put down the flowers and spoke to him first; then placed his hand inside the bag and removed the tobacco and cigarettes.

"Signore, er, I mean, sir, please accept these gifts in the spirit of friendship." Arthur, the girl's father was well and truly taken aback, and not wanting to offend this young sailor, or, indeed, miss out on the tobacco and cigarettes, simply took Stephano's hand and shook it.

"Are these flowers meant for me as well?" Arthur asked jokingly to the bemused Stephano.

"I am sorry, sir, but these are for your beautiful daughter, who I would like to meet – under strict chaperoned conditions, obviously," replied the nervous sailor.

Linda's dad thought he may have been too abrupt with the young handsome man on the previous occasion. His daughter was now at the age of meeting young men, and eventually marrying. In his neighbourhood, there weren't many men he'd wish for as a son-in-law. Running the café kept his daughter very busy, and she never seemed to take an interest in men – especially those she encountered locally.

At this juncture, Linda emerged from the kitchen only to see her father chatting away with the man who only yesterday he'd threatened. What had brought about this sudden change? But seeing the flowers and gifts on the table, all became clear. "Aren't you going to introduce me to your *friend*, Father?"

Suddenly, hearing her lovely voice, Stephano stood up and introduced himself to the pair as Stephano Capuano, but was sometimes called Stephan by his friends. From here on in, all seemed to go well for Stephano; being invited to meet Linda's mother and other family members was a triumph for the young Sicilian. How easily a gift of flowers, cigarettes and tobacco can change what was previously an impossibility, 24 hours earlier. But to be fair, after meeting and chatting together, Arthur took a liking to this well-mannered young sailor... Especially the gifts he could acquire without too much difficulty. The ground rules were laid out to him about the custom of being chaperoned, and not being alone with a young lady until they were well acquainted. Stephano realised this and was in complete agreement.

His pluck and tenacity had really paid off on this occasion. His good luck also played a huge part in this romance; upon returning to his ship, he was told that it wouldn't sail for another week because of problems in the engine room. A huge oil leak occurred, and the engine needed a complete overhaul that would take at least a week to complete. This unexpected extension of shore leave succeeded greatly in bringing the two young people together. Stephano visited Linda's house on many occasions, and he even offered to help in the café, cooking Italian dishes that most people hadn't heard of, but took an instant liking to. As it was, Linda and Stephano weren't lovers, but in the short space of a couple of weeks, that changed, and they became obsessed with each other.

After two weeks, the ship was still not ready to sail; an engine component was not available and had to be shipped from Italy where it was built. The skipper told the men they wouldn't be paid for the time off that was forced on them, so Stephano asked to be freed from his contract, as he intended marrying and needed a job. The ship's captain wasn't too happy about this, but being an old romantic Neapolitan, agreed to Stephano's request. And so it was, this young Sicilian quit the sea to settle down to married life... All aided by of a bunch of flowers and a bagful of cigarettes and tobacco.

Chapter 12

Gang War!

Events happened at an immensely fast pace after Stephano first introduced himself to his future wife's family. Linda never had much experience with boys before, and was completely smitten by the young Italian who was also head over heels with her. Anxious not to lose him to the sea – as most sailors never stay ashore for too long – she asked her father's advice on whether to marry him or not. Her dad got on well with Stephano and found him to be honest and hard-working; but, like his daughter, he didn't wish him to return to his life as a seaman, believing, if that happened, they'd all lose him forever.

Linda's mum and dad, along with Stephano, came together to discuss the young couple's marriage. It seemed the pair hadn't known each long, but if Stephano took to his old life once more, it was possible they'd not only lose a future son-in-law, but a daughter as well, believing Linda would follow him wherever he chose to go. The canny café owner wanted the pair to run the café, as, not being in the best of health, this arrangement would take much responsibility from him.

Shortly after this little get-together, a marriage was arranged, resulting in the happy couple getting wed some three months later. Less than a year after the wedding, their son was born, who they named Alberto. His birth was followed about a year later by twin girls, who were christened Lisa and Gina. Of course, both grandparents were delighted with these happy events, wondering how many more grandchildren would arrive on the scene in the future.

Unfortunately for everyone, in 1914 war broke out with Germany and Austria against the Allied Powers of Great Britain, France and Russia. Although Italy wasn't involved at first, it joined Britain and France the following year. Being an Italian national, Stephano thought it his duty to join-up and serve in the Italian army's fight against Austria. He fought at the Battle of Caporetto, where Italy beat the Austrians. However, this victory was short lived – Italy was defeated by a counter offensive later in 1917. Although slightly wounded, he carried on fighting until Italy finally beat the Austrians at Vittorio Veneto in 1918, which helped bring an end not only to the war, but the Austrian Empire as well.

After the war, Stephano returned to England and took a job at the docks. The café went into liquidation because of food shortages, and Linda's dad took a turn for the worse. A little later, he sadly died, although happy in the knowledge he'd a son-in-law and grandchildren who'd look after the most important people in his life, Linda and her mum.

When the children were old enough, Stephano took the whole family to where he was born, Palermo in Sicily. They had an extended stay with relatives, and Gina, one of the twins, asked to stay there and live with Stephano's relatives. How could he refuse – Sicily was such a beautiful place, and his daughter simply fell in love with it, having no wish to return to London's East End. Fortunately, Alberto and his other sister, Lisa, had no wish to live there, and returned to England with their mum and dad, where he later found work in London's dockland.

Alberto married around the year 1932, followed shortly after by Lisa, who married and moved to Bedfordshire with her new husband. Alberto and his wife produced two sons and a daughter, thus ensuring the continuation of the family name. All seemed to go well for a while; but, as happened with his father, war broke out once more between Britain and Germany, with France fighting on the side of Great Britain and her Allies. This time around, Italy joined the war and fought with Germany against Britain. Alberto hadn't the appetite to fight against members of his father's family but was conscripted into the army anyway, and posted to North Africa. Because Stephano was an Italian national, he was forcibly interned on the Isle of Man with people from other foreign nations who'd pose a danger to Great Britain's security. Rather than be separated from her husband for the duration of the war, his wife, Linda, joined him in the internment, but sadly died there after contracting tuberculosis.

It seemed Italy didn't have the appetite to fight, as the allies took 38,000 prisoners at the Battle of Sidi Barrani in Egypt in December 1940. It was here that Alberto's fluency in Italian became useful, when he was asked to take a position of translator, which brought with it a promotion to sergeant. He was content in the knowledge he'd not have to kill any Italian relations, and even happier when Italy finally surrendered in September 1943.

Being unscathed and unscarred, Alberto Capuano came home from the war late in 1945. His wife and three children had been living in Bedford with his sister's family, where it was much safer than London, with the heavy bombing of the capital and its docklands. His two sons and his daughter attended school in Bedford and loved living there. They soon had to return home to London, where their dad found work rebuilding the mass of bombed out buildings.

Finding the labouring job too much like hard work, it wasn't long before Alberto found work at the docks. He very soon became involved in illegal dealings with a gang consisting mainly of Italians; many of whom were ex-prisoners of war, deciding to stay on in England rather than return home to a life of poverty. There was much money to be made in London's docklands, and knowing the right people, as well as having good connections, could make them all rich.

The Italian mob weren't the only gang operating there; one or two East End gangs were in competition with the Italians or 'Ites and Ities', as they called them. Trouble boiled over when they entered each other's territories. The main business operating at that time was 'black market' trading. Certain goods found their way to gang-owned warehouses, instead of the legitimate ones for which they were intended. Dockworkers such as stevedores and longshoremen were involved, along with certain ship's captains and crews.

Alberto became active in similar operations whilst working in Naples during the war. Shiploads of foreign aid goods were sent there from America and Great Britain after Italy surrendered. Many of these goods were never delivered to their intended destinations because certain crooked operators got to them first. The Camorra – a Mafia organisation – had much of this illegal trade well sewn up. All transactions went through them, and anyone working independently, if discovered, usually ended up dead. Having a Sicilian background, where the local Mafia was the Cosa Nostra, went someway to being accepted into dealings with the Camorra; being a member of the British Army working as translator and coordinator, was also an advantage to the Mob. Alberto was able to furnish information such as cargos and ships' arrival times, which were most useful to the men who were going to steal their loads. It enabled the transport and destinations of these goods to run smoothly when prior knowledge of arrival times and contents of cargos were available.

Although he wasn't a member of the Mob, he was trusted and rewarded greatly by them for the information he provided. Alberto couldn't bank this money, but after changing it into gold, he'd take a trip across the water to Palermo in Sicily, where he'd deposit it at his sister Gina's home for safe keeping, with the intention of collecting it long after the war had ended.

With these dodgy dealings and pay-offs, there was quite a sizeable sum awaiting him when the time was right to collect it.

Alberto's sons, Franco and Eduardo, after first finding work at the docks, later joined their father in the illegal operations he and the gang were involved in; much to the annoyance of their mother. There were a few confrontations with the other gangs, but overall, they managed to keep out of each other's way, carrying on with their respective unlawful activities.

There existed one or two members of the East End mob who'd taken a huge dislike to the Italian gang, especially as they were doing much better than them, and allegedly encroaching upon their territory. Two of the mobsters – Longboat and Boxer – took it upon themselves to start what later became a gang war. Longboat was so nicknamed because he was lanky and had a long face – cockney rhyming slang for face being 'boat race'. Boxer was given his nickname not because of his pugilistic abilities, but for being aggressive and thickset, with a face that matched the features of that particular canine breed.

Carefully choosing their target as the leader of the Italians, and knowing his usual whereabouts, they decided one dark evening to lie in wait for him. Not content to just give him a beating as a warning to keep off their territory, they gave him both barrels of a twelve-bore shotgun at point blank range. Poor Alberto never had a chance; the shotgun blasts killed him outright, leaving his body terribly disfigured.

The noise of the gunshots brought others swiftly to the scene, and it wasn't long before the police arrived. By then, the two assassins had made their quick getaway, laughing callously at what they'd just done. "That'll teach them Itie bastards to stray onto our patch," snarled the cowardly Boxer.

"We gotta get rid o' that bleedin' gun; what d'ya reckon we should do wi' it?" asked Longboat a little anxiously.

"Sling it in the bleedin' river, no one's ever gonna find it!" replied his accomplice sneeringly.

Waiting for the opportunity, the killers threw the shotgun into the middle of the River Thames, assured in the knowledge it wouldn't be found. After their evil night's work, they made off to their favourite pub on the Wapping high street, The Town of Ramsgate, to join their mates and brag about what they'd just done.

"You silly pair of fuckers, don't you realise what you've just done – you've only gone and started a gang war with them Italians!" called out the boss of the East End gang. "We're well and truly fucked now; them Ites won't take this lyin' down!"

"But, boss," protested Boxer, "we wuz doin' everyone a favour getting rid o' that Ite."

"You pair 'ad better watch your backs if that crowd find out you shot one of 'em," warned their boss.

"Well, a bunch of Ities don't frighten me," responded Longboat haughtily, "let 'em come and try owt, we'll be ready for 'em!"

Indeed, 'them Ities' had no intention of taking this cowardly ambush of their leader lying down; after discovering Alberto's badly disfigured body, they were already planning their revenge. Hearing the news of her husband's murder, his wife, now a widow went to pieces. Why had someone done this terrible thing to her beloved husband and father of her three children? Her children did everything they could to comfort her, but she was totally inconsolable.

The funeral was a huge affair, attracting many of the Italians living in that area, as well as other dockside workers and associates of the various factions operating there. During the funeral, and at the wake, Alberto's favourite music was played. He loved Puccini, and in particularly the plaintive strains of 'Oh Mio Babbino Caro' and 'Un Bel Di Vedremo' from *Madam Butterfly*; these sad pieces of music did much to create a sorrowful atmosphere.

No one seemed to know the reason for this callous act, but gang members were warned by the police not to take matters into their own hands. They were advised to let the police handle things and leave it to *them* to bring the killers to justice.

The Italians had other ideas, and when Grandfather Stephano took the boys to one side whilst peering into the open coffin at his late son's wake, he reminded them it was their duty under the traditional unwritten Sicilian law, to avenge their father's murder; the die was cast, there would be no going back. It wasn't long before the killer's identities were discovered, owing to their constant bragging. Anyone with the slightest modicum of common sense would have remained quiet and kept their heads down; not these two cowardly killers, who seemed to bask in the adoration of fellow gang members, plying them with drinks, asking to retell how they 'did it'. Each time the account of the killing was retold, it became ridiculously exaggerated. The killers implied it was their victim who confronted *them*, and it was only by the chance they were carrying a twelve-bore shotgun, that they were able to defend themselves. Of course, no one believed this ridiculous excuse, but it made for great entertainment, hearing the ludicrous claims from these two clowns, that their part in the murder was simply self-defence. Incredibly, the police didn't seem to take any action after hearing about these preposterous claims from their informers, and simply put it down to 'boastful bragging'.

Whilst the East End gang members were having a laugh at the Italian's expense, wheels were turning in their organisation about what action should be taken. It was agreed Alberto's two sons would have to honour their father by avenging his death. They'd decided who, they now had to plan where and when, as well as what would happen later. Taking the boys to one side, the man now in charge of the gang, Pietro Falconi reminded them that, after doing their duty by killing those responsible for their father's murder, it would be a very long time before they could return to England after they'd fled the country.

"Boys, leave it to us to arrange things, but it must be left to you to avenge your father's death and defend the honour of the Capuano family." The boys simply nodded in agreement. Falconi went on to explain the plan and arrangements. "After you've made the hit, you'll get away as quick as you can and board a ship, hopefully one that'll take you to Naples or another Italian port. You'll get yourselves over to Sicily where you will contact family and friends of your dad; they'll do the rest, believe me, you'll be in safe hands, my boys."

"What about Mum and our sister?" asked Eduardo.

"Don't worry, they'll be taken care of. We've got to get this hit sorted first; most of the details are sorted except for the ship and when it sails. Is that okay, fellas?"

"*Capisco*," answered Franco in Italian.

"Yes, and you'd better start using our mother tongue after this, as no one speaks any English where you two are going," responded Pietro with a laugh.

The boys were given a small gun, a snub-nosed Smith and Wesson .38 calibre, with which to carry out their revenge killing. Lessons were given in a deserted quarry on how to load, unload and fire it. They were advised to get as close to their targets as possible, with the 3" short-barrelled gun, nicknamed 'The Bulldog', and aim at the head, firing off two rounds apiece to make sure. Pietro also advised the boys, if possible, to shoot one of the killers each; that would automatically share the burden, and the act of revenge, between them.

The place chosen for the shooting was a pub on the Wapping high street, near to the appropriately named Execution Docks. "Have everything you wish to take with you when you do a 'runner' on the night," reminded Pietro, "things like passports and money; you'll need 'em when you get off the ship at Naples, or wherever the ship takes you. *Capisco?*"

"Yes, we understand," answered the brothers solemnly as one.

"Well, that just about takes care of it, except for the 'getaway' ship; and by the way, ditch that bloody gun overboard when you're in the English Channel; nobody'll ever find it there," suggested Pietro.

The boys were as ready as they'd ever be, and had enough time to say their farewells to their sister, mother and grandfather. All they had to do was wait for final instructions, which would take them on a journey away from England, possibly for a very long time... Or even forever.

Chapter 13

Execution Dock

In the afternoon of 23rd of May 1701, at 5pm, being low tide on the River Thames during that period, the infamous pirate, privateer and buccaneer, Captain William Kidd, was hanged at the appropriately named Execution Dock in Wapping, London.

Crimes committed at sea, including piracy, mutiny, and murder, came under the jurisdiction of the Admiralty, and it was *they* who were responsible for trying, convicting, and punishing these criminals. Because these crimes were committed at sea, it was decided, appropriately, the punishments should be administered at sea.

The River Thames being a tidal river, was the location for executions by hanging. Permanent gallows were erected offshore in the Thames, qualifying the term 'at sea' to be observed. The Admiralty looked unfavourably at those who committed crimes at sea, and to display their revulsion to such crimes, made the punishment harsher than those committed on land. Instead of using a rope long enough to execute the convicted criminal by snapping the neck instantly after 'the drop', a special method of hanging was reserved for these maritime offenders.

A shorter rope was used on these hapless criminals, which instead of delivering a swift death, ensured a long, slow, and lingering suffocation, causing the half-dead souls to kick their arms and legs in the air, imitating a macabre sort of dance; 'the dance of death', as it was known.

In the unfortunate Captain Kidd's case, the rope snapped instead of his neck, causing him to fall to the dry riverbed in a drunken and dazed state. There were calls from the crowd that this unusual occurrence was divine intervention, implying Kidd was innocent. These cries were ignored by the officials, who quickly acquired a replacement rope, and proceeded with the execution, thus condemning the unfortunate victim to a slow death by strangulation. After Kidd's excruciatingly painful and extended death, his body was tied to a post on the foreshore until, as was customary, three tides had washed over it. After this, his body was placed in a steel gibbet, and displayed at Tilbury Point for three years, as a warning to pirates, mutineers and other criminals who'd choose to commit crimes at sea.

A few yards from where these barbaric executions took place on the riverbank, stood a public house with a truly interesting history. Built around the time of the Wars of the Roses in the 15th century and known as The Red Cow – because of the antics of a ginger-haired barmaid of the period – it was later renamed The Town of Ramsgate, in honour of the Kentish fishermen based in that town. Choosing to unload their catches nearby at the Wapping Old Stairs, instead of Billingsgate where they'd pay higher taxes, saved them an enormous amount of money – possibly some of which they'd spend in the pub.

Condemned prisoners would descend to their horrific 'stretched out' deaths by way of the Wapping Old Stairs, which ran alongside the inn. As custom had it, each condemned prisoner was allowed a last 'quart of ale' before being hanged. This was taken at The Turk's Head Inn en route, or sometimes The Town of Ramsgate would be used to serve them their last drink of ale.

The inn's cellars housed those men unfortunate enough to be press-ganged into serving in the Royal Navy before they went to sea. Convicted prisoners deported to the colonies were housed in the same cellars whilst awaiting transportation. Captain Bligh and Fletcher Christian had a drink together here before embarking upon their fateful voyage on the *Bounty*.

With such an interesting history as a favourite drinking establishment of the period's infamous characters, together with the many macabre goings on in and around its perimeters, it was no wonder this infamous establishment was favoured by the present-day rogues and villains, of whom the East End gang was amongst its numbers.

Longboat and Boxer could always be seen drinking and boasting there, to anyone who was foolish enough to buy drinks for them, simply to hear the far-fetched stories of their supposed misdeeds. They never boasted or bragged to strangers about their recent and actual killing of Alberto Capuano, father of Franco and Eduardo. His two sons were given the unenviable task of taking retribution against this nefarious pair, preserving their family honour by doing so. If it needed to be known where to find this evil duo, one only had to look in at the Town of Ramsgate on a Friday or Saturday evening, to watch them downing their pints, standing at the far end of the bar. Being a creature of habit can sometimes be one's downfall; on this occasion, it might well have been for Longboat and Boxer.

Chapter 14

Honour Thy Father

The brothers were at home, spending their last few hours together with their mother, sister, and grandfather. Not knowing when they'd see each other again meant for a tearful and final farewell.

"Do your stuff, boys, and make your family proud!" encouraged their grandfather, Stephano. "We'll all meet up together in 'the old country' when things die down." With that, he gave both boys a big squeeze and hug, trying to hold back the tears that began to run down his craggy weather-beaten old face. He had to quickly let go of them before he broke down and wept outwardly.

Mum and Lisa, upon seeing Grandad's reaction to his two grandson's departures, began to cry, only not supressed as the older member of the family, but outwardly and uncontrollable wailing.

"Must it be like this, my boys? Is there no other way we can sort out this terrible situation?"

"No, Mother, what has to be done must be done by us and us alone. We'd prefer not to do it and keep our family together, but *che deve essere, deve essere;* what must be, must be!

A knock on the door suddenly interrupted this tearful farewell; after opening, it revealed a sombre and serious looking Pietro. "Okay, boys, are we ready to go?"

"As ready as we'll ever be," replied an even more serious Eduardo, slowly wiping the tears from his puffed-up eyes.

"Right, lads, here we go, better to talk on our own and not include family members to what's going on. What they don't know, they can't tell if questioned by the police... And they will be, believe me. So, it's a last goodbye and off to our briefing down at the docks."

A final blow of a kiss to Mum and sister – Grandfather couldn't bear to see their departure – accompanied by a sad lingering look, and that was it; away to do what duty required of them. It would result with either a police apprehension, and a possible trial, conviction and hanging, or a swift departure to places and experiences unknown. This was to be the destiny of the two young Anglo Italian lads, into a fate unknown.

Arriving at the docks and inside one of the buildings owned by the gang, Pietro began explaining the plan to the nervous brothers. "Listen up, boys; now I take it you know the name of the pub, and where it's situated?"

"Yes," answered Franco, "we did a recce the other day to make sure we knew the way. We went down Thomas

More Street and joined Wapping high street; we followed the old cobbled road for about a mile until we came to Oliver's Wharf. It's tucked away on the corner of Wapping Old Stairs where the condemned prisoners were marched down before they were executed. Am I correct?"

"You're right," answered Pietro, "but remember, it's dark now, so don't get bloody lost, okay!"

The boys simply nodded, saying, "How can anyone get lost in that short distance?"

"You'd be surprised," replied the Italian, "but will you be able to identify your targets; one's a lanky, long-faced geezer; his oppo's short, well-built and very ugly!"

"With a description like that, who could miss 'em?" replied Eduardo.

"Okay, but whatever you do, don't lose your way... Y'hear?"

"Right, boss, we won't!"

"Now listen, and listen hard; unfortunately, there's no rehearsal, which we would've liked, but I've gone over the ground and made all of the preparations." The brothers listened intently to what Pietro had to say. "There's only us here, because the rest of the gang are up town in pubs and clubs getting their alibis sorted out; it's just us three."

"What about your alibi, Pietro, won't you be questioned by the police?"

"Don't you worry about me; I've got my alibi sorted out already. I'm not really here, but up town in a club where half the members will swear I'd been all night."

"Very clever, my friend, but don't get caught out!" replied Franco to his late father's trusted friend.

"Right, here's the plan. You have the gun?" Franco patted his pocket and nodded. "Made sure it's loaded?" Once more, he got a nod to his question, "Okay then, here we go at last." Looking at his wristwatch, he informed the boys that he had a passage on a ship sorted out which would leave St Katharine Dock precisely at high tide, midnight. "Unfortunately, it's destination is Marseille, and not Naples, as we wished, but nevertheless, you'll be somewhere safe... For a while."

"That gives us four hours," said Eduardo, looking at his watch, "long enough to do what we have to."

"You'll be amazed at how time flies when you don't want it to; for the ship to sail at midnight means you'll have to be aboard by 11.30pm at the latest," replied Pietro, again checking his watch, "and our time's running out as we speak!" The brothers were getting a little nervous, but hearing the next instruction, made them even more apprehensive. "Getting to the pub from here will take you less than a half hour. Enter and leave the bar by the front door."

"Will they be in there?" asked one of the brothers.

"It's Saturday night, they're always in there; take my word for it!" The thought of doing as planned began to hit home, and Eduardo almost asked Pietro to accompany them, but swiftly changed his mind when he heard the next part of the plan. "Enter the bar and look to see where the ugly pair of fuckers are supping, usually at the far end, so I've been told. You walk up to them, making sure no one is in your line of fire; you put your hand inside your jacket pocket, calling out their names as you do it; slowly cock the gun as you take it from your pocket, and as they turn to face you, let 'em have it. Two bullets each in the head; as they slump down dead, you make your exit from the door you came in, making sure you turn left into the alley. Hurry along the 20 or 30 yards to the steps leading down to the river. The tide will be in, so don't bloody well fall into the river. When you reach the water, look towards your left and you'll see a little boat waiting by Oliver's Wharf; I'll be in it. After hearing the gunshots, I'll be at the ready, and whisk you to St. Katharine Docks where you'll board the *Emperor Vespasian*. Any questions?"

Of course, there were many questions to ask, but the boys simply had to go over the instructions in their heads for the plan to become clearer. This well thought out scheme, after being absorbed, brought up something which was unclear, and needed to be clarified by Franco, who asked, "It sounds a good plan, but what about the other drinkers standing at the bar and sitting at the tables?"

"Oh, don't worry about them, as soon as they see you with a gun in your hand, they'll all be on the floor, covering up their heads. There they'll stay until you leave the bar, then it'll be a mad scramble to get out; so, bear that in mind."

"What if one of the East End Gang pulls a gun on us?" asked Eduardo.

"Look, you've got the element of surprise, if anyone pulls a gun on you, shoot the bastard before he shoots you. This ain't a game of cowboys you used to play as kids, this is real life!" exclaimed Pietro. "I'd do the bloody job for you with pleasure, but this is something you have to do, so accept your responsibility; *capisco?*"

"*Si, si,*" replied the brothers together, "*si, si.*"

"And just in case you suddenly go soft on these killers, and they start begging for mercy, remember how cowardly and ruthlessly they gunned down your brave father, making your lovely mother a widow, and depriving you and your sister of a really fantastic dad... Bear this in mind when you squeeze that trigger!"

Chapter 15

First Blood

The two brothers shook hands with Pietro, who wished them good luck, vowing to see them again, hopefully within the hour. Eduardo wished for something that had been troubling him to be cleared up. "Can you clear something up for me, Pietro. The plan is to pick us up at the rear of Oliver's Wharf after you hear the gunshots and bring us back here to board the ship you've sorted out to make our getaway. Why can't you take us there with you in the boat as well as bring us back?"

The canny Italian rubbed his bristly chin and thought for a while but didn't give an answer to the question; instead, he promised he'd tell him on the way back. This didn't go down well with the brothers and left them slightly suspicious of Pietro's motives. "Boys, don't worry, you can rely on me completely; I swear I'll not let you down, believe me!"

Still not convinced, the brothers began the half hour or so walk to their date with destiny. It was fully dark now, but streetlights showed the way. They didn't speak for a while, until, simply to break the stony silence between them, Eduardo asked about the strange shaped iron bollards fixed into paved areas. "I've always wondered why those iron bollards are shaped like cannons with a cannonball stuck inside the top."

Franco thought for a while, then, with a smile, answered, "I don't know, bro; it all seems like a load of old bollards to me!"

Hearing the unexpected but humorous reply from his sarcastic brother, Eduardo suddenly burst out laughing. This little bit of humour lightened the sombre mood a little, as they were tensed up and unhappy with the task ahead of them. "I tell you what, brother, if I had my way, we'd both carry on walking when we get to that pub, find another further down the road, and get pissed."

"I feel the same as you, but we'd never be able to face any of Dad's mates or our Italian family again. This rotten job's got to be done. Face it, even if we never had Sicilian connections, we'd still have to avenge our dad's cowardly murder," replied Franco. Neither of them had the heart or intention of doing what was planned, but knew killing these two thugs and risking the consequences, was preferable to living the rest of their lives in shame.

Still walking in the cobbled roadway – with its cast iron bollards – The Town of Ramsgate's swinging pub sign in the distance indicated their short journey was at an end. If all went to plan, they'd return to St Katharine Dock by boat... If it arrived, which was questionable, owing to Pietro's refusal to answer their question.

Peering through the glass panels of the brightly painted pub door, they looked intently for their prey. "Look! Just in front of us at this end of the bar, it's Longboat, but I can't see his mate, Boxer," whispered Franco a little excitedly.

"We've gotta kill 'em both; one without the other won't do!" replied Ed despondently.

"He's probably gone for a slash... Just wait a while, he'll be back. Those two are never apart for long," said Franco, a little optimistically.

Suddenly, a voice behind them called out, "You two gonna stand there all bloody night or are ya goin' inside?"

Looking around, the boys were met by the unfriendly faces of two men desperate to get inside the pub, and angry at the brothers for blocking their way. "Sorry, gents, we were just looking to see if our mates are in here or up the road at the Prospect of Whitby," replied Eduardo apologetically.

"We just come from up there, but never seen 'em," laughed one of the men.

The brothers stood aside, allowing them to enter. When the door was fully open, they spotted Boxer, further along the bar, chatting to someone... A friend, possibly. This gave them a chance to discuss strategy. Franco, being a quick thinker, told his brother to walk up to Boxer and tell him his mate, Longboat, needed to have a word with him. "When they're together, get yourself by the door and be ready to run... Bloody quickly. I'll do the business; none of this swapping the gun between us; it'll be me who'll pull the trigger. Now let's get this fuckin' job done. Okay, bruv?"

"Okay," replied a very nervous Eduardo.

His brother checked the gun in his pocket was loaded and ready to fire. The next couple of minutes would be crucial to this situation, and many lives would be affected by the result of their actions. Eduardo entered the bar, which was absolutely heaving with drinkers, all enjoying their usual Saturday night's entertainment and a get-together with friends. It was a happy, party atmosphere... But that was about to change.

Eduardo slowly made his way to where Boxer was chatting to an acquaintance. "Excuse me, Boxer, but your mate, Longboat, at the other end of the bar wants an urgent word with you."

Boxer turned around to see the slightly agitated figure of Eduardo looking directly at him. "What the fuck's that lanky bastard want now; tell him to fuck off, I'm busy!" Unfortunately, eloquence and refinement were not virtues attributable to Boxer, however, he always seemed to get his point across somehow.

Poor Eduardo hadn't banked on it being this difficult, but with a quick flash of inspiration, replied, "He mentioned a big deal coming off that could earn you both a lot of money."

"'Ow d'you know, who the fuck are you?" answered Boxer, slightly bewildered but suspicious.

Eduardo raised the game a little by saying, "There's a job going down concerning them Italians; either we get in first or they take it off us."

That did it; the mere mention of 'them Italians' sent Boxer scurrying to where his pal was, at the other end of the bar, downing his sixth pint that evening. Pushing his way past the throng of thirsty customers, he got to where his mate was and asked, "What's all this about takin' a job off them Ities?"

Longboat turned to face his pal, asking, "What fuckin' job, what fuckin' Ities?"

He never got an answer, as the man behind said, "Longboat, Boxer, this is for murdering our father," accompanied by two shots, and then a further two, which sent the pair of cowardly thugs crashing to the floor, each with fatal gunshot wounds to their heads.

Hearing the four shots ring out, and seeing a gunman standing over his two victims, the place erupted, people dropped to the floor fearing more gunshots to come, women screamed, glasses on the tables smashed, spilling drinks, and covering those trying to protect themselves by hiding beneath the furniture. A mad dash for the door caused countless casualties, as everyone tried to get out and far away from the scene of carnage as possible. The unfortunate drinkers standing near to the victims were covered in blood and gore that spurted from the victims' exit wounds; it was absolute pandemonium.

By now, the brothers were out of the door and sprinting down the side alley towards the steps leading to the river. Some people, not realising it was a dead end, followed but made a swift about-turn when Franco paused and fired a shot above their heads.

Arriving at the steps almost breathless after their 30-yard sprint, they desperately looked for Pietro. "Where the bloody hell is he?" called out Franco, when suddenly, out of the shadows appeared a small dinghy, powered by an outboard motor with Pietro at the tiller.

Getting as close to the steps as possible, he called them to quickly hop aboard. Scrambling to get in the small boat almost made it capsize; it took a while to settle the rocking motion caused by the pair jumping in. Needing to manoeuvre the small craft as close to the steps as possible caused the dinghy's propeller to hit one, stalling the outboard engine in the process. Pietro hastily yanked on the engine's pull cord in a vain effort to restart it. His hurried attempts caused the carburettor to flood, making it impossible to start the temperamental little motor. "Grab one of them fucking oars apiece and get rowing as quick as you can," he shouted at the lads. "Come on, get your fuckin' backs into it… We'll 'ave the bloody coppers on our backs any minute." This was the first time they'd seen Pietro – usually calm and collected – in a state of panic. "Use an oar to shove us off away from them bloody steps, else we'll never get away!" he called out again anxiously.

Eduardo took an oar and leaned out of the boat, attempting to push it away from the steps; unfortunately, by pushing too hard, the oar slipped out of his hands, and whilst trying to retrieve it, he almost went overboard himself.

"*Dio mio*, what the fuck you playin' at? If you lose that oar, we're all well and truly buggered; try and get it back… Jump in if you 'ave to!"

"Leave it to me," chipped in Franco as he took the other oar to try and reach the one which was now floating away.

"NO, NO, NO! For God's sake, leave it. We can paddle like a canoe with one oar, but with no oars, we can't move. *Idioti*!"

Whilst this little drama was playing out, not far away, an even bigger one was in motion at the Town of Ramsgate. The police had arrived, as well as an ambulance, whose medics were busily attending to the injured. The two victims of the shooting were beyond help, but there were others needing medical assistance. One or two of the pub's clientele suffered broken bones in the mad rush to get out of the bar where the shooting took place. Others sustained cuts and bruises, which needed looking at.

The police were trying to discover what happened, as well as asking for descriptions of the gunmen. Most of the drinkers inside the pub had made a quick departure, not wishing to get involved in what appeared to them as a gang war shooting. The prospect of having to stand in a witness box later and give evidence against dangerous gang members didn't appeal to them; so, they put as much distance as they could between themselves and the scene of the shooting. The police did, however, discover the direction which the gunmen took, and after going to the end of the alley and seeing nothing, decided to bring the Thames River Police into the search for the suspects.

How on earth the police never noticed the shenanigans going on at the bottom of the Wapping Old Stairs, had to be put down to complete incompetence on their part. The boat had fortunately drifted away from the scene and was hidden from view behind another riverside building. They were too far from shore to disembark from the small dinghy, so they had to do what they could with only one oar. The slight current was flowing in the direction they were heading, towards the Pool of London, as it was not yet high tide. They needed to be at St. Katharine Dock at around 11.30pm, before their ship sailed.

Pietro had 'shipped' the small outboard motor into the boat, and left it rest on its hinge fixed to the stern. He inspected it for damage and found the drive shaft buckled as well as damage to the propeller. This discovery didn't make him happy at all, but as the engine had been at rest for a while, possibly the excess flooding caused by persistent yanking of the starter cord had evaporated. Hoping for a little success instead of the failures that seemed to haunt them, Pietro had one more go at starting the engine. After returning it to the normal position in the water to ensure it would get a good supply of fuel – if it started – he gave a gentle tug on the starter cord, but nothing happened. Allowing the pull cord to recoil to its normal position, he said a silent prayer and 'crossed' himself.

This time, he gave one more gentle pull, and after hearing it splutter into life, called out in Italian, "*Ecco il successo*." He'd done it but didn't like the sound the small 4hp engine made, or the judder which accompanied it. Obviously, the contact with the stone steps back at the wharf caused the drive shaft to buckle, throwing it out of balance. However, the motor was running – in a fashion – and the prop was turning, which would get them on their way. "Keep your fingers crossed, boys, I reckon we'll make it after all and not have to swim for it." The boys never said much, but congratulated Pietro on his mechanical skills – and great patience.

Although they were running on half power, the impressive sight of Tower Bridge looming into view gave them the boost they needed. Almost at the Pool of London now, they soon arrived at St. Katharine Dock, where their ship awaited them. The *Emperor Vespasian* was fully loaded and almost ready to leave. Having a huge cargo of heavy pig iron necessitated the ship to have as much water under its hull as possible, hence the wait for high tide.

After tying up the dinghy amongst other small boats in the harbour's tiny marina, Pietro motioned the boys to a quiet little spot where they had a last chat together. Looking towards their ship and noticing a small crowd waiting by the ship's gangway, prompted the Italian to caution the brothers and wait until it was clear before they slipped aboard. Hopefully someone would be waiting to help them climb on and show them to their 'quarters'.

"You will not meet the skipper, because, as far as he's concerned, if you're discovered, you are simply a couple of stowaways who boarded his ship without permission. When you are instructed where to settle down, remain there until the ship docks; under no circumstances go on deck." The brothers nodded their understanding of what they'd been told. "From the beginning of this bloody caper, things have gone wrong. The reason I never brought you by boat and let you walk to the pub instead was because I wanted to give you the chance, whilst you were alone, to 'bottle out', if need be. If that had been the case, it'd be left to me to do the 'job' instead; but I'm proud of you boys and what you did. Your father would be too."

"Well, that's cleared that mystery up; we did wonder," replied Franco.

"I must tell you this though, boys, whilst waiting at the wharf and tying up to one of those rotting wooden posts, I experienced all sorts of weird occurrences."

"How do you mean?" asked Eduardo, a little puzzled.

"Well, the boat began to rock back and forth, but no other boats could be seen to cause any rippling; then I heard wailings and a gurgling noise. Very, very eerie!" The brothers listened intently to what their mentor had to say as he continued. "I've read up about the history of that place before, and how it got the name 'Execution Dock."

"Go on," urged the boys, a little more curious at this stage.

"Well, just a couple of yards from where I was tied up, used to be some gallows; erected by the Admiralty to hang pirates and mutineers. Those posts I tied up to were the 'death posts', where they chained the half dead convicts after hanging them. They slowly drowned as the tide came in and washed over them."

"So, what do you reckon the gurgling noises were?" asked Franco, slightly sceptical of what he'd just heard.

"Why, it was the spirits of the convicts, slowly drowning; I must have disturbed them!"

"Get away with you, fancy believing in ghosts; there are no ghosts, they don't exist!" exclaimed Eduardo.

"Those steps you came down to get aboard the boat were the same ones the condemned men walked down on their way to the gallows. All our problems started from there. I'll tell you, we disturbed some ghostly spirits, and they did their best to punish us... And they almost finished us off!"

The brothers were still not convinced of what Pietro had told them, but later, after having plenty of time to recollect their near fatal journey from the execution site, they began to wonder if there *was* any truth in what

Piero experienced. The words of William Shakespeare came to mind when he wrote, 'There are more things in Heaven and Earth, Horatio, than are dreamt of in your philosophies.'

After their extraordinary encounters with the spirit world, the brothers were ready to begin their next adventure. Because they'd disembark at Marseille instead of an Italian port, a thoughtful Pietro had with him a sizable number of French francs to give the brothers, which hopefully would see them clear for a few weeks. He also gave them the same amount in Italian lire.

After things had died down, he advised them to head for Sicily where they'd meet later; but in the meantime, he asked them to correspond somehow to let their mother, sister and grandfather know about their circumstances. "Apart from that, boys, there's not much more for me to do except wish you *buona fortuna,* and *fink a quando ci incontriano di nuovo* – Good luck, until we meet again."

After giving each other hugs, along with kisses – which was not the done thing for English men, but normal practice in Italy – tears began to well in the eyes of the three men, not knowing when or if they would meet again. In the short time they were together, a small bond of friendship had developed between them, which they hoped would mature as time went by. "Don't forget to look after our mum and sister – and our old grandad; especially Grandad" called out Eduardo as they made ready for their sea journey.

The gangway was clear now, except for a seaman who was nervously looking around... Trying to spot his two invited passengers. Pietro thought he'd accompany them to the gangway, simply to ensure they were meeting the right man. The seaman was relieved at the sight of the three men, and hurried the brothers along the gangplank, but not before he accepted a package from Pietro... Payment for the passage. Leading the boys down to the cargo hold, he advised them to stay there until told otherwise. The journey to Marseille would take about three days, so it was imperative they remained where they were during that period. The same seaman brought pillows and blankets for the boys, informing them he'd bring breakfast and coffee in the morning. It was past midnight when they sailed so all they had to do was settle down for a good night's sleep and wait and see what the morning would bring.

"Hey, brother, what about this for tomorrow's newspaper headline?" suggested Franco.

"Go on, let's have it," replied Eduardo.

"Bulldog Kills Boxer at Execution Docks."

Feeling very exhausted now, and after hearing his brother's witty account of the evening's events, he laughingly dropped off to sleep; followed later by his equally exhausted big brother.

Chapter 16

Marseille

The SS *Emperor Vespasian* cleared the busy River Thames and continued its journey along the Thames Estuary into the English Channel, en route for the port of Marseille. Thankfully, there were no holdups or complications as the brothers anticipated, and, most importantly, their ship wasn't boarded by the Thames River Police. This likelihood crossed their minds, as a double murder had been committed in the vicinity of the river. The perpetrators of this crime made their escape by boat along the Thames, heading towards the docklands, which could have led to their intervention. It may have later crossed the River Police's minds, that an escape could have been made by ship *out* of the docklands, but this possibility was never acted upon... Much to the relief of the brothers.

The seaman helping in their escape, Alfredo, ensured the boys had enough to eat, as well as looking after their general well-being, washing, shaving and toilet facilities. The voyage went smoothly with no rough seas or bad weather to spoil it. After only a couple of nights aboard the freighter, the port of Marseille was reached without any unpleasant occurrences.

Alfredo had to help with the docking of the huge ship and assist in unloading its cargo. Having a period of free time, he was able to get the brothers ashore, and clear them through the busy docks to a place of refuge he'd sorted out previously. After being approached by Pietro to help the brothers escape and find a suitable hideout, Alfredo made a phone call to Guido, an old friend. Guido ran a café/restaurant located near the Old Port, overlooked by the magnificent Fort Saint-Nicholas.

The Café Caligula was favoured by the legionnaire garrison of the fort, and its soldiers could always be seen availing themselves of its many facilities – which were not always food and drink. Indeed, apart from the restaurant and bars, there was a small stage area where various shows were performed. These were mainly female dancers, performing whilst scantily clad. Although the audience was predominately male – legionnaires, in particular – touching or body contact in any form was not only frowned upon but forbidden. To ensure this rule was observed, Bruno, a six-foot-six giant of a man was on hand to ensure the safety of the girls, and deal with anyone who acted out of hand. Of course, certain liaisons did occur, but not on the premises; usually by predominately wealthy clients. To ensure the café maintained its licence, and was able to remain open at all hours, along with the continuation of the sometimes-risqué dance routines, certain city officials were given sweeteners, which sometimes involved trysts with some of the performers – male and female.

Needing a place to lie low for a week or two until suitable passage could be arranged to take them to

Sicily, the Café Caligula was ideal for the two young men. Until they were taken there and introduced to Guido, its owner, the brothers had no idea what awaited them. "I can only put them up for a couple of weeks at the most," Guido told his seaman friend.

"That'll do fine; by then they should be on a boat out of here on their way to Sicily... With any luck!" replied Alfredo.

Looking around and rubbing his hands with glee, Eduardo said triumphantly, "I think we are going to enjoy our stay here; even if it is only for a couple of weeks." Alfredo reminded the brothers that a payment for lodging would be expected, which needed sorting out with Guido.

Satisfied and relieved he'd done as requested by Pietro, Alfredo bade the brothers goodbye, after downing a huge brandy and slamming the empty glass on the bar counter. He gave his chum, Guido, a hug and kiss on the cheek, thanking him for the huge favour he'd done for him. Finally returning to his ship, he left the brothers to enjoy the delights of the Café Caligula.

"No luggage then, boys?" asked Guido, looking down at the floor where the brothers stood.

"Er, no," replied Franco, "we never really had time to do any packing!"

Guido gave a puzzled look and asked them to follow him up a couple of flights of stairs to where they would be accommodated. "We'll sort the money out later," said Guido after opening a door leading to a small bedroom in the attic space. "By the way, I'm not interested in what you've done or why you are on the run. If anything should happen resulting in your apprehension, remember I don't know you or anything about you; I am simply renting out my attic space to a couple of guys looking to work a passage on a boat out of here, *capisco?*"

"*Si, si, capisco,*" replied the brothers as one.

Finally on their own, and with no unpacking to do apart from the contents of the small holdall they were carrying, their first move was to have a good wash. Unfortunately, there was no shower at this level of the building. There were fresh towels but no soap or toiletries. "We'll buy all the stuff we need tomorrow when we go for a walk around the harbour; we'll then plan our next move. What do you say, bruv?" Eduardo received no reply to his question, just a gentle snoring from his brother, who was fast asleep on one of the beds. Not to be outdone, he lay down on the other and joined him in a well-deserved sleep.

Their slumbers were disturbed after closing their eyes for what seemed a few minutes but was in fact four hours. Hearing loud music brought the brothers back to reality after their brief nap. "Let's go down and see what all the noise is about; sounds like there's some type of show going on," suggested Franco.

Reaching the restaurant, they were confronted by a group of dancers on the small stage, apparently going through their routine, which was due to begin at 9pm. The girls looked beautiful and alluring in their skimpy costumes; the boys couldn't take their eyes off them. "Get a load of those gorgeous legs on the tall blonde; boy, could I do her some good," said Eduardo whilst leering at the dancers. He spoke to the tall blonde, asking, "What are you doing after the show; how about we have a drink together or something?" He repeated suggestively, "*Or something!*"

"Put your eyes back in their sockets, fellas, those dames are out of bounds to you or anyone else that fancies their chances with them." Turning around to see who was giving the warning, they saw Guido looking directly at them, appearing to be unhappy with their comments. "Follow me into the office, we need to have a bit of a chat concerning the ground rules I've set out." The brothers did as suggested, and once in the office, were invited to sit down. "Okay, boys let's get things straight. I don't know what you did back in England that was bad enough to make you go on the run; in fact, I don't particularly care. When my friend, Alfredo, rang and asked if I'd put you guys up for a week or two, I agreed with no conditions attached, except that you don't attract attention, and only go out when you are searching for transport to take you to Sicily."

Franco interrupted, saying, "We appreciate what you've done for us so far, and we'll do our best to be unobtrusive and keep a low profile; all we were doing was looking at those beautiful girls as any young, hot-blooded men would do."

"That's just it, you mentioned young, hot-blooded men, who, if left to their own devices, could upset the routine of my café by trying to screw my dancers." Franco was still a little niggled that they were being accused of something which they hadn't done... Yet! "I have a suggestion to make. Normally I'd charge you 5000 francs each a week for renting that room (at that time, £1 sterling was equivalent to 1000 French francs), but if you agree to clear and clean tables, help in the kitchen, take orders to customers and such, you can stay here rent-free, but only for two weeks. After that, you must either have found your transport, or move to other accommodation. And to make it completely clear, keep your eyes off my girls; is that clear, boys?"

"Absolutely clear, boss, when do we start work?" replied Eduardo whilst getting a nod from his brother.

The last thing they wanted was to cause trouble for the man responsible for giving them shelter. On hearing this, Guido produced a bottle from a cabinet, along with three glasses, and poured a generous amount of cognac into each one; after which the three men raised them and gave a toast to 'friendship'.

"Okay, guys, I'll find you an apron apiece and get you working; you can begin to earn your keep," remarked their host whilst giving a smile and a wink.

Guido led the boys into the kitchen, where, after having a word with the chef, they were given aprons and a breakdown of what their duties would involve. They were mainly clearing away tables and cleaning them down; generally making sure everywhere was tidy. Waiting on the tables in the restaurant and outside terrace were among their duties too. The position the boys held was not only for them to be kept occupied during their brief stay at the café, but mainly keep them away from the dancing girls. Guido didn't trust them one bit, and he had good cause not to. Franco was a lady's man, possessing the looks and the charm to go with it.

Through their duties, they came across Bruno the bouncer and general caretaker of the premises. This giant of a man never smiled or gave signs of any emotion, standing no nonsense from anyone. He was a man to be feared and respected.

Being in the proximity of the fort overlooking the harbour made the café an ideal place for the legionnaire garrison to meet and drink. The fort was used as a staging post, introducing raw recruits to the Legion whilst awaiting transportation to Oran in Algeria. After their thirty-six-hour journey by boat across the Mediterranean, the recruits would be transported to the camp at Sidi Bel Abbès. Here they'd undergo another induction process before once more being transported to one of the two training camps in Mascara or Saida. They'd spend four months special training before joining a brigade of their own choosing; usually the Parachute Brigade. The French Indochina War had been in operation since 1946 and was costing many thousands of lives of both the French and Vietnamese. The Legion recruiting officers were always on the lookout for foreign, young, and fit men to fight their wars for them.

Technically, Frenchmen were not allowed to serve in the Foreign Legion, by virtue of its name. Many Frenchmen did fight and die in the Legion, by joining on the pretext of being Belgian, Swiss, or other French speaking nationalities... Sometimes Canadian. The garrison stationed at the fort were usually long-serving legionnaires and were given a reasonable amount of freedom when off duty. They loved having a few drinks at the Café Caligula, not just because of its proximity to their barracks, but they loved the atmosphere, and, of course, the dancing girls.

The brothers were doing reasonably well at the café; they'd been there almost two weeks, yet still couldn't locate a ship to take them to Naples. They'd discussed other possibilities, such as taking the train, but realised they'd need to show their passports when crossing the border into Italy from France. It was more than likely the Italian police would be on the lookout because of their connections with Sicily. Being happy and content to carry on as they were, the pair decided to stay put, if possible, and hope something would soon turn up.

One exceptionally warm evening, four legionnaires were having a drink together inside the café, annoying no one. They sat inside, hoping to see the show, especially the girl dancers. From outside, a group of American marines, slightly the worse for drink, strolled in. Seeing the legionnaires, they proceeded to mock and call them toy soldiers, as well as make other derogatory remarks. The four legionnaires took no notice and carried on drinking. This annoyed the marines, so they intensified their nasty comments. By now, Bruno caught

wind of what was afoot, and politely showed the
marines the door, only to be to be told by one of them,
"Who d'you think you are, you big ugly bastard, fuck
off before we sort you out, along with them tin soldiers
sat there!"

Bruno weighed up the odds before making his move,
and believing he had a good chance against six fit
looking marines, grabbed the smaller of the group,
lifted him above his head and threw him out the door.
"Okay," growled Bruno, "who's next?" No one moved
except Bruno, who pushed another two outside, and
returned for the remaining three marines, dragging
them out with him.

As ill luck had it, another group of marines were passing
at the same time. Seeing their buddies being shoved
around, they set upon Bruno, who hadn't reckoned on
there being so many to contend with. As the fight
progressed, and seeing poor Bruno savagely kicked whilst
on the floor, the legionnaires waged in to help him.

"Watch out, guys," called out a marine, "the tin soldiers
have arrived!" With that, they all set upon the four
outnumbered legionnaires.

Franco and Eduardo came quickly on the scene, and
just to even up the odds, waded into the marines. It was
almost a pitched battle underway outside the café, with
tables, chairs, glasses, and bottles flying everywhere.
Police sirens could be heard, followed by the arrival of
the Military Police, who waded into their own men,
using clubs and sticks to get them under control. After

seeing the police van, the brothers quickly disappeared, and hid inside the kitchen, away from it all. A good while later, order was restored, bringing everything back to normality.

The legionnaires carried on with their drinks, and the place began to fill up once more. Immediately after the police left, the brothers came out of hiding and proceeded to clear the mess up with the help of Bruno, who, despite the rough treatment he'd received, wasn't badly hurt... Just a few bruises.

The four legionnaires gave a hand with the clear-up and invited the brothers to join them in a drink. Guido was on the scene, and seeing him standing there, Franco asked if it would be okay to take up their offer. "Yes, no problem, fellas, enjoy your drink, you've earned it, but come and have a chat with me later, we really need to talk." This sounded a little ominous, and together with the warning they'd received concerning the girls, thought something was about to erupt.

"How long have you guys been working here; we've not seen you before," asked a legionnaire out of curiosity.

"Oh, this is just a stopgap before moving on; we are slowly working our way towards Italy," replied Franco.

"We need fit healthy young guys like you in the Legion; ever thought about joining?"

"No, we're not French so they wouldn't take us," answered Franco.

"You cannot join the Foreign Legion if you are French, buddy, that's why it's so called, get it?" The boys thought for a while, making sense of what they'd just been told. "None of us here are French, although we must speak French when on the parade ground or on duty."

"It's getting complicated, I'm afraid," said Franco, "seems it wouldn't suit us at all."

"Well, you speak English and I heard you speaking Italian during the punch-up, so learning French wouldn't be a problem for you guys."

The boys looked at each other, not knowing what to make of it. If they were back home and hadn't committed any crimes, they'd have to register for National Service, but that eventuality was unlikely in the present circumstances. Laughingly, Franco asked the soldiers, "By the way, guys, you aren't recruiting officers by any chance... Are you?"

"*We're* not, but one comes down here a couple of times a week if you want to see him." This was the last thing the boys wanted – to join a French army of any kind. They thanked the soldiers for the drinks, saying they'd have to resume their duties shortly or they'd be getting the sack. "Okay, fellas, but remember, you could do a lot worse than join the Legion. You receive the best military training in the world, you'll receive a litre of red wine a day, along with four cartons of cigarettes weekly; free uniform; fantastic food; foreign travel and yes, most importantly, a new identity, meaning you'll be given a completely new name and domicile."

"That sounds good," commented Franco, a little patronisingly, "but surely there must be some disadvantages." One of the legionnaires thought for a while, mentioning he couldn't think of any, except the pay was bad, and you had to sign a contract for five years. "Five fuckin' years!" exclaimed Franco. "We'll be old men by then!"

"You'll be looked after and protected during that time, many of us sign on again after serving our time; it's a great life, believe me, fellas." The brothers didn't know what to make of it all, but the last thing on their mind at that time was joining the French Foreign Legion.

Chapter 17

Café Caligula

After their chat with the legionnaires, the brothers began to think about what had been discussed. They were on the run and unsure of their next destination; plans had to be made for their future. Whilst they still had somewhere to sleep, eat, and drink in relative safety and comfort, there was no reason for them to make a move. They remembered what Guido asked them to do before they finished for the night, so they called in at his office for the chat he'd suggested previously.

"Hi there, fellas, make yourselves comfortable; fancy a drink or anything to eat?" asked their landlord and benefactor.

The brother's response was to look at each other, decline the offer of refreshment and get straight down to business. "Is it something we've done to upset you, Guido? We realise we overstepped the mark after wading into those drunken marines, but we couldn't stand by and watch poor Bruno take a beating."

Guido smiled and shook his head, saying, "No, fellas, you've done nothing wrong, but what just happened got me thinking; suppose the police had run you in along with those marines and asked you for identification or what your business is; I could visualise problems arising." He then went on to say, "I've been doing a little checking up on you guys. There's a pal of mine in London who I chat with now and then; I asked if anything big had gone down there lately and were the police looking for anyone. Basically, guys, I asked about you two, and the reply I received has me very worried indeed."

"What lies have you been listening to, what's he been saying about us?" asked Eduardo.

"Guys, let's not beat about the bush or play silly bloody games with each other; I know exactly what you did, and I salute you for it, but I'm in a position where I could lose everything if the authorities discover I've been harbouring two Englishmen wanted for a double murder. Let's not deny it but accept my position."

An uncomfortable hush befell the tiny office, as the brothers realised the game was up; but to put the man who'd sheltered them in danger, with the possibly of losing his livelihood and freedom, was not the honourable thing to do. "Okay Guido, we'll come clean, what your pal told you is true. We're on the run because of an 'honour killing' and don't wish you to be involved, so we'll be out by the end of the week!" promised Franco.

"Sorry, guys, I want you out sooner than that, tomorrow is what I'm thinking; I just cannot take a chance."

"Can't you give us an extra day, say, the day after tomorrow, please, just one last favour then we'll be out of your hair forever," pleaded Eduardo.

Sucking through his teeth and taking a deep breath, Guido reluctantly agreed to the brothers' request, but warned them, "Not one day more; you must be out of here by Friday." Then, laughingly, he added, "If you're not out by then, I'll get Bruno to throw you out!"

"That clinches it," said Franco with a laugh, "anything but that, we'll be gone at the crack of dawn." It was accepted that in less than two days' time they'd have no roof over their heads and needed to do something about it.

It was an uncomfortable sleep for the boys that night, and reality really kicked in with a thud. They had all day tomorrow to find accommodation, if not, they'd be on the streets... Quite literally. Not much was spoken between them during their wash and shave period, and little more spoken whilst supping their coffee and eating their salami-filled rolls at breakfast time. Guido happened to show his face, but simply gave the brothers a forced smile.

"Let's take a walk along the harbour, perhaps we may come across some cheap lodgings that seamen use," suggested Franco. His brother simply nodded in agreement.

Strolling along the front and sitting down at a harbourside café, they ordered a couple of coffees with brandies to accompany them. Sitting there, enjoying the warmth of the sunshine, prompted Eduardo to take more than a little interest in the motor yachts moored in the marina. "Just look at those fantastic boats anchored out there with no one in 'em. I'll bet they've got everything you could want; beds, showers, galleys, sun lounges; all the comfort you'd need. Let's break into one and spend a couple of nights inside, just to see how those rich bastards live."

Franco began thinking and suggested, "Why only a couple of nights, lets steal a bugger and set sail for Sicily, it can't be all that far from here as the crow flies – or even as the fish swims."

"Ever sailed a boat, bruv?" asked Eduardo. And after seeing his brother shake his head, replied, "Me neither!"

"I suppose we could break into one just for the fun of it."

"What if we're caught?" responded Eduardo. "We'd lose everything, especially our freedom, and if we get extradited to the UK, it'd be the rope or long prison sentence; I don't fancy either. No, we'll have to think again."

Whilst the brothers were planning their next move, they were being watched by two attractive young ladies. Franco soon noticed them, and lifted his brandy glass, giving them a lingering smile. Returning the smile, along with a little wave, was all the encouragement Franco needed. "Pick your cup and glass up, bruv, I think we're in with a chance if we play our cards right."

Walking up to their table, Franco asked if they might join them, offering to buy a drink. "I'll bet you ladies only drink champagne; am I correct?"

"A little too early for us, monsieur, but I would like to take you up on your kind offer this evening." Franco was flabbergasted; he'd 'pulled' without even trying.

The other lady introduced themselves as Lucie and Celine. Franco reciprocated, giving the girls their names. "Oh, what lovely names, ladies; are you both French?" he asked.

"Oui, monsieur. Your names sound Italian, are you from there?"

"How very perceptive of you, Mademoiselle, is it so obvious?"

The small talk went on for a while, eventually becoming a little boring for the two young ladies, as one said suddenly, "Oh dear, just look at the time, we have appointments for lunch, but when we meet up this evening, we'll take you up on your kind offer of that champagne."

After arranging a time and place, the ladies stood up, blew both brothers a kiss saying, "*jusqu'à ce soir, messieurs.*" The brothers understood and wished them the same in Italian.

When both ladies were out of sight, a victorious Franco clapped his hands, saying, "How about that, then! Your brother hasn't lost his touch; we're well and truly in now, problem solved. They're bound to have a flat or room where we can bunk down for a couple of nights; we can begin to breathe a little easier now!"

Feeling elated at their apparent conquest, the brothers returned to the café to freshen up for the evening's assignation with their new lady friends. Their ardour was soon dampened when a glum looking Guido beckoned them into the office. "Each time we come inside here we usually get bad news," said Franco, "is now any exception?"

"I'm afraid not, boys," answered Guido seriously, "we've got big trouble, seriously big trouble!" He went on to tell the boys of his phone call from the gendarmerie, regarding the previous evening's fracas outside the café. "Apparently, one of the marines involved in the scuffle is in a coma; the hospital authorities are doubtful of his recovery."

"How does that affect us?" asked Franco.

The café owner stared at him in disbelief. "How does it affect you? Are you bloody serious? You pair were involved in the fight; you, the four legionnaires and our own Bruno. An American lies in hospital in a coma with every chance of not coming out of it, and you fucking pair ask, 'What's it got to do with us?'" Guido was becoming very annoyed and agitated at the response received from the brothers. "I wished to heaven I hadn't anything to do with you fucking pair; I only put you up as a favour to an old pal, and look where it's got me; right up the fucking creek!"

The boys knew when to be quiet and simply waited for their host's next words – which followed a pause for Guido to regain his composure. "The police asked me for your names and addresses. They became annoyed when I told them I didn't know; so, unless you present yourselves at the gendarmerie by tomorrow at the latest, they're gonna pay me a visit! I'm fucked boys, well and truly fucked!"

This bad news put the brothers into panic mode; what could they do? "What exactly did you tell them, boss?" asked Eduardo, a little patronisingly.

"I could hardly tell them I didn't know your names; the fact you were wearing aprons bearing Café Caligula's logo on at the time convinced the cops I must know you! All I told them was you asked for a job with accommodation. I paid you in cash, and knew your names to be Ed and Fred, or something like that. The cops weren't convinced with my story, that's why they want you to go down to the gendarmerie to give them your version of what happened."

"You know we can't do that, Guido; it's for sure they'll have some sort of wanted notices out on us. If we set foot in that cop shop, we'll be doomed!"

"You'll be doomed? What about me, I could lose everything!" called out Guido in exasperation. "I tell you what, boys, I want you out of here right now, d'you hear, RIGHT NOW!" Nothing more was said between the three men as the meeting broke up suddenly, with more than a little acrimony between the two parties.

Hurrying up to their attic room, the brothers decided the sooner they were away from there, the better. There was a chance Guido could turn on them in a bid to curry favour with the police. Denouncing them and pleading he knew nothing of their previous exploits would be better than insisting he knew nothing of their criminal past. If he decided on this, he'd enlist the help of Bruno the bouncer, to make sure they stayed around to face the police; in doing so he'd take the blame off himself. These thoughts were foremost in their minds as they packed away their meagre belongings into the small holdalls.

Stashing their money into one of the bags, Eduardo came across the gun they'd used to shoot their dad's killers. They were told to ditch it in the English Channel once aboard the ship they escaped in. Not being allowed on deck made them forget these instructions. Showing it to his brother, Franco asked how many bullets were left. After spinning the chamber, Eduardo told him there was only one left.

"We really need to get rid of that gun, y'know, bruv, if the cops get hold of it, they'll know for sure it was used to kill those two East End clowns. Ballistics will prove it for sure."

"I know that, but if we are going on the run, and won't know what or who we come across out there, this little beauty will protect us," said Eduardo, patting the gun. Franco still wasn't convinced but had no wish to argue with his brother; there were more important things going on in his head. He changed the subject, asking what they should do about their date with the two mademoiselles.

"I say we keep the date with them; it's for sure they'll have some sort of apartment where we can crash, so let's stick with it. It's for sure we'll be guaranteed a good night's sex with them; we can't fail."

Having a quick look around their tiny room, making sure they hadn't left anything, Franco suddenly realised that if the police called at the café, they would surely inspect their room, and possibly dust it for fingerprints. "Hang on there, brother, there's something we've not done!"

"What now?" asked Eduardo.

"We haven't wiped our prints off the fittings, door handles, etc." They grabbed towels and a duster, then wiped over every conceivable article they came into contact with. "That should do it!" said Franco. "As clean as a whistle, let's get out of here while we can."

The time spent with their father and his gang taught them to leave no trace of their comings and goings, such as leaving cigarette butts, food wrappers and especially fingerprints. "Good advice from dear old Dad. God bless you, Dad, wherever you are," uttered Eduardo, looking up as he closed the door.

Reaching the ground floor, they looked around to see if Bruno was waiting for them. Seeing the coast was clear, they left through the kitchen by way of the delivery door. Needing to distance themselves from the café was crucial, as there was no telling if, in order to save his own skin, Guido hadn't contacted the police, and informed them of their whereabouts.

"Look, brother, the cops don't know what we look like, and as far as we know, they won't make a move until the morning, when we fail to show up at the gendarmerie. Keeping our date with those two beauties is the wisest thing we can do. Two couples dining and drinking together won't attract as much attention as two guys on their own." Getting the answer he wanted, they made their way to the arranged meeting place, and were amazed that their dates were already there, a half hour early.

"Good afternoon, ladies, lovely to see you again. What would you like to drink, as if I didn't know?"

Celine answered Franco's question, saying, "Champagne, of course, what else!" Attracting the waiter's attention, Franco ordered a bottle of champagne. It arrived soon after, whereupon the waiter placed four glasses on the table, half-filling them before he left.

"Cheers, and good health to us all; here's to a delightful evening in the presence of two of Marseille's most beautiful ladies." Eduardo thought his brother was going slightly over the top with his salutations, and speaking in Italian, told him so.

After finishing the bottle, they ordered another, and continued with their conversation, enquiring of each other's' occupations. The ladies looked at each other, and speaking in French, Celine said, "Devrions-nous leur dire?" This meant in English, 'should we tell them'.

Her friend, Lucie, shook her head, saying, "Pas encore."

A little tired of all this speaking in different languages, Franco suggested, as they all knew English, they should continue to converse accordingly... In English. He understood a couple of the French words the girls spoke to each other, and was not only becoming a little annoyed, but suspicious, too; what if they were drinking champagne with a couple of female cops?

Chapter 18

Femmes Fatale

Poor Guido, by doing a pal a favour accommodating a couple of men at his request, he could now face going to prison for harbouring two criminals. Not only that, but his beloved café and everything that went with it was also at stake. At the very least, even if he wasn't prosecuted, he could lose his trading licence as well as his business and livelihood; just because of a couple of strangers he never knew.

Sitting alone in his office, this problem worried him immensely; what action should he take? If the brothers failed to go to the gendarmerie in the morning to report to the police as requested, it was certain they'd pay him a visit, wanting to know why. Realising they'd do just that, convinced him to come clean and phone the police straight away; he'd give his version of events, before being taken into custody. An early confession would stand him in greater stead with the authorities, than having one forced out of him later. Not being a member of a Mafia family, would he be guilty of breaking the sacred 'omertà code', the most sacred code of conduct in all Mafia organisations? If a Mafia member informed on another member to the police, he was in fact inflicting a death sentence upon himself. The death involved was not a quick bullet in the head or anything as expedient; it involved gruesome torture resulting in a long, lingering death, with the body later immersed into a pit of quicklime. Needless to say, few Mafia members were guilty of breaking this code, and those who did, quickly regretted it, along with family members who would also suffer, though not as harshly as the 'snitch' or 'grass', as the informers were known.

Despite not being directly associated with any Mafia organisation, he encountered many who were, including his friend, Alfredo, who introduced two loosely Mafia-affiliated members into his care. Had he realised this, he would rather have lost his business and livelihood than suffer the consequences of his intended actions. Before picking up his phone, he should have considered the consequences of his actions; but he didn't.

"Hello, monsieur, can you put me touch with the officer responsible for investigating the fracas outside Café Caligula a couple of nights ago?" Guido waited to be connected to the officer in in charge. Once connected, he gave his name and details, asking if they could pay him a visit as he had some important information for them. When told he could expect a visit within the hour, he sat back on his chair and thought very hard of what he was going to say.

There was still time to back out and possibly save his own life, but he knew the die was cast, and he'd go all out to put himself in the clear. The thought never crossed his mind that, by contacting the police right away instead of later the next day, he'd effectively robbed the brothers of a half day's start ahead of the police. This was merely academic at the time, as the last thing on the brother's minds was making a run for it... Not yet, at least!

At the harbourside café, it was 'question time', or 'guess one's occupation' quiz. The two pretty girls told the brothers they were working girls, leaving the boys puzzled as to what they meant by the term 'working'. Usually in England, that term amongst certain circles meant the ladies were prostitutes, but in this case, it referred to them being high-class escorts.

"Do you mean to say that we are going to be charged for the privilege of buying you ladies champagne, with the possibility of buying dinner too?" asked Franco on hearing the girls' occupation, unable to believe it.

"Yes, of course, gentlemen, we thought you'd realised that before now!" exclaimed Lucie.

The brothers had the wind blown out of their sails with this confession. There they were, believing they had just charmed a couple of beautiful women into having a drink and a meal together, with the possibility of a night of passion to follow, only to discover they were a couple of hookers.

"I can't believe this!" called out Eduardo, sounding very annoyed. "You misled us not mentioning you charge for your services!"

The ladies became very coy and a little embarrassed – although that's the impression they wanted to make with the brothers.

He was about to get up and leave when Franco pulled him back saying, "Sit down, bruv, all is not lost; we could make some good come out of this. Where would we go if we got up and walked away; we can't go back to the café. Let's cut our losses and go for the jackpot... It's not as if we haven't got enough to pay them. Ask what they charge, and if there's a discount for two of us, especially if we spend the night with them."

Negotiations were in progress as the nightly rate was discussed, and the conversion from French francs into English pounds. Whilst the two ladies showed their business acumen in negotiating with the boys, they were obviously no strangers to dealing and bartering. Eventually, a figure was agreed between the four, on an all-night session, with breakfast and coffee included in the morning. It just required their clients paying 50% of the fee up front, with the balance payable later. "Do we get a receipt for that?" asked Franco after taking the wad of notes from the holdall and paying the agreed amount of French francs.

"If you wish, but it will not be an official tax-deductible receipt, merely a piece of paper with the amount paid on it," answered Lucie whilst folding the money away and concealing it in her handbag. "Boys, we'll give you a night to remember, one you won't forget in a hurry!" Getting up from the table, she gave Celine a wink, telling the boys who were becoming excited now,

"I suppose buying us a champagne dinner is not going to happen now."

"You can bet your fucking life it ain't, sweetheart, no fucking way!" answered Franco with great determination. With transactions completed, the girls decided they needed to powder their noses; telling the boys they wouldn't be long, perhaps ten minutes or so.

"Er, just hold on a minute, ladies, why do you both need to go together for a pee and freshen up?" asked Eduardo.

"We always go together... We sometimes have a chat," answered Celine.

"How do we know you won't run off with our money!" persisted Eduardo.

"Boys, please, we are professional girls, we don't run off with our client's money!"

"Well, as a sign of good faith, leave your handbags behind until you return," suggested Franco.

Lucie thought for a while then replied, "What is to prevent you two from running off with our bags?"

"Precisely," continued Franco, "to settle this, either we follow you in there, or you take it in turns."

Eventually it was agreed that one of the ladies would visit the toilet on her own, whilst the other would go when her friend returned. Speaking in Italian, Franco leaned over to his brother and said, "They must think we were born yesterday!" Eduardo just gave him a wink.

It was only a few streets away from the harbour to the tiny one-bedroomed apartment occupied by the girls. It comprised of a double bed, and a single pull-out in the bedroom, and a kitchen complete with table and chairs, with a lavatory tucked away. Basically, it was a place used to sleep, have breakfast, and get dressed for the day's work.

"Only one bloody bed!" called out Eduardo after inspecting the furniture.

"I'm afraid so," answered Celine, "what do you expect for what you are paying; we have given you a special rate as we like you so much."

"Who gets the bed, and who has that grotty-looking divan in the corner?" asked Franco.

"When there are two couples, we change over halfway, and swap beds in the process." explained one of the girls. "You get value for your money that way." She gave her friend a knowing wink.

"Change over at half-time?" questioned Franco, "What the hell *is this,* a bloody football match, where we change ends after the half-time whistle?"

"Stop complaining, please, we are doing the best we can for you; you English always insist on getting value for your money!"

After deciding who would take the double bed, the ladies began undressing. Once down to their undies, they motioned the boys to do the same, which seemed very strange for them, as this was their first time 'doing it' with professionals.

"Is there a lock on that outside door?" asked Eduardo, still a little wary of the two women.

"You men are so suspicious, just relax and we'll take care of everything you need."

"All the same, I want that bloody door locked... From the inside!" As he followed her to make sure the door was bolted from inside, Eduardo found the toilet and had a pee.

When he returned, Celine dangled two condoms in front of them. "We require you to wear one of these during penetration, if you don't mind, gentlemen," she insisted. The boys simply took one each and nodded their heads.

"Okay, gentlemen, we want you to relax whilst we go about our business, we will give you a night to remember," uttered Celine in a seductive whisper. The boys, now feeling relaxed, waited for their hostesses to go about their business.

Around the time the bedroom activities commenced in the tiny apartment, not far away, at Café Caligula, the police had just arrived. Apologising to Guido for being later than planned, the inspector in charge suggested they go somewhere quieter to talk, as the cabaret was in progress.

Leading them to his office, Guido offered the police officers a chair, and asked if they'd like a drink. "Thank you, but, no, monsieur, we are both on duty, but some other evening we'll accept your kind offer; we like the look of this place and would like to spend time here."

"You'd be only too welcome, Officers; I'll ensure you are well looked after when you do," responded the café's owner, a little patronisingly.

"Right, down to business!" stressed the inspector. "We need to find out what happened to your two employees."

"Ex-employees," corrected Guido as he gave the police officers chapter and verse about his association with the two Englishmen.

"You realise, do you not, monsieur, that the same two men we speak of are wanted for a double shooting in England, where two innocent men died."

Poor Guido began to tremble at the thought of being implicated in the men's' escape from justice. Now realising they were wanted killers; he was guilty of sheltering them! "Inspector, please believe me, I knew nothing of this; I simply agreed to a request from an old seaman friend of mine, asking to put up two of his pals for a couple of nights... Which incidentally turned out to be almost two weeks. I knew nothing of their past, or even their names!" pleaded Guido, now stressed out more than before.

Noticing how harassed he was, the policeman went on to ask his friend's, name as well as the ship he arrived in. The devastated café owner, realising he'd gone so far in giving information to the police, must now go all the way and tell them everything they wanted to know. After writing this information down, the inspector got up from his chair, and, looking around at the ornate and well-equipped office, said, "It would be a great pity to lose all of this for the sake of a couple of English gangsters, would it not, monsieur? We'll be in touch, and may we wish you a very pleasant evening." With that, they walked out of the café, leaving its owner a very worried man indeed. Ironically, the two men they wished to question were but a short distance from where the police officers stood, and their chances of arresting them were increasing at a most propitious rate.

After experiencing sex acts they never dreamed existed, the brothers were naturally exhausted, and the thought of changing partners for another session was unthinkable. They were worn out by the different positions adopted, as well as the multiple variations they were happily forced to adopt. All they wished for at this stage was simply to rest and regain their strength. "Would you gentlemen like a drink?" asked one of the seemingly indefatigable hostesses.

"I'd love a cold beer please."

"Me too," echoed Franco.

Celine left the pair to regain their strength and catch their breath. Turning around, looking at them whilst she went for the drinks, and realising how helpless both men looked, she quietly slipped the bolt of the door undone. Going over to the curtains, which were drawn shut, she slowly opened them, only to turn around to see Franco standing there.

"You're taking your time with those drinks!"

"So sorry," she replied apologetically, "I'm opening a window to let in some fresh air; It's so stuffy in here with four people participating in the Sex Olympics." Franco just smiled as he took the two ice-cold bottles of beer from her sweaty hands and returned to his brother relaxing on the bed.

Lucie was simply reclining, smoking a cigarette. "Phew, it's so damned hot in here, open a window, Celine."

"I just have," replied her friend, I opened the one in the kitchen." Watching their clients slowly sipping their beers, she asked, "When will you two guys want to resume?"

"Just let us get our bloody breath back!" replied Eduardo, a little annoyed.

Being anxious to resume with the activities, she held out her hand for the empty bottles. "You're in a bit of a hurry, what's up?" asked Franco. "You haven't got more clients waiting, surely?" No sooner had the words left his lips, two men barged into the bedroom, one wielding a knife, the other threatening them with a club. "I fucking well knew it!" called out Franco. "You pair of crafty fuckers have been lining us up. Come on, what's it about, we've paid our money, what are you after?"

The ugly brute wielding the knife answered for her, threateningly demanding, "We want the rest of the money in that bag, as well as your watches and anything else of value."

"How did you know about the money?" asked Franco, pausing, and suddenly remembering the girls' session visiting the toilet whist at the café. Realising this, he went on, saying, "I've got it, you crafty bitch, you made a phone call, didn't you? You undid the bolt on the door and signalled by drawing the curtains; what a stupid pair of bastards we are, falling for the oldest trick in the book!" Then, reaching down for the holdall, he pleaded with the knifeman, "You can take the cash, but leave us enough for taxi fare to get out of here, and please let us put our clothes on!"

"Just hand it over, all you're gonna get from us is a good beating, so be quick about it!"

Frank gave his brother a look and a wink, apologising to him, saying, "Sorry, brother, but I'll have to let 'em have it!" With that, he put his hand in the bag, felt around, and triumphantly pulled out the little snub-nosed revolver. Pointing it at the knifeman, he told him threateningly, "Anyone moves, and you'll get it. That includes you, ladies, in fact, *especially* you ladies."

Waving the gun around at the intruders, he motioned them to kneel with their hands behind their backs. Quickly complying, afraid of being shot, they did as ordered. Pointing to the women, he told them to use their stockings to tie their wrists. "And tie them tight... Very tight," ordered Franco. "When you've done that, tie up their ankles... Very tight!"

As the women were doing this, the brothers quickly dressed. Still holding the gun, Franco told the girls to get dressed and give him both sets of keys to the flat. Seeing the two thugs safely trussed up, Franco, trying to plan their next move, told the women to hand back their money, as they weren't happy with the service they'd received. After grudgingly handing it over to them, Celine said, "We are very sorry it turned out like this, boys, but we were forced into it by these two." She pointed at the thugs trussed up on the floor. "Please, I beg of you, don't report this to the police, if you do it'll mean a prison sentence for us both."

"How can we believe anything you tell us; you are a pair of liars. I've a good mind to drag you both to the gendarmerie myself and let them deal with you!" Celine began to cry and again pleaded with Franco, who relented by saying, "If you pair release those two goons before we've got a good distance away, we'll call the cops and send them around here."

"No, no, we will not let them escape; thank you for being so understanding, thank you very much!" she said pleadingly.

"All the same, I'm keeping the keys until we're away from here, and you'll have to follow us if you want 'em, okay?"

"Yes, yes, that'll be great, we'll follow you for a good distance, then take the keys from you. If we don't release those men they'll beat us, so we'll take our time getting back and give you time to get away. They won't come after you as you have a gun, and that scared them. Once more, can I thank you both!"

With the pleading and promising out of the way, the flat door was locked from the outside, leaving the would-be robbers trussed up, lying on the floor. As agreed, the boys gave back the keys when they were a safe distance away, leaving them to decide on their next move. "I almost feel sorry for those two girls, all that work and not a penny for it," said Eduardo.

"I felt sorry for them too," replied his brother, "but only for a few seconds, because if it hadn't been for Bulldog down here, who knows what would have happened to us; I dread to think."

They found a quiet out of the way place to sit down and decide upon their next move. "Any ideas, brother?" asked Eduardo.

"Not a bloody sausage, kid, not even a bloody chipolata!"

Chapter 19

The French Foreign Legion

After spending the remainder of the night in a cramped and cold shelter near the harbour, the brothers had some serious thinking to do regarding their immediate future. As usual, they weighed one thing against the other, realising, unless definite action was taken, they'd be arrested by the police, with the possibility of being extradited to England, where they'd stand trial for murder.

The idea of joining the Foreign Legion seemed an option, after all other alternatives were discussed. Faced with the grim reality of capture and possible conviction, they were left with no others. Look, brother, it can't be all that bad in the Legion; those guys we spoke to said it was a great life, food, travel, expert training, as well as cigarette and wine allowances. How can we fail?"

"You did hear them mention we'd be compelled to sign a contract for five years, with no option of being released before then!" reminded Franco, to his brother's somewhat optimistic impression of what could be awaiting them, *should* they intend to join up.

"What do you suggest, we are out in the open with the chance of being picked up at any minute, and the solution is staring down at us from that fortress up there," stressed Eduardo, pointing to the impressive structure of Fort Saint-Nicholas. "We have no choice, it's either that or nothing. If we hadn't fooled around with those two hookers, we could have been far away from here by now!"

"You must admit, though, we had a fantastic time with those girls; they did things to me I never knew existed. Did Celine do that thing where you had to—"

Franco was stopped in his tracks when his brother reminded him, "Just forget those bloody girls, they almost got us a good beating as well as losing all our money. By the way, did Guido ever pay us for the work we did at the Café Caligula?"

Franco simply shook his head and continued weighing up their options on what to do next to extricate them from their present predicament. "You're correct as usual; we don't have a choice. If we hang about here much longer, there's bound to be a patrol car driving around, possibly searching for *us*. Come on, let's get up to that bloody fort; what've we got to lose?"

"Five years of our lives, brother, that's all!"

Before making their way to the fort, they had to get rid of the revolver they'd used to kill the two members of the East End gang. They were advised to do this back in at the docks in London; had they done so, it was highly possible they'd have had no protection from the two hoodlums who tried to rob them back at the girls' flat. He produced the small, snub-nosed .38, which had saved them from being robbed, as well receiving a hiding. So, it was with deep regret they had to throw it out to sea as far as they could; ensuring the remaining bullet was removed, and the gun was carefully wiped to remove their fingerprints beforehand. There was just the large amount of money they had to consider, as it was certain they'd have to account for it if searched at the Legion HQ.

Clambering up the steep road leading to the fort, they had a breather and went through any implications should they continue and apply to join the Legion. After making their unanimous decision, they banged on the huge door, and waited for a hatch to open. "What do you want?" barked the sentry who was on duty inside the fort.

"We want to apply to join the Legion," answered Eduardo.

After a long pause, a small personnel door opened and the sentry beckoned them inside, slamming and bolting it shut behind them, saying, "So, you want to join up. Have you given it much thought?"

"Yes, sir, we have; our minds are made up!" replied Eduardo with conviction.

"Follow me and I'll see if the duty sergeant can look after you." The brothers were shown to a sparse-looking lobby and told to sit down and wait.

"I'm getting bloody hungry, bruv, I wonder if they serve breakfast here," muttered Eduardo. "At least you'd think they'd give us a mug of coffee while we wait." The words had hardly left his mouth when an orderly appeared with two steaming mugs of coffee.

"Thank you very much indeed, these are just what we needed," responded Franco after receiving his coffee from the orderly.

"Well, you may have a while to wait until the sergeant arrives. They do not ordinarily recruit applicants here, so a medical team will have to be summoned to make sure you are fit enough to join before we carry on."

"Okay, we'll wait, we've nothing else to do at the moment," replied Eduardo, whose response prompted the orderly to bring them some food.

"Will bread, cheese and salami do?" asked the orderly. "I'll see what I can rustle up. Please be patient while I see what's left in the kitchen." Hearing this brought a huge smile to the brothers' faces; it was the best news they'd had so far.

After an hour's wait, during which they ate their food, the pair were summoned into a well-furnished office. Quite a contrast to the lobby they'd been in while waiting to be interviewed. A dapper-looking, well-dressed and immaculately coiffured NCO beckoned them inside. "Good morning, gentlemen, or is it the afternoon, one has difficulty distinguishing one from the other at times."

"I believe it is mid-morning," replied Eduardo, looking at his watch.

"Ah yes," replied the NCO, affirming Eduardo's answer, "so it is. Okay, gentlemen, being Saturday, we do not usually convene to interview candidates for enlistment; had it been Sunday you would not have been considered at all. Being two fine-looking and healthy specimens of manhood, we are making an exception. Now, down to brass tacks, as the English say, why do you wish to join the Legion?" The sergeant NCO stared intently at the pair, as they delivered their answer.

"Well, sir, as you realise, we are both English, and because of our ages, we are required by the authorities to register for national service," explained Franco.

"Continue," replied the sergeant, watching them both intently, "I'm becoming very interested."

"Well, sir, rather than that, we'd prefer to join the Legion, as we'll have better training, food and wine as well as more adventure… Which we both crave."

Getting up from his chair, the officer took a cigarette from the ornately carved wooden box on his desk, tapped both ends and popped it into his mouth. Twirling it around his lips a couple of times, then lighting it from an equally ornate silver cigarette desk lighter, he took a long draw and said, rather cynically, "Do you two gentlemen take me for a bloody fool? I don't mind being given fictitious reasons for joining up, so long as they are believable. What you've just told me is the biggest load of horse manure I have ever heard. Now, no more horse shit, *why* do you want to join the most disciplined and best trained military force in the world... And no more lies!"

This reaction took the brothers by surprise; they simply hadn't a clue what to do next. There was a pause as the sergeant drew on his cigarette and responded by saying, "I know exactly who you are and why you are here. We have bulletins all the time from foreign police forces, warning us of criminals on the run from the law. It wasn't hard for us to recognise you two as being wanted in England for gangland shooting offences. Had it been a normal recruiting day, a member of the Deuxième Bureau would be sitting here beside me, and it wouldn't take him long to recognise you both."

"Well, that's it," said Franco, resigning them to their fate, "you'll probably call the police now; that's us well and truly fucked!"

"Not necessarily," replied the sergeant, now halfway down his cigarette. Taking another long slow draw and exhaling a cloud of blue smoke, he turned to the brothers and said, "We heard of what you did at the Café Caligula the other evening, and how you intervened to help four of our legionnaires when hopelessly out numbered. This is the spirit we are looking for in recruits, and I'm not concerned with what transgressed previously. You are both young, fit agile and seemingly fearless; you'll go a long way with us and have a bright future to boot. Just don't insult our intelligence by lying."

"Does that mean you'll accept us, sir?" asked Franco.

"Subject to a medical examination, which I will arrange. Should you pass, I'll have you back here and sign you both up."

The recruiting officer said he did not want lies or duplicity, but he didn't tell the brothers the real reason for overlooking their dark past. The French military was losing personnel at an alarming rate because of their war in Indochina. They had survived WW2 with heavy losses, as well as fighting in Morocco, where they were obliged to grant it independence. The FLN in Algeria were causing problems in *their* fight for independence, which needed more men to enforce French law. In a nutshell, the Legion needed recruits desperately at that time, and weren't too concerned with their past. If they were fit, young and willing to be trained, that was enough to qualify them for enlistment.

With the preliminary interview finished, the brothers were taken to a medical ward. Two orderlies in white coats were on hand to give them a thorough check-over – obligatory before the final enlistment. The results of this medical were crucial to the boys' future, as if one or both failed, they wouldn't be considered for the next phase.

When the medical was over, they were told to dress and wait outside in the draughty lobby once more. They didn't have long to wait, as after only a half hour, the brothers were ushered into the NCO's office once more. "Sit down please, gentlemen, I'm just going through your results, and they look okay. No bad medical ailments. Blood pressure okay, blood test good, heart condition satisfactory." He continued flicking through the papers, then stood up to congratulate the lads, saying, "You've both passed with flying colours; once I select new identities for each of you, I'll get you signed up." He wandered over to a bookshelf and returned with a huge leather-bound volume, which contained hundreds of names and addresses. After placing it on his desk, he sat down and flicked through the pages. "Have you any preferences regarding your new identities?" he asked them.

"We'd like to have a different surname please, the same for each of us. Could you keep our first names as similar to what they are now... If that's possible... Sir?" suggested Franco.

"Let me see now, Franco and Eduardo... Hmm." After a brief pause, he suggested, "What about Frank and Edward, or Eddie?"

"Eddie sounds fine," replied the bearer of his new name.

"And Frank's okay by me," answered his brother.

"All I need to do now is give you a surname, a nice, short, English name." Perusing through the list once more, he stopped suddenly and suggested, "What about Best...It's the best one I could find." The sergeant laughed, watching to see if his new recruits appreciated his little joke.

"That's fine with us, Sergeant, Frank and Eddie Best... Brilliant!"

Giving another smile whilst twirling his magnificent moustache, the sergeant placed two documents in front of the boys and said, after they'd signed them, "That's it, gentlemen, welcome to the French Foreign Legion; congratulations!" After which he summoned an orderly, telling him to 'kit out' and find accommodation for the new recruits. Finally, shaking their hands, he parted by saying, "You will not regret your decision, you are now part of the greatest military establishment in the world... Good luck!"

"Follow me, men," invited the orderly, "I'll get you some dungarees, and a place to bunk down; soon lunch will be ready, so we'll get you both sorted out before then." The new recruits were taken to the quartermaster's department and issued with the scruffiest and filthiest uniforms imaginable. They couldn't help noticing the grins on the faces of the orderly and quartermaster as they tried them on. "Don't worry, lads, these are only temporary until you reach Sidi Bel Abbès. You'll find out later why we don't give you fresh uniforms, as these old denims will serve their purpose; you see if they don't"

"Mine stinks of vomit and urine; have they been cleaned after the previous owner had finished with them?" asked Eddie concernedly.

"I told you, lads; these are only temporary for a few days before you reach your first base camp... You'll soon get used to the smell," replied the orderly, giving a grin. The brothers were very disappointed with their uniforms, but decided to accept them without more complaining as they'd only have to be worn for a short time.

"I reckon this is some sort of initiation process," muttered Frank, "we'll see what the other recruits are wearing." Sure enough, in the dining room, everyone there was dressed the same, except for regular soldiers and NCOs.

A ritual had to be observed at mealtimes, which involved standing by one's chair, singing Legion songs, and finally being requested to sit down and be wished *bon appétit*. The food was very good indeed, which was more than could be said for the sleeping accommodation they were led to after the meal was over. The bunk beds allotted were damp and very old; the whole of the sleeping quarters was cold and draughty. Out in the yard, they were given a tour of their washing facilities, which comprised a couple of cold-water taps – or faucets, as they were called - situated outdoors in the open air. "Don't worry too much about the sanitary or sleeping facilities here as they are most exceptional. When you've been allotted an operational HQ, you'll discover conditions are far superior to these; this is just a transit camp, nobody spends more than a couple of weeks here whilst awaiting transport over to Algeria," commented the cheery orderly whilst showing the pair around the fort.

"Two bloody weeks!" called out Eddie. "What are you trying to do us? We haven't even spent one night in this place yet, and the thought of a couple of weeks here would just about see us off!"

"You won't need to be here long," chirped the orderly, "the troop ship arrives in less than two weeks' time, so stop complaining. You've only been with us a couple of hours and all you've done is moan and complain. Lose that attitude with the NCOs or they'll make your lives a bloody misery. Just accept and get on with it; you haven't even started your basic training yet!" Frank elbowed his brother, advising him against rocking the boat, echoed by the orderly, who said with a huge smile, "There'll be plenty of that when you take the 36-hour journey across the Mediterranean to North Africa." This left the brothers feeling a little puzzled as to what the orderly meant, but in a couple of weeks' time, they'd find out themselves.

Time spent at the fort seemed to pass slowly but making acquaintances with some of the other recruits helped it go a little more swiftly. Meeting different men who all had their own reasons for joining up gave them a common bond with each other. Although it was not considered courteous to ask other recruits their reasons for joining up, some of them were only too eager to tell of their reasons, if simply to unburden themselves of the huge problems they were having.

Whilst serving time in prison, the same protocol applies; one never asks a fellow prisoner what he did to warrant a prison sentence. If a cellmate decides to reveal to you the reason for his imprisonment, he'd expect you to tell him why you were there. If you didn't wish him to know what crime you'd committed, and therefore refused to tell him, he'd assume you didn't trust him, so creating a difficult relationship whilst serving time together. The unwritten rule was to keep quiet about previous misdeeds and avoid the subject if approached. This was the policy adopted by the brothers, so they agreed to keep schtum.

There were two new recruits who'd struck up a relationship with each other, but the brothers were puzzled as to their identities, even though they spoke English with each other. One who they assumed to be Swedish because of his dialect, was indeed an Englishman, who later revealed he was from a small mining town in Warwickshire called Bedworth. Being tall, blond, with a swarthy appearance and having bright blue eyes, gave one the impression he was Scandinavian. The other fellow, slightly diminutive with bushy brown hair and staring eyes came from Belfast. Standing side by side, with their huge differences in stature and general appearance, one couldn't imagine them as being friends or even comrades in arms; although it's said that opposites do tend to attract one another.

"Let's go over and have a natter with those two guys," suggested Eddie, "they look pally enough and we need to strike up a few acquaintances. I don't like the looks of most of the others, they look as if they're on the run from somewhere or have committed terrible crimes."

"You mean like us?" suggested Frank as they ambled over the square to introduce themselves to the two men.

"Hi there, fellas, any idea when are we going to get away from this shithole, and out of these crappy uniforms? They're makin' me and my brother stink like hell!" enquired Eddie cheerfully.

"We ain't gorra clue, me babby, no one's told us nothin'," replied the taller of the two, who introduced himself as Jorge, and his friend as Paddy.

After the introductions, Eddie was curious as to where Jorge came from because of his unfamiliar dialect; he'd guessed Paddy was from Ireland, but not sure whether it was the north or south. Later that evening, in the bar, the four men got together and continued their chat, but didn't mention their reasons for joining up. However, Jorge, after having one or two beers, began to dominate the conversation, and seemed only too happy to tell of his adventures, culminating in the reasons for his present predicament.

Chapter 20

The Miner from Bedworth

The town of Bedworth, is situated halfway between Coventry and Nuneaton in North Warwickshire. Born there in 1930, George Stubbs had not the slightest idea his name would be changed to that of a Swedish citizen some twenty years later; nor did he realise he'd have to abandon his English language and speak only French when on duty.

I mention English language, but there are many non-Bedworth citizens, who, after hearing it spoken, would believe it to be anything but. Bedworth is unique in so much as it has its very own patois, a slang flowing dialect laced with undiscernible idioms, which only the locals can understand.

It's possible this dialect came about with the influx of people from the north, mainly Scots, and people from Northumberland, arriving in their thousands to this small town in search of work in the nineteenth and early twentieth centuries.

Bedworth is well known for its unique spirit of community and caring for others, as well as themselves. Although quite parochial, it is very welcoming to strangers, often making them feel at home. These attributes possibly emerged in the mining community, where accidents and disasters were commonplace amongst the tough, hard-working pit workers. Communities had to help each other in times of great stress and hardship and share whatever they had with those who needed it.

Around the period George was born, twenty or more coal mines were in operation. But Bedworth, or Bed'uth, as the locals call it, was equally famous for the huge number of drinking establishments that flourished there; indeed, at one count there were, over 84 pubs and many more clubs and associations, where the citizens could satisfy their huge thirsts. The jewels in Bedworth's crown are the Nicholas Chamberlaine Alms Houses, rebuilt in 1840; also, a magnificent example of nineteenth century architecture, the huge brick-built 45-meter-high water tower. Built in 1898, this huge building stands proud and overlooks the town; it is recognised as a prominent landmark for the surrounding areas. In the centre of town is the charming seventeenth century All Saints Church, rebuilt in the late nineteenth century, and takes prime position in the square bearing its name.

George was educated to a minimal standard, and never attended a grammar school as such. Coventry was the place to attain a higher education but travelling there at that time was a problem. During George's formative years, there was a war on, and because Coventry was an industrial city, it sustained bombing on a tremendous scale, making it a place to avoid. Our man was not too concerned with higher, or indeed any education, as his career, along with his fathers and grandfathers before him, was predetermined... Working down the pit. In fact, most of Bedworth's male population spent their entire lives as miners. As soon as George left school, he was given a job 'darn pit', as the locals would say. He was lucky enough to work alongside his father, who, with his twenty years' experience spent as a coal miner, was able to give valuable advice to his son. When on the same shift, they'd leave home together, and depending on their work allocation of the day, work side by side.

Father and son were on different shifts on this occasion, so George had to ride to work alone. It was a warm spring morning when George took his bike out of the garden shed, squeezed the tyres, ensuring there was enough air in them, and set off on the mile-and-a-half bike ride to the pit, just on the outskirts of town. There would be many others on their bikes doing the same thing.

Jumping off his bike after passing through the huge iron gates, George left it in the cycle shed, and reported to the shift overman, who'd be there sorting out the jobs as you drew your tally. The tally carried your own personal number, which was duplicated on the payroll. The purpose of the tally, or disc, was to receive them at the beginning of the shift, and hand them back at the end of it. This would indicate you'd returned safely to the pithead and weren't left down at the coalface.

After receiving his tally, George got changed into pit gear, filled his tin water bottle, and walked to the lamp room where he received his freshly charged-up helmet lamp; this would last for the duration of his shift. Before entering the cage to descend to the coalface, George, as usual, entered the airlock and underwent a search for any contraband he may have forgotten to leave at the pithead. The deputy would be searching for cigarettes and, primarily, matches.

On occasions, pit disasters occurred when miners smuggled matches and cigarettes down to the coalface, intending to 'light up' secretly when alone. A water bottle and 'snap tin' (food container) were the only items allowed to be taken to the coalface, as gas pockets often formed, and would ignite easily by lighting a match whilst having a 'quick drag'. The gas explosions caused horrific injuries and sometimes death to the men working at the coalface, and other areas at the pit. Anyone caught carrying contraband on their person faced immediate dismissal, with perhaps a criminal charge to follow later.

This shift was the same as any other; George, after undergoing the routine search, entered the cage and descended to the coalface, where he'd spend the shift working on his job allocation. What a difference in the atmosphere, when stepping out of the cage and taking a good look around. The roof was black along with the pit bottom. The coalface loomed in front of you, and pit props and boards held up the roof behind. As the coalface advanced ever slowly forward after being blasted and shovelled away, the pit props were pulled down, allowing the area it was holding up to collapse, bringing hazardous lumps of coal with it as it fell. There were safety procedures in this operation, but it never prevented accidents from happening.

Coal dust lingered in the atmosphere permanently, contaminating miners' eyes, noses, chests, stomachs, and lungs; in fact, every part of one's body that wasn't protected was invaded by coal dust. Each time a miner breathed, he inhaled this dust into his lungs, where it remained, causing sickness, and breathing problems later in life. Some miners wore a neckerchief over their mouths and noses to help alleviate the direct and immediate effects of what they'd otherwise inhale. It was a dangerous and unhealthy occupation, with unseen hazards occurring when one least expected.

On the previous shift, the coalface had been drilled, loaded with explosives, and blown up to form sizable lumps of coal, which could easily be handled and shovelled. Miners on the following shift would do this. After the exploding operation, strippers would move in and make the area ready for the men with shovels – George and his mates.

George had been allocated his working space, after a deputy marked out an area of approximately five yards square with chalk on the coalface. This expanse would need 15 tons of coal shovelling and take the whole of his shift to do it. About halfway through the shift, he noticed his workmate, Heinz – a German ex-prisoner of war – take a packet of Polo mints from his trouser pocket. He proceeded to unwrap the silver paper, intending to have a mint to suck on. After having a good swig of water from his flask, which never cured the dryness of his throat, George asked Heinz for one of his mints.

Being an unfriendly and uncharitable sort of man, Heinz replied, "Buy your own fuckin' mints!"

Responding to the German's nastiness, George made a grab for the mints and snatched the packet from his workmate's hands, saying, "Tight fisted Jerry bastard, I'll 'elp me sen then!" All hell broke loose after that. Heinz did his best to snatch his property back, but his opponent was bigger and stronger than him, so his attempt to retrieve his mints failed. "I'm really gonna enjoy these sucks," bragged George, "stolen fruit always tastes better. Ha ha!" This annoyed Heinz, and seeing his opponent continue to open his stolen packet of mints, slowly retreated to the end of his emplacement.

After fully peeling back the silver wrapper, and about to take a mint out of the packet, George was aghast at what he'd discovered. Neatly packed into the centre hole of the mint packet was a thinly rolled cigarette and two matches. "Ya sly German bastard, smugglin' in snout and bloody matches so's ya can and 'ave a crafty drag; ya bastard, I'll learn ya." Upon discovering the hidden tobacco, he walked up to Heinz and confronted him, shaking him and expecting to find more. The German took issue with this, and pushed him away, prompting George to lash out with a punch. Unfortunately, the deputy saw it happen and stepped in to prevent any escalation of the incident.

"Right, lads, break it up; you know what you'll get if you're caught fightin' darn 'ere. What's it all abart?"

Both men stood silent, not saying a word. The deputy tried again to find the cause of the fight, and not being satisfied with the response, told both men to report to his office when the shift was over. The two men, after being chastised, carried on with their allotted tasks, refusing to speak with each other for the remainder of the shift.

After emerging from the cage and returning to the pithead – always a huge relief to the miners seeing daylight and breathing fresh air – George and Heinz stood outside the deputy's office, waiting to be called. As ill luck had it, the German was interviewed first, giving him the opportunity to make up a false story, blaming George for the incident and accusing him of smuggling the contraband. For some unknown reason, the deputy took his word against George's, as he didn't want to be accused of prejudice against an ex-POW. When the hapless Bed'uth man was interviewed, he was asked to turn out his pockets, which revealed the mints, tobacco and matches inside. The deputy ignored George's pleas of innocence when being confronted with the evidence and sacked him on the spot. George looked for the union man to help in his defence but was told he'd gone home after finishing his shift. Returning to the deputy's office, he had a row, finally threatening him with, "I'll put yer fuckin' light out, yer slimy bastard! Siding with them lousy Germans wot wus killin' decent Bed'uth blokes not two-year ago!"

"Stubbs, get yersen 'ome 'afore I call security!"

"You call 'em an' I'll sort them fuckers art too, same as I'll sort you art!"

The deputy had no choice but to call security, who escorted George and his bike to the gates, ordering him not to set foot at the mine again except to collect his cards and wages from the gatehouse.

On the lonely bike ride home, George muttered to himself, "Wor am I gonna say to the old mon, this'll bloody kill 'im; 'is only son booted art o' the pit cos 'e thumped a Jerry!"

Chapter 21

The Argyll and
Southerland Highlanders

George's father didn't take the news of his son's dismissal from the colliery very well at all. He tore into his son – verbally, not physically – telling him he should have reported the discovery of the contraband to the deputy straightaway. "If you 'ad done, we wouldn't be in this bloody mess nar. They should've sacked that bleedin' Kraut, not you!"

Both parents were convinced of their son's innocence, but annoyed with him, because it was George's hot temper that brought about his dismissal. His dad was ready to go to the colliery and plead his son's case, citing him as a victim of circumstance, and completely innocent of the crime he'd been dismissed for. "You realise you'll never get a job in this tarn, cos o' what they've accused you of!"

"Dad, I don't gi' a damn abart this tarn anymore, in fact I'm gettin' art the bloody pits... I'm gonna join the army; me mind's med up!" This sudden and unexpected news only worsened the atmosphere in the Stubbs' house, as the last thing they wished for their son, was a career in the army... Much too dangerous for him! After telling him their feelings, his reply was, "What job cud be much wuss than bloody wokin' darn the soddin' pit?"

Mother and Father realised their son had been treated badly, and somehow sympathised with him, eventually giving their blessing to pursue a different career. However, George's choice of the army wasn't received at all well. Eventually, they accepted defeat, realising the more they dissuaded him from his ambition, the more he'd dig his heels in; besides, the war was over now, so it was highly unlikely their son would be placed in any danger.

After paying a visit to the Army careers office in Coventry, telling the recruiting sergeant his reason for leaving the coalmine, and hoping for an army career, his story was accepted. "I've been fighting those bloody Germans for five bloody years, and I wouldn't put what you've just told me past any of 'em... The bastards!" The sergeant made known his feelings for his old enemy and backed up George's version of the story completely. He went on to advise this potential recruit which regiment he should join.

After having the whole of the young male population of towns and villages wiped out in WWI, because they were all in the same local regiments, it was decided to scatter recruits of a town or village to different regiments, thus preventing the same disaster reoccurring;

leaving communities without their young men after hostilities had ceased. It was on this basis that the sergeant extolled the virtues and battle honours of one regiment, The Argyll and Southerland Highlanders.

After hearing about this famous regiment, and being acquainted with its colourful history, instead of going home and discussing it with his parents as advised, George, being over 18 years, asked to sign up straightway. He was given forms to sign and pamphlets to read, along with a train pass, and told to report to Stirling Castle in Scotland to attend a medical examination, then undergo an induction process after enlistment procedures were completed.

"Why the bloody 'ell didn't you come an' discus it wi' your mam 'n' dad fust, instead o' signin' your life away to somewhere in bloody Scotland?" shouted his dad after hearing his son's news. No amount of trying to put him off would have any effect on George's decision; besides, he lied to his parents that he'd signed up for four years, and there was no getting out of it. He hadn't passed his physical examination yet, and the outcome of *that* would determine whether he'd be eligible to sign on for four years.

"Yer either like it or bloody lump it, I ain't' bothered no more; I'm off to bonnie Scotland in a couple o' days' time, an' there's nawt yer can do abart it, so there!"

Eventually, both parents accepted their son's decision, realising his mind was made up, and the last thing they wished for was to part company with ill feeling; they loved their son and only wanted what was best for him. Father, Mother, and son went to the local Labour Club for a final drink together, and to say goodbye to his friends.

These old pals of George's were not happy with the Coal Board's decision to sack their fellow miner, and even unhappier to see him leave Bedworth and go to Scotland. They had a singsong together joining in with all the Scottish songs they knew, finally ending with 'Auld Lang Syne', which brought many a tear to the revellers in that cheery little Bedworth working men's club that evening. "Dun't forget to come and see us all when you come on leave; and dun't forget to wear yer kilt!" shouted the sozzled up group of well-wishers. George took note of this and promised he wouldn't forget them.

After saying goodbye at the train station with his mum sobbing her heart out, Dad shook hands whilst Mum gave him a final hug, leaving the two bereft parents to wave their goodbyes until the steam train disappeared into the distance. George settled down in his compartment seat and readied himself for his great adventure.

After arriving at his destination, Stirling Castle in Argyllshire, Scotland, it didn't take long for George to settle in and undergo the induction process, outlining the routine of a recruit. The medical examination went well, resulting in him passing with flying colours. He wasn't keen on the injections which followed, making his arms sore as well as his backside. After being given a billet which he shared with other recruits, he settled down for a nap. They were each allotted a bed, with a cupboard alongside to house their personal possessions, as well as the new kit they'd been issued. For the first part of his induction, he was given ordinary dungarees to wear, but later issued with a dress uniform and battledress.

He loved the dress uniform, consisting of a dark green jacket with yellow facings, a kilt in the tartan of the Black Watch, a Glengarry bonnet, socks and shoes; in effect, everything a soldier of the Argyll and Southerland Highlanders would need. He never wore this around the barracks, only on special occasions, but delighted in returning home to Bedworth where he wore it on every occasion... Especially when he visited his local club where he had to put up with a lot of 'stick' from his mates. Along with wolf whistles and the singing of every Scottish song they knew the words to, George had to fight off attempts by his mates trying to put their hands up his kilt, eager to discover if the rumour was true about what the Scotsman wore under it. They never discovered then, and as far as George was concerned, they never would!

He also had to get used to his new nickname, Jock, which wasn't so bad considering what he might have been called. Later, it was revealed George was completely exonerated from the charge of carrying contraband down to the coalface. This was why George got fired, and the reason he joined the Argylls. Apparently, when he quit the coalmine, his workmates down the pit – convinced of their mate's innocence – kept watch on the man who denounced him. George's dismissal for smuggling cigarettes and matches down the mine was attributed solely to this man's false statement. Heinz the German – or Baked Bean, as they called him – was seen by another miner emptying his water flask and shaking out a thin, aluminium container, which previously contained sore throat tablets. When empty, this little tube could hold a couple of thinly rolled cigarettes along with matches, and was just thin enough *and* watertight to fit into the neck of the water bottle.

After discovery, Heinz was sacked immediately, and as a gesture of reconciliation – and for his own safety – he owned up to the false accusation made against George, taking the blame for the offence himself. The management tried in vain to reach the innocent miner they'd wrongly dismissed, and when George heard they wanted to reinstate him, his exact words were, "Tell the bastards to get stuffed!" He was never going down a coalmine again... Ever!

Training in the Argylls was most arduous, as the regiment had a fierce reputation to maintain. They'd won many battle honours in the Napoleonic and Crimean wars, along with the Indian Rebellion. Although their weaponry had changed, bravery and valour hadn't. This hard training and drilling didn't bother George; he was a Bed'uth man, tough and fearless, and couldn't wait for a war to start so he could get in on some action – unknown to him at the time, he wouldn't have long to wait.

Being a regular soldier as opposed to a two-year national serviceman, the military were always looking for ideal candidates to promote to NCOs, or in rare circumstances, officers. George's enthusiasm and ferocity were noticed by his superiors, and it was mentioned to him about the possibility of a promotion. The factor preventing this from materialising swiftly was his accent and strange idioms, indigenous to George's hometown of Bedworth. There were others in the regiment with hard-to-understand accents, namely Geordies, Liverpudlians and certain Scots, who could benefit from English and elocution lessons. Such a class was formed with the intention of standardising an accent which all could understand and be understood by. George enrolled for these lessons, deciding to give them his best shot. He was a quick learner in most things and was no exception in mastering the King's English, with reasonable fluency. When going home on leave, however, he tended to slip back into his old Bed'uth slang. 'You can take a man out of Bed'uth, but you can't take Bed'uth out of a man', as they'd say in those days.

Chapter 22

Action in Korea

In June 1950, Communist North Korea invaded the South, beginning what would be known as the Korean War. America was the first country to go to the aid of the outnumbered South Koreans, but soon made it plain they too needed help in driving the invaders back across their border; the 38th Parallel.

The Argyll Regiment at that time was stationed in Hong Kong, and were ordered to Korea in support of United Nations forces. Sailing from Hong Kong on 24th August 1950, after a few adventures en route, they landed in Pusan, South Korea, some days later. Without having much time to settle in, they were ordered to meet up with the Americans, and help repel the North Koreans. Private Stubbs was excited by this and couldn't wait to get into the action, which came in droves. Arriving at the Nakdong River, they came between North Korean forces on one side, and US troops on the other. They narrowly missed having casualties when both sides opened fire, causing them to retreat, but later joined the Americans on the correct side of the river. Another incident involving friendly fire occurred at Hill 282, during September 1950.

After surprising a North Korean patrol and driving them from the hill, with losses to their own forces, they were attacked by US propeller-driven Mustangs. Mistaking them for the enemy, the Americans bombarded them with napalm, killing some of their wounded, and severely burning others. Fortunately, their position was on a slope which enabled the napalm to flow down. Believing the onslaught was over, they were horrified to see the Mustangs returning; this time machine-gunning their position. Their signaller had been killed, and it was only due to the bravery of two Argylls, who managed to locate the correct red flare, they were able to fire it into the air with a Very signalling gun. This flare alerted the Americans of the presence of friendly forces. The aircraft finally broke off the attack and returned to their base, after being responsible for killing and injuring many of their allies. With the counterattack by the N. Koreans which followed, the Argylls were forced to retreat to the bottom of the hill, which had been retaken by the enemy.

That day, the Argylls, after starting out with 180 men, suffered 90-plus casualties, with 13 dead. George was one of the lucky ones and escaped injury, but unfortunately there was more action to follow, which for a time had him wishing he was back down the pit. After suffering lice, 22-inch tapeworms and below zero temperatures, life was becoming unbearable. When they left Hong Kong, the regiment were dressed in their tropical clothing. Luckily, they weren't wearing kilts, but nevertheless, their attire was quite inadequate. The Americans came to their rescue and allocated them appropriate winter battledress, consisting of long woollen trousers, fur-lined hats, jackets with warm, quilted linings, along with fur-lined gloves and thick winter socks. They were also kitted out with unbelievably warm sleeping bags, which kept them from freezing to death in temperatures of minus 40, to minus 50 degrees. They were forced to sleep outside, having no cover at all except for 18 inches to 20 inches of snow. These were the conditions the soldiers had to endure, as well as fight the enemy.

The regiment was coming to the end of their tour, and whilst making their way south, George's platoon was warned to be on the lookout for snipers hiding in trees and amongst the rocky terrain. They'd endured many battles during their tour where they faced their enemy, which were noted in the annals of the regiment. However, one incident that wasn't recorded in the Battle Honours list, but nonetheless well remembered by those involved, occurred on a clear, but cold March morning.

The platoon was on the march, heading in the direction of Pusan from where they hoped to be shipped home. Being so close to their departure day, they became careless and unalert, except for Private Stubbs. Suddenly, a shot rang out, causing a soldier to scream with pain and hold his right shoulder. He'd been hit by a sniper's bullet; fortunately, not too seriously. "Hit the bloody deck! Everyone down!" called out the officer in charge, a Lt. Barrington. The men didn't need telling twice as they all 'hit the dirt' together.

"Anyone see where it came from?" called out the lieutenant.

"I saw it where it come from, sir!" answered one of the men.

"Ah, Stubbs, glad to see you were on the alert," responded the officer, "now, tell us where." George pointed to a haystack in the distance, about 250 yards away. "A haystack?" said the officer, quite unbelievably, whilst peering up into the distance. "Ah, I see it now, but its only small; how can a sniper hide himself in that little pile of hay?"

"Well, I definitely saw a puff of smoke come out of it, sir, little pile of hay or not!" The lieutenant wasn't happy being corrected by one of his men, and not particularly liking George, told him to go and investigate. "On me own, sir?" questioned George.

"Of course, on your bloody own, you're the one who saw it, so you are the one to investigate it."

Under his breath so the officer couldn't hear, George muttered, "Wish I'd kept me bleedin' mouth shut now."

"Did you say something, Stubbs?"

"Er, no, sir, just talking to myself... Sort off hyping myself up, that's all."

"Well, hype yourself up to that pile of bloody hay then... Come along... Hurry up!"

George's mates, or indeed any of the men, said nothing; they didn't wish to be chosen to accompany their comrade on the dangerous mission the officer had given him.

Checking his kit whilst taking a good look in the direction of where he saw the puff of smoke, the unhappy soldier began crawling on his knees towards the target. Every now and then, he'd stop and assess the distance ahead of him, but to his horror, the undergrowth and grass that had hidden him, became shorter; hence where the grass was taken to make the haystack. He was now more or less in the open, with no cover at all save for a few clumps of what appeared to be reeds.

He realised by now, if there was a sniper about, he'd have taken a shot at him. Maintaining a low profile kept him out of a sniper's sight. Heading towards the haystack, flat on his belly, he approached it from the rear.

Whilst recovering his breath and rubbing his badly scraped elbows, a shot rang out. Raising his head very slowly, he looked towards the position of his platoon, and spotted a hat bobbing up and down. One of the men was ordered to fix a bayonet, place his hat on the point, and move it up and down to provoke the sniper to reveal his position. It did the trick, as George saw where the shot came from straightway... Inside the haystack!

Reaching for his rifle, he was horrified to discover it wasn't on his shoulder where he'd hastily slung it before making his crawl towards the haystack... It had slipped off somewhere along the way. "That's me on a bleedin' charge when I get back... If I get back!" he muttered to himself. Now right up to the target and planning his next move, he checked to see what weapons he had with him. All he came up with was a bayonet. *Perhaps I can prod him with this, make him come out of that bleedin' haystack, and stab him with it*, he thought, *that's what I'll do*! But thinking and doing it were two different things; so, he changed his mind after suddenly having a brainwave. *I'll set fire to the bloody haystack, wait for the bastard to come out, and then... I'll swipe him wi' me shovel*! Luckily for George, he made his way to the target in full kit, which included the small shovel soldiers used for 'digging in' on their positions.

Assured the sniper was still inside and couldn't see him, George struck a match, grabbed a clump of straw, lit it, and crawled around the haystack lighting it in several places. Smoke began to rise with the flames following, when, slowly, a small hatch opened at the top of the stack, and a little head appeared, looking around to see what was going on. Seeing the flames surrounding him, the sniper quickly closed the top flap, and opened another on ground level, almost where George was kneeling.

The smoke was getting thicker and becoming very hot, when George saw the flap open, and the head of the sniper slowly emerge. Believing no one was out there, the sniper pushed his head out at full stretch, turned to look at the sky... And was met with the sharp edge of George's shovel bearing down on him at full force. The first blow never severed his head completely, but the second and third did, splattering blood, gore and entrails all around him.

As the severed head rolled off, George kicked it away, having just enough time to enter through the hatch and poke around, looking for items of value. Seeing the sniper rifle, he threw it outside, followed by a canvas pouch, which, on later inspection, held maps and other papers. He'd just time to remove these items and crawl back through the hatch to safety, kicking his trophies, including the severed head, away from the fire, which by now was in full flame.

"What the bloody hell's going on up there?" called out the lieutenant, looking through his binoculars and talking to his sergeant. "Where the hell's Stubbs?"

"I think he's on the other side of that haystack, sir, out of view now, but we'll spot him when the fire burns down," replied the sergeant.

"How did that fire start? Did he get the sniper or what; I haven't heard any gunfire lately!"

Suddenly, one of the soldiers spotted George and called out, "I can see him, sir, he's making his way back from the other side of that burnt-out stack. Indeed, George was on his way back, he'd gone through his victim's pockets and found nothing of value, so he took the maps and papers from the canvas pouch and dropped the severed head inside, shaking it down to the bottom. As there was not enough room for the maps, he stuffed them in his tunic. Admiring the Russian rifle as he picked it up, he slung it across his shoulder and headed back to the platoon. Fortunately, by taking the same route back as he did going up to the stack, he came across his own rifle and slung that over his shoulder.

"Where the hell have you been, and who started that bloody fire... Come on, man, make your report!"

George was annoyed at his superior for not thanking him for what he'd just done and felt like telling him, but thought better of it. "Sorry, sir, but I just want to say the mission is complete, and I've eliminated the enemy sniper."

"Well, where is he; what have you done with the body?"

George was a little surprised at this; what did the officer expect him to do, drag the body back down behind him, just so he could look at it? "I left it up there, sir, it was too 'eavy to bring down 'ere."

The lieutenant still wasn't happy; impatiently he asked, "Well, what did this sniper look like, was it a man or woman; was he Chinese, Russian or North Korean? Come along, Private, give me a description to report back to the Intelligence Section. How tall was he, big, small, fat, thin; come along man!"

George was becoming angry at this officer's aggressive questioning; he hadn't even said well done or given any sign of gratitude for his efforts. The sergeant felt the same way. "Well, 'e wasn't a tall man, sir, not very big at all!" said George, tired of the grilling he was getting. So, he put his hand in the pouch and pulled out the severed head, thrust it out at arm's length aimed directly at the lieutenant, saying, "He was about this tall, sir!" Almost shoving the head up the officer's nose, he said, "They ain't very big, are they, sir, them Koreans!"

The startled officer was lost for words, peering down at this gruesome sight still dripping blood with entrails hanging from it. "My God, man, what the bloody hell do you think you're playing at; get rid of that hideous bloody object right away!"

"Well, you did ask, sir," replied George a little sheepishly.

"GET BLOODY RID OF IT NOW; I'LL HAVE YOU ON A CHARGE FOR INSUBORDINATION," shouted the angry officer at the as loud as he could.

Meanwhile, the men in the platoon couldn't help themselves, rolling on the ground in hysterics. Some were holding their stomachs, faces turning red, howling with laughter. "Here, George, chuck it over to me!" called one of them.

"Head it this way!" called out another.

"On me head, George, kick it to me and I'll head it back to you!"

"Which way you are heading for mate, give us a kick!"

These calls and hollers continued until the lieutenant, now almost blue in the face, looked as if he was about to burst a blood vessel. The timely intervention of the grinning sergeant prevented this, sidling up to the officer and having a quiet word in his ear, saying, "With your permission, sir, may I suggest you let the men carry on having a bit of fun. They've been under stress for days now, and this incident, grotesque as it is, will help relieve it. Just indulge them, sir, it won't be for long." Then, looking at the officer's purple face, advised him, "We can't have our officer getting a stroke now, sir, especially as we are on our way home." These words of wisdom from an experienced and worldly NCO did the trick and calmed his superior down. "And by the way, sir, why not thank Stubbs for his brave action, killing that sniper single handed, and possibly saving more of our lives."

Lieutenant Barrington took this advice on board, but after George had finished his antics with the head, and handed the maps and papers to him, he changed his attitude completely. Quickly scanning through the maps, he realised they indicated positions of the enemy forces, and where other snipers were situated. Swallowing his pride and with genuine gratitude, he thanked George, and assured him his actions would be reported to high command, with a recommendation for an award. "When Intelligence sees these papers, they'll go wild. The enemy positions are all indicated making it easy for our forces to take appropriate action. Thank goodness you rescued them from the fire. By the way, Stubbs, how did that fire start, and why chop that sniper's head off?" After seeing the puzzled look on George's face, he decided not to continue with his questioning.

Although George wasn't aware of it at that time, the taking of heads for identification purposes, rather than having to produce the whole body, was usual practice in the Foreign Legion. Fellagha bandits in Algeria with prices on their heads – quite literally – if shot dead by legionnaires, had their heads severed and taken back to HQ for inspection by officers of the intelligence department or Deuxième Bureau. They were photographed and catalogued to keep track of who was still alive and active in the various regions.

Rather more gruesome and distressing was the practice of the Legion putting prices on the heads of their own legionnaire deserters. Once again. it was a 'dead or alive' price paid to the bounty hunters, who, after capturing a deserter, found it more expedient and simpler to kill their victim and produce only the head to claim their prizemoney.

Chapter 23

Mrs Agnes Tweedsmuir

The Argylls left Korea in April 1951, returning home with fewer men than left Hong Kong eight months previously. As a result of his actions whilst under fire, George not only received a bravery medal, but was promoted to full corporal, so bypassing the lance corporal grade. Because of his initiative and ability to perform under extreme conditions, his commanding officer, Major Robert Tweedsmuir – 'Old Robbie', as he was called by his men – took an exceptional liking to him. He believed he was good promotion material, and with the correct grooming, could reach officer class. To keep an eye on him he was given a job on Old Robbie's staff, which included running errands as well as performing certain office duties.

As he had some leave owed and hadn't been home since he returned from Korea some weeks previously, George planned to travel south to his hometown of Bedworth. He telegrammed his parents to let them know of his homecoming and arranged to meet them at the station.

On arrival, instead of being met by just his mum and dad, it was a brass band and members of the council, including the mayor of Bedworth, who were there to welcome him back. Although only a small town, it knew how to greet and look after its heroes. The Warwickshire town of Bedworth is the only town outside of London to have observed the two minutes' silence at 11.00 on November 11th every year since 1921, earning the nickname, or title, 'The Town That Never Forgets'. The week's leave was spent attending functions organized by the council some weeks previously, after hearing of George's exploits in Korea. All was made ready for the day he returned, and only a few of his pals were in on the surprise... And surprise it was, due to what they'd planned for him.

Apart from attending one or two banquets, he not only planted a couple of trees in the Miners' Welfare Park, but opened a small supermarket, and was guest of honour at various functions. His period of leave flew by and having little time to spend with his parents and friends was a disappointment to him; these were the people he was anxious to see, not council members and notaries.

Before realising it, he was back on the train to Scotland and his HQ in Stirling Castle where his return wasn't as lavish as he'd experienced in Bedworth. The newly promoted corporal soon got down to work in the major's office and immersed himself in the routine of a staff NCO.

One sunny afternoon, he was called into the CO's office and asked to deliver a message to his wife, Mrs Tweedsmuir. "I'd go myself, laddie, but it would mean spending too much time explaining my absence, so I'll leave it to you to take the flack... What!" Apparently, her husband spent a lot of time away from home in his determination to obtain the position he'd always wanted... Colonel. The quest required him to perform duties above and beyond those required of an ordinary major and CO. It was at the expense of his married life, which didn't receive the attention it should have. This caused much friction and annoyance in the Tweedsmuir household, especially with the lady of the house.

When they first married, the CO was a mere second lieutenant with huge ambitions to better himself, and so give Mrs Tweedsmuir a lifestyle to which she was accustomed. She was the daughter of a Scottish industrialist and used to the finer things in life; these couldn't be provided on a second lieutenant's pay. However, she was in love with him and wasn't concerned about material things at that time; she'd enjoyed these whilst living at home with her parents. They gave her everything she asked for... Except love. Being married to Robbie Tweedsmuir would provide this... She thought.

Their sex life wasn't much to write home about, but she imagined this would improve as her husband progressed and achieved his ambitions. They didn't have children, though not for the lack of trying... On her part. In fact, if her husband's performances in the bedroom were anything to go by, they'd be forever childless. It came to the point where she craved for a lover, but the junior officers had the same ambitions as her husband – to attain promotion; playing around with their CO's wife would certainly get in the way of achieving that.

She'd stand in front of the mirror some days after showering and look at her figure... Which wasn't at all bad for a 45-year-old. Twisting one way and half turning the other, she'd think to herself. *You're in good shape for your age, Agnes, slim waist, nicely shaped hips and bottom, gorgeous legs and thighs, and such a beautifully firm bust; why the hell can't you excite that husband of yours?*

Agnes was everything the mirror reflected and perhaps more. She ate sensibly and exercised regularly to maintain her beautiful shape, but found her efforts in vain, as no man dared complement her. Fearing the wrath of their CO who had a reputation for losing his temper, flirting with his wife would be most unwise.

"Before you go to the house, Corporal," enquired the CO, "are you any good at DIY, you know, fixing household items, putting up shelves, doing a bit of gardening and that sort of stuff?"

George thought for a moment and replied, "Why yes, sir, owt like that I can do. A bit o' painting and carpentry, sure, even doin' electrics and that sort o' stuff... Why d'you ask, sir?"

"I'll let you know in due course, leave it with me."

These remarks from the CO started George thinking. *What 'ave I let me sen in for now; what's 'e got lined up for me?*

George didn't have long to wait for his answer. He should've heeded the sensible advice given by old soldiers through the ages, "Never volunteer for anything!"

Instead of leaving the task of informing his wife of his impending absence to someone else, the CO changed his mind and asked George to accompany him to the house, as there were one or two small jobs for him to do; this came about because of his revelation of being a handyman. "Come inside, Corporal, I'll introduce you to the lady of the house... My wife," said the major quite jovially, "she'll give you a list of what needs doing. You'll be doing me a favour sorting out these jobs, as I'm far too busy to spend my time knocking nails in and screwing bits of wood together. Besides, it would be demeaning for the CO to be seen doing these things... What!" They walked into the lounge but there was no sign of Mrs Tweedsmuir. "Hello, darling, I'm home; I have someone here I want you to meet!" he called out. Looking around, there was no sign of her, but looking into the garden they saw her kneeling, doing some weeding. "Don't bother with that anymore, my love, I've someone here to do it for you."

George thought, *So I'm to be the bloody gardener as well as the soddin' major's dogsbody. They can bloody well stuff that, I signed up to be a soldier!*

However, he soon changed his mind when he saw the major's wife. She dropped her trowel, and after wiping her hands on an attractive apron, held one out, greeting George with a huge smile. "Pleased to meet you, Corporal, did I hear you like gardening?"

George quickly changed his attitude and replied, "I love gardening, ma'am, really enjoy it!"

"Oh, I'm so pleased to hear it; the major hates it, as well as anything to do with household chores. It would be nice to have someone who doesn't mind getting his hands dirty." The lady of the house then proceeded to give George a little tour of the garden, asking his opinion of certain flowers, and whether they were too much in the sunlight or not, leaving him nonplussed, and wondering what she was going on about, but nodding his agreement here and there.

Whilst this was happening, the major looked impatiently at his watch, reminding his wife he had to be in Edinburgh within the hour, and he was late. "What time shall you return, my dear, will you be dining here tonight or what?" asked his wife anxiously.

"I doubt it; I'll probably eat at the officers' mess at the other barracks, so I advise you do the same here."

"When will you return, darling?"

"Oh, gone midnight, I should think... Don't wait up for me. Corporal Stubbs, I'll leave you in my wife's capable hands, she'll tell you what needs doing." Then, taking another quick look at his watch called out, "I'll be off now, cheerio!" With that, he was gone, leaving George in the capable hands of his wife... Or so he wished.

George was struck by the beauty of this woman, and her amazing figure. He guessed her age to be in the low forties – old enough to be his mother. *My crikey!* he thought. *If my mum had a figure like that, I'd never have left home!* Such lascivious thoughts going through his wicked mind. Having had many girlfriends previously, he lost his virginity at the tender age of fourteen. Being well endowed in the 'lower quarters', and with the local girls knowing of this, he had a job fighting them off. The vision before him, however, was an unknown; he'd never been placed in such a position before.

"Okay, my man, er, what's your name? I don't want to be calling you 'Corporal' each time we speak; you can call me Agnes, but only at home and not in the barracks."

"My name's George, ma'am, and if it's okay with you, I'd prefer to address you as 'ma'am'... That's if you don't mind, ma'am," replied George in his posh, would-be officer's voice.

"Oh, we are a stickler for propriety, aren't we now?" she responded sarcastically.

"It's not that, ma'am, but I do have the deepest respect for you and the major, and I don't want to become too familiar, ma'am," again in his posh voice.

The CO's wife simply nodded in approval, but secretly wished this handsome well-tanned hunk standing before her would chill out a little, as the last thing on her mind was gardening. Bringing this man around to be at her beck and call was like an early Christmas present; a well-built, handsome hunk of a man; very earthy and not in the least corrupted by propriety or false gentility. It could be said of her, 'she liked 'em rough'.

"Fancy a drink, Corporal?" she offered.

"Don't mind if I do, ma'am," replied George, not knowing what to make of this most attractive woman... No, she wasn't a woman... She was a lady, a proper lady.

"Let's cut out this bloody 'ma'am' business, call me Agnes; I hate being called ma'am."

George got the message, and thought this to be the first clue of her being familiar with him; who knows where it would lead? He fancied her 'something rotten', as he'd say, but didn't want to spoil his chances... Not at this stage. Entering the lounge, he sat opposite her after she brought him a beer and sat down. He had a choice of tea, coffee, wine or beer; so, he chose a bottle of the major's favourite.

"Will 'e mind me drinking 'is beer, ma'am, I mean Agnes?" he asked.

"Too bad if he does, I don't care what he minds and doesn't mind."

George detected a note of friction between them and wondered where it might lead. He didn't wish to make the first move, so he waited to hear more signs of discord. He'd known previously that when women begin to berate their spouses, particularly in front of a stranger, a predatory male like him, all out to have his wicked way with her, would stand a fair chance... If he played his cards right. Here he was, at his superior officer's residence – at his request – having a beer with his wife, and listening to her complaining about him, instead of praising him up, as most women would.

Staring at George's muscular legs and taking a glimpse of his thighs above his kilt, Agnes remarked how fit he looked, and what lovely legs he had. These were complements a man would make to a woman... But she was no ordinary woman. George became slightly unnerved as events were proceeding a little too fast for him, and he didn't wish to fall into a trap.

"What about that cupboard in the kitchen and the shelves you want putting up?" asked George.

"Oh, stuff the bloody cupboard, and the shelves. Is there nothing else on your mind except putting things up?" Realising what she'd said and how it could be misconstrued, caused them both to laugh. It looked as if things were beginning to come George's way. However, to make a move on the first occasion was asking for trouble, even though she did seem, 'up for it'.

"Ma'am, I mean Agnes, I really think I should do the jobs my CO asked me to do, cos if he returns 'ome and sees nowt done, I'll be in for it... Understand what I mean?"

"Oh, I suppose you are correct; if his bloody Highness gets back and sees nothing has been done, he'll wonder what we've been playing at, won't he, George?

And the fact is, we've not been playing at anything... *Have we now?*"

George just nodded and got on with doing what the major told him to do. "Agnes, while I'm standin' on this step ladder, could you support me please?" he asked, needing her assistance in case he fell off. Agnes was only too pleased to get her hands on George's manly legs and reached a little higher, holding around his waist. *What would the major do if he suddenly appeared and saw us in such a compromising position?* he thought.

"Is that okay, George; do you feel safer now?" she asked, holding him tightly around his waist. His answer was simply a grunt, as he was lost for the correct words to say in response.

George finished marking out the positions where he would drill holes and fit the plugs, and asked Agnes to pass the drill. Ensuring the drill bit was the correct size, he carried on drilling the four holes he'd marked previously. Now finished drilling, he tapped the plugs in, ready to fit the screws. All the time, this seductive and very suggestive woman had her arms clasped around George's waist, resisting the temptation to put her hands up his kilt, and stroke his muscly thighs.

He needed help to lift the cupboard up, and got it from his willing assistant, who wanted nothing more than to get her soft, warm hands anywhere on George's body. After screwing the cupboard to the wall, running the spirit level over it and standing back to admire his work, Agnes jumped with joy and threw her arms around him, giving a huge kiss as she did so. "What a clever man we have here! Oh, you are so clever; and highly skilled too!" she called out, whilst giving George another kiss, and hoping he'd respond.

George was a bit too wily to respond in the way she wished; instead, he looked at his watch while extricating himself from her boa constrictor-type grip, saying, "Oh dear, is that the time, I'll miss the evening mess call! Best get back, else I'll be late!"

This attitude had Agnes puzzled; was he not interested in her advances, or simply playing the 'long game', waiting for a more positive response from her as if she hadn't done enough already. Giving him a little kiss – on his cheek – she whispered, "Hope this isn't the last time we'll do things together; we worked very well as a pair, did we not, my dear?"

It was the 'my dear' endearment which gave George a little signal that his 'services' would be needed again, and glad he'd not jumped the gun and made a play for her on this first occasion. If the truth was known, he had 'the hots' for the major's wife, and she definitely had the same feelings for him.

Major Tweedsmuir was very happy with his corporal's performance putting the cupboard up for him, as well as sorting out one or two other little jobs. His wife, Agnes, was pleased with his efforts and mentioned this, as well as his exceptional behaviour, along with his carpentry skills. Agnes craftily made it known she'd not be averse to George doing other jobs for her in the future. "If that's the case, and he's proved himself to you, there's a few more jobs we'll have him do... That's if it's okay with him!" suggested the major.

A week later, George was called to the major's office and asked if he didn't mind doing a few more little jobs around the house. He mentioned how pleased Mrs Tweedsmuir was with his last performance and would like him to come over to the house again. "By Jove, what a difference it made when I returned home the other night, instead of the usual nagging for being away for too long, she was in a most pleasant mood, and cooked me supper, as I missed it in Edinburgh."

"I'm glad to have been of service, sir, and only too glad your charming wife was pleased with what I did," replied George, feeling proud of himself; proud, that is, that he didn't succumb to his wife's advances. It would be a different story next time if his wife behaved as she did previously.

"In a couple of days' time, along with some other officers, I have to go to Catterick army base to attend an important meeting of military staff. I had the chance to take you along, but I'd rather you got on with one or two jobs which need doing around the house; how do you feel about that?"

George had difficulty stifling his excitement; an opportunity for him to be alone with that seductive beauty once more. "That's okay, sir, you can rely on me to get things done for you," he answered with a straight face.

Chapter 24

A fall From Grace

George's first meeting with the major's wife left quite an impression on her. Thinking of him, she began to scrutinise his actions, as well as form an opinion. He lacked finesse and refinement, but exuded earthiness... Which excited her! He'd a certain charm about him, which possibly worked well with girls of *his* class, but not with refined women such as herself. The brief time spent together left her feeling very excited, wondering what his performance would be like in the bedroom. His interests were few, hence his limited conversation; she wasn't interested in conversation, she wanted *facta non verba,* or 'deeds not words', as she'd learnt in her Latin lessons at finishing school.

Previously, as they made a joint effort to fix the cupboard to the wall, and having her hands around his waist, steadying him, she resisted the temptation to put her hands up his kilt. *How would he have reacted had I done so*, she asked herself. Her imagination began to run wild with all sorts of fantasies emerging, exciting her more and more. Knowing he was to spend most of the day with her, fixing shelves and doing other little jobs her husband couldn't be bothered with, would give her the chance to act out some of her fantasies... Her sexual fantasies. He did seem keen to participate, but the fear his actions would be discovered might prevent him from taking part. She must do her best to excite this hunk of man, beginning with her choice of underwear.

George had no idea what awaited him as he strode up the path leading to the major's house. He didn't have long to wait for the door to open after ringing the bell; in fact, she was waiting for him. Opening the polished oak door, he was amazed to see the transformation in her appearance. On the previous occasion, she wore an apron over a long skirt with her hair in a mess; she *was* in the middle of gardening, after all! Today he was greeted by her wearing a short, gossamer, flowered skirt, and a close-fitting sweater, accentuating her ample curves. Her hair was much tidier, and only a hint of makeup, with lipstick applied sparingly. Wearing too much of either caused many a broken marriage, when wives discovered it on some hapless husband's clothes, especially shirt collars.

George, in contrast, was wearing a pair of dungarees; overalls he thought more appropriate if he was about to do some painting. "No kilt today? Shame, I was looking forward to seeing those magnificent legs of yours... Especially your huge thighs," she whispered seductively.

"No, ma'am, I dressed like this to do some work." George thought he'd try his luck when he uttered the next few words. "The only way you'll get see my legs is if I take me trousers off."

That did it. If he was trying to push open the metaphoric door, the reply from Mrs Tweedsmuir pulled it wide open when she said, "That can be arranged, Corporal, believe me, no problem at all."

The die was cast, cards were on the table. This sexy woman, after taking George's hint, realised no more silly innuendos or *double entendres* were necessary. She pulled him inside the doorway, slammed the door shut and threw her arms around him, kissing him wildly. She was now going to get what she'd been deprived of for too many years... Excitement, passion pleasure and sex... Especially sex.

"Close the door and follow me upstairs, there's something I want you to do for me... And for heaven's sake, stop calling me bloody ma'am, it makes me so mad!"

"The madder the better," called out George. "Come on, let's do something bloody wild, I haven't been with a woman for months, and I don't want to waste any more time playing silly games. You want it and I want it, so let's bloody well get on with *it*!" These were the words Agnes wanted to hear and added to her wild expectations.

It didn't take George long to remove his clothes, but he took his time whilst undressing Agnes. What a delight for this ordinary working-class soldier, slowly taking the clothes off an upper-class lady. He never in his wildest dreams imagined a 'posh bird' would take an interest in *him,* and here he was, getting ready to go to bed with one. He remembered the advice on the fine arts of lovemaking and seduction given to him by one of his older and experienced pals - treat a tart like a lady, and a lady like a tart. He was about to put this into practice. The more he undressed her, the more he became excited; her too. Down to her underwear now, he decided to leave it on as the sight of her black silky panties and matching bra was a sight to relish. She had a most glorious figure, and after gently laying her flat on the soft bed sheets, proceeded to kiss every inch of her semi-naked body. Her skin was smooth and soft, just asking to be stroked and caressed, which he did whilst kissing her.

These sensual movements had an effect she'd never experienced before, and rather than wait for him to continue undressing her, she tore the remaining clothes off herself, grabbing hold of George, putting her hands below him and taking hold of his manhood. Feeling her soft warm hands stroking his upper thighs drove him wild. He stopped kissing and proceeded to do what he was meant to do; couple up and make wild and passionate love to this goddess of a woman.

In her wildest dreams she hadn't imagined there existed so many ways to enjoy sex, in so many different positions too. It was like being pulled out of one dull and tedious existence into a new wild abandonment of another world; a world she never knew existed. Soft lights and sweet music weren't necessary to experience what she was enjoying now; complete abandonment of all decency and propriety. "My God, they never taught me anything like this at finishing school, Corporal. Which school did you attend to learn such deviations of the simple sex act, and discover so many ways to achieve an orgasm?"

George had difficulty understanding the words being spoken but grasped the full meaning of them and how his partner was behaving, enjoying everything he could deliver. "I don't fully understand what you are saying, ma'am, I mean Agnes, but I've got the gist of it. I never went to no posh school like you, so I never learned 'ow to talk as you do, but I certainly know 'ow to treat a woman and find out what she really wants; and most women, apart from wanting love and affection, just want sex and a bloody good time."

Still using their formal titles for each other, Agnes answered, "Most succinctly put, Corporal, I couldn't agree with you more; pity most of the men in my life didn't attend the same school as you."

Both participants, now feeling exhausted by their over exertions, decided to have a rest, and let nature take its course... As it had done with their previous performances. They became tired and needed a nap, which they had. Sinking into George's muscular arms, Agnes drifted into a gentle slumber, feeling more satisfied than she'd ever been. George needed breathing space, so he dropped off as well.

The major arrived in Catterick, accompanied by an officer companion and a sergeant driver. He'd been up early and was a little tired. They were too late for breakfast and had to contend with coffee and toast, which the chef swiftly prepared for them. The 160-mile journey from Stirling Castle to Catterick in Richmond, Yorkshire took about four hours. The major believed they would need overnight accommodation if the meeting went on for too long. After discovering the meeting had been called off due to the high-ranking officer's absence concerning highly confidential military matters, the major and his escorts decided to make the journey back. Being fully refreshed and hopeful of an early return to base, it would be a pleasant surprise to their wives who expected them to be away much longer.

"My wife will be pleased," said the lieutenant, "I told her we wouldn't be back 'til late; now we can have a pleasant evening together."

"Me too," agreed the sergeant, "a nice curry washed down with a couple of cans of lager, what could be nicer than that, except an early night with the missus!"

"What about you, sir," enquired the lieutenant, "have you any plans for this unexpected early return?"

"I don't quite know what awaits me, Lieutenant, I'll just have to wait and see; nothing unpleasant, I hope." All three men laughed at this, and settled down for the journey back to camp, each looking forward to the surprise their early return would give their loved ones.

The four-hour drive back to Scotland was uneventful and gave the two officers ample time for a nap; the sergeant did the driving, so he had to remain alert. Driving through the gates of Stirling Castle and towards the married quarters, the major invited both men inside for a drink and a light snack, which his wife would prepare.

Unlocking the front door, he suggested the lieutenant and sergeant sit outside on the terrace whilst he'd sort out some drinks, after which he'd ask his wife to prepare snacks for them. "Before I ask you what you'll want to eat and drink gentlemen, I must go straightway to visit the toilet. I'm dying for a pee." Both men laughed politely at their COs remark and settled down into a pair of comfortable reclining chairs on the terrace.

"This is the life, what, sergeant! I'm just about ready for a decent drink; hopefully the CO's got a decent malt whisky, eh?"

"I'd prefer a lager myself, sir," replied the sergeant, "but right now anything will do!"

The major returned from his call of nature in the convenient downstairs toilet and took the orders for the men's drinks. "I can't think where my wife's gone; there's no sign of her, or that corporal who's supposed to be fixing up some shelves. I'd better give them a shout. Perhaps they're in the garden or somewhere. Agnes! Are you about, darling, there are three hungry men needing your culinary skills here!"

Nothing stirred; no sign of life at all. The major looking around and seeing the shelves exactly where they were before he left that morning, and the paint tins yet to be opened, should have given him a clue that something was amiss... But no. In his naivete, he assumed the corporal failed to turn up for the minor work detail he'd planned, or a more important matter required him to be elsewhere. Calling out once more failed to bring a response, and he was about to give up when he heard strange noises coming from upstairs.

The two lovers were too involved with each other to hear what was happening below. Agnes had been introduced to the world of sexual deviation, and, with the various contortions and different positions involved, she failed to notice, or even hear, the presence of anyone else in the house. She was about to experience another deviation, which involved her sitting astride her partner, assuming the position a of a western rodeo rider on an unbroken mustang. "Where on earth did you learn such disgustingly deviant and perverted positions of the sex act, Corporal?"

"It's just summat we always done, ma'am; I never really went nowhere to learn 'em, it's just doin' what comes naturally, I suppose," replied George nonchalantly.

"My God, the things you working-class lot get up to; seems you've had more fun and excitement than we ever did!" she uttered quietly, not really wanting George to hear. Preparing herself for the next lesson in what the lower classes regarded as normal practice, she threw the bedclothes off, and to George's great delight, wriggled herself down upon him, connecting once more, bouncing up and down in slow jerking movements. She and George were oblivious to what was going on elsewhere, and continued to twist, bounce and cavort themselves into a world of sexual pleasure and sensual fantasy.

Slowly climbing the stairs, the major couldn't make out the strange noises coming from his bedroom. At first, it sounded like an injured animal in distress, moaning, purring, and whining, as an injured cat would. But no, it can't have been an animal, as they didn't keep pets of any sort. Approaching nearer the bedroom door, the noises changed to a heavy breathing, more human than animal. Suddenly, hearing softly spoken words of affection, it dawned upon him two people were inside, making such noises that could only be made whilst having sex together.

Pausing outside the door, he really didn't want to see who he was inside, as subconsciously he realised it might be Agnes with another man; but who? Whilst slowly pushing the bedroom door open, and seeing his naked wife astride another man, everything became apparent. His heart was racing, and his throat was dry. Still unaware of his presence, the pair continued to indulge in more sexual deviations. "Come along, Corporal, it's time for a change over; your turn to get on top, this position is tiring me out!" Hearing this from his wife, and witnessing her indulging in this thoroughly disgusting display of salaciousness, put the major into shock; he was too astounded and unable to make any sound at all to betray his presence. In shock, the major may have been, but nowhere near as shocked as his wife was, after climbing off George and seeing him standing there, open mouthed and purple with rage.

Neither made a move nor said a word; each completely astounded at what they saw; they just could not believe it. Agnes made the first move – a treacherous one at that. "Robbie, thank God you're here; it has been terrible what this man has done to me, and what he's making me do now!"

George was the next of the *ménage à trois* to surface, seeing his CO standing at the end of the bed, almost boiling over with anger. Realising he'd not a stitch of clothing on, he tried to throw a sheet over him. Hearing Agnes' pleas and blaming him for what had transpired made him feel powerless, and unable to say a word.

"You must punish him for what he's done, Robbie, he's thoroughly debased me and made me feel cheap and full of shame!" She began to sob as she shamelessly lied.

The major simply pushed her to one side, vowing to deal with her later, once he's sorted out her lover. "Stay over in the corner, you disgusting bitch, I'll give this swine his just deserts, then you'll get yours!" he threatened.

"Please, Robbie, no, it was nothing to do with me, this lout forced me to do it... Honestly!"

Now fully able to speak coherently, he addressed George, who was still standing there with a white sheet draped over him, looking rather like a Roman emperor who'd just indulged in an orgy. "You absolute bloody scoundrel, taking advantage of my wife as soon as my back was turned; did you plan this?" George remained silent. "After all I've done for you; treated you like a son, dragging you from the ranks to make an officer of you. I had big things planned, and this is how you treat me, but you won't get away with it, no way will you escape my wrath. Prepare yourself for a bloody sound beating... And take that ridiculous sheet off!" the major shouted. He proceeded to remove the thick leather belt from around his jacket, threateningly saying, "It's a bloody good job I'm not wearing my pistol, otherwise I'd SHOOT YOU!"

Downstairs on the terrace, the officer and NCO, hearing the noise, assumed it was their NCO having a 'domestic' with his wife and didn't wish to interfere; had they done so, they'd have witnessed their CO beating his wife's seducer. After being whipped a half-dozen times, George decided the maddened major had gone too far. Pausing for breath before his next onslaught on the unfortunate corporal, gave George an opportunity to grab hold of the vicious belt, and yank it out of his trembling hands. "You'll pay for that, you swine, give it back here and take your punishment like a man!" called out the purple-faced commanding officer.

"If I give it back, sir, promise you won't 'it me again," said George anxiously.

"Promise... Promise? Who are you to ask me to promise, you back street bloody layabout, dragged up in some grotty slum, I'll promise you nothing... Now give it here!" called out the major with outstretched hands. Still refusing, and with his superior officer almost black with rage now, George tucked the belt under the pillows, and told the major to calm down.

Constantly being told what to do by the man he'd just found in bed with his wife maddened him more; the CO grabbed a walking stick leaning against the wardrobe and proceeded to strike out again at George, hitting him sharply across his chest, causing him to uncover himself and stand there cowering, completely naked. Aiming to strike down below at his opponent's naked body, the major aimed his blows at his uncovered manhood shouting, "I'll make sure you never seduce anyone else, you low life reprobate!"

Being hit with a stick in these delicate parts of the body caused George to call out, "Hit me again with that bloody stick, and I'll whack you a 'bleeder', officer or no officer!" With that, the major aimed another blow in the same area, causing his opponent much pain. He shouted out, "That's it, I've had enough, drop that bloody stick or I'll drop you, you cowardly old bastard!"

That did it, getting ready to take another swipe, George grabbed hold of the stick and threw it down. Squaring up to the major, he delivered a single well-aimed punch to his face, knocking him to the floor and breaking his nose in the process. Agnes, who'd been cowering in the corner, let out a huge scream upon seeing her husband knocked out cold, fearing he was dead. This scream prompted the lieutenant and sergeant to go rushing up the stairs, believing someone was badly hurt.

Seeing their CO flat out on the bedroom floor and George stark naked, with the CO's wife attending to her husband, prompted them to call for a medical officer. "While you're at it, Sergeant, call for a couple of

Military Policemen – we're going to need them. Looks as if our commanding officer has been severely injured by his corporal."

The medics and MPs soon arrived, and taking stock of the situation, ordered their CO's assailant to get dressed, then dragged him away to the guardhouse where he was locked in a cell. "Your days are numbered, soldier; striking a superior officer is gonna get you 20 years; and shagging his wife as well, will get you hard labour. If it was wartime, you'd be shot immediately," said one of the MPs as he pushed George into the cell, locking the door behind him. Alone now in the damp, darkened cell, suffering in great pain from the severe beating he'd received from his CO, poor George could not believe what had just happened. The events which suddenly occurred were his fault entirely; he didn't have to go to bed with Agnes, but what man could resist the charms and promiscuity of such a temptress like her. Had he been sensible and did what he was supposed to, this disaster wouldn't have occurred; but this man was anything but sensible, and this disaster *did* occur!

What happened in the major's household after this unfortunate incident was typical of what a military man and an upper-class lady would do. Behaving very adult and professional, they decided to pretend that the version of events given by her were what they must adhere to in order to preserve the good name of their families, as well as their military reputation. This was to be a damage limitation exercise, to save their marriage and retain each other's integrities. Corporal Stubbs was to be the sacrificial lamb, and all blame would be attributed to him, painting Mrs Tweedsmuir as whiter than white; completely blameless.

In preparation for the court martial, the prosecution lawyer advised the couple to adhere to this version of events and instructed the major not to contest his wife's testimony – although he knew it to be untrue. The court would be told Corporal Stubbs was the main protagonist in this matter, and Mrs Tweedsmuir was forced to go along with what he instructed, fearing he'd become violent. The full description of the sexual deviations, as well as the other sordid details, were not to be mentioned. She'd maintain molestation occurred after she undressed to begin painting, whilst helping the corporal to go about his duties. In other words – according to her – no sexual intercourse occurred, but would have had it not been for the timely arrival and subsequent intervention of her dutiful and loving husband. Not many people – sensible people – would believe a word of this, as most officers knew of Mrs Tweedsmuir's attempts to bed *them*, but the honour of the regiment was at stake, and this version of events would protect it. After all, it was only a mere enlisted man who'd suffer, and what did he matter?

It took a couple of weeks to convene the court martial. A judge advocate would preside along with five other officers, who'd pass judgement on the accused. Normally a panel of seven officers would be called along with the judge, but only in more serious cases. This trial was to be as low-key as possible, and it was already decided the defendant would be found guilty, along with the appropriate punishment which would follow. All that was needed now was to 'prime' the accused and offer him some sort of deal if he kept his mouth shut, and not mention what *really* occurred. Part of the deal would be to keep quiet about the lady concerned, and not mention the beating he received from his CO.

As with civil courts, the accused was given a defence council; in this case, a lieutenant who'd just finished his course at law school and passed with flying colours. This was to be his first case. However, there was a reason for this. George was told if he pleaded guilty as charged, for striking a superior officer after being found *in flagrante,* molesting his wife, he would receive only six months in prison, but lose his corporal's stripes. The court martial was to be brief, as at all costs, it was crucial to preserve the reputation of the lady concerned, also, the integrity of her husband.

George was a little naïve about such matters, and well out of his league, but decided to go along with what this well-educated, well-spoken defence lawyer suggested. He was told by his lawyer that six months would soon pass, and by pleading guilty, he'd obviate the chance of receiving a harsher sentence than if he pleaded not guilty, so causing distress to the lady concerned, as well as her husband, the CO.

On the day of his trial, George looked very smart his corporal's uniform, and by now, most of his bruises had disappeared. A good lawyer would have taken photographs of his client's injuries to help prove his case. Had he been instructed to do so by a senior defence council, such evidence would help prove why his client struck his superior after being viciously provoked, but that was considered unnecessary in this case.

There was hardly anyone in the courtroom, except those immediately concerned with the trial. The witnesses present need not have been there at all, as the accused had agreed to plead guilty for the reasons outlined to him. The major and his wife sat together, holding hands, looking most concerned and innocent of any wrongdoing.

The judge advocate read out the charges and asked the accused how he pleaded – guilty or not guilty. George thought for a while, and whilst standing up and in a clear voice said, "Guilty, Your Honour." There was a little discussion between the members of the panel, and the shuffling of papers, after which the judge announced there would be an interval before punishment was announced.

Back in his cell, George wondered what it would be like in a military prison, and what treatment he'd receive from inmates and warders. *It's only going to be for six months, so I reckon I'll be able to handle that, but only just*, he thought to himself.

After a ridiculously short recess, the prisoner was taken back to the courtroom to hear his punishment. The judge advocate read out the charge sheet once more, saying, "Striking a superior officer is a very serious matter. In wartime it would demand a death sentence.

Fortunately for you, we are not at war, so the maximum sentence allowed for such a serious offence is 10 years in prison."

George gulped when he heard this, thinking, *thank the Lord I'm only gonna get 6 months.*

"The offence you pleaded guilty to was committed whilst forcing yourself on a defenceless woman, and only because of the timely intervention of her husband preventing you from doing real damage to her. You then struck him down, rendering him unconscious and leaving him with a broken nose. I am therefore passing down the maximum punishment allowed of 10 years in prison. Because I cannot give more, I recommend it be served with hard labour. That is the judgement of this panel, and you will begin your sentence as soon as escorts arrive to convey you to be detained at the Military Corrective Training Centre, Colchester. Case closed."

On hearing this unexpected and frightening sentence, George was speechless. His throat was dry, and his head spun around; he just couldn't believe it. He was told he'd only receive 6 months, and was given 10 years, *and* hard labour to boot. He finally came out of his stupor, looked at his defence lawyer and said, "You promised me I'd only get 6 months, and I've been given 10 fuckin' years; what the fuck are you playin' at, you slimy two-faced bastard!"

Moving away from his client and fearing violence, the lawyer replied in a trembling voice, "I'm so sorry; I was told by senior council that they didn't want a nasty drawn-out trial for the regiment's sake, as well as for the reputation of the CO and his wife. It was hinted you'd get a lighter sentence by pleading guilty!"

George began to compose himself by now, saying, "Whadya mean, 'it was hinted', and what did they mean by 'lighter sentence'? TEN FUCKIN' YEARS; what would I have got if they gave me a harsher sentence, LIFE?" The nervous lawyer advised George to calm down and not use profanities as there were ladies present. "CALM DOWN? PROFANITIES?" he called out loudly. "I'LL GIVE YOU SOME FUCKIN' PROFANITIES!"

Hearing the shouting, along with swearing, coming from the defence lawyer and his client, motivated the judge to call for the guards to take George to his cell... Immediately, because he was causing distress to the major's wife. Hearing this caused George to grab his defence lawyer by the throat, threatening to strangle him. When he saw the major and his wife get up to leave, he called out, "You ain't 'eard the last of this, you pair of slimy twats, not by a long chalk; I'll tell everyone what a lyin' cheatin' connivin' bloody pair of perverts you are..." He was prevented from saying more as the guards and two burly MPs grabbed him from behind and dragged him screaming out of the courtroom.

Now in his cell and much calmer, George realised he'd been well and truly 'stitched up' by the system. He'd been tricked on a huge scale and led along like a lamb to the slaughter. Speaking quietly now, he told himself, "George, me lad, you've been well and truly 'done up like a kipper'; they've made a bloody mug out of you and they're laughin' at you. Now stay calm and use your noddle to get yourself out of this bloody mess. You won't get anywhere losin' your temper." Having remonstrated with himself, he became calmer with the knowledge he'd been badly wronged, and it was now up to him to put it right. He needed a plan, and to devise one required him to remain cool, calm, and collected. "You'll beat the bastards, my boy", he told himself. "No one puts one over George Stubbs and gets off light."

The guards opened the cell door and asked if he needed anything to eat and drink. They also told him he'd be leaving for Colchester in the next day or two. Asking for his uniform, they told him he was to be provided with prison clothes instead. "Certainly, gentlemen, anything to oblige." The guards were surprised at his sudden change in attitude, and if they were wise, they would have been suspicious.

"What do you think that mad bastard's got planned?" asked one of the guards. "There's nothing he can do now. Two burly NCOs will take him to Colchester in handcuffs; any funny stuff will be met by a whack over the head with one of their truncheons. Those guys won't take any messing from anyone."

The other guard agreed with his colleague but felt sorry for their prisoner and the way he'd been tricked, feeling scorn for those who'd treated him so badly.

The guards made sure George had everything he asked for, including cigarettes and a bottle of beer. They left him to settle down and await transportation to the military prison, where he'd spend the next ten years, much longer than the six months he was promised if he'd cooperated.

Chapter 25

An Incident on
the Road to Colchester

George was not one to give up too easily. He'd been sentenced to 10 years in a military prison with a recommendation of hard labour; 'well and truly shafted', as he'd say. In fact, the military had made him a scapegoat to preserve the fine reputation of the commanding officer and his treacherous wife. She'd made all the moves on George, and him being who he was, fell for them and was snared by her deviousness.

At present, he had to plan how to extricate himself from this ugly mess. He'd no intention of serving his sentence but hadn't a clue of how to avoid it. The prison van sent from Colchester to escort him to the military prison was on its way but wouldn't arrive until late evening. It was a 450-mile journey, which could take the best part of a day to reach Stirling Castle, requiring the drivers to spend the night there, and begin their return journey early the next day. The transfer could have been made by rail, but the military were a little uneasy about using public transport to convey convicted prisoners to penal institutions, and therefore preferred to use one of their own vehicles instead.

As George was polite and offered no resistance to his guards, he was treated courteously and given more or less what he asked for in the way of food and tobacco; they even smuggled in another bottle of beer to cheer him up. There would be no such perks at Colchester, and in many ways, his comrades admired him, and felt sorry for the way he'd been treated; this included the guards too.

After a long, gruelling journey to Scotland, the escorts arrived late in the evening. Once refreshed, they decided to visit their prisoner, still languishing in his cell. "Stand up when I'm talking to you, soldier; you are still in the army, and as such, continue to behave like a soldier when the occasions arise… Understand?" barked the senior of the two escorts, a Sergeant Cook.

George stood up and saluted, saying, "Yes, Sergeant, I understand!"

"Right then, laddie, just so we are clear; you have been convicted of using violence against a superior officer whilst he was preventing you from assaulting his wife, and have been given a 10-year prison sentence with recommendation for hard labour… Understand?"

"I understand, Sergeant!"

"You'll be taken to the Military Corrective Training Centre at Colchester and will be ready to leave at 0600 hours tomorrow morning. Is that understood, soldier?"

"Yes, Sergeant, I understand fully," replied George once more, resigned to the fact he was finally on his way to prison... A military prison.

After informing the prisoner of their intentions, the two NCOs were invited to the sergeant's mess, where they spent the remainder of the evening as guests of the regiment. Addressing his hosts at a dinner specially prepared for them, Sergeant Cook went on to say, "Thank you for your fine hospitality, gentlemen, and don't worry about your prisoner, he'll be in safe hands. And this time tomorrow, we'll have him safely tucked up in his new cell, where he'll be our guest for the next 10 years."

His hosts applauded with one NCO shouting, "Make sure you take good care of him, and keep him away from the CO's wife!" This caused everyone to laugh aloud.

During the last night in his cell, George's attitude changed from being submissive to defiant. He wished to convey to his escorts that he'd do whatever was required of him and give them no trouble: the opposite was his intention. There was a germ of a plan in his head, which needed more thought and attention to detail. Being one not to give in easily, feeling betrayed and left to serve out a long prison sentence, he made up his mind to attempt an escape... Or die trying. He noticed both escorts were carrying side arms.

Realising the distance he'd have to travel – around 450 miles – they'd need to stop about halfway to refuel, take lunch and use the toilet. This is when he'd make his attempt. But on reflection, he realised that's exactly what his escort would expect; they were professionals, specially chosen for this job. *No*, he thought, *making a break then would be a mistake, they'd anticipate it and be ready. No, think again, George, come up with something better.* Whilst his escorts were being feted by their hosts, their prisoner was planning an escape. It was in the early hours when he'd finally 'cracked it', giving just enough time to catch a couple of hours sleep before being awakened at 5am.

After a huge breakfast and lots of tea, the prisoner finished his ablutions and was ready. The escort left on time at 6am, hoping to be in Colchester twelve hours later. Their intention was to have a break at Manchester, and head south-east after reaching Birmingham. The corporal was at the wheel, whilst his sergeant sat in the rear with the prisoner – they didn't want him to harm himself if left alone, as happened on a previous occasion. To ensure this, he was handcuffed, giving George cause to complain that the cuffs were too tight on his wrist, causing him pain. Sergeant Cook's remedy for this was to squeeze them tighter, hurting his prisoner even more. "One thing you must learn with us lot laddie, is you don't complain about nowt; d'you understand?"

"Yes, Sarge," replied George, easing the pain in his wrists by slowly massaging them.

"And don't call me fucking 'sarge', d'you hear; you address me as 'sergeant' from now on!" barked the unpleasant NCO.

"Yes, Sergeant," replied George, sharply standing to attention, although the handcuffs were cutting into his wrists causing him great pain.

Nearing Preston in Lancashire, George asked to have a pee – he'd drank a lot of tea at breakfast and needed one badly. "Use the bucket in the corner," barked the sergeant, "it's got a lid on it, so it won't spill out!" George did so, but had great difficulty in achieving it, as being handcuffed made a simple function very difficult... And painful.

"Cor blimey, my bleedin' guts are bad, I dunno what they put in that breakfast, but it's givin' me the shits, I reckon I've got bloody diarrhoea!"

"Well go in the bucket!" shouted the sergeant.

"Wot, with these bleedin' handcuffs on, the van shakin' about, with you watching me... No thank you!"

Being annoyed at this, the sergeant slid open a small flap in the bulkhead to speak to the driver, asking him to be on the lookout for a layby or a pull-in somewhere.

"What for, Sarge?" asked the driver.

"Laddie here has the shits and needs to go very quickly, otherwise he'll crap himself."

"What's wrong with using the bucket?" suggested the driver.

"Because he's got diarrhoea, and I don't want the bloody smell of it wafting about in here all the way to bloody Colchester... Now find a fuckin' layby and be quick about it... Y'hear!" The corporal never responded but kept his eyes peeled for somewhere to stop on the busy road.

Meanwhile, George was going through the motions of one needing to defecate badly, to the point of rolling around on the van floor. "Hurry up, Sarge, me guts is achin' very badly now; I reckon it's that bloody dysentery I got when I was in Hong bloody Kong. Oh my God, I think I'm gonna crap...'Urry up, Sarge!"

"Stop the fucking van any-bloody-where; we've an emergency back here!" called out the harassed NCO to the driver.

Pulling over to a rough piece of ground at the roadside, the corporal shouted through the hatch, "Will this do, Sarge?!

"Yes... Fine; now hang on whilst I sort the prisoner out!"

George was still rolling about in great pain and discomfort as the sergeant helped him up, opened the back doors and led him outside. Being too close to the roadside, both men had to mount a small fence to get to a clump of bushes near to a small bunch of small trees.

The rolling around in pain had ceased, as George was about to make a miraculous recovery. "Take the cuffs off, would you, Sarge, you can't expect me to do me business chained up!"

Ignoring the fact he'd just told his prisoner *not* to address him as 'sarge', he took the key from his pocket and unlocked the handcuffs, holding them ready for when his prisoner had finished his 'business'.

"You'll need this, laddie," he said to his prisoner, handing him a newspaper he'd brought with him. George quickly grabbed it, thanking him in the process. He headed towards a clump of trees with the sergeant closely following.

"Don't get out of my sight, soldier… I'll be watching you!" threatened the sergeant.

"You some kind of bloody pervert, watching a man go about 'is business?" called out George. Feeling guilty, the NCO turned away, giving his prisoner the privacy he asked for.

Now unwatched, George scurried around, looking for a suitable weapon with which to hit the sergeant, intending only to disable him. After a quick forage around, he picked up a heavy piece of fallen branch, and seeing the sergeant with his back turned, crept up and hit him across the back of his head, rendering him unconscious. Working swiftly, George took the handcuffs and slapped one half on the sergeant's wrist, removing his revolver at the same time, leaving his other hand free.

He had to work quickly now to lure the other escort out of the van, where he'd been sitting at the wheel. "Hey, Corporal," shouted George to the unsuspecting escort, "come quickly, the sergeant's slipped on some wet leaves and hit his head on a tree trunk; he looks quite bad!" Straightway, the corporal jumped out of the van to where his sergeant was last seen. Being too concerned at what he'd been told, he failed to notice his prisoner waiting behind a tree with a huge piece of wood at the ready. "He's down here!" shouted George, popping out and directing him to where the sergeant lay. As he stooped to look, George hit him on the back of his head, causing him to fall, unconscious, almost on top of his sergeant.

Standing across the pair, holding his makeshift weapon, and feeling very satisfied at what he'd achieved, he muttered quietly, "That'll teach you bastards to mess with George Stubbs; no one makes a monkey out of me and gets away with it!" He took the corporal's revolver, and along with the sergeant's, removed the bullets and threw them into the undergrowth where they were out of reach. His predicament now was what to do with his unconscious escorts.

Searching both men, he took their money, and was pleased to find another pair of handcuffs on the corporal. Looking around the copse for a suitable tree, he dragged both bodies towards a sapling around 12 inches in diameter, and placed them head-to-head with arms outstretched.

Ensuring the sapling was central to his two victims, he handcuffed both together, with the tree trunk in the middle, making escape impossible. Whilst on the ground, he listened for breathing and was satisfied they were both alive; after verifying this, he was ready to make his getaway. The keys to the prison vehicle were in place and, looking at the fuel gauge, he estimated how long before he'd need to refuel. His intention was to head for a port and stow away on a ship, taking him far away from the UK. With his assault on the two NCOS, along with his 10-year prison sentence, he calculated he'd be looking to serve 20 years, if caught, before he'd see the light of day again. Effectively, he had nothing to lose now, unless he'd killed one of them, in which case it would be his life... A hanging offence!

Now sitting in the driver's seat and heading due south, he was on the lookout for road signs directing him to Liverpool, hoping there'd be enough fuel to get there. It was a while since he'd driven a truck, but after a few miles, soon got used to it. In the distance he saw a road sign and was overjoyed when he saw Liverpool displayed, but a little concerned at the distance – 50 miles. Having a quick look at the gauge, which was showing a quarter full, and calculating the approximate distance they'd travelled since that morning, he estimated he'd have enough to get him there without having to refuel, which he wanted to avoid. After about an hour and a half, he was following the signs to Liverpool Docks... He was almost there.

Meanwhile, back at the little woodland copse close to the main highway, the two victims of George's successful escape attempt had regained consciousness. They were both suffering from tremendous headaches, but apart from that were relatively unscathed. Using their knees in a concerted effort, they were able to get to their feet, but were left in the uncomfortable position of being handcuffed together around a tree trunk, leaving them with little room to manoeuvre as they both faced each other.

"Good grief, Sarge, how the hell did you let him get the better of you?" asked the corporal.

"I might ask you the same bloody question, Corporal; he played us for a pair of suckers, and we fell for it, hook, line and bloody sinker. We'll never bloody well live this down; we'll be the laughing stocks of the regiment. That's of course if they don't demote the pair of us first."

Both men felt really stupid, that their prisoner fooled them into pretending to need a call of nature; now it was they who needed a pee, and with both their hands cuffed together, that simple human function became impossible. "Our only hope is that some motorist will need to stop where we had our truck, needing a piss," said the sergeant.

"That could take hours," replied his corporal. Both men, now resigned to their fate and hearing traffic roar by, could only hope one would stop.

After about an hour being tethered together, with both bladders at bursting point, the sound of a vehicle slowing down was heard close by. Waiting for the engine to stop, both men shouted as loud as they could, hoping to attract the attention of the driver. Luckily for them, the driver heard their shouts and rushed over to find out what the noise was about. Seeing them both chained to a tree made him wary at first, not knowing if anyone was waiting to pounce on him. Assured they were the only ones there, he hurried over to assist them. "What can I do to help, gentlemen?" asked the curious driver."

First you can undo my flies and help me have a piss; I'm bursting!" called out Sergeant Cook. Seeing their predicament and wishing to help them, he agreed to the sergeant's plea, and helped both men with their calls of nature.

"Good job I didn't turn out to be a lady driver," said the stranger with a smile.

"Oh, I don't know, that would have been even better for us, what do you say, Sarge?"

The sergeant wasn't in the mood for jokes and got right down to business. Addressing the stranger, he asked if he'd find a phone box, dial 999 to get the police and fire brigade out to them as quickly as they could. Realising their sidearms were missing, he told the driver to inform the police there was a prisoner on the loose, armed and dangerous. He was asked to be as quick as possible and gave him a description and registration number of the prison van to pass on to the police.

With the driver gone, and both men being relieved in more ways than one, they planned their strategy... And their revenge. "Let's hope we get that bastard before the cops, because I'm gonna give him the beating of his worthless life. I'll crucify the bastard, you see if I don't," vowed the sergeant, bent on revenge.

Once at the docks, George needed to get rid of the army truck belonging to the prison. On the assumption the best place to hide a tree is in a forest, he drove the truck to the centre of a lorry park and left it there. Tidying himself up, and thankfully not being dressed too much like a military prisoner, but attired in denims and wearing a donkey jacket, he realised he'd fit in well if he made enquiries about working his passage, in a dockside café or pub.

Finding a decent looking café, he went in and ordered a mug of tea. After stirring it and replacing the spoon, he looked around for a place to sit. It was very busy with most tables full, but seeing a spare seat at a table occupied by half a dozen workers, he asked if the seat was unoccupied. After looking him up and down, and being suspicious, the bigger of the group nodded his head and offered him the seat. George was the first to speak, addressing the group saying, "Thanks a lot, gents, very nice of you makin' a stranger feel welcome."

This opener was met with silence, after which they resumed their conversation, except for one man who kept staring at George, looking him up and down and finally asking, "You on the run, mate?" George was surprised and wondered why he said it.

"What makes you say that matey?" asked George in a friendly manner. Everyone stopped talking now, waiting for a response from their workmate.

"Lookin' at your wrists, I'd say you been wearin' handcuffs on 'em!" replied the man.

George straightway examined his wrists, seeing the cuts and bruising caused by wearing handcuffs, which were slapped on too tightly. Indeed, the man was correct in his assumption, so he admitted it in a whispered voice, saying, "I ain't gonna deny it, matey, but you're right, so if you don't mind, I'm off now... Bye!"

"Not so fast, pal," ordered the bigger of the five men, "we might be able to help you. We're no friends of the bizzies around 'ere. Wot they got ya for?"

"Well, it ain't the civilian police I'm on the run from, It's the MPs, the military.

"Wot ya done then, pal; nowt serious, I 'ope?"

George then went on to tell them of his woes regarding his brief association with the CO's wife, and the circumstances of his arrest, trial, and subsequent absconding; looking at the door each time anyone entered or left. Telling of his trial, verdict, and punishment, prompted a response from another of the men who until now had remained silent. "Look here, mister, you ain't got nowt to worry about wi' us lot. Most on us 'ave done time, and I done 6 months in an army nick when I wuz doin' me national service. MPs, I fucking 'ate the bastards, all of em!"

After that outburst, he asked George how he wanted them to help him. A suggestion came from another of the men, which received the approval of his fellow workmates. Now getting their heads down and deciding what was best for the escaped prisoner, they decided on a plan, which they put to George. "Right, me old mate, what you do is this; get yourself on a boat to Marseille, or another French port. Once there, look up the recruitment office for the French Foreign Legion. If they accept you – which they will – they'll give you a new identity, train you, feed you and look after you. All you do in return is sign on for 5 years and risk your bloody life for 'em. Simple as that, your problem's solved."

Poor George couldn't believe how quickly this fantastic bunch of dock workers had simply and speedily sorted out his problem. It was only by chance he chose to sit amongst them, and discovered, by being honest and straight, they rallied to his cry for help.

"And to show you we mean what we say, follow us and we'll get you on a boat this very evening," assured another of this obliging group. "We always 'elp those that need it most, and, brother, you really need some 'elp. If and when those NCOs get hold of you, they'll half beat you to death and get away with it; and we won't let that happen to one of our own."

George was a little suspicious when he left the café, and was alone with the men, but, true to their word, and with their local knowledge of shipping arrivals and departures, they sorted a passage for him on a ship leaving for Toulon that very evening.

"Before you disappear, old matey, do us a favour. will you?"

"Why, sure," replied George, "what is it?"

"Tell us where you left that army truck you nicked and give us the keys; we've got mates in the scrap business who'll jump at a chance to strip it down for spare parts. They'll never find it after they've done with it." George put his hands in his pockets, shuffled around and gave the man the keys, wishing him and the others all the best, and thanked them for their combined effort in helping him make his escape, and the beginning of a new life.

Back by the roadside, the NCOs had to wait almost an hour for their 'messenger' to access a phone, inform the police and fire brigade, and for them to get there. There was a call put out for the stolen vehicle, but it was never found. Later, in Colchester, at an enquiry into the loss of their prisoner, two sidearms and a prison vehicle, both NCOs were found guilty of gross negligence along with dereliction of duty and had their ranks reduced; now both privates, they were transferred to another regiment.

At Stirling Castle, Major and Mrs Tweedsmuir separated and began divorce proceedings. She went to live a life of luxury with her parents, who later found her another husband – not in the military this time. The major kept his rank but was relieved of the position of commanding officer.

Regarding the court martial, an enquiry ruled it to be a farce. Officers on the panel were reprimanded, and the defending officer was disbarred from being a lawyer because of the underhanded way he treated his client. It was decided that no soldier accused of striking a superior officer caught *in flagrante* with his wife, would attack the husband without good reason i.e., to defend himself. It was further decided no soldier accused of such a crime, knowing the punishment would be in the region of 10 years penal servitude with hard labour, would plead guilty, knowing there was a chance he might get off or indeed receive a smaller sentence. It was discovered the accused had been duped into pleading guilty, by telling him he'd receive just 6 months ordinary prison time without hard labour.

Although the cards were stacked against Corporal George Stubbs, and every nefarious trick was brought into play to convict and punish him severely, it was those who used treachery and duplicity against him, as well as his tormentors, who came off worse... Much worse, in fact. The victim of this disastrous affair was about to begin a new life in the Foreign Legion, with a new identity and clean slate... But knowing George, how long would that last?

Chapter 26

The Crossing

The two weeks spent at the fort passed relatively quickly, as the recruits were always kept busy with one menial task or another. Time spent at the woodyard was always tiring, where some of the men received serious injuries whilst chopping and sawing wood. Being unused to the huge saws and axes made the work most precarious, where the slightest mistake in handling these dangerous tools could easily cause a man to lose a finger or even his hand. "Cheap bloody labour if you ask me!" grumbled Jorge after a hard day's graft at the woodyard.

"Never mind, buddy, I heard we're getting paid when we get back to the fort, so we'll be able to have a bloody good piss-up tonight," chipped in one of the men after hearing his fellow recruit's complaints. In fact, they all received their first two weeks' pay, which amounted to the equivalent of three pounds sterling. Not a huge amount, but enough for a couple of nights beer drinking in the bar, or foyer, as it was called.

The following morning, the whole company was given the Legion haircut, le *boule à zéro*, which combined with their scruffy dirty appearances made them look more like convicts, and less like legionnaire recruits. However, if the truth were known, amongst those receiving their shaven heads were men who truly deserved the title 'convict' more than others; our present company accepted.

The order was given for half the recruits at the fort – some 150 men – to be shipped out to Algeria the next morning. Reveille would be at 5am when a small fleet of trucks would ferry the men down to the harbour, where the 5000-ton troop carrier, SS *Sidi-Bel-Abbès*, would be waiting to transport them to Oran. With fair weather, the crossing would take approximately 36 hours, but it was only on rare occasions it went without incident. During one of the drinking sessions in the bar a few nights previously, a couple of the regular legionnaires gave a group of recruits some good advice on preparing for the sea crossing. "Stick together in little groups and watch out for each other. When you get below deck, find a position joining a bulkhead or side of the deck to place your chairs. Take more of the crappy little deckchairs than you need and stow your gear on 'em. Don't put your gear on the deck – you'll see why when you've been at sea for a few hours." The wily old legionnaire kept looking at his near empty beer glass before imparting more of his valuable advice. After having it replenished by an eager recruit, he continued, "Don't eat or drink too much before or during the journey; it'll all come back one way or another before you reach Oran; that's assuming you reach Oran."

"I reckon you're doin' your best to put the shits up us, ain't ya', mate?" called out a cynical and disbelieving Jorge.

Ignoring Jorge's remark, the sagacious legionnaire carried on with his pearls of wisdom. "With each crossing we lose around half a dozen men overboard."

"Ah, fuck off, we know your takin' the piss now!" yelled another of the drinkers.

"Those who ended up being washed overboard were those who ignored our advice, so I'll tell you guys the same as we tell them that wants to listen. Once you've cleared land, do not under any circumstances go up on deck. When it gets to the point you can't stand it below 'cos of the shit, piss, spew and 'owt else that's washing about, don't go up for air on deck. If you do, unless you can fly or swim like a bloody dolphin, it'll be the last breath of fresh air you'll breath; believe me, fellers, I've done a few crossings and seen it all. That's not just advice I'm givin' ya all, it's a bloody deadly serious warning." Draining his glass one further time, he handed it to a recruit, saying, "Same again, my man, if you don't mind."

Arriving at the dock the next morning, as the four new friends clambered out of one of the trucks and boarded the rickety old troop ship, the advice given to them a couple of nights previously now became apparent. Was the old legionnaire simply trying to put the wind up them by telling a pack of lies in order to scrounge a few free beers, or was he giving them some valuable advice? Only time would tell.

The deck allocated to the legionnaires was at the bottom of the ship. Iron stairs had to be carefully manoeuvred, as their steepness could easily cause a stumble; so great care was taken on the descent. When the men reached the bottom, they realised the veteran legionnaire's description on the seating arrangements was perfectly correct. Heeding his advice, the four pals grabbed two seats apiece and headed over towards the bulkhead at the end of the crowded deck.

"How about getting as near as we can to the toilet," suggested Frank, "thirty-six hours without a piss is going to be a long time!"

"If you take my advice," said Jorge, "you'll keep as far away from those bogs as you can. When they get used a lot – and they will be – the stench will knock you out." A slight exaggeration from the well-travelled ex-serviceman, but good advice that needed to be taken on board... Literally!

As the four headed towards their chosen spot to stow their gear and other belongings, the whole place began to fill with grumbling and dissatisfied recruits. They hadn't reckoned on their seating arrangements being so basic and crude. Seeing the lads had two seats apiece and some hadn't any – yet – caused a little friction between the men. Being told to 'fuck off and get your own bleedin' chairs the same as I just done' by an irate Jorge almost caused the first fight of the crossing.

A corporal intervened and advised the man without a chair to get one from the huge stack folded up against the side of the deck. "There's plenty of chairs, enough for two each if you want them – stop causing trouble and do as this man advised – 'fuck off and get your own bloody chairs'." With that, the corporal mingled with the other men, trying to get them into some kind of order for this long and sometimes uncomfortable crossing. Returning to where Jorge and the others were getting settled, he remarked, "I see some veteran has been giving you advice; am I correct?"

"Yes, Corporal," replied Eddie, standing to attention.

"Nice to see you are heeding it. You've got a good spot here, just make sure you don't lose it."

"Yes, Corporal, thank you, Corporal," said Jorge, also standing to attention. As he walked away, Jorge remarked, "First impressions the NCOs get of you are very important. If they take a disliking to you, they can make your life a bloody misery... I know!"

The ship was now underway, and a few men went up on deck to see the French shoreline disappear into the distance. "I wonder when we'll see France or Europe again," said one man to his chum.

"Not so much *when*, but *if*," replied his mate. These two men then made the hazardous return to the lower deck but found it tricky as the ship was now moving. However, with much care and managing to keep their balance, they finally made it to the berthing area, only to discover their chairs, along with their belongings, had disappeared. Not a very good start for this hapless pair, but once among a huge group of rough, undisciplined and lawless individuals, it always pays to be on one's guard.

The word soon got around that thieves were at work, and it was vital to watch out for any belongings that weren't being carried. The four pals decided to go in pairs when moving from their seats to visit the toilets, or go to the canteen for food. As it was, an NCO called out that soup was being served, and anyone who wanted some had to pick it up from the canteen. "What flavour is it, Corp?" called out one of the men jokingly.

Taking a long look at his questioner, the corporal sauntered over to him with a bowl of soup he'd brought from the canteen. "First, let me remind you, that in future you address me as corporal, not corp. Secondly, in answer to your question as to the flavour of this fine soup, how about you try some yourself and let us all know." With that, he grabbed the man's head, thrust it into the bowl of soup, held it there until he nearly choked and said, "Well, soldier, what flavour was it, and would you recommend it?" He then threw the choking, gurgling, hapless recruit, covered from head to foot in hot soup, onto the floor, ordering him to bring a fresh bowl for himself. As a punishment, he told him, "You are now soup waiter for the rest of the crossing, to anyone who wishes to try it; okay!"

"Yes, Corporal!" answered the unfortunate recruit, wiping the soup from his eyes.

"See what I mean about respecting NCOs; you never want to be too familiar or seem as if you're taking the piss out of 'em. That's what happens when you do," warned Jorge, who'd had experience with non-coms during his army service.

Jorge and Frank got up to go to the canteen for the soup and, remembering the advice they'd been given, agreed it would be the last thing they'd eat until they reached dry land. Looking around to make sure the corporal wasn't near, Jorge called out to the man covered in soup, who was just getting to his feet, "Well, pal, what flavour was it, pal, and what's it taste like?" This started everyone laughing out loud; except the new soup waiter.

Until then, the sea was very calm, prompting some men to tuck into the food they'd brought with them, finding the helping of soup insufficient. All types of refreshments were brought out, and the hungry men tucked in with great relish. Beer, along with their wine allowance, was also drunk to wash down cheese, salami, sausage and other cold meats. To some it seemed like a holiday outing with caution cast to the wind... Wind being a very important factor later in the voyage. After the food and drink was consumed, what the men wished for was simply to settle down on their deck chairs and enjoy a decent sleep as they'd been up since 5am that morning.

It was late afternoon when the first unusual movements of the ship were felt. Most men were in deep slumber or merely dozing, enjoying the gentle rolling and pitching of the ship's progress through the seemingly calm sea. At first there was a little laughter, with some men exaggerating the movements, pretending to be drunk. The first pitching movement came and went, leading the passengers to believe it was simply an abnormality, or a heavy wave the ship had encountered. Waiting for it to settle, most men returned to their slumbers, but, unfortunately, they had been given a false sense of security. The wise men remained in their seats and waited for another wave to break.

"Okay, lads, I reckon we're in for a rough ride," warned Jorge. "Move your chairs with the backs touching the bulkhead so they don't move about."

"What you on about, mate, there was only a little shudder and it's gone now!" protested Paddy. The words had barely left his lips when the ship lurched downward at such a steep angle, many of the men were thrown from their seats, and landed on the floor.

"Stay on the bloody floor, mates; what goes down must come up again!" called out Jorge, warning those lying on the floor. Many ignored his warning and tried to get back into their seats, but just as Jorge warned, the ships bow, after diving forward, returned with a vengeance to its normal level, then dived once more, throwing men, chairs and belongings onto the heavy steel deck. This action caused quite a few injuries and seeing it was safer by the bulkheads of the deck, many tried to reposition their chairs.

As if this wasn't enough, with the forward and rearward movements of the ship, it then took another turn, pitching from side to side with equal ferocity. The whole ship and all its passengers were at the mercy of the ferocious, unforgiving ocean. The four comrades had managed to avoid any mishaps, simply because of Jorge's guidance in these unusual wave movements.

In a panic to reposition their seats, the rolling action, as well as the forward and rearward pitching of the ship, caught many unfortunates by surprise, leaving them rolling about the hard deck. Many men were beginning to throw up, causing the floor to be horribly slippery and hard to walk on. Those needing the lavatories found them to be occupied with people retching up. Those needing to defecate or urinate had the same problems. Within the time span of a half hour, from when the first downward thrust occurred, the whole deck was awash with every conceivable human and non-human fluid existent, along with those whom this human detritus emanated from. To call it chaos was an understatement.

The conditions below decks were absolutely appalling. Hardly any of the seats were occupied, and the occupants of those that were, found themselves to be sliding back and forth across the deck, to the movement of the ship's tossing and pitching. After one long, steep dive, followed by its equally steep return, some of the men believed the ship was about to sink and called on others to follow them to the boat deck above and search out a lifeboat.

"Don't be so bloody stupid," called out one of the others, "even if you get topside and launch a lifeboat, what makes you think you'll last five minutes in the open sea in a storm like this; get back to your seats and weather the storm like the rest of us!"

Ignoring this advice, three others followed the man up the steel stairway to the boat deck, in search of a lifeboat. Whether or not these men made it to the upper deck and secured a lifeboat to escape the utter turmoil below wasn't known. What in fact was known was that none were seen again; four men who ignored the advice of their comrades, ultimately costing them their lives.

Jorge, along with the others, managed to weather the storm, and, unbelievably, Frank fell asleep. He tended to 'drop off' in times of turmoil and strife. When the storm had almost abated, one or two corporals appeared from their allotted cabin, where they comfortably sat out the storm from the comfort of their bunks. They now went about organising the cleaning-up operation. Although it was an unpleasant job, Eddie and Paddy stepped forward to volunteer, prompting others to do the same. Buckets of sand and sawdust, along with huge brooms and shovels came onto the scene, and the volunteers went about this most disgusting but necessary task, to restore the deck to its previous condition.

The sick bay had been very busy, with cuts, bruises, and one or two broken limbs to reset. The main complaint was seasickness; this caused more discomfort to most men unprepared for such an uncomfortable voyage, by either eating or drinking too much before and during the crossing.

With the sea much calmer now, and the deck restored to its previous cleanliness, things began to return to normal, except for the loss of four good men, and those who received serious injuries. If only they'd heeded the sound advice offered to them, these tragic events could have been avoided. The remainder of the crossing passed relatively smoothly. It wasn't long before the ship docked at the harbour in Oran, where another small fleet of trucks ferried the tired and weary recruits to a transit camp... Of sorts. The function of this camp was merely to give the men a bowl of soup and chunk of bread, then have a roll call to see how many of them had succumbed to the harshness of the cruel sea. There was an ambulance in attendance to ferry those too badly injured to make the three-hour train journey to Sidi Bel Abbès; these men would join their comrades later, after returning to full fitness.

Once fed, and the brief period of recuperation over, the men boarded the trucks and were driven to the station for the three-hour train journey to Camp CP3, nerve centre of the Foreign Legion at Sidi Bel Abbès. Here, once more, they were given refreshments on arrival and allowed to bed down on the parade ground, until dawn's early light brought about another roll call. This was to ensure they hadn't left any stragglers behind, or to establish whether some had decided, after that terrible sea crossing, the Legion wasn't the place for them, and deserted.

After a couple of hours sleep, the men were lined up and given a talking to regarding their time spent at this camp, and where they would be transferred to in a few days' time. Unfortunately for most of the recruits, these instructions were given in French. Those who couldn't understand the language were advised to get together with someone who did.

"What the bloody hell are we gonna do now?" asked Frank. "I can speak Italian and English, but buggered if

I can speak a word of French!" Jorge and Eddie were in the same predicament and turned to the Irishman.

"What about you, Paddy," asked Jorge, "I don't expect you know any French words, do ya?"

Paddy's reply had the others absolutely stunned when he answered their questions in almost perfect French, leaving them astonished. It transpired that his father, whilst serving in the British Army during WWI, met and fell in love with a local French girl from Normandy. They were married in Arras and returned to Ireland two years after the war ended, which at that time was undergoing the partition process. The separation of northern and southern Ireland meant Paddy and his family remained in Great Britain, because they lived in Belfast.

Paddy wasn't born until 1929, and after leaving school, took a job on the railway, working with his father. The family travelled frequently to France, and sometimes as a youngster, Paddy stayed on with his mother's family in Arras. It was here, and with the tutoring of his mother, he learnt to speak French.

"You're a bloody dark 'oss, ain't ya, me old mate. Fancy you being half Froggy!" said a very surprised but pleased Jorge.

"This means we can all stick together with Paddy speaking French; this is what the Legion wants, to make sure their orders are understood," called out an elated Eddie.

"Stick with me, fellas, I'll put you all right, and do my best to help you speak the language," promised Paddy.

However, if his three new comrades knew about his dark past, it's doubtful they'd want anything to do with him, considering the nature and magnitude of the crimes he'd committed. It was a consequence of one of these crimes that motivated his enlistment in the Legion. Fortunately for him, discussions of past life and the reason for joining up were a taboo subject, and rarely spoken about; except for Jorge, who couldn't help bragging about why he left England in a hurry, and his reasons for enlisting.

The lads let it be known to the NCOs that they had a French speaker in their company and asked to remain together for the period of their training. They were reminded that learning French was on the curriculum as well as learning French history.

The men were glad to discover they were about to lose their disgusting travelling attire, and were to be kitted out with everything from boots to hats, and all things in between. The downside of this was they had to hand over their personal effects, which would be returned to them after completing their five-year contract. Eddie and Frank decided to hand half of their money in for safe keeping and divide the remainder between the four of them. This decision went well in cementing an already good relationship with the little group, and was a sign of good faith and friendship. "Just make sure you keep it well hidden, boys; the safest place is where you wouldn't expect to hide it. I was told this by some guys who'd spent time in a French nick. They put me right about a few things, and the method they told me about is fool proof... Well, almost," advised Jorge, who later gave instructions for the safekeeping of folding money.

The men were allotted beds in the huge dormitory and began to settle into their new surroundings – which wouldn't be for long. The final part of their journey would be the allocation to one of the two centres of instruction: one at Saida and the other at Mascara. The contingent of 150 – less those hospitalised, and the men washed overboard – were to be divided. Half would spend their four months of basic training at one of these centres, prior to choosing their final regiment, where they'd spend the remainder of their time in the Legion.

The time spent at in the camp at Sidi Bel Abbès was mainly in classrooms and on the parade ground. The new recruits were taught the history of the Legion and its traditions. French lessons, along with history, were taught, and in particular the events occurring in French Indochina. Special emphasis was given to this subject, as it seemed the recruits were being trained to serve there eventually.

After a week spent at Sidi Bel Abbès, the word came through that Frank and the other three were amongst the group who'd travel to Mascara to complete their training. Discovering this was welcome news amongst the four new comrades. They'd be staying together at Mascara, a town some 80 miles to the east. Their final night at Sidi was spent enjoying themselves in the camp bar, but they needed to be on parade at 5am, where a small fleet of Simca trucks would carry them to the final destination of their long and tiring journey.

Chapter 27

Intense Training, Legion-style

It was a bright sunny morning when the recruits lined up on the parade ground, each awaiting the allocation of their particular truck. There were seventy men and six trucks, with a jeep placed at each end of the convoy, acting as escorts. Two fully armed legionnaires rode in each of these jeeps to protect the trucks and their passengers. With the trucks now fully loaded with eager recruits, the convoy set off to Mascara. The journey would take around three hours, with a stop halfway to give the men an opportunity to stretch their legs. Hopefully, the small convoy would arrive at the camp in time for lunch. There were eight others in the truck with Jorge and co., along with a corporal sitting in the cab with the driver. The terrain was rough and hilly, making progress difficult for the Simca trucks and their occupants. The exteriors of trucks were covered with canvas, and a curtain at the rear which could be laced up to prevent dust entering inside. Despite this, dust had a way of getting inside, making it uncomfortable for the occupants.

An hour passed, when suddenly the leading jeep came to a halt. The four corporals with the convoy got together to have a conversation with the jeep's forward escorts.

"What d'you think's the matter?" asked Eddie. "Why are we stopping?"

"Ain't gorra clue, mate, but I 'ope it ain't trouble; only the corporals and escorts have guns."

This revelation began to worry the men, but a command shouted by one of the corporals almost caused a panic amongst them. "Okay, men, everyone out of the trucks and take cover!" ordered one of the corporals, sounding very concerned. He'd good reason to be worried, as they'd heard the local bandits – the fellagha – were active in that area.

"Hey, Corporal, we ain't got no guns!" called out Jorge. The corporal returned to the truck with a sub-machine gun, asking if anyone aboard could use it. "Give it to me, Corporal, it looks like the Sten gun I used in Korea!"

Handing Jorge the gun, he put the group's minds at rest saying confidently, "With any luck, we won't need them. The lead jeep stopped because he thought he saw some movement ahead. It could be an ambush or simply a shepherd moving his flock; either way, we need to be on our guard."

"What should *we* do, Corporal? We haven't got a gun," called out Frank.

"Just keep your fucking heads down as soon as any shooting starts." This piece of advice didn't help much, in fact, the mere use of the word *shooting* caused some of the men to panic.

In fact, it was the NCOs who were in a slight panic. They dreaded this journey, carrying unarmed recruits who had no weapon training. If they *were* given guns for protection during the journey, and not knowing how to use them correctly, they'd be more of a danger to themselves than the enemy. The fellagha had a way of finding out about convoys and the type of troops or cargo being carried. If they knew it was carrying unarmed recruits, it would be easy pickings for them. Mounting an ambush and fighting off just a half dozen armed men would be comparatively easy, meaning *their* casualties would be considerably light.

The NCOs were fully aware of how the fells – as they were known – treated their prisoners, especially legionnaires. Legionnaires in return treated them much worse – torturing them mercilessly whilst extracting information. These details weren't given to new recruits, for fear of creating a panic; and who wouldn't panic if they knew a simple journey from one camp to another could come to an end by being tortured to death at the hands of barbaric Arab tribesmen?! When recruits were later instructed on procedures during their basic training, they were told to save their last bullet to use on themselves, rather than be taken prisoner by the fellagha.

Leaving the rear guards on the alert, the other escorts, along with the corporals, had to decide whether it would be more prudent to turn around and head back to Sidi or continue to Mascara. Their combined firepower would be insufficient to hold off a concentrated attack, and, although they'd be able to pick off a few fells, they couldn't guarantee the safety of seventy unarmed recruits.

There was a similar situation a few years back when a convoy carrying unarmed recruits was attacked, leaving half dead and the others captured, along with the escorts. Thankfully for those captives, the fells offered them up for ransom, and without hesitation, the French military paid up. Almost all were returned unharmed, but a couple were horribly tortured in front of their comrades, leaving them with terrible memories and nightmares, with the urge to quit the Legion before beginning their training. Requests to have their five-year contracts annulled were turned down unreservedly, with orders to continue serving their time or be treated as deserters, and therefore outside the protection of the Legion.

The safest and most sensible action to take would be to turn around and return to base; there they could arrange a much bigger and more heavily armed escort to accompany them to Mascara. If however, it was discovered later that in fact it wasn't fellagha, but simply a shepherd or goatherd moving their animals, those in charge, namely the corporals, would find themselves reduced to the ranks, or be court-martialled for cowardice – carrying a prison sentence if convicted. The unfortunate corporals were in a tricky situation, between the Devil and the deep blue sea.

It was finally decided to send two of the escorts ahead on foot to spy out the land, and report back whether there were fells about, or simply movements of animals. They left one rifle behind with both of their pistols – just in case. The rifles issued were a complete waste of time: 7.5 mm bolt action rifles with a magazine holding three cartridges and a killing range of 300 yards – unbelievably underpowered and incapable of inflicting any real damage. The submachine guns fared slightly better, but only had an effective range of 50 yards, leaving the pistols with a greater range but less accuracy.

Making their way ahead very slowly, and being on the lookout for anything unusual, the escorts left the rest of the convoy to take cover, but stay on the alert. Each of the corporals and drivers were armed with sub-machine guns, but nothing more powerful. The escorts had rifles *and* sub-machine guns, along with a sidearm apiece. Trucks now had to be arranged into some form of defensive formation, rather like the covered wagons in certain Western movies.

The men were sheltering underneath the trucks in the shade, and out the line of direct fire, should there be any. Although their firepower was inadequate and only minimal, the discovery of a case of hand grenades used on a previous exercise, but mistakenly left in one of the trucks, would help even the odds should they be attacked. It was all down to what weapons the fellagha would use on them, should the shooting start, as their weaponry was the result of attacks on weapon convoys, and the guns they plundered. Ironically, the legionnaires would be fighting men with guns stolen from *themselves.*

All this preparation was academic, as it wasn't even known if an enemy existed. This action could be one huge panic, but precautions always had to be taken when such occasions arose; it was better to be safe than sorry. The sun was getting higher now, making it very hot for the men sheltering beneath the trucks. Even so, they fared better than the sentries and corporals out in the open keeping watch. All eyes were pointed to where the escorts were last seen.

This situation had lasted around half an hour but seemed much longer to the recruits lying in the dust, which was gluing itself to their sweating faces and exposed arms. Their uniforms were beginning to stick to the rest of their bodies, as fear, as well as heat from the sun, began to overpower them. Some men were beginning to panic, and had to be restrained and calmed down by their more stable comrades. The atmosphere was tense indeed, and problems would surely arise if it went on much longer.

"What the fuck's happened to those two escorts; surely they should have found out if anything's amiss by now!" muttered one of the corporals.

"Unless the unthinkable has happened," replied another NCO, "in which case, may the good Lord have mercy on them."

Overhearing this brief exchange, one of the recruits panicked and climbed from beneath the truck and headed back to where they'd come from. Fortunately, one of the rear guards grabbed him before he could get too far and dragged him back, pushing him under the truck. "Now stay there and keep bloody still, otherwise, if the fells don't put a bullet in you, I fucking well will!" The frightened recruit stayed where he was thrown and never made another move.

"I fear the worst," said a corporal, "we'd better get in position to resist an attack. Get those bloody hand grenades out, hopefully they're impact fuses and won't have a time delay on 'em!"

Panic really was setting in now with the appearance of the grenades, and the men were given quick instructions on how to withdraw the pins and throw them. The drivers, who also had sidearms, went up and down the line of recruits, asking if anyone knew how to use one. Frank and Eddie came forward and took one apiece, but instead of receiving a revolver as expected, they were given automatic pistols. "No time to give you guys instructions on their use, just make sure the safety catch is off and point it to the enemy, then squeeze the bloody trigger. They'll come at us yelling and screaming like fucking madmen, but take no bloody notice, that's just to scare you!"

Those without weapons lined up for a grenade and were told quickly how to use it. The whole convoy was in a state of preparation rather than blind panic, and the men's stoicism began to shine through with fine examples of self-control and impassiveness. This behaviour, the corporals took note of, and were pleased they had men in their midst who wouldn't buckle under at the first sign of trouble.

A defensive stance was taken, unlike the 'British square' at Waterloo, but, nonetheless, it was organised and disciplined. There were those amongst the men who were about to relish the fight and seemingly had little fear as to the outcome. These would be the men the Legion were keen to enlist; fearful and indomitable.

Suddenly, the cry went out, "Men approaching from ahead!" This caused tenseness among the waiting men, all on full alert, ready and spoiling for a fight. Those with firearms checked their safety catches, and those with grenades came out from beneath the trucks, taking a stance allowing them to throw them once the pins were pulled. Sweat was rolling down their faces and the previous fear they'd experience seemed to disappear with an adrenalin rush.

"We're all ready, Corporal!" called out one of the men nervously. "Give us the order."

"Shh, all in good time. These could be our men approaching, or the fellagha dressed in their uniforms. Keep it quiet," ordered the corporal whilst straining his eyes ahead.

"Call out the challenge to them," suggested a driver, ready with his finger on the trigger of his gun.

"Identify yourselves or we fire!" shouted a corporal.

The approaching men stopped suddenly and called out, "Don't bloody shoot; it's us, the escort!"

"How do we know that?" replied the corporal.

"For fuck's sake, stop playing silly buggers and lower your guns and let us advance."

"What do you reckon; are they our guys or what?" asked another of the NCOs.

"Why has it taken you so long to see if it's all clear ahead?" asked the corporal.

"For Christ's sake, let us carry on and we'll tell you; we can't stand here all fuckin' day chatting. We'll drop our guns and come in." After they'd lowered their guns and walked toward the convoy, a corporal walked out to meet them, still ready with his gun cocked and pointing to the two men. Just twenty yards away from them, he recognised them as being the escorts and couldn't hide his joy at seeing them well and all in one piece.

"You had us all worried for a moment; why on earth has it taken you so long to report back? We were sure the fells had got you and using your uniforms to trick us," said the relieved corporal.

"Let's get out of this bloody sun and get a drink before we dry up completely; we'll report what happened then."

As they returned to the convoy, the corporal gave the order, "Stand down, crisis over, hand in your weapons and board the trucks." This was much to the relief of those standing by, all primed to face an attack.

It later transpired there *was* in fact movement ahead, but, as suspected, it was some shepherds moving their flock from one side of the road to the other, where the grazing was better. The escorts questioned them, asking if they'd seen any movement of fellagha ahead, to which they answered no. As is the custom in that part of the country, if you are offered food or drink by these tribesmen, it was courtesy not to refuse. It transpired these shepherds were about to eat their lunch and invited the legionnaires to join them. Reluctantly, whilst remaining on their guard, they joined their hosts in a meal of sorts, and chatted politely to them, hoping to gain intelligence of enemy movements ahead, but to no avail. "What else could we do, Corporal; they offered us food and drink, and protocol requires us to accept... And we did," replied one of the escorts when questioned why it took them so long to do a simple scouting job.

Convinced all was clear ahead, but nonetheless still on the alert, the convoy continued its journey towards Mascara. They decided to forgo the halfway break, and instead continue to the camp. As the convoy drove across the plain of Mascara, to the corporal's relief, they were in sight of their destination – 5th Company of the Instruction Battalion of Mascara. Once through the massive wrought-iron gates of the camp, the convoy of trucks pulled into a muddy section of the parade ground, alongside a huge trough, which later turned out to be the communal washbasin.

The recruits were ordered out of the trucks and formed into some sort of order, after which names were read out, assigning them into sections and barracks. Once more, the four friends were assigned to Group 4, Barrack-room 12. Twelve men were assigned to six barrack- rooms, leaving one with just four occupants. Metal beds with straw mattresses, along with an open metal locker, were assigned to each of the men. All kit had to be stored in these lockers, with each item folded and stacked immaculately to form a rectangle, awaiting inspection at evening roll call or Appel. Before lights out, a sergeant wearing white gloves came along to each hut to inspect cleanliness and tidiness. Heaven help the occupants if everything wasn't up to his standard of cleanliness, with penalties of loss of liberty and extra fatigues imposed on all.

At the evening meal, 'la soupe,' everything had to be done in an orderly fashion, with diners waiting outside. A whistle was blown, after which they were all led inside in an orderly fashion and told to remove their kepis, then shown to their allotted tables. When all was still and quiet with no one left wandering about, a corporal would enter, and call for a song – 'La tone'. After the count of one, two, three, four, the whole of the refectory burst into singing, 'La Legion Marche'. When this was done, they were told, "Asseyez-vous. Bon appetite."

With that last order, everyone shouted back, "Merci, Caporal." Then everyone dug into the food, shovelling it down as fast as they could. The food was exceptional, along with the wine, which came with the meal.

When the evening meal was over, there was a brief period of about an hour where the men were allowed free time in the bar for a beer or two, after which, everyone returned to their barracks to prepare their kit for inspection during Appel. Although all orders were given in French, it was permitted to use one's own language whilst in the bar, which made it sound very much like the Tower of Babel, with some twenty different languages spoken all at once. Once inspection was over to the satisfaction of the visiting sergeant, it was lights out until the morning call at 6am. The breakfasts never amounted to much, usually a coffee, bread or rolls and perhaps some cold meat on occasions, depending on what – if any – was left over from the previous evening meal.

Now the classroom events would begin. Each man had an intelligence test along with a visit from the French special branch – the Deuxième Bureau. When being questioned by these men, it was crucial they were given the same answers they were given on their previous interrogation. Heaven help anyone who didn't furnish them with the right answers. There was a certain amount of levity, but only from recruits whose services were desperately needed.

The brothers, along with Jorge and Paddy, became nervous when asked about their past. The intelligence officers knew all these recruits had good reason to join the Legion, and didn't bother too much if their transgressions were minimal. Jorge came clean with them when telling why he was on the run, although there was no Interpol enquiry concerning him. Paddy made up some yarn about dodging the draft and wanted to serve France as his mother was French. His story held out as it was easy to remember. When it was the brothers' turn to be questioned, for some reason they were always last in the queue and had only a cursory round of questions to answer. If the truth was known, the DB knew about the killings in London, but because of their young age, apparent fitness and the fact they'd stood in when some legionnaires were having the stuffing kicked out of them, they made allowances. Besides, the Legion needed young, fit men to fight wars for France, and there was every possibility these two would die whilst serving.

The camp in general needed a spring clean, so all the new internees were mobilised to do it. This operation took just over a week to accomplish. With this out of the way, they were back in the classroom learning French and French history; and most enlightening it was too, especially as these men learning it were about to be part of it.

The training outside was beginning to become more intense. Five-mile runs to begin with, increasing by another five each week. Sometimes with a backpack, others without. Once the trainees became used to the routine, running with full kit including weapons came next. Unarmed combat followed hand-to-hand combat with knives. Rope climbing, crawling under barbed wire in mud, sometimes with, others without, gunfire overhead. Much time was spent on the rifle range using different weapons from the Legion armoury, including bayonets, handguns, and mortars. The five-mile and ten-mile runs increased to a long twenty-mile run, with sacks of sand on their backs. Many of the men were beginning to buckle under the intensity of these exercises, but alternate days spent in the classroom helped alleviate the general fatigue of constant heavy training.

Guns were taken apart and reassembled, sometimes in the light, others in a darkened classroom. French language lesson followed French history, which some believed was being forced down their throats. Map reading was practised in and out of the classrooms, and woe betide any group who found themselves lost during an exercise out in the hills. Marching formation was also conducted on the parade ground. The Legion had its own style of marching at a pace two thirds that of the regular French Military. This slow pace gave the marchers a sinister appearance, a little frightening, in fact, which intrigued observers at local and national parades. History and proud traditions of the Legion were taught, especially the battle of Camarón in Mexico during 1863. Here, 60 legionnaires faced a Mexican army of 2000, and after fighting to their last bullet, attempted to charge the enemy with fixed bayonets. They were finally overpowered and surrendered on condition their injured lieutenant would be treated for his wounds, and they would be allowed to retain their weapons. Incredibly, the Mexicans agreed, and allowed the remaining five legionnaires, along with their officer, to go free. Unfortunately, the lieutenant died of his wounds later, but his wooden hand was retrieved and displayed in the Legion Museum. The anniversary of the Battle of Camarón was held in very high esteem amongst all Legion brigades, and the only celebration that came anywhere near to it was Christmas day. When this piece of history was taught to trainees, the importance of fighting to your last bullet, but to save it for yourself, was stressed. When fighting a savage enemy, such as the fellagha, you must never allow yourself to be taken alive. If you are, a slow and painful death awaits you at their hands, whilst they inflict the most barbaric torture imaginable. The recruits had heard this before but took special notice of the dire warning.

The soon to be fully trained legionnaires were ending their four-month training period and would soon pass out. They had many ups and downs, as well conflicts with their trainers during this period, but in general, they'd managed to come through it relatively unscathed. There was one unfortunate incident concerning two deserters, which put a dampener on the whole situation. These two men decided they'd had enough of the tough regime imposed on them by the Legion, and couldn't bear the thought of serving another four and a half years of it. Until then, they hadn't experienced combat, and the thought of it made them decide to desert during a night out in Mascara. No real preparations were made for this move, and it wasn't long before they ran out of food and water, and, in general, suffered from exhaustion. They handed themselves in at a local gendarmerie, pleading for food and water, and somewhere to sleep. Their expectations to be given what they asked for and be allowed to continue their journey were soon dashed, when a prisoner escort arrived from Mascara to take them back to the camp. The corporal in charge of the escort detail made sure they had a good beating after they'd left the shelter of the police station.

Arriving back at the camp, battered and bruised from the beatings they'd received, was only a part of the nightmare which awaited them. After being stripped of their clothes apart from underwear, they were made to crawl around the parade ground on their hands and knees, in full view of the whole camp, who were brought out to witness the ghastly spectacle.

After the first part of their punishment, they were made to don rucksacks loaded with rocks, and ordered to 'quick march' around the perimeter of the camp until complete exhaustion caused them to collapse from the ordeal. Mercifully, they were allowed a half hour's rest where these unfortunates had buckets of water thrown over them.

Those legionnaires witnessing this punishment were aghast at the cruelty inflicted upon their fellow recruits, but were powerless to stop it. The deserters were made to crawl out to a rough piece of ground along the edge of the camp. A corporal brought two spades and a metre rule. Some of those watching thought at first that they were going to be made to dig their own graves, and relieved when the NCO drew lines in the sand, exactly a meter square. The unfortunates were told to dig this square exactly one meter deep, keeping to the lines he'd marked out. If the hole deviated in any way, they were ordered to fill in the hole, and begin again.

This mindless exercise continued for over two hours until the square hole was completed to the corporal's satisfaction. They were then told to fill in the hole, after which they were made to crawl to the guard house and thrown into the cells, where they sustained another beating.

The witnesses to this macabre display – the entire camp – were due to spend an evening out in Mascara. Because of this incident, it became too late to give them time to go there and enjoy themselves and return before inspection. The outing was cancelled, and most men returned dismally to their billets, many feeling very disturbed at what they'd been forced to watch.

Chapter 28

Talk of Desertion

In one of their quieter off-duty moments, the four friends discussed witnessing the punishment of two fellow recruits who were apprehended after deserting. Desertion was considered to be acceptable in the Legion, but being caught was absolutely beyond contempt.

Many of those enlisting in the Legion had their own reasons for doing so, and considered it to be the best option, rather than face the consequences of some demeaner they were guilty of in civilian life. Jorge believed he'd be better off in the Legion than waiting to be apprehended and made to serve ten years hard labour in an austere and brutal military prison. The brothers knew if they'd remained in England, it wouldn't have been long before the authorities caught up with them and charged them with murder. If found guilty they'd face the death penalty, or a very long time in prison. As far as Paddy was concerned, he had very good reason to seek sanctuary in the Legion, and considered it preferable than face punishment in Ireland for his crimes, which he was very reluctant to reveal to anyone – especially his three new comrades.

The life they'd signed up for was anything but what they'd imagined it to be. The constant drilling, running for miles with a pack of sand or rocks on their backs seemed to them to be anything but useful. The constant bullying by NCOs was getting on their nerves, and living up to the traditions of one of the strictest and toughest military forces in the world took a lot of getting used to.

The previous night's escapade was about the last straw for them; although they'd just witnessed the brutal treatment of two deserters, or escapees, as they were called; it didn't put them off considering doing it themselves. "The only problem with that," said Frank, referring to desertion, "is if you are caught, not only will you have to endure the physical beatings and torture from the non-coms, but you'll have to serve hard time in a military nick, after which you'll continue to serve out the remainder of your contract. Apart from that, the non-coms will have it in for you, and make your lives a misery for the duration of your service."

"You could always fuck off again," replied Jorge, "by that time you should have learned how to get it right on your next attempt." The lads just laughed and accused Jorge of not taking the discussion seriously.

Discussions about desertion were extremely dangerous, and if overheard or reported to the non-coms or officers, you'd be considered as guilty as if you'd done it. So the topic was dropped, and talk about pleasanter subjects discussed instead.

A couple of days later, during morning assembly, a request for volunteers who wished to join a parachute regiment was announced. "Now that would suit me," said Jorge enthusiastically. "I've always wanted to float through the air on one of them things." It was also announced that those volunteering would get better pay and the absolute best of conditions if accepted. Much travelling around the world in aeroplanes was also promised – quite cynically. "That does it, I'm gonna apply after breakfast... Definitely," declared Jorge. "What about you lot – are you gonna join me?" he asked, looking expectantly at his pals who remained nonplussed at their friend's suggestion. No consideration was given to the subject, in fact, it was the last thing on their minds to jump from an aircraft thousands of feet up, and not know where you'd land.

"Let's talk about this sensibly, Jorge; we haven't considered the implications of this move, so we're not in a position to give an answer," replied Eddie.

Paddy never uttered a word, although he was deep in thought about what his hero and mentor had suggested. After a few minutes, he broke his silence, calling out in his strong Northern Irish dialect, "Tell you what, Jorge, me ald mate, if you're up for it, then so am I; count me in!" It was as if he didn't wish to part company from the man he admired and liked so much since joining up; whatever was good enough for Jorge, was good enough for Paddy. He simply wished not to be parted from him. The brothers, as yet, were ambivalent and had yet to give an answer to their friend's question; their decisions seemed to be made too quickly and without enough consideration.

After a 30-mile jaunt with full backpacks, the group were given the rest of the day off. The bar was open, so the foursome checked their finances and decided on having a beer or two before lunch. The subject of applying to join the parachute training course was discussed, and after having downed a few beers, and much arm-twisting, the brothers agreed to join up with their two pals. "That's great!" called out an elated Jorge, "the fantastic four sticking together!" 'Stick' being the operative word, as that's what a group of parachutists were known as, although the 'fantastic four' had no idea of this yet.

The following day, before a session on the shooting range, the four approached their corporal and told him of their wishes to enter for the parachute course, with the option later to join a parachute regiment. "That's good news and bad news, boys," replied the corporal. "The good news is we need a lot of you guys to train for the parachute regiment, and you four will help make up the numbers."

"What's the bad news, Corporal?" asked Jorge.

"Well, it means I won't have your company anymore, and I had wonderful things planned for you four guys," replied the corporal with a sardonic smile.

The next day, without delay, after packing their kit, they joined another dozen men and boarded a truck which took them to Sully, just ten miles from Sidi Bel Abbès, where they would undergo a ten-week course in parachute training.

After arriving around early evening, and climbing down from the truck, the look of utter disappointment and disgust was written over just about everyone's face. Instead of a neat and tidy training camp like the one they'd just left, they were faced with a scruffy, disorderly abandoned farmyard, complete with water troughs and huge barns. It was soon discovered that the troughs were the washing facilities, and their beds were in a draughty old barn, with the refectory situated above it in the loft. To visit the lavatories, the men had to walk 350 meters to a huge trench. The thought of spending ten weeks in this disgusting excuse for a training camp didn't bear thinking about.

"It looks as if we've jumped out of the frying pan and into the fire, boys," groaned Frank to the rest of the lads.

"Talking about frying pan, where's the kitchen?" asked Paddy.

"Over by the pigsty, where you'll go to collect your evening meal... You've missed the *soupe,* because of your late arrival; now pick up your kit and I'll show you to your accommodation for this evening," barked out a sergeant who'd been listening to their comments.

After being acquainted with where they'd bed down for the next ten weeks, they took their *gamelles,* or food tins, and queued at the kitchen for their evening meal. What they received tasted almost as bad as it looked. It was as if all the leftovers from the evening meal had been mixed together and dished out, together with a chunk of bread.

"What a load of bleedin' crap!" called out Jorge, whilst looking around to see there were no non-coms within hearing distance. "Do they expect us to eat this shite!"

"Get it down ya and stop bellyaching," remonstrated Paddy, "you're the one who talked us into coming here, so get on with it; it's only for ten weeks!" Hearing this, Jorge just laughed and did what his pal advised… Got on with it.

After the meal of sorts was over, they washed their tins and joined the rest of their group, being pleased to discover this 'camp' had a bar. They asked permission from their appointed corporal to visit this drinking establishment, and were surprised he granted it, with the warning that the following day would be strenuous, so make the best of it.

Reveille was at 5am and after washing and shaving in the pig troughs, they assembled in the refectory for coffee, cold meat and brown bread. After roll call, they were assigned to one of the two groups – Section 1. Another group of twenty men, Section 2, had been at the camp for around a month, so were well ahead of the other group in their training. They were issued with new kit, which included a very good pair of boots – which later they'd be very glad of.

The whole day's events consisted of a five- mile jog, fully kited, press-ups, rope climbs, carrying each other on their backs, sprints and marching in formation. This went on for days, until it was decided to go out into the wild and practice tracking, evading, and finding one's way back to camp, after being dropped off in the middle of nowhere. Hand-to-hand combat, wrestling, boxing, and judo were all practised and perfected.

"We've been 'ere almost a bleedin' month and not even seen a bloody plane never mind a parachute!" complained Jorge. "When are we gonna get some proper training?" Once more, because of his loud voice, his complaining was overheard by a corporal who decided to give Jorge something to moan about.

"Legionnaire Jenson get in full kit and do twenty laps around the parade ground; after that do twenty press ups, followed by on-the-spot running. Oh, yes, and all in full kit!" After he'd completed this, he was on his last legs and had to be helped to bed by his pals. Before he left the parade ground, the corporal informed him he'd be having his first taste of parachute training in the morning, along with the rest of the Section 1 team.

As his pals laid him into bed, Jorge, forever the optimist and referring to the next day's events, managed to say, "See what I mean, lads, if you don't complain, you get nawt done; we're gonna get down to some proper parachute training tomorrow." With that, he collapsed and sank into a deep slumber.

There was an air of excitement in the section at the thought of training for what they signed up for – to be a parachutist. That day they were driven to an airfield and taken on a flight in an antique Nord Noratlas aeroplane. This was the aircraft favoured for first-time jumpers, but would give the beginners a taste of what it would be like when their turn came to leap from an aeroplane. Fortunately, none of the beginners were expected to do this straight away, as their parachute training was anything but completed thus far.

There were parachutists accompanying the non-jumpers, but they were only there to demonstrate the procedure to adopt when their turn came around. If anything, this short exercise did much to boost the morale of the men, as until then, many were becoming disenchanted with the mundane exercises they were forced to do day in, day out. After returning to base, it was discovered two men had deserted, and a search party dispatched to try to bring them back. "Woe betide them when they're captured; a fate worse than death will be waiting for them!" promised one of the sergeants angrily.

This incident put a dampener on the proceedings, as everyone hoped the two deserters would evade capture, and the terrible punishment awaiting them if brought back. "If those two lads get away with it, I'm gonna be next to go," promised Jorge. "I've had enough of this place and the bully boys that run it; it's not what I signed up for!"

"If you go, I'll go wid you, me ald pal; I'm sick and tired of dis place and all dat goes wid it!" groused Paddy in a quiet tone. Usually a man of few words, when the occasion arose, Paddy, or Pat, as he was sometimes referred to as, let his feelings be known, and this occasion was no exception. In fact, he thought the world of his new English pal, and everywhere that Jorge went, Paddy would follow.

"Okay, Paddy and Jorge, keep your voices down; there are some around here who'd dob you in as soon as look at you; trust no one," whispered Frank. After the brief discussion on dissent with the arrangements in the training camp, word came that training would begin on learning how to land correctly after reaching the ground from your chute.

The whole section was grouped together and given instructions for their next part of the training programme. Once more, they were taken in trucks to the airfield where a piece of apparatus known as the 'stop chute' was situated. This consisted of a platform some twenty-five feet up, where the jumper would be strapped into a harness. On command, he would leap from the platform into the air, then just before contact with the ground, the harness would pull him up. After being left to swing, suspended in the harness, it would be released, leaving him to land with a thud like a bag of potatoes. This exercise was intended to show the would-be parachutist how it feels when hitting the ground, and the best way to deal with it without getting hurt or breaking his legs or ankles. The intention was to teach the students how to roll forward instead of remaining still.

This exercise continued for the whole of the day, and indeed the rest of the week, until the instructors were satisfied with the results, and believed the whole section had perfected the jumping and landing technique. There were occasions, whilst on the platform, one or two of the reluctant students hesitated and refused to jump. This action was met with a good push from the instructor, and a good kicking from an NCO when he reached the ground. Shocking treatment of a nervous learner frightened the onlookers that much, that none of them dare refuse to jump once up there. After returning to camp, the man who refused to jump was put on fatigues, and made to do press-ups and circuits around the perimeter in full kit – with extra rocks in his backpack. Whilst the remainder of the section were in attendance, the sergeant informed them menacingly that anyone who refused to jump from an aircraft whilst in flight would have his static line cut, and be booted from the plane without a chute. This was a threat, but it made those watching take note. Once more, these bullying tactics fuelled the fire in Jorge's belly, giving him more reason to desert.

Day after day, the harsh training continued. A twenty-mile run to Sidi Bel Abbès was made before breakfast daily. Exercises in the hills became commonplace, as well as learning of the booby traps used by the fellagha. Trip wires setting off a grenade which could blow a man's leg off. An innocent-looking article left on the roadside, if picked up, would explode, causing horrific injuries to the unfortunate soldier who happened to pick it up. All these lessons were taught to the legionnaires to prevent such incidents. Whilst walking through the wooded areas, the lead man had to walk ahead, with a long, thin twig held in front to locate any tripwires, which, if broken, would activate an explosive device capable of causing terrible injuries to those unfortunate enough to be in its path.

The results of these exercises left many men traumatised and shaken. They'd been driven almost to breaking point, when the decision came to give them passes for days out in Sidi to recuperate, ready for the next round of arduous training. It was at this juncture, and because of all which transpired previously, that Jorge came to the decision to make his move and go 'over the wall', as he succinctly put it. The others tried to dissuade him, but his mind was made up.

His plan was to visit Sidi, as allowed, but whilst there, commandeer a vehicle and drive to Oran where he'd buy different clothes. He'd visit a few bars or cafes along the dock and locate a ship sailing for America or South America, in fact anywhere but Europe. The money the brothers had given him would help buy a passage on a freighter, and hopefully the others would lend him a little more to help make a success of his 'departure'. After consulting with Paddy – who was in full agreement – his plans were almost complete. The brothers agreed to give him more money, and that evening retrieved it from its secure location in their bodies – their anuses. This was a chosen place for many French convicts who used a thin cylindrical device, similar to an aluminium cigar tube called a 'charger'. This device could hold most small articles of value, including folding money, and was placed in this most personal orifice of their anatomy, guaranteed to avoid detection, even from a medical examination. The only disadvantage of this uncomfortable device was the wearer always had to remember to remove it before defecating. The results of failing to do this were most unthinkable to contemplate.

With plans made, everything was in place for their premature exit from the Legion. There was some concern about how the brothers would be treated after the pair's departure, as they were all part of the same foursome who did almost everything together. "We'll cross that bridge when we come to it," said Frank resignedly. "If those rats take it out on us, there'll be another two candidates for a trip 'over the wall'."

"At this bloody rate, this shithole of a camp will soon be empty," quipped Eddie.

"And a bleedin' good job too!" responded Jorge.

These mumblings were akin to the beginning of the French Revolution, which brought with it much violence and many deaths. Hopefully, there'd be no such terrible events in this minor revolution, which was happening at Sully like a slowly burning fuse.

With decisions made and *almost* everything in place, the only item needed now was to receive their passes, as promised, for some well-earned leave in Sidi Bel Abbès. All was going well, but an event occurred which scuttled everything that was planned. The two deserters had been captured – luckily for them, by a body of French regular soldiers, who were approached by the absconders asking for help. They were taken in chains to Sidi and awaited the arrival of an escort from Sully, from where they deserted. As fate had it, Jorge was selected to drive two non-coms to Sidi and bring them back. Not knowing whether to be elated or disappointed, he realised he couldn't desert without his escape pal, Paddy.

Arriving at the barracks in Sidi, the two non-coms set about punching the hapless pair almost unconscious. "That's nothing to what you'll receive when we get you back to Sully," growled one of the non-coms. Jorge felt helpless to do anything for his fellow trainees, and simply stood by to witness their beatings.

Arriving back at Sully, it was announced all promised leave was now cancelled, as the whole camp was ordered to watch the punishment of the two deserters – as if they hadn't received enough already. The punishment – a legal and official punishment – to be administered to this unfortunate duo, was to be *la pelote*. Anyone not knowing about the administering of this gruesome form of punitive treatment, would soon be familiar with it.

After another cruel beating, the men were dragged out and forced to carry rucksacks filled with rocks, the shoulder straps of which were made of thick wire instead of canvas; then don a steel helmet with the soft interior removed so the heavy steel rubbed against the wearer's skull. They were made to begin running around the parade ground to the sound of a whistle blown by a sergeant. Different blasts of the whistle meant different actions to take. It took a while for each different blast to be recognised and acted upon. A short blast meant do a forward gambol, a longer blast, crawl on the knees, an even longer blast signalled get up and run, followed by an extremely fast blast, indicating an even faster run. If these actions weren't carried out to the NCO's satisfaction, he whacked them across their bodies with a knotted piece of rope.

The men witnessing this terrible punishment for the first time were truly traumatised, believing this punishment was sanctioned by the military regime they'd signed on for; it seemed illegal and criminal. The punishment was far from over, as the two men almost beaten and worked to death were made to crawl through an open sewer, then, on their bellies, crawl across the parade ground in front of their comrades. There was not a man present who didn't feel pity or compassion for this unfortunate pair, but this disgusting spectacle was specially demonstrated as a warning to others who contemplated deserting – and there were many who had. But after watching this display, thought again, in particular, Jorge and his buddy.

The camp punishment was to be four hours of *la pelote* for four days; administered two hours in the morning, and two in the afternoon – the hottest part of the day. By the end of their punishments, both men had no resemblance at all of being human. Both had lost their will to live and tried to commit suicide; one did, leaving the other to face more wrath from the sadistic and inhuman NCOs. His punishment of a twelve-month prison sentence later was more preferential to what he'd experienced previously; and was accepted readily.

The atmosphere in the camp was at an all-time low, along with the morale. Everything began to change, and instead of being classed as trainees, they felt like inmates in a concentration camp, but all this was about to change... Dramatically. With their performances on the 'high wire' – as they called it – executed to the satisfaction of the instructors, the final part of their training was about to begin. The whole of Section 1 was about to be transferred to a regular army parachute training centre, where they'd make six perfect jumps and earn their wings. After receiving them, they could apply to serve in a regiment of their choice. They were finally to be rid of this notorious training camp, its cruel and barbaric NCOs, and the unpleasant memories it held. They'd be in the company of regular professional soldiers, who'd show them how to successfully jump from an aircraft, and land safely on the ground. After their time spent at this camp, they would call themselves parachutists.

Chapter 29

Blida, Home of
The Parachute Regiment

Most recruits believed the time spent at Sully would be purely for parachute training. In fact, it was anything but. They had one flight in an aircraft, and spent a full week leaping into the air whilst being restrained from above, and learning how to land on the ground. What they did learn, however, was of man's inhumanity towards his fellow man. After witnessing the barbaric spectacle of *la pelote,* the men were under no misapprehension of how one man could treat another, and the enthusiasm and pleasure they'd derive from it. To give a punishment an official name, have it dispensed without any control, and without apparent supervision, is in the realms of barbarity and degradation. It was later discovered there existed a punishment named *la crapaudine,* which was considered so cruel and inhumane its use was banned. Those unfortunate enough to receive it often became crippled for life, or died later due to its severity, and its effect on the body muscles. If this was how the Legion treated its own soldiers, God only knows what they'd do to their enemies!

Being a regular army camp, Blida's facilities were far superior to those at Sully. The canteen and food were much better than any they'd experienced elsewhere. Dormitories had beds instead of bunks as in some camps, and washrooms were equipped with hot and cold running water.

There was a captain in charge of the camp who seemed amiable, and possibly because of his just administration, the NCOs weren't as bullying as those in the Legion. In fact, the whole atmosphere was pleasant. The four friends settled in nicely, and talk of 'rebellion' was put on hold... For the time being, at least. The whole of the group had learnt how to land from a harness dangling some twenty-five feet up in the air; they were now to learn how to don a parachute, and land successfully with it strapped to their backs.

There were the regular drill sessions, and time spent in the classroom learning theory. Each recruit was taught how to fold his own parachute under the expert eye of their instructors; there was no margin for error in this procedure. During a classroom discussion, the trainees were told of the failure rate of parachutes not opening during the last war. The failure rate at one time was running as high as 20%. That meant one in five chutes didn't open. Fortunately, the parachutists had a reserve chute strapped to their chests, but delay in pulling the ripcords, and the chute not opening out, caused many unnecessary deaths.

It was decided by the high command that, occasionally, a parachute would be chosen at random, along with one of those responsible for folding it, and ordered to wear it on a test flight. After this test was in operation for a week or two, the failure rate had dramatically dropped from 20%, to an amazing 2%, which was considered acceptable.

The ground equipment used for practising was different to that at Sully. Candidates were strapped into a harness and swung through the air on a rope attached to a pulley. How to land, and the procedure of using the rope lines once in the air after your chute has opened, were practised repeatedly until the instructor was happy with your performance.

Facilities at the camp included two cinemas, four dining halls and three bars. The whole atmosphere was one of camaraderie and bonhomie. After the preliminaries spent on the ground were well and truly practised to perfection, the time had come to put them into practice. The group – or stick, as they were called – were given their chutes and driven to an airfield. After putting on their chutes, and their straps tested and adjusted, they were taken off again and laid in a row, whilst the stick awaited the arrival of an aircraft. On arrival, the instructors told everyone to don their chutes and check all straps were in order. There were thirty men in this stick, and all sat opposite each other in the aircraft. The four friends sat in the same row together, all as nervous as hell, wondering what would happen if they refused to jump when the order was given.

With everyone aboard, the plane took off and began climbing until it finally levelled off to a pre-determined height of some 2500 feet. Every man in the group was feeling fearful of what the next order would involve, even though they'd been through the procedure many times. They sat nervously watching the light on the bulkhead. Suddenly, it glowed red, and the men were given the order to stand up and hook up. Everyone stood up and secured the webbing static lines protruding from their chutes to a parallel overhead cable by way of a spring hook. Once on the move to the doorway, their lines would follow them along the cable, ready for their next move.

The atmosphere on board intensified, as they waited for the red light to change colour. Some were trembling, others shaking; all were desperately trying to hide their nervousness. One would indeed have to be devoid of all feeling to not to be fearful at the thought of leaping out of an aircraft some 2500 feet up and travelling at over a hundred miles an hour. Now on their feet and hooked up, an instructor passed along the line, checking straps and buckles on the parachutes and harness. All eyes were on the red light, then suddenly a buzzer sounded, and it changed to green. With the exit door open and the air rushing in, the first man leapt out after being patted on the back by an instructor, followed by another and then another until half of the stick had left the aircraft. Unfortunately, the man in front of Jorge had a change of heart and refused to jump. "JUMP!" called out the jump master, whose order fell on deaf ears. "JUMP, YOU YELLOW BASTARD!" he shouted once more.

FUCKING WELL JUMP, OR I'LL SHOVE YOU OUT!" yelled Jorge, just behind him, all fired up and ready for his turn to jump.

Jorge had no need to carry out his threat, as an enormous kick from the instructor's boot propelled him out of the doorway, and into the slipstream of the aircraft. With the growing number of static lines whipping and slapping at the corners of the open doorway, and the wind rushing in, the remainder of the stick followed Jorge and leapt out of the plane in textbook order, with no one else refusing to jump.

Now emptied of its reluctant passengers, the instructors gazed out of the open doorway to see them all land safely, one by one without any 'Roman candles' – failure of the chute opening. Many found themselves on flat ground, others weren't as lucky and landed amongst trees and in thick undergrowth. The failure of one man to jump, threw the drop zones (DZs) into disarray, and it took longer for the jumpers to assemble at a rendezvous point (RP). There were one or two injuries sustained amongst the group, but nothing life changing. Eventually, they gathered their parachutes together and made their way to the RP.

Once back at base, the 'non-jumper' was singled out and ridiculed by the instructors, accusing him of cowardice. "If you'd done that on operations, you'd have put the lives of all those behind you in immediate danger. The delay you caused could have meant those who followed would land in drop zones miles apart, and possibly behind enemy lines. Your cowardice could have threatened the lives of your comrades. I hope you feel proud of yourself!" bellowed the instructor so all could hear.

This occurrence was common with first-time jumpers, who were later grouped together and put on training jumps apart from the others. With the first jump out of the way, the stick was lectured on what they did right or wrong, and monitored again on their next five jumps, which included jumping with heavy gear, without gear, and one jump during darkness. After successfully completing the remaining jumps, their parachute training was over. All that remained was to be presented with their wings, qualifying them to be competent parachutists.

Reluctantly, after receiving their wings, they returned to Camp Sully to await being sent to a parachute regiment. Which one, would depend on the number of vacancies needing filling due to losses during operations. After hearing this news, Frank's comment was, "It looks as if we're going to have to fill some dead men's shoes." Not a pleasant expectation, by any means, after all their months of exhaustive training, but quite true.

France's involvement in the war in French Indochina required an unending number of soldiers to fight in the many battles with the Vietminh – followers of Ho Chi Minh. He was a Vietnamese revolutionary, intent on evicting the French from Vietnam, and ultimately Indochina. With the backing of China, and later Russia, the Vietminh were giving the French a hard time, causing the deaths of many of their fighting men. As long as the men dying were not French – mainly Legionnaires, Vietnamese National Army, Laotian Forces and a dozen other smaller factions paid and supplied by the French – the French public back home were not too concerned by the losses. As soon as regular French Army troops began to suffer, the public's attitude changed, along with political interventions.

Chapter 30

Na San, French Indochina

France colonised Vietnam in 1887, and six years later, along with Laos and Cambodia, formed French Indochina. The official language was French, but Vietnamese, Laotian and Khmer were spoken freely along with many other local dialects from the different tribes and settlements.

The religion was Buddhism, Confucianism, Vietnamese Folk Religion and, of course, Roman Catholicism. The official currency was the French Indochinese piastre, commonly used in all three countries.

With France's collapse and subsequent surrender to Germany in 1940, Japan lost no time in demanding the use of airfields in Indochina, along with the installation of garrisons and the free movement of Japanese soldiers through French territory. When the French governor general refused, he was replaced with a more cooperative administrator by the newly formed Vichy government, led by Marshal Petain.

Soon after this humiliation of the French administration, the Japanese expelled the French completely, after much bloodshed and slaughter, including the beheading of two French officials after they were made to dig their own graves. Obtaining assurances from the Vietnamese not to attack any Japanese troops, they were given administrative control of their country, under certain conditions. The Communist, revolutionary Vietminh leapt at this chance, and gradually built their army up from a clandestine guerrilla movement, into a conventional army, which later proved to be capable of taking on any who opposed to it.

Once more, all was about to change with the defeat of Japan in 1945. They lost control of Indochina, along with other countries they'd conquered, leaving the puppet government it installed to negotiate with France after the war ended. France, of course, was in no mood to negotiate with a Communist government, installed by an enemy who'd expelled them from *their* colony some five years earlier. The failure to reach an agreement led to the declaration of war between the Vietminh, led by revolutionary leader, Ho Chi Minh, and the French government and its forces.

Sharing a common border with China was a great advantage to the Vietminh (VM), as their hosts, the Chinese, armed and supplied them. Chinese experts were able to train the VM, as well as give them all they needed to help defeat the French, and subsequently expel them from Indochina, as the Japanese had done five years previously. France, in return, built a series of block houses along its borders with China and garrisoned them with soldiers from the local hill tribes, under French supervision.

In mid-October 1952, Ho Chi Minh's army, led by General Vo Nguyen Giap, ahead of an army of three divisions trained and equipped in China – an excess of 60000 men – invaded North Vietnam and the Thai highlands, attacking French garrisons in their wake. The French formulated a strategy to block their invasion route, by creating a huge fortress across its path. The place chosen was a small outpost called Na San, situated in a valley around three miles long and a mile across, surrounded by two dozen hills which if fortified, would act as defence points.

The outpost at the time was guarded by a small company of men under the control of a single NCO. This was all about to change when after the sappers moved in to strengthen and lengthen the small airstrip with steel plate; C-47 Dakotas, Bristol 170 heavy transport planes, and a host of other aircraft from the Hanoi-based French Air Force, began bringing in everything a reasonably sized defensive army would need to hold off, and hopefully defeat, a much larger enemy.

With its newly strengthened airstrip, the outpost now resembled an air-land base, with men and armaments being flown in on a regular basis. Heavy transport planes flew in trucks and jeeps, heavy artillery, howitzers, timber, tons of barbed wire, as well as ammunition and other supplies. Each of the overlooking hilltops were converted into defensive points called 'position armees', or strongpoints (PAs). These were surrounded by barbed wire and entrenchments, along with outer minefields. Around a hundred men defended each of these hilltop entrenchments, which were intended to provoke the enemy into launching full-frontal attacks, instead of using hit and run tactics as done previously.

On the night of 23/24th November, the Vietminh launched their attack on strongpoint PA8, with mortar and heavy machine gun fire. The battle lasted several hours, with the attackers unable to break the French defences, leaving many dead and wounded behind after they broke off the attack. These attacks and repulses carried on for several days, resulting in the deaths and serious injuries of many French soldiers, mainly legionnaires.

With the help of circling Dakotas dropping parachute flares at night, and B-26s, Hellcats and Privateer fighter planes coming in from Hanoi, bombing and strafing the enemy with napalm, the battle was going mainly in the French's favour. By 2nd of December, the VM broke off the attack after failing to overwhelm and capture any of the PAs. Their losses were great, and mounting by the day, so General Giap, the Vietminh leader, reluctantly decided to withdraw and lick his wounds, whilst determining what went wrong. Although he lost a good many of his forces, he learned valuable lessons from this battle, lessons he'd remember and implement during further engagements with the French.

The French victory came at a heavy cost with the loss of nearly two battalions, almost 2000 men killed and wounded. Clearing up after the battle took many weeks, but despite this, they needed to keep up a sizeable presence at the outpost to deter the VM attempting another unannounced attack. Although the bulk of the Vietminh army was now some 200 miles away, near to the Chinese border, they left a sizeable battalion behind to monitor movements, waiting for their chance to mount another attack; although it would be a low-key affair. After a few months, this battalion shrunk to around a couple of hundred men, as the bulk of the army was needed elsewhere.

It was early August 1953 when the French decided that remaining in Na San would be of no advantage. They'd had no attacks for at least a couple of months, and it was believed the Vietminh had lost interest in that area, although they kept their presence with a small garrison based in Son La, a village some 20 miles to the north. It was decided by the French High Command to abandon their outpost – the maintenance of which tied up too much manpower and equipment – and withdraw by flying out the whole company, munitions, guns, equipment and anything which could be loaded onto a Dakota or larger aircraft.

Disengagement under fire is one of the most dangerous movements that soldiers could attempt. Although not quite under fire, they very soon would be if the enemy discovered they were withdrawing. To overcome this possibility, it was planned to circulate a rumour amongst the VM that, instead of pulling out, they were indeed going to reinforce the outpost by sending in two legionnaire parachute regiments. Arriving by parachute would reinforce their rumour of the reinforcement, and at the same time allow fresh troops to arrive to act as a rear guard whilst the evacuation was underway.

It is at this juncture our four heroes return to the story. Having just completed their parachute training and being awarded the much-coveted wings, they were waiting to be assigned to a parachute regiment. Unfortunately for them, the regiment they were about to be assigned to was that chosen to drop into Na San and act as rear guard, whilst everyone else was in the process of packing up and leaving. How they'd return to their base after guarding the withdrawal, wasn't yet decided, but it was determined they'd have to link up with the partisans and other friendly tribes of the high region and make their own way back. The nearest friendly airfield from Na San was over the border in Laos, some 130 miles away. To get there, they'd have to cross the high region, travelling through hostile jungle and all the perils that lurked within. Quite a feat for the young, newly trained legionnaires, but with the harsh discipline and strenuous training they'd received, it would stand them in good stead to cope.

Chapter 31

The Descent into Hell

Back in Sully, with their parachute training complete, the newly qualified legionnaires were awaiting orders to join a parachute brigade – they didn't have long to wait. The whole section was summoned to assemble at Camp Pehaut, home to the *3e Régiment de Parachutistes*, outside the coastal town of Philippeville, near Tunisia. There was an emergency in progress, and it needed the presence of the Third Parachute Regiment 3REP to take part in an evacuation in Northern Vietnam.

Having had hardly enough time to settle into their new surroundings, they were called to a briefing with others of the regiment – around a hundred men – and the part it would play. Companies of the regiment were already in Vietnam, and many had either been killed or badly wounded at the battle of Na San. Although this battle with the Vietminh had taken place some months earlier, the survivors were needed in place to help stop the advance of the Communist forces under General Giap, and their leader, Ho Chi Minh.

"Okay, men, at ease," instructed the officer responsible for this briefing. "What you are about to hear is top secret, and not one word of it must be divulged outside this building!" He then went on to discuss the evacuation plan, and the part those men listening would play in it. There was much deception needed to convince the enemy that, instead of withdrawing, the garrison would in fact be reinforcing. To emphasise this ruse, ten planeloads of parachutists would be dropped into the outpost, giving a visual display of its intention to indeed strengthen the garrison.

The major impressed upon the men that this would be on a need-to-know basis, and more would be disclosed after their arrival at Na San. The atmosphere in the assembly hall was one of excitement and nervousness combined, as many had heard of the previous battle there, but were not familiar with the reasons for *them* being there. With the preliminary briefing over, the officer asked for any questions – unusual for a secret briefing.

"When do we ship out, sir, and how long will it take to get there?" called out one of the men.

The major paused for a moment, and decided that, as departure was imminent, the men going on this mission should know a little more. "We won't *ship out*. In fact, we are *flying out*; tomorrow morning!" Much nodding and agreeing followed this disclosure.

"Excuse me, sir, but you'll need a bloody big plane, or a lot of smaller ones to get us there, and how far is it to Vietnam?"

The major was beginning to wish he hadn't given the men the chance to question him, however, as there was no need at present to inform them of their role in the operation, he relented... With reservations. He didn't let them know they'd be left to defend the settlement when the others had left, and subsequently left to find their own way to liaise with friendly forces. The men weren't told they'd have to march through thick jungle, and cope with the hidden dangers that lay therein. Just as well, otherwise the Legion would have had more than a few deserters to contend with after discovering they'd be subjected to tiger attacks, poisonous snake bites, deadly spiders, leeches, as well as malaria and jungle fever. There was good reason to keep the men ignorant of these dangers, but he decided on informing them of the luxurious transport chartered to fly them there instead. "Has anyone heard of the luxury passenger plane built by the British?" he asked, not expecting an answer. "It's called the Comet, and we are borrowing two from the Royal Air Force. These jets will make the 6000-mile journey with four refuelling stops, in about 18 hours. It flies at a speed of 450 mph and is the last word in comfort, unlike the C-47 Dakotas you'll fly in to reach Na San. The Comets will fly us to Hanoi Airfield where we have a military supply base, and there we'll await further orders."

The mere mention of flying to war in a luxury jet put most of the men in a relaxed frame of mind, and they weren't too concerned about later developments. One man, however, wasn't as happy as everyone else, and his griping and constant complaining got on the men's nerves. "We've got to fly out to God knows where, to stand guard while others pull out, leaving us the last to fly back after facing the shit storm when it comes!" he complained angrily.

An NCO present happened to hear him and called him out in front of the men. "What do you expect, soldier? The Legion take you in with no questions asked about your background, or if you're on the run – as many here are! Apart from giving you a new identity, they put a roof over your head, they feed you, clothe you, supply you with cigarettes and wine, free of charge. You're given the best training any army could get, along with free healthcare, and to top it all, they pay you so you can visit the camp bar as well as the brothel. What's there to complain about? Stop your bloody moaning!"

Nearly everyone agreed with the non-com and thought the complainant to be lucky he wasn't put on fatigues; he would have been if they weren't flying out the next day. The four pals were excited about the assignment they were about to embark upon, but Frank, being a realist, mentioned to his pals, "I dare say what the major informed us was all true, but from his tone and attitude, I felt it wasn't *what* he told us, but what he *failed* to tell us that set a few doubts in my mind about this mission… I don't like the sound of it!"

"Stop worrying, bro, we are going to do something worthwhile at last. Whatever it is, it'll be exciting working with other trained and experienced legionnaires. You can't spend all of your time marching and going on training exercises with bullying NCOs; this is our chance for a bit of excitement." The others agreed with Eddie and assured his brother all would be well.

Hardly any of those about to embark on this venture had any sleep that night, and with dawn's early light, the whole group paraded on the airfield, waiting to receive their allotted places on one of the luxury passenger jets. As usual, the four found themselves together, and despite Frank's misgivings, decided to relax and enjoy what the future held for them. Had any of them known what really lay ahead, it was almost certain that the frame of mind they were in would have been anything but *relaxed*.

The estimated flight time from Algiers to Hanoi was more than the sixteen hours envisaged; in fact, with the stops necessary for refuelling these huge passenger jets, another five hours was added to that figure. In all, from departing from Philippeville Air Base, it was almost a day later they arrived in Hanoi. To complicate matters further, Vietnam was six hours ahead of North Africa, which meant there would be a certain amount of jetlag experienced by the legionnaires.

Despite these trivialities, the weary travellers were given sleeping facilities and told to rest as much as possible, as the next day there'd be final briefings, and familiarising with parachutes and weapons. Early next morning, they were acquainted with other groups of legionnaires already at the base, to make up a total of 240 men, who together would parachute into Na San and form the rear guard. It was all dreamlike, as the men didn't have enough time to acclimatise themselves with their new surroundings, or acquaintances. All legionnaires were issued with new weapons; instead of the MAT-49 sub-machine guns they were used to, each received an M1 Garand semi-automatic rifle. These rifles had a far superior range than their normal guns – 300-500 yards.

They were far more accurate than a MAT and were widely used by American forces in WW1. Once again, the men became suspicious as to why they were changing from guns they were used to, and being equipped with unfamiliar weapons at such short notice. As before, Frank let his feelings be known by telling his mates there was more to this assignment that met the eye. "They're keeping us in the dark about something, and I'd really like to know what we are letting ourselves in for!"

A corporal heard Frank's complaint and straightway challenged him, saying, "Look here, soldier, it's not what you are letting yourself in for... You have no say in the matter! You, along with the rest of this group, are on a mission to reinforce an outpost by parachute. What your final orders will be, you'll find out when we arrive. So, for now, keep your big fucking mouth shut and behave like a legionnaire – await orders, and to the best of your ability, carry them out... Savvy?"

"Yes, Corporal, sorry, Corporal; just that it's our first time on active duty, and I was feeling a little apprehensive, but you've put my mind at ease. Thanks, Corporal!" responded Frank sheepishly, remembering the old piece of advice about not getting on the wrong side of the non-coms or officers. The corporal simply gave him a long stare and nodded, implying he understood the concerns of the young soldier.

Having completed a short two-hour session on the firing range to acquaint themselves with their new weapons, the men were taken to the parachute stores where they received their final piece of equipment... A parachute. So, with their rifles, parachutes, and other equipment, the 240 men were given final instructions before climbing aboard their designated aircraft. The most favoured aeroplane used by the paras was the Douglas C-47 Dakota, used widely by the American and British forces during WW1. It was a little poky inside but thoroughly dependable.

"We haven't any orders on what to do after we land!" called out one of the men to a long-suffering sergeant, who was becoming a little tired of the unnecessary questioning he was receiving from the men.

"Look here, soldier, the less you know the better. If, for example, your plane crashes or you happen to drop into enemy territory and are captured; under torture you won't reveal what your orders are, because you won't know until you land safely, and group up with the rest of your outfit... Understand?"

"Yes, Sergeant, sorry, Sergeant," replied the curious, but now better-informed legionnaire.

In fact, there was a heightened atmosphere of activity amongst the men as they stood outside their allotted aircraft waiting for the order to climb aboard. After a final count by an NCO, the order came to get on board and take positions. There was a final pep talk from the jumpmaster, reminding them that a refusal to jump, or even a hesitation, could cost the lives of their comrades; so, anyone who refused would be shoved out when his turn came, whether he was ready or not. "This is not an exercise but an important and most decisive drop we've ahead of us. Much will depend on what we do today to ensure this mission is a success, so we want no fuck-ups... Understand?"

"Yes, sir!" shouted back the men as one, above the whirring of the Dakota's unmistakable engine sound. The atmosphere was electric; hardly anyone spoke as the plane and its complement of twenty-four parachutists taxied toward the runway, ready to wait for the final flight instructions. The men were briefed previously as to which of the ten Dakotas they'd be in, as well as the weather conditions and general visibility; all were pleased to discover both favourable with no wind forecast for this operation. They'd arrive in under an hour from take-off, and should make themselves ready to jump on the jumpmaster's instruction. This was it; Na San would be their next destination.

Twelve men sat either side of the aircraft, watching those opposite, knowing what feelings were running through their heads... Most likely the same as theirs... Fear and sheer terror. Some men chewed gum, acting nonchalantly without a care in the world, but deep down they were as scared as hell. Their throats were dry, the back of their heads began to throb, some felt their hands trembling, others shook uncontrollably.

It was the jumpmaster's job to try and keep the stick as calm as possible. The last thing he wished for was to have a couple of non-jumpers to deal with. "Okay, men, at ease; some of you have jumped into action before, others haven't. Believe me," he lied, "it's no different than doing one of those exercise jumps you did to earn your wings." This revelation did little to put the minds at ease of those thinking they could be jumping to their death. A 'Roman candle' caused by bad parachute packing, or a stray bullet from the enemy on the ground, could easily achieve this. They'd be an easy target for snipers, especially being unable to shoot back whilst floating slowly to the ground.

"I'm gonna give you your final briefing now, so listen up, y'hear!" Those listening intently momentarily forgot their nervousness, and paid attention to the jumpmaster's instructions. "When I give the word, stand up and hook up, you'll all know what to do. Make sure those hooks on your static lines are snapped tight; yank the bastards hard to make sure. Check the man in front of you to see his gear is in order; I'll check the last man's myself."

The roaring from the engine of the C-47 made it difficult to hear what was being said, but despite this, the leader carried on. "When you see the red light, get ready. When you hear the buzzer sound, followed by the green light, keep moving toward the door, and when it's your turn, jump out as far as you can and wait for the chute to open. If it fails to open, which is very rare," he lied once more, "deploy your reserve chute by yanking the handle situated on your chest."

All the jumpers listened intently to the next piece of advice. "If your lines get tangled, which is very rare, cut them with your knife which you must keep handy, and deploy your reserve. Any questions?" The throats of those listening were too dry to shout above the noise of the engine, and they were too busy unfastening their knives and placing them in an accessible position, tucked into their belts.

Seeing this frantic activity from the nervous jumpers, the master called out above the engine noise, "Believe me, fellas, you won't need those knives, it's only a precaution. As jumpmaster I've been on hundreds of jumps, and only once have I seen two chutes get into a tangle; so, relax, it won't happen!"

After giving the men those necessary instructions, the jumpmaster gave them enough time to settle before his final and most important briefing. "There are three rendezvous points on this drop zone; three smoke grenades on the ground will show red smoke, green smoke and yellow smoke. The colour of your smoke is red, so after you land, unhitch yourself from your chute, leaving it where you land. Unpack your rifle and keep your head down. Look around for your colour – RED – and head straight for it to regroup and await further orders."

He made his way to the pilot's cabin, and after returning a couple of minutes later, told the men, "Okay, guys, it won't be long now, the plane's levelled off to 2500 feet, with the speed down to 105 mph; wait for the word from me and do exactly what I've told you. Good luck, guys, and God be with you all." He returned to the cabin a final time and when he emerged shouted the order, "STAND UP, HOOK UP!" Two dozen men got out of their seats and nervously hooked their webbed static lines to the overhead cable running the length of the inside of the aircraft. "CHECK 'EM TO MAKE

SURE THEY'RE TIGHT!" he called out once more, just before the red light appeared.

Those not nervous before sure as hell were now, knowing what the next light would mean. Jorge, Frank and the others hardly spoke, but they whispered to each other, "Goodbye, matey, and good luck. See you on *terra firma*."

The men were bunched tightly together now in the cramped space of the Dakota, all waiting for the order. The red light was aglow, with the exit door wide open, allowing the wind to gush in and refresh those nervously waiting to jump. Suddenly, the buzzer sounded, followed by the green light glowing bright. The first jumper heard, "GO!" With a slap on his back, he leapt through the exit door as fast and far as he could. Seconds later, he was followed by another... And another... And then another, until the whole stick had exited the aircraft in record time with no refusals. With the 24 empty static lines whipping and slapping the door frame, and the wind blowing in his face, the jumpmaster peered out of the door with great satisfaction, noticing every man in his stick was floating to the ground with fully opened canopies. He called out to them, "Good luck, my beauties, good luck and may the good Lord be with you all; you're gonna need all the luck you can get on *your* mission."

Job done, the plane circled to head back to Hanoi, leaving the two dozen men – and the remainder of their company – to cope with the many dangers of which they were unaware and, indeed, deliberately uninformed of.

Chapter 32

Abandoned!

After exiting the plane and taking a huge leap forward, with the successful opening of his parachute, Andy was horrified to discover the suspension lines tangled up. This was a common occurrence, and after a little twisting and turning the lines usually corrected themselves. He looked up to see his canopy fully open and functioning correctly, but the twisted lines worried him as he was falling downwards quite swiftly and had just two minutes before he would reach the ground. Looking around him, he noticed the others were floating and descending in reasonable order, but he now had a decision to make. Should he try manually to untwist the cords, or cut himself free and deploy his reserve chute? The seconds were ticking by, allowing him little time to decide. He'd made up his mind and reached for his knife, and was about to cut himself free, when, literally from out of the blue, a voice in his head said, "Do not cut the lines, my son." In fact, the shock of hearing this caused him to drop his knife, oblivious of his proximity to the ground. A minute later the touchdown caused him to tumble over, but, nevertheless, he landed safely.

Forgetting this 'voice incident', he reverted to last orders, and after freeing himself of the parachute harness, unpacked his rifle and looked for the red smoke of his rendezvous point. There was a certain amount of gunfire as the Vietminh snipers seized the opportunity to take pot-shots of the helpless soldiers, dropping slowly to the ground. Once down, the men unpacked their weapons and fired back. By now, all 240 paratroopers of the company had landed... Some less successfully than others. One or two twisted ankles and bruised bodies occurred, but at least no one had been hit by the sniper gunfire.

Jorge spotted Andy, and it wasn't long before all four joined others of their group at the rendezvous point, where they took orders from an NCO. Grouped together with their guns at the ready, they swiftly made their way to the command post (CP). Those legionnaires already there made swift work of the sniper threat by firing short bursts of heavy machine-gun rounds at their positions; the snipers soon made off, back to the cover of the jungle.

Now all grouped together, the men were greeted by the CO of the outpost. He told them how pleased he was with their presence and offered every assistance he could. "He's buttering us up for something; I can tell by his patronising attitude towards us," quipped Frank. "Just wait for what's coming next!" he warned. Frank's perfectly accurate perception of the situation indeed turned out to be correct; what they were about to hear following the false welcome by the CO sent a few shockwaves through the group of freshly arrived paratroopers.

Bunched together inside the huge canteen, and behind closed doors, Major Foret, the CO, laid bare the evacuation plan he'd formulated and coordinated with the high command in Hanoi for the entire withdrawal of men and equipment from Na San. It was a clever and complex plan, which required perfect planning and coordination from everyone if it was to be a success without *too* much loss of life.

The CO went on to remind the men that disengagement under fire would be one of the most dangerous manoeuvres any army could attempt. The rear guard could be overrun, leaving the retreating forces helpless before they could make their escape. Looking at his watch, he went on to tell them more of the plan. "Everything which cannot be removed safely must be destroyed, leaving nothing of value to the enemy. Light machine guns and mortars, along with hand weapons and grenades will be carried back with us. Heavy artillery must be put out of action and their shells defused. Over 100 trucks and jeeps will need to be made unserviceable. We've a survivor of the retreat from Dunkirk in 1940 to oversee this; he did an excellent job of decommissioning the British Army's vehicles, rather than leave them serviceable to be used by the advancing Germans. Radio communication will be broken, along with their sets, at the last minute."

The CO went on to inform his open-mouthed audience of further plans for this precise and complicated withdrawal of men, women, children, machinery, and armaments. "This must be achieved without the knowledge of the four or five hundred Vietminh, who've been watching us for the last eight months. As soon as they get wind of our departure, they'll radio in to their divisions up north, and we'll have them descending on us like a swarm of locusts. It'll end up in a bloodbath, with most of our weapons destroyed, and most fighting men back in Hanoi. Secrecy is paramount to ensure everything goes to plan, without any hitches.

Many men listening thought the whole idea farfetched and wouldn't even get off the ground. How could they attempt a full-scale departure without the knowledge of the VM, who were watching every move? Na San was situated in a valley with the command post, stores and hospital surrounding an airfield with direct links to Hanoi, the base of the French Airforce.

Situated around this outpost were a series of hills, which, during their last battle, were heavily armed and surrounded by barbed wire and entrenchments. A hundred legionnaires occupied these armed positions (PAs), and it was because of them and their heavy machine guns, as well as unswerving courage, that the enemy was prevented from breaking through to the command post, which in turn was guarded by ten other smaller PAs.

The layout and planning of this outpost was complex, but prevented the VM from gaining a victory, despite their overwhelming numbers of troops. However, it had to be seen if the overly complex plan of the withdrawal from Na San would be as successful as its defence.

"Men, I know you must be a little confused by now," droned on the CO, "but time is of the essence as

I previously emphasised, and we have no time to waste, so I'll cut to the chase. Now you are all here, and the enemy believe we are being reinforced, our big deception plan will take effect. Three companies of legionnaires will sweep out these unsuspecting Vietminh who've been keeping watch on us, and after meeting up with around 700 partisans, they'll drive them back to Son La, a village about 20 miles away that they are using as their HQ. Once surrounded, the legionnaires will return to base, leaving the partisans to box them in, fully unaware of our withdrawal".

Where does this leave us? were the thoughts of the 240 men assembled there who'd take up position of the rear guard. That question was about to be answered by the CO, and would send shockwaves through their ranks. After discovering they'd be abandoned, left to fight the enemy on their own, with perhaps the help of some of the Thai, Meo and Muong tribesmen, those chosen as the rear guard were far from happy with their allotted task. The formidable hill country fighters, who'd be alongside them, formed the greater part of the partisans and maquis guerrilla bands, all loyal to the French who armed and supplied them in their fight against their Communist enemies. Between them, they'd possibly have to hold off the enemy whilst all other personnel were being flown to safety. The confident CO maintained it wouldn't come to this as he believed his plan was fool-proof… Well, almost.

As the exodus was being discussed, large groups of legionnaires were already making a huge sweep of the outer perimeter and jungle, to herd and drive off the VM who'd been keeping watch there. Grenades and flamethrowers certainly helped root out the enemy and drive them through the jungle, away from their observation positions. Many were burned to death or blown up by the grenades. Believing this was a full-blown advance by the French, they swiftly retreated to their temporary HQ in Son La, pursued by the legionnaires.

As prearranged, a battalion of partisans, led by French officers and NCOs, met up en route to Son La, to continue the pursuit of the fleeing enemy. Having arrived at the Vietminh temporary HQ, the French allowed them to settle in after taking up positions around the village. Once boxed in completely, word was sent back to Na San HQ of their successful operation, now allowing 'Operation Pegasus' to commence.

Back at Na San, the operational code name of the winged horse was set in motion. Dakotas from Hanoi arrived at frequent intervals, loading personnel and equipment on board, and flying them to the French Airforce base and safety. It was to be a long-drawn-out process, with much air traffic needing good weather to make this operation a success. The English survivor of Dunkirk, Big Baz, went to work with his little team of vehicle saboteurs, destroying the many motor vehicles forced to be abandoned, ensuring their handiwork left each vehicle unserviceable to the enemy. "Get plenty of rocks," he called out to his team. "Once the engine's racing at full speed, bung a rock on its accelerator to keep it running. Unscrew the sump screws and let the oil gush out. We did the same in France in 1940, it worked then, so it'll work now."

Other acts of sabotage included removing the fuses from abandoned artillery shells, smashing heavy mortars; removing gun sights and breechblocks from heavy guns and throwing them in the nearby river; after that, an exploding hand grenade was dropped down the barrel, to make sure it'd never fire again. Anything left behind had to be made completely useless to the enemy. Stocks of food and medical supplies were taken away, except for a small amount necessary for the rear guard, should they have casualties to care for.

The deployment of the rear guard was next on the list. Outer armed positions normally manned by more than a hundred men, would now have only ten, plus a heavy machine gun or Bren gun, whichever was available. Food, water, and medical supplies had to be provided for the defenders, as well as ammunition for the guns. The four outer armed positions, PA21 to PA24, were the most susceptible to attack, being farther away from the airstrip and enjoying a higher position. The enemy tried in vain to capture these PAs during the last battle, eight months previously, as their elevated positions gave a strategic advantage over the entire outpost, especially the airstrip.

Ten inner PAs were in a slightly less perilous position, but, nonetheless, still vulnerable to attack. It was at one of these positions, PA8, that the four pals were allocated to defend. The four, along with six more legionnaires, were joined by a half-dozen Meo tribesmen from the local partisans. These men were spread around each of the armed positions to give the legionnaires greater numbers, but still left them perilously undermanned.

The Dakotas continued to fly in and out, gradually diminishing the garrison and laying the outpost bare of personnel and equipment. Major Foret and his entourage did a tour of the manned PAs, giving advice and encouragement to the defenders. Arriving at PA8, he told the men it was unlikely they would come under attack, and there was a slim chance that once the planned airlift was complete and there was no sign of the enemy, room could be found for some, if not all, the men acting as rear guard. Failing that, they would join the Meos and Muong tribesmen, who would guide them through the jungle to Laos, where they'd be escorted further to one of the airstrips located there. Airfield Muong Sai in Laos was a helicopter base as well as having a few aeroplanes. Muong Nam Bac was specifically used for aeroplanes. Either of these bases would ensure the stranded legionnaires got back to Hanoi in the event of them not being airlifted from Na San – after negotiating what perils the jungle held for them.

"In the most unlikely event of you coming under attack, and possibly being overwhelmed, rather than fight to your last bullet and be killed, surrender to the enemy and take your chances with them," he continued. "You'll be taken as prisoners of war, and treated accordingly under the terms laid down by the Geneva Convention. This statement really unsettled the tiny band of defenders, especially Frank, who waited for the CO to disappear before making his feelings known. "Of course, men, this situation is highly unlikely, and improbable, but nevertheless, possible." This little pep talk was meant to put the men's minds at ease and prepare them for what he insisted was highly unlikely. But it was what he said to them just before he climbed over the sandbags and barbed wire that really alarmed the men in that tiny dugout. "Oh yes, men, should you be overwhelmed and take a decision to surrender, have a white flag available to indicate to the enemy of your intentions... Oh yes, don't forget to decommission your weapons. Push your rifles in the ground as far as they'll go... And pull the trigger, ensuring you have a bullet in the breech. The machine gun or Bren should have their breeches smashed with the heavy hammer my adjutant will give you. Apart from that, men, good luck and God be with you all."

That was it, advice, and encouragement over, leaving those who listened to this sermon more nervous and jittery than before. After the CO and his little band had left and were on their way to give encouragement to the occupants of the next PA, Frank now had his say. "If that talk was meant to put our minds at ease, he made a fucking bad job of it!"

"I'm as nervous as hell now after that, can't we just fuck off into the jungle now instead of waiting here for the VM to come and kill us?" fumed Eddie.

"Don't worry, lads, you'll be okay with your Uncle Jorge to look after you!" responded the old soldier.

Paddy didn't utter a word, neither did the other men present, except for the Meos who hardly understood a word of what had been spoken by the CO, and continued to chat together in their native tongue.

After his morale-boosting tour of the armed positions – armed, maybe, but terribly undermanned – the CO, now feeling proud of how the operation was going, invited his officers to a meal and a chat whilst going over the situation thus far. Everything was fine and running to schedule, apart from the early morning mist, which hampered the aircraft flying in and out. When asked how many days before complete evacuation, his adjutant told him a couple, three at most. This news brought a huge smile to the major's weather-beaten face, and made him smugger than ever. He could almost envisage the ceremony held in Paris, where he would be guest of honour receiving his *colonel's* pips. "Colonel Foret; that sounds fitting for the man who organised and administered the evacuation from Na San."

It was at this point the words of Scottish poet, Robert Burns, came to mind; 'The best laid schemes o' mice an' men...' Major Foret's planning and administration had been perfect, meticulous, in fact. There was no controlling the weather, but men and machinery, he was good at. What he failed to do was 'see the forest for the tree', another aphorism which could apply to this situation.

Had he taken the trouble to look up into the trees surrounding his base, he may just have spotted the Vietminh watchers who'd been up there since Operation Pegasus took flight. Armed only with outdated binoculars, and a supply of food and water, these camouflaged figures were well placed to report back anything unusual occurring at the outpost. What they never had, fortunately, was a radio with which to report their findings. Those sets located on the ground were destroyed by the legionnaires' flamethrowers, leaving them without communication. They came down from their tree positions at night, carefully avoiding the French sentries patrolling the perimeter. After realising they had been tricked, it was decided that two of them would reach Son La, and report what they'd seen. Avoiding the partisans making up the perimeter encirclement was tricky, but one of these tiny spotters managed to break through to the VM headquarters, and give his information to the officer in charge. After being interviewed by the commissars to determine if the spotter's observations were worth following up, it was decided to get in touch with General Giap's HQ and report to him.

Although his divisions were located at Bac Kan, in the Tonkin region of Vietnam, it was decided to force-march a couple of his brigades to Na San, some 80 miles away. These soldiers of the People's Army were experts in navigating the jungle paths and terrain, and it was believed if they travelled 25 to 30 miles a day and night, they could make it in three days. Their armaments would only be lightweight to enable them to cover such a distance in that short time. Although lightly armed, they would ensure they had enough guns and ammunition to hamper an army that was in retreat.

It was left to Jorge to supervise their position and arrange for the placing of the guns, should they come under attack – which their CO said would be unlikely. They were left with a belt-fed machine gun, similar to a Thompson sub-machine gun, and a British Bren used in

WW2. They already had their previously allocated Garand rifles, and a supply of hand grenades. "If all the other strong points are as armed as well as we are, it should be easy holding off any army," assured Jorge.

"What about when our ammo runs out?" asked one of the other legionnaires. Jorge ignored this question, simply having no answer to it. With time to spare, he went for a stroll around the camp to watch the demolition in progress, but was quickly told by an NCO to return to his emplacement and always be at the ready, instead of interrupting other men in their work.

Most of the withdrawal plans were nearing completion, and Hanoi asked how many more flights were needed to finish the abandonment. The CO did not wish to order too many or too few, but with the help of his NCOs, he decided upon a final figure which he believed would transport everything else that was left.

Receiving an important radio message from the partisans was about to spoil the CO's plans. The partisan leader informed Major Foret that, because of the arrival of a sizable advanced guard from General Giap's army, they could no longer hold out and prevent the Vietminh from heading back to the outpost. There was a good chance the whole Vietminh army could reassemble and be ready to march on Na San, where they would carry out an attack. On hearing this devastating news, all hell broke at the camp. Major Foret was hoping to evacuate all the legionnaires forming the rear guard. He swiftly radioed the PAs giving them the bad news, and at the same time put them on full alert.

Parked up on the airstrip was a Dakota, fully loaded and ready to go. Nearby, another was taking on passengers at an alarming rate, with everyone pushing and shoving to get on, and an NCO shouting orders to maintain discipline.

The flight organiser told the CO that four more empty planes were due in within twenty minutes, by which time the runway would be clear for their arrival. It was a logistical nightmare. With the last four empty planes due in less than fifteen minutes, and the chance of an advance army arriving within an hour or two, the situation was desperate. "How long before they arrive?" he asked one of the officers, who was impatiently looking at his watch.

"I don't expect the full army to arrive for a while now, but some frontline skirmishers may get here within the hour. It depends upon when the partisans left their encirclement position, and whether or not they engaged with the enemy."

The major nervously looked at his wristwatch once more, and at the same time glanced up at the sky looking for the four Dakotas. "How on earth did the enemy discover we were in the middle of an evacuation so soon?" asked the harassed major.

"I can only assume that some spies avoided the clear out we had when we drove the enemy back to Son La and waited around, watching our movements. They somehow got the news back to their battalion headquarters, and relayed the information to General Giap," explained his adjutant.

"Well, if that's so, and they had the information earlier, why did they wait until now before deciding to attack?" the major replied.

"I'm sorry, sir, but not knowing when Giap actually received the intel about our withdrawal, I can only assume they waited until most of us had gone, as well as destroying our armaments, leaving us at their mercy."

In fact, General Giap hadn't received the intelligence on the retreat from Na San for a few days after it commenced. To reach the outpost in time with a couple, or just one, of his divisions would take too long. What he decided instead was to dispatch a lightly armed contingent ahead of the main army to create as much havoc to the French as possible. This advance contingent had to travel as light as possible through the dense jungle paths, armed only with a few mortars and rocket-propelled grenades (RPGs). Arriving well before the main army and concentrating on destroying aircraft where they stood on the airstrip, would make it impossible for other planes to land, and hold up the evacuation until reinforcements arrived, perhaps a day or two later.

The waiting plane on the airstrip was fully loaded and took off immediately. This left it clear for the others to land straightway, obviating the need to circle around, waiting for a slot. The vehicle demolition was complete, along with the destruction of the artillery and heavy guns; they were now quite helpless if the impending attack began before the Dakotas could be loaded up.

All was in a panic, with everything being done in double time. The CO had graciously ordered two of the four incoming Dakotas to fly out some of the rear guard – around a hundred or so men. With two more planes behind them, a total of six were expected at different intervals; this would just about complete the evacuation of the entire personnel.

Communication had now ceased, due to the last-minute destruction of the radio equipment; it was too late to inform the aircraft crews of the situation on the ground. Once more, the major looked at his timepiece; after hearing the distinctive sound of the Dakotas, he strained his eyes, and counted four in formation, ready to land. "Order the rear guard from the six southern PAs to smash their weapons and get themselves out here as quickly as they can," he ordered his officer. "At least we'll be able to evacuate a hundred of those who won't be needed. After doing that, the men of the northern and western PAs should be informed they have a good chance of being flown out too... If we don't get attacked!"

The officer and two NCOs quickly headed in the direction of the six-armed positions to give the good news to the defenders, just as the Dakotas came into land. Then he had to run up to the northern PAs, telling the men to wait for a signal from the airstrip, but not to destroy their weapons at all costs. When a CO arrived at PA8 with the orders, Frank called out, "What the fuck's going on? Are we staying or going?"

"Just wait for the signal from the airstrip after the last two planes land, then run like bloody hell to get on board," called out the harassed non-com as he climbed over the sandbags and barbed wire. Next, he had to inform the other groups of defenders. Everyone in the dugout suddenly jumped for joy at the thought of being airlifted out, and not having to stay behind to fight off the enemy, or make the hundred-mile journey over hills and through jungle to an airport in Laos.

After giving orders to the lower PAs, the NCO had to reach one of those on the highest and most northern position. As he'd just made it to the top of the hill, a terrible noise filled his ears as a mortar shell landed just in front of where he stood. He never had a chance and was blown to pieces. Another shell followed, and then another, making a full-blown barrage of mortars zeroed in on this, the most strategic position. Those inside didn't stand a chance as they too took a direct hit, but, nevertheless, those not killed or injured fired back and threw grenades at an unseen enemy.

On the airstrip, as luck had it, three of the Dakotas had landed, loaded up and were ready for take-off, just before a cluster of mortar shells exploded around them. Luckily, these shells landed haphazardly, as the enemy were not in position to zero- in in these mini artillery pieces. Without hesitation, the fourth plane was speedily loaded and took off instantly, in the opposite direction to where the barrage was coming from. "That'll be the *avant-garde* of the main VM army, trying to get a high position to mount their mortars, giving them a direct line of fire onto our airstrip!" called out the major as he watched the Vietminh advance squads storming up the hill to PA24. "If they take that hill, we'll be well and truly fucked!"

The final two Dakotas were coming in to land as arranged, despite the exploding mortar shells peppering the airstrip, which would soon be unsuitable for landing and taking off. The harassed CO was herding his last personnel towards the first plane, giving the pilot orders to fly out as soon as he got the okay. The plane behind had landed and was waiting to be loaded.

The little group of defenders on PA24 were hopelessly outnumbered. Being overwhelmed, they put up a good fight and reverted to hand-to-hand fighting but were all killed without having the chance to surrender. The position was quickly taken over, with rocket-propelled grenade launchers being brought into position, to mount an attack on the airstrip.

Major Foret was the last man to climb aboard the Dakota C-47, slamming the door behind and calling out to get the aircraft moving. The engine was running at full revs and just beginning to taxi for take-off, when a direct hit on its port side engine caused it to explode and burst into flames. Another rocket followed close by, but fortunately passed over the now burning aircraft. "ABANDON SHIP!" called out an officer. "EVERYONE OFF!"

With the CO being last man on, but now the first one off, he quickly ran towards the empty plane behind which was fortunately positioned at an angle to the other Dakota, now in full flame. Because of the offset angle of the static aircraft, and the smoke belching from the other plane, it was impossible to get a good sighting to send another couple of rockets over to finish both aircraft off. Despite the flames, smoke and acrid fumes emanating from the burning C-47, the fleeing passengers managed to clamber out of one plane and into the other. The pilot couldn't see a thing as the smoke was blowing in the same direction as his take-off heading. "Hang on, everyone, I'm about to make a blind take off... Here goes!" called out the flustered pilot as he taxied out of the smoke and into the clearness of the empty airstrip.

Seeing the plane making its escape, the RPG launchers sent another two rockets in its direction, but good luck and bad aiming caused the rockets to miss the moving target. As a grouse or clay pigeon shooter would tell you, 'Always shoot in front of a moving target'. Fortunately, game bird shooting was not a sport favoured by the average Vietnamese rifleman.

With the explosions of rockets and mortar shells around them, Jorge and the other defenders of PA8 made themselves ready to ward off an attack. This was the first time the brothers had been in action and were, at that moment, petrified. Paddy, as usual, was calm, collected, and unphased at the events happening around him. "You must have blood like ice, Paddy, ain't you scared?" asked Eddie.

"Of course I fuckin' am... It's just that I don't show it," he declared calmly.

Jorge was now organising everyone to take up arms and be ready to repel invaders. The main army had yet to arrive, and only the occupants of six PAs were left to defend the outpost. Looking in the direction of the airstrip and affirming everyone had escaped the carnage, one legionnaire suggested, as there was no one to defend, they should surrender without firing a shot.

"Not on your fuckin' life!" responded Jorge. "Those Vietminh are merciless and would stick a bayonet into ya rather than look at ya. Anyway, there ain't many of 'em that we can't 'andle."

"I reckon we should take a vote," replied the legionnaire, whose words had no sooner left his lips when an RPG plunged itself into the outer barbed wire encirclement, throwing up great clouds of turf, soil, and wire fragments.

"There's you answer, matey, the fight is on, get behind them weapons. I'm on the Bren, Paddy an' Eddie, man the machine gun. Let's give the fuckers hell, men!" called out Jorge as he took aim at the dozens of men running towards them.

Sending a couple of short bursts to get his aim and direction right, he then opened right up and emptied his first magazine on the first line of attackers, dropping them like flies. He quickly reloaded and did the same again. Paddy and Eddie gave a few short bursts of their machine gun, as one fed the ammo belt and the other squeezed the trigger and fanned the gun around, dropping everything in its path. The others in the dugout did their share with the rifles they were allocated, and between the indomitable little band, and the defenders in the other PAs, it wasn't long before they'd wiped out the first wave of attackers. Peering through the sandbags and wire which formed their defences, Paddy informed the rest of the group that all he could see were dead bodies, and wounded men crying out in pain.

"That'll learn them bastards that we don't give up without a good fight. Tell you what, boys, get yourselves sorted out to fend off another attack. We ain't killed 'em all, so it won't be long before they come back for some more of the same... And we'll be here to give it 'em!" vowed Jorge. The others in the dugout being happy with the way things had gone, agreed to let Jorge take command and make decisions, as there wasn't an officer or NCO to make any. This pleased him greatly, so he immediately went about organising the defences, and what their next move would be. Looking around at the ammunition they had left was a little disturbing. They had one machine gun belt, about two Bren gun magazines and close to ten cartridge clips for the Garand rifles. They still had a good supply of hand grenades, and decided to use them first whilst they were able to get a good throw.

"What do we do when the ammo runs out?" asked one of the other legionnaires. Jorge was unable to answer the question – once more – as the thought had crossed *his* mind too.

By now it was becoming dark, and as most of the frontrunners of the *avant guarde* had been wiped out by the defenders, they decided to wait for reinforcements before mounting another attack. Fortunately for the defenders, the front wave Vietminh were lightly armed, as speed was the main criteria in their attack plan. They'd used up their supply of RPGs and mortar shells in trying to prevent the aircraft from leaving, however, they'd been successful in destroying one of the C-47s. Although the plane had exploded and caught fire, all passengers survived, and, to the COs credit, not one man was injured or killed during the evacuation. Those of the rear guard didn't fare as well, as they took the brunt of the fighting while trying to defend a crucial position.

As darkness fell, the defenders were all on full alert, as this was the time when unexpected attacks were favoured by the VM, trying to catch them off guard. Jorge informed the men, "We ain't gonna get much sleep tonight lads, as it's more than likely them sly bastards will try to launch a sneak attack!" That was the last thing the VM intended, as all they had to do was wait for reinforcements to arrive, and the remaining defenders would be completely outnumbered and easily overwhelmed.

With the evacuation of those occupants in most armed positions thought not to be necessary in the defence of the now empty outpost, only four – including Jorge's group – were left. They did their share of the fighting and helped defeat the Vietminh in the first attack. Now they too were deciding upon their next move. With communication between them non-existent, Frank decided to take advantage of the darkness, and visit the other PAs to find out their next move. Moving around slowly, and making it known to the other defenders of his presence, Frank organised an impromptu meeting at PA8 with leaders of the other armed positions to decide what to do next.

At the meeting, the leaders, including two corporals, discussed their options. With full knowledge the main VM army would arrive by morning – if not already there – attempting to defend an empty outpost with no strategic value would be pointless. There were no families of women and children along with non-combatants there – they'd all fled to safety. "What's the point of getting killed defending an empty position, which has no people or serviceable arms for the enemy to get their hands on?" asked a corporal.

"I agree, Corporal, no point at all. We should take our chance surrendering to the enemy as the major ordered," pointed out one of the men.

"Or take our chance escaping through the jungle," suggested another.

On hearing this, the corporal stressed the dangers of navigating through the jungle, especially at night and ruled against it. "However," he added, "if anyone is brave or foolish enough to attempt it, I won't stand in their way. On returning to our respective positions, we leaders should point this out to the others and give them a chance to escape if they wish. Other than that, I suggest, rather than fight to our last bullet, we should make plans to surrender. This will include the destruction of our weapons before doing so." The mood amongst the defenders was sombre with some agreeing, and others preferring to fight on.

Each PA had a brief discussion between its defenders, with around two from each deciding upon escape through the jungle. Fortunately, one who decided to take his chance was a Muong tribesman who talked most of the other Muongs and Meos into doing the same. Grouping together, and taking with them food, water, and weapons, they slipped silently and slowly away into the darkness, careful to avoid any sentries posted by the Vietminh who'd thought of the possibility of a breakout by the defenders.

There was more than one occasion when a sentry was alerted by the escapers, but these mainly backward, unpaid, and coerced conscripts, were no match for the Muongs, who were masters in their own territory. After creeping up on a sentry and plunging a knife in him, the legionnaires looked on in horror as the Muong swiftly removed his head, keeping it as a trophy.

Chapter 33

Surrender or Fight On

At the French Airforce base at Hanoi, Major Foret was basking in the praise and laudation of his fellow officers on his magnificent achievement. To evacuate an entire garrison of men and their families under extremely difficult conditions was by no means an easy task. It was considered an even greater accomplishment to arrange and expedite a withdrawal whilst under attack from the enemy. Bringing off such a hazardous feat without the loss of life or serious injury, was indeed something unexpected in the circumstances, and it could only be attributed to the skill and proficiency of one man... Major Foret. He was so certain he'd be given the promotion he deserved. Nothing was mentioned of those left behind, or their part in warding off the attackers to make the evacuation such a success. After all, he'd given them orders to surrender, rather than fight to the death, and have faith in the terms of the Geneva Convention – which, to a large extent, the Vietminh completely ignored.

Back in PA8, plans were afoot to make ready for a surrender; hopeful their enemy would be gracious enough to adhere to the conditions laid down on the treatment of prisoners of war. "I'm afraid you blokes ain't got a bloody clue how these Oriental bastards operate. They'll completely ignore any convention and treat their prisoners as they wish... Very badly!" warned Jorge, as the others began their preparations.

"If that's the case, me old mate, why the fuck are you gonna surrender with us if it's that bad!" retorted Paddy.

"If you lot had agreed to come with me, I'd have taken me chances out in the jungle wi' them Muongy blokes. They seem to know what they're doin'," replied Jorge.

Every now and then, gunshots could be heard coming from the direction of the jungle, indicating possibly the escapees had been discovered and were shooting it out, or were being executed. Hearing these gunshots, Frank suggested to Jorge that it was safer where they were than in the jungle where those who chose to escape were indeed having to fight for their lives. Jorge simply sneered, adding, "The only reason I stayed behind was to look after you blokes, cos I've an idea you're all gonna need Uncle Jorge's expertise in dealing wi' these Vietnamese Commie bastards if you surrender." Happy in the knowledge their good friend Jorge, was going to look after them, the little band of defenders continued with their preparations.

It was still dark when they were paid a final visit from the corporal, who'd take it upon himself to arrange for their surrender. "To fight on in these circumstances would be tantamount to suicide. We have nothing to protect except our lives. Come daylight, it's for sure the VM will mount another attack, and if they've been reinforced and resupplied, it won't take long to overrun our PAs." The sombre-sounding NCO went on to tell his small audience that their last order from Major Foret was to surrender, so there would be no disgrace in carrying it out. "Now we've decided not to fight on, destroy your weapons as you were informed by the CO, and leave nothing of use to the enemy. Eat and drink as much as you can, because everything will be taken away from you, especially food and medical supplies. You'll be searched thoroughly, so don't hide anything they'll easily find on you... It only makes them mad and gives them an excuse to beat you. Do not put up any resistance when they search you, just let the bastards do as they like." There were tears in the eyes of this long-serving veteran as he gave the last instructions before surrendering. "Oh yes, hoist your white flag up now, assuming you made one on the major's instructions. So, I'll say a final good luck, and God be with us all." With his final words, he tried his hardest to hold back his tears along with the others, but finding it so difficult, simply wept uncontrollably.

With the corporal gone, it was Jorge's words that brought the situation back to reality, "And there's me believing these corporals are tough and have no feelings; just shows 'ow wrong you can be!" After a short pause for reflection, the men went about destroying their weapons in the manner suggested by their CO before he made his departure to safety.

The lump hammer was used on the Bren gun and the machine gun, rendering them useless. Garand rifles were shoved into the soft soil, and their triggers squeezed, making them to unable to be fired again. Grenades had their fuses removed and destroyed under the hammer – being careful to do so. Food was eaten and water drunk, along with a couple of bottles of Legion red wine. Jorge suggested hiding some medicaments, such as quinine tablets or other small objects, down their underpants, hoping the searchers wouldn't make them strip off completely.

"I wonder where they'll take us all," asked one of the other legionnaires.

"I expect they'll have some sort of prison camp to keep their captives. I did hear that quite a few men disappeared after some of the battles fought over here in the last year or two." replied Eddie.

"Let's hope it's more humane than them Korean prisons!" commented Jorge. "Not only that, but 'ow far is it to the nearest one, and 'ow will we get there?"

Such questions did nothing to put the men's minds at ease, making them all very nervous. Whilst this speculation as to their impending incarceration was discussed, one legionnaire was on his knees, holding a crucifix close to his chest, eyes closed, hands clasped together, reciting a prayer. One or two others followed suit and joined him, hoping for spiritual guidance and divine help. Jorge refused to go down on his knees, and instead stared upwards in search of something, but was unable to find it.

The whole atmosphere in PA8 was mournful if nothing else. It was as if everyone present was in the condemned cell, waiting for the hangman to appear with a priest. Each man there was used to some form of hardship, and had experienced dangerous situations before, especially Jorge, but this was entirely different. Everyone seemed to be impotent, powerless to save themselves, and relying upon an unknown pitiless enemy to decide their fate; what a hopeless position they were all in.

Dawn had just broken, bringing with it a heavy mist, which was always prevalent in the low-lying valleys. Not much could be seen from the dugouts in the PAs. Jorge suggested they could have taken advantage of this by slipping away into the jungle. "It's the same every morning, so why the hell didn't we think about it!" he called out.

"For fuck's sake, Jorge, you had your chance to fuck off, and you never took it... So, leave it at that!" called out Frank, who by now was becoming tired of everything which came out of Jorge's mouth.

"Now then, lads, let's just calm it down a little; we're all on edge and the last thing we want now is to fall out with each other!" uttered a calm and collected Paddy. The two men turned to face one another other, giving a huge hug, and apologising, saying it wouldn't happen again.

"Save your anger for the enemy, not each other!" called out one of the wiser legionnaires. "We're gonna need to stick together with no falling out; we're all on edge, and

now is the time to put our Legion training to the test!"
Everyone agreed. It was the waiting which made
everyone a little tetchy.

"I 'ope them fuckers out there 'ave got decent eyesight,"
uttered Jorge

"Why?" asked Eddie.

"So they can see our white flags in this bleedin' fog!" he
replied in his inimitable manner.

This bit of banter brought one or two laughs in the
dugout but didn't do much to alleviate the tenseness
pervading the atmosphere. However, they didn't have
long to wait, as events were about to commence.
A Vietminh officer, along with a group of his men,
approached the defenders in their dugouts, brandishing a
white flag. The moment when surrendering soldiers are
trying to have their capitulation recognised and accepted
by the enemy can be the most dangerous. In this case, it
was more so, as their weapons had all been destroyed or
de-commissioned. This made them particularly vulnerable
should the enemy decide not to recognise their white flag.
Not knowing what to do caused the atmosphere inside
the bunker to be very tense. This was it; the defenders
were completely at the mercy of the attackers.

"What do we do now?" asked Eddie to the others.

"Just sit tight and wait… All will be well," replied one
of the wiser of the legionnaires once more, trying to
sound optimistic, and alleviate the fears of the others.

The words had hardly left his lips, when two heavily armed Vietminh burst into to their dugout, forcing its defenders outside at gunpoint. Stern-faced and aggressive, these young soldiers were almost as nervous as those they were pointing their guns at.

The men walked slowly out into the early morning mist, clambering over the barbed wire and turf barricades, with their hands held high above their heads, giving their enemy no cause to squeeze the triggers of their guns. All was solemn and ceremonial, as if the situation followed an agreed and rehearsed pattern between the victors and the vanquished... Each knew his part and how to play it. The same scene was enacted along the line, as each strong point surrendered in turn. As soon as the legionnaires came out of their dugouts, Vietminh soldiers stormed in to make sure everyone was out, including the wounded. Whilst this macabre ceremony was underway, Frank looked along the line and counted over fifty men with their hands in the air, and another four, wounded and lying on the ground.

Satisfied everyone was out of their defensive positions, and no one was left inside, the men were searched from head to toe, being 'patted down' clumsily by the stony-faced enemy. One legionnaire objected to this personal search, and made his feelings known to his searchers. He was immediately forced to the ground, followed by a beating from the butts of the VM rifles, and a few heavy kicks to make sure. This treatment caused the unfortunate soldier to lose consciousness, whereupon he received more kicks to make sure he wasn't faking. Those looking on helplessly knew it would be futile to object to anything the enemy wished to do, and to refuse would earn them a good beating.

Following this incident, the VM officer ordered the defenders to squat on the ground with their hands on their heads after they'd been searched. They were forced to watch ashamedly as a red and gold embroidered Vietminh flag was hoisted above their headquarters, amidst the cheers and hat-waving of their enemy. This ignominious ceremony did much to dampen the spirits and morale of the defeated men... As it was meant to.

After being searched and checked over by various VM officials, they were led away and ordered to squat once more and listen to a speech from a political commissar. Being criminals and murderers, they would be under sentence of death and be executed within the hour. This completely unnerved those listening, believing they would be treated as prisoners of war. One or two protested, but were quickly hushed by their comrades, as this outburst could bring on the executions prematurely. The leading legionnaire corporal protested to the VM commissar, pointing out the conditions laid down by the Geneva Convention. After being told the capitalist-inspired convention wasn't recognised by the Vietminh, the corporal realised he was wasting his time and made no further protests.

This statement may well have caused a demonstration and uproar, but the corporal advised against it, as it would give the enemy the excuse to fire on them. One man present realised the intentions of these political commissars, as he'd come across something similar previously in Korea. Reassuring his chums this was a big ruse helped ease the seriousness of the situation, but it still had the men feeling ill at ease.

"Because of the infinite goodness, generosity and understanding of our great lord, Uncle Ho, we have been advised that rather than execute you as criminals and murderers, His Greatness has instructed us to take you to a place of rehabilitation and fulfilment, where you will be shown the error of your ways, and have plenty of time to atone for your sins."

"What a complete load of bollocks!" retorted Jorge, after hearing the speech spoken in perfect French by one of the young, well-educated commissars. Luckily, Jorge's remarks were out of earshot of the political officer, otherwise it would have warranted him a good beating, assuming he understood what was being said... Not many did! Speaking softly, Jorge advised his group to go along with everything the commissars said, and not to argue with them. "It's the only way to survive, lads, just nod and do what these slimy little bastards tell you; disobeying will only get you shot.

The VM officer took the legionnaire corporal to one side, and after giving a long talk, allowed him to address the squatting men on their next move, and how to go about it. "We are all being taken to a camp some 60 miles from here where we'll be kept until we have 'atoned' for our sins," advised the corporal. "At a rate of around 10 miles a day, a week should see us there. If anyone tries to escape *en route,* he'll be severely dealt with. That's them talking, not me," he insisted. "Personally, I wouldn't recommend it, as, without food, water or a weapon, you won't stand a chance." Apart from fifty fit men, there were four wounded. The commissar advised that unless they were taken along with the others, they would be bayoneted.

This prompted the corporal to insist they do everything possible to help these wounded, and if necessary, carry them the 60 miles to the prison camp. This caused a few groans from the men, but eventually they accepted that rather than standby and watch them be executed, they would take their turn helping them. Three of the wounded were able to hobble along on their own two feet, but one severely wounded soldier needed a stretcher, which was swiftly sourced with the permission of the VM officer in charge. Six of the men, which included a corporal, were pulled out of the group and ordered to squat down and wait for orders. There was a little tension within the group as no one knew what the enemy intended to do with them. The six men singled out would soon learn their fate.

The remaining prisoners were forced to stand in line along with the wounded, and begin the long slow march to Camp No. 4E, otherwise known as Chao Mung ('welcome' in Vietnamese). Surprisingly, there were only around ten men guarding the column, but they all had guns, and were under orders to shoot anyone who broke out of line or tried to escape. With a full week's march ahead of them, through rough jungle terrain crawling with poisonous snakes and spiders, along with the occasional tiger, the prisoners were resigned to their fate, and soldiered on, wondering what the next day would bring. Jorge couldn't help looking behind him at the six men ordered to remain, believing they might be executed, but for what reason?

Chapter 34

The Suicide Squad

The six men left behind from the main column were about to learn their fate. With two nervous guards pointing guns at them, there was little they could do if they were facing execution. They remembered the words of the commissar, calling them criminals who deserved to be shot, but instead they would be taken to a place of re-education and fulfilment. Unfortunately, they were separated from the main group, which led them to believe their treatment would be different; harsher, perhaps.

Speculation was rife as to their fate, but with the arrival of the commissar, accompanied by a half-dozen stony-faced soldiers, it was soon revealed. "Gentlemen, I imagine you are all wondering why you have been left behind." He paused for a moment awaiting a response. "Well, let me put you out of your misery." There were a few gasps from the waiting men, wondering if the accompanying soldiers were about to form a firing squad. "You six have been selected for a very important and dangerous assignment." One or two relieved gasps came from the prisoners, assuming they'd need to be alive to perform an *assignment*. The commissar continued with his long-awaited delivery, "Yes, you have been selected to carry out very important and dangerous work for the brave soldiers of Uncle Ho."

"Hurry up and get on with it, you pompous little twit!" muttered one the squatting prisoners.

"You have all been selected to clear the mines and booby traps that I'm sure were planted by your predecessors. I assume you know of their whereabouts, so the job should be relatively safe and easy for you," he continued, with a sarcastic smirk on his face.

The corporal was first to respond, saying, "We only arrived here a couple of days ago, so we have no idea what or where these devices were planted... If at all."

"If that is the case, Corporal, you shouldn't have anything to worry about. So, get on your feet and begin the search. And by the way, should any of you decide to make a run for it, my men's orders are shoot to kill!"

The other captives had been on the march for around four hours, all feeling very weary. They took it in turns helping the wounded but realised it would be impossible to carry those who couldn't walk the whole of the distance to the camp, some 60 miles along rough jungle paths. Fortunately, their guards were tiring too, so a brief halt was called. Water was in short supply and not much was given to them, making matters worse. Fortunately, their Legion training made the march easier, as 20 or even 30 miles a day was commonplace to them, but with rest periods, plus food and drink in between to sustain them.

After a half hour, they were on the march again, slowly but surely plodding on through the dense jungle, doing their best to cheer one another up, but not appearing too cheerful lest their guards disapproved and made it harder for them. It began to darken, making an overnight stop inevitable. They were forced to remove their boots and leave them in a pile until morning, leaving them to settle down to a night's sleep, oblivious to what awaited them in the morning.

The six 'chosen ones' at Na San had finished their day's work at the outpost, finding no hidden landmines or booby traps, leading their oppressors to believe they weren't trying hard enough. Losing his slightly friendly tone now, the commissar let the six men know he was displeased with their efforts, informing them that unless things improved the next day, a punishment would be administered – although failing to describe what form it would take.

They were ordered into one of the PAs for the night with a single guard outside watching over them. Plans were afoot to put an end to this futile charade, so the corporal made suggestions as to what their next move would be. Lots of mumbling went on through the night, with each man making his suggestions, and weighing up their options, as well as the consequences, should they fail. After delivering his final plan to the other five, the corporal took a show of hands which decided unanimously what they intended.

The six were rudely awakened at around 6am and forced out of their bunker into the cold early morning mist. The guards gave them a very weak tea and a handful of rice to begin their day, after which they were ordered out to the perimeter to look for landmines. Unfortunately, their search was becoming futile, until one legionnaire, after inspecting the inside of one of the decommissioned trucks, came upon a hidden - or forgotten - cache of hand grenades. He quickly reported back to the corporal, along with a plan he'd quickly formulated. This plan was to set a couple of grenades off, indicating the presence of booby traps hidden in the trucks. Hopefully, this would deter any of the VM guards from entering inside the trucks, giving the legionnaires time and opportunity to make thorough searches of them, and possibly finding more arms inside. After demonstrating to the VM the trucks were booby trapped by exploding a couple of grenades – at a safe distance from them – they were allowed to continue their search.

Sure enough, after checking a few more trucks, a couple of sub-machine guns and half a dozen handguns were discovered. As luck had it, a first aid kit and a few tins of beef, along with some biscuits were found. The corporal's brain was working overtime, thinking quickly of a plan to make their discoveries come into use for the planned escape they'd formulated the night before. Insisting on a break because of the pressure in discovering more booby traps – four more grenades were exploded to validate the fact that a dangerous threat existed – the men were given time to rest and regain their composure. A plan made by the corporal was revealed to the other five men.

With the indiscriminate explosions occurring around them, the guards, and indeed their officers, were too reticent to go anywhere near the men whilst engaged in their search for more booby traps. This gave the plotters ample time to store away the guns, ammunition, first aid kit, and food they'd foraged for their intended break-out planned for that night. A couple more grenades were exploded, giving the legionnaires the excuse to finish for the day, for without a good night's rest, they'd be unable to continue with their hazardous job the following morning. Miraculously, no VM guards dared enter anywhere near to the area where the explosions came from; had they done so, they'd have wondered why so many trucks were still intact. However, the officers were content to let their captives continue their highly dangerous task, provided none of their men, or indeed themselves, were injured in the process.

Before entering their makeshift prison cell – the PA dugout – the six legionnaires were searched thoroughly and given what amounted to the evening meal... A handful of coarse rice and mug of weak tea. The well-spoken commissar entered the dugout and congratulated them on their discoveries. "It seems quite a few booby traps are becoming evident, and there's lots more for you men to do. With this in mind, I am allowing a team of my own men to accompany you tomorrow – at a safe distance – to learn the techniques you are familiar with, and the safe way you go about discovering and detonating these devices without any injuries being sustained." The commissar droned on in his boring tone, "Tomorrow I shall be there with you to discover how you manage to do it so well; although we are enemies, I have the greatest admiration for you all. Well done!"

Waiting until he'd gone, the corporal muttered, "He's turned out to be such a nice bloke, it's a bloody shame we have to leave tonight, but after hearing what he had to say, it won't be a moment too soon."

One of the others quipped, whilst looking at his handful of rice, "I can't wait to be on the run tomorrow, so we can have some of that tinned beef instead of this rice crap!" The others just laughed but became serious as the corporal delegated their separate tasks.

"We have guns and ammo. A couple of tins of beef which won't last us long, but our biggest problem will be finding water. If we are heading to Mung Sai in Laos, it's at least a hundred-mile hike."

One of the men, smiling all over his weather-beaten face, stuffed his hand down his trousers and withdrew it, producing a piece of paper. Handing it to the corporal, he said with a smile, "Do I get a special prize for this, Corp?"

His superior was taken aback when he unfolded it, saying, "Fuck me; I don't believe it. It's a map of North Vietnam and Laos! Well done, that man, you'll sure enough get a bloody prize when we get back to civilisation. I'll buy you drinks for a month. How you smuggled it past those bloody goons is a miracle. You didn't manage to find a compass as well, did you?"

The soldier once more slipped his hand inside his pants, saying, "Er no, Corp, very sorry."

This bit of humour put the men's minds at ease, as they were fully aware as to the danger of their mission taking effect in six hours' time; enough to go over the plan and get some sleep into the bargain. Unfortunately, prisoner guarding arrangements had changed, which was a concern for the six men planning a break-out. Instead of *one* VM keeping watch of them, suddenly it was doubled up, which caused a little anxiety to the plotters. "Do you think they suspect anything?" one man asked the corporal. "The commissar did mention the VMs would be following us tomorrow to learn our techniques."

"Don't worry about it, they'll have more to worry about than us if they open any of those truck doors. I've wired a couple of 'em up, so that if they open the driver's door, a grenade will explode. That should keep 'em busy for a while. Now get some kip; I've got to figure out how to silence those two guards before we make our break. And by the way, none of you open any doors on the trucks; leave it to me, I know exactly which are booby-trapped"

The corporal's dilemma was how to silence the guards. He didn't really wish to kill them, but realised if he overpowered and tied them up – which would be an easy task for him, an experienced soldier – when their officer discovered they'd allowed the prisoners to escape with *their own* guns, killing them would be preferable to the punishment metered out by the officers, in particular the commissar. His mind was made up as he searched around for something to use as a garotte. Luckily, there were plenty of parachute cords lying about, so he carefully selected two, cutting them to size with a blade he'd found during his daily tasks.

The time selected for the break-out was 3am; one of the quietest times of the night – or early morning. The men were all ready to leave after the guards had been 'silenced'. Creeping up behind them, coiling the cords around their necks and pulling tight, not only squeezed the life out of them, but crushed their voice boxes, making it impossible to call for help. Dragging them into the dugout and going through their pockets, earned them nothing, but they were rewarded with two Russian automatic rifles. Ensuring no one else was about, the six men scurried towards the truck where their cache of arms and other findings were stored. Now fully loaded up, they made their way across to the perimeter and the jungle.

They encountered a sentry near to the jungle's edge, but being surprised and confused, he didn't feel the whack across his head which came from the butt of one of the newly acquired rifles. They had ample time to set a few more booby traps with the hand grenades found hidden in one of the trucks. This technique was taught during their basic training in Algeria, causing the deaths or mutilation of many an unsuspecting fellagha terrorist.

With a clear run ahead of them and a good distance from the outpost, they decided to rest up until daylight. They needed to take a bearing from the early sunrise to plot their southwestern approach towards Laos, and eventually the airstrip at Muong Sai. Here, they hoped to be picked up by one of the helicopter patrols operating from the airbase. However, being more than 100 miles away, but with determination and extreme resolution, they intended to make the journey in less than a week, allowing nothing or no one to get in their way.

Chapter 35

Camp Chao Mung

Out of the forty-eight men who were force marched through the jungle to the Vietminh prison camp some 60 miles away, only thirty-six arrived at the camp alive. Of the twelve who didn't make it, the wounded were the first to perish. The gruelling seven-day march through dense jungle paths with little or no food and water was too much for them. Some asked to be left behind, but after doing so were shot by their pitiless guards. Some men succumbed to poisonous snake bites as well as being stung by all types of insects.

Huge rats, much bigger than our domestic cats, would appear at night, gnawing through the boots of the men, who, being tied up, were helpless to drive them off. There were men who, rather than carry on with the punishing march, decided to break off on their own and try to escape. None of them got far and were bludgeoned to death on the spot where they were discovered. Jorge and the other three kept together, each doing his best to help his comrades when required.

Trying to eat leaves from the variety of tropical plants made many men ill, forcing them to throw up everything inside their stomachs, leaving nothing sustainable to replace the meagre ration of rice they'd been given. The whole scene was one of horror and dismay, as none of the wretched legionnaires knew if they'd survive the arduous journey or not. There seemed no end to this nightmare, and even when the pitiful and forlorn little band arrived at Camp Chao Mung, the sight of the prison where they'd spend their incarceration plunged them into the depths of despair.

The actual outpost had a low perimeter around it, and a gateway adjoining the dirt track road. Situated inside this garrison was a compound, surrounded by bamboo and barbed wire, where the captured soldiers were held. A series of little huts made from bamboo, with banana tree leaves for their roofs, were where the inmates slept or sheltered from the heavy rains, which flooded the whole area at certain times of the year. Those men not out in work parties – mostly the sick – just lay about in the huts or wandered around the camp to keep their limbs from seizing up. Disease was rife, and many men suffered from malaria, dysentery, or typhoid. These men had no medical aid whatsoever, not even a dose of quinine. They were simply left to starve, as those who couldn't or wouldn't work, received no food. Their comrades helped by sharing their meagre allowance of rough unwashed rice with them, but it meant depriving themselves of any nutrition they'd need when in the work details. The whole situation was one of hopelessness and despair.

The gates of the compound were opened when the newcomers arrived, leaving them to fend for themselves with no instructions or orders on what they should do. Their guards merely herded them all inside, locked the gates and ambled over to the guard room where they reported the arrival of the newcomers to the commandant.

The four pals spread out, trying to get the feel of the place, regarding food, sleeping arrangements and washing facilities. When asked about these, one of the regulars simply replied, "There ain't none! No food, no beds, no medicines, no nothing. What you see is what you get, a big balloon with no skin around it... Sweet fuck all!"

Surprisingly, there were tiny fires burning with steel pans full of water slowly simmering. Here, the water from a little brook which flowed through the camp was boiled before drinking, or used to boil the unwashed rice they were given at the end of the day. It wasn't long before an official-looking group, comprising of an officer, two armed guards and the camp commandant, made an appearance. The newcomers were ordered to form a line where each man's name was recorded in a ledger. Instructions were given that a roll call would be called each day when the names of everyone present – including those who died overnight – were checked with those in the ledger. Preparations would be made to bury the dead by the appointed gravediggers, and those remaining would be allotted tasks in the various work parties. Rules about punishments for misconduct, such as attempting to escape, theft or fighting with each other, were read out, as well as the camp regime concerning hygiene, sleeping and general behaviour. Any inmate accused of insulting or striking a guard would automatically face execution. A political commissar would visit twice weekly for 're-education' sessions. Those who did well earned points, which would be exchanged for extra rice at the end of each session. After being informed of these and other rules and regulations, the commandant and his team left the compound for the officers' building, situated far away from the compound... And the offensive smell.

"What do we do when we want a crap or a piss?" asked a new intern.

"Follow me and I'll give you a tour of our humble abode," replied one of the regulars. "It ain't much, but it's all we 'ave." He told them to follow him as he pointed out places of 'interest'. The lavatory was a huge open cesspit, buzzing with thousands of flies and other insects. "We call this the 'bog' or the 'shit pit', whichever you wish to call it," he told his disgusted onlookers.

After being shown the toilet facilities, the new boys were conducted to the dormitories, an odd mixture of homemade huts built from bamboo. Two large huts at the end of the row were known at hospital wards, where the sick and dying were carried to lay on a floor of banana leaves. Here they'd spend their last few days, or hours, which was often the case. When asked about food once more – as they hadn't been fed that day – they were told, "No work, no rice." It was as simple as that. "It's not all bad, though," went on the self-appointed tour guide, "sometimes the cooks in the camp kitchens empty their bins in the compound. They just roll up and throw their rubbish at the wire; some gets through, some doesn't, it's just your luck." He went on to tell them of a Dutchman, who, as a boy in Holland during the German occupation, was forced to eat rat meat his father had caught and cooked for the family. "It was either that or starve. Sometimes one of the lads will catch one here; he'd skin it, chop it up and cook it, sharing it with everyone; or them that wanted to eat it."

"Rat meat? Urrgh," called out one of the men. "What's it taste like?" he asked.

"Just like rabbit – lovely!" the tour guide replied, smacking his lips.

Suddenly, a noise outside the gates took everyone's attention. The work parties had returned and were being given their daily rice ration. After receiving it, they made their way through the gates to where those who hadn't worked that day had the water prepared to cook it. Each had a particular comrade who *had* worked, and kindly shared his rations with one who couldn't. This occurred regularly, and had it not been the case, many men would have died prematurely.

The work parties were engaged in cutting down trees, and producing logs for building entrenchments, digging out pathways and roads, or planting and harvesting rice from one of the many small villages out in the flat, wet areas. At times, a friendly villager would give some of the prisoners a little food, but were harshly punished if found out.

So it was that the newcomers were familiarised with their new home, and told of the dos and don'ts, which, if adhered to, did much to keep harmony in the compound, and not set man against man, which is what the camp authorities wanted. When Frank asked one of the working parties about food, he was simply told the same. "No work, no food," he replied nonchalantly.

Occasionally, a couple of guards would enter inside the compound looking for a little sport. They'd be smoking a cigarette whilst walking around, attracting a few followers. When the cigarette was down to its last few puffs, they'd toss it to the ground and delight in watching the inmates wrestle each other for the stub. Sometimes they'd throw a little food around simply to see the same reaction, then wade in with their batons if the situation got out of hand.

Whilst hearing of this sickening practice, Eddie asked if this was a regular occurrence. "Oh yes," he was told, "it gets worse than this at times." He went on to tell Eddie of other odious and sickening events which occurred there, simply for the entertainment of the bored guards. They would enter the compound and choose a prisoner at random to give them a 'little fun'. The guards would escort this unfortunate prisoner out of the compound and into the jungle. He would be told if he could outrun the two guards, he'd go free; they'd even give him a ten-minute start. Being half starved and in bad health, the hapless prisoner would fall to the ground in less than ten minutes. When the brutal guards came upon him, he was kicked most savagely, and dragged back to camp where after a couple of days he would die.

"Does this occur regularly?" asked Frank.

"Oh yes, at least once a week. They always pick on someone who's ill and can't work. That way they get rid of the sick ones who have no value to them... Except entertainment."

After hearing this, Jorge agreed that none of them should ever be allowed to get in such a situation, and if they were anywhere close to being that ill, the others would look after them. The storyteller went on to relate to other occasions when more hideous events occurred. He told his little audience of the time a man was accused of attacking a guard, which was false. "They tied his hands, laid him across a log on the ground, and simply hacked him to pieces." There were gasps from those listening, in utter horror and disbelief.

The four comrades swore that none of the barbaric practices would happen to them, and one way or another, they would do anything to prevent it. They sorted themselves out with a hut for the night, wondering what the next day would bring. All they had for breakfast was hot water with a little rice some of the regulars had collected for them. On this diet they were expected to do a day's work.

The assembly was called by a guard blowing a trumpet, when the camp commandant and his entourage called out everyone's name, ticking them off in his ledger. Work detail parties were called out, including the names of the men designated. Jorge and Paddy were given work at the village, planting rice, whilst Frank and Eddie drew the wood cutting detail. There was no transport to any of the worksites, and each man had to make his way there by foot, in boots or shoes which were just about worn right through. No gloves or other protective garments were issued, which left the men with very sore hands as well as feet – especially after the long march back to camp from their day's work.

Before entering the gates to their compound, each man received his rice ration. This meagre amount was wholly inadequate for the needs of one who has worked all day and had to walk there and back from his work site... In rough terrain. Luckily, on that day, the garbage bins had been emptied outside the camp, where the brutal guards got their pleasure from kicking it around, whilst watching the starving men desperately trying to gather it up. They did, however, manage to scoop up a certain amount of potato peelings, along with other tops and tails of root vegetables. They even discovered two chicken heads, along with their insides, which had been discarded by the camp cooks. These valuable findings were carefully sorted out and made into a stew which the whole camp could enjoy... Including the sick and dying.

The whole routine continued, day in, day out, with the occasional visit from a commissar who'd give 'enlightenment' sessions to the prisoners. The rule was to go along with everything they were told and be in complete agreement with the Communist philosophy. This meant points were earned, giving those who attended the classes an extra ration of food.

Jorge got on very well with the commissar, congratulating him on his good work of enlightening the working classes, and debunking the ways of the capitalist society. In fact, Jorge got on well with everyone, including the two guards nicknamed Vu Phu and Du Con, or, in English, Brute and Thug. This pair were selected for executions and other brutal forms of punishments; therefore, Jorge did his best to stay on good terms with them. He'd perform little tricks and acts of magic, as one would at children's parties. Jorge would juggle with two, three and sometimes four round stones to the delight of these two brutes. Sometimes 'the magician' would put a stone in his mouth and pretend to swallow it; then it would reappear from behind either Brute or Thug's ear. This delighted them to the extent that they always searched Jorge out for a little light entertainment; that is when they weren't beating some hapless inmate half to death. It had its rewards too, as quite often the two merciless beasts would reward their entertainer with a cigarette or slice of meat, and even a whole bag of leftovers, which the camp enjoyed, careful to be out of sight of the terrible duo.

As the days of their incarceration passed by, Jorge had less to do with the brothers, but spent more time with Paddy and a Muong prisoner, who the Vietminh allowed to live because of his local knowledge. It was this that Jorge was after, and quite often, tucked away in the corner of the compound, he could be seen drawing diagrams in the rough soil, being most careful to scrub them out later, leaving no evidence of what had been discussed.

"What's that old bastard up to?" asked Frank to his brother.

"Search me, bruv, but you can bet your life he's up to no good!"

One morning at roll call, the bodies of those who'd died in the night were brought out, awaiting burial after they were accounted for. The two men who formed the burying detail were nowhere to be found, until it was discovered that, after digging eight graves between them the previous day, one collapsed with fatigue, whilst the other died of sheer exhaustion. Being undernourished and overworked put these two gravediggers out of action permanently. After a little discussion, the commandant asked Brute and Thug to find another detail to dig the men's graves. Seizing this opportunity, Jorge volunteered, stating he was qualified for the job, as his grandfather, Horace, was the gravedigger at his local church back in Bedworth. Of course, this revelation made little difference to qualify for the job, but as it was Jorge, the deadly duo granted him the job – along with Paddy as his helpmate.

Indeed, Jorge's grandad, Horace, *was* the local gravedigger at St. Giles Church, and passed on little tips to his grandson about the gravedigging business. One such tip was to always to keep one's spade sharpened well, as it made the digging much easier; a piece of information his grandson never forgot.

"What the fuck's going on, you old bastard, what are you up to?" asked Frank.

Without looking at his friend and comrade, Jorge replied, "The less you're seen talking to me, the better it'll be for you. Just ignore me and I'll do the same for you." A strange reaction to a simple question, but Frank knew better than to challenge his friend's motives, realising Jorge had something planned, and didn't wish his friends to be involved should it go wrong.

The work details marched off to their various assignments, whilst Jorge and Paddy remained behind to begin their gravedigging project. There were only two graves to dig that morning, but Paddy suggested they should have one or two more dug to keep in reserve. Constantly being watched by the 'Devil's duo', Jorge asked permission to return inside the camp to assess the condition of future 'customers'. Once inside, they paid a visit to the 'hospital' shacks where those waiting to die lay, being attended to by volunteer – but wholly unqualified – medics. Sizing up the situation, it was decided to dig a further two graves only, to make their job easier for the next day.

The death rates in the camp were totally unacceptable by any reasonable standard, as medicines and qualified medical treatment was non-existent. Men died from all types of tropical diseases, including cholera and typhus, plus other diseases brought on by drinking water contaminated by rat and other animal faeces. Once struck down with either of these ailments, recovery was unachievable, impossible, in fact. With the lack of medicines, along with poor, or in some cases, no diet, death was inevitable. It was as if, rather than execute their prisoners, the captors preferred to work them to death, either by disease or starvation.

The rules of war, and treatment of captives, were completely ignored by the Vietminh regime.

This routine of working, eating little or no food of nutritional value, fighting off diseases, without washing or change of clothes, simply went on, day after day. New prisoners were brought in, whilst the older ones died. It was this which drew the brothers to organise something to break this tedium and deadlock. Pretty soon, the brothers realised, it would be them lying outside the compound waiting to be buried – possibly by Jorge and Paddy. The critical aim was to remain alive and as fit as they could, eating and keeping their strength up. Fortunately, when they joined the Legion, they were given a cocktail of vaccinations and injections to protect them from most diseases. Why, they thought, had so many legionnaires, after being immunised against most diseases, contracted them, and died as a result. All they could think of was that a poor diet affected their immune system, making them more vulnerable. The brothers knew rescue was impossible, and unless something drastic was to happen, organised by them alone, they would spend the rest of their miserable days in Camp Chao Mung.

Chapter 36

Heads Will Roll

By stark contrast to the misfortunes of the remainder of the rear guard, who were incarcerated in Camp Chao Mung, the six who broke out of the outpost at Na San, where they were forced to search out booby traps and landmines, fared much better. After leaving a trail of devastation in their wake, by mere chance they came upon a friendly Meo village. Once fed and watered, the Meos contacted the local partisan group who led them out of the jungle and set them on the road to Muong Sai in Laos. Being in friendlier territory, they were soon picked up by a helicopter patrol operating from the airbase. They were in the best of health when rescued, and after a long period of recouperation, found themselves back in action, but not in Vietnam. Had they been captured a second time, they would have faced instant execution. They were, however, able to report on the other men in their group who were marched away, but unable to state where they were taken to.

Such good fortune wasn't to be for the inmates of the Vietminh prison camp, as all they had to look forward to was a slow and lingering death, brought on by starvation. This wasn't to be for Jorge and his good pal, Paddy. For weeks he'd worked on an escape plan, and very soon, if circumstances prevailed, he would activate it... Quite subtly by Jorge's standards. The pair had been scraping together a little food that might see them through for a couple of days, in the hope of finding more once on the run. The futility of making an escape had been discussed frequently by the captives, and the result of such a foolhardy venture was made evident by the capture, torture and finally beheading by their cruel and sadistic guards, of some who did. Anyone deciding to make a break into the jungle without having a workable plan of action, was simply asking for trouble.

Legionnaire Jorge Jenson wasn't the brightest of men, but he was shrewd. He studied people and their habits; in particular, he'd made a careful study of the two most feared and brutal guards in the camp, Vu Thu and Du Con. He'd got on the good side of these two brutes, and amused them with his puerile party tricks, particularly the disappearing and reappearing of objects, which delighted this pair of ghouls. They loved to watch his tricks, as well as his adept skill juggling stones in various numbers. He earned little treats from them for his entertainment, and he'd earned their trust... Though not altogether.

Paddy and Jorge did their best to avoid the other two in their quartet of good friends, and although this could be misconstrued as unfriendly, Frank and Eddie knew something was afoot; what, they didn't know, or found hard to imagine. "Something's going on with that pair," remarked Frank. "I hope they don't do something stupid and get their heads chopped off!" Eddie agreed there was something going on, but knowing Jorge, it would be anything *but* stupid.

It was a sunny, humid day in the area where Camp Welcome – or Chao Mung – was situated. The Monsoon season was over – just about – and the weather outlook much drier – ideal weather for an escape. The roll call was completed, and each detail had been despatched to their various workstations where they'd spend the day – as every other day – working for the army of Ho Chi Minh. The sick and disabled were left behind to perform menial tasks, such as boiling water, preparing what little food they had for the evening meal, and caring for the sick and dying; speaking of who, those that passed away in the night were left outside the camp, awaiting burial, in the ever-increasing graveyard outside the camp perimeter.

The two gravediggers, also acting as undertakers, went about their grim task of giving the departed as good a Christian burial as possible. After internment, Jorge would close his eyes and say a prayer whilst looking up at the sky to where he assumed the Almighty dwelt. Even the brutish guards joined in the brief service – being of the Catholic faith – hoping they'd gain some forgiveness for repenting their many sins. Two graves had been dug on the previous shift and as there were only two bodies to inter; they set about digging two more. "Okay, me old Irish mate, this is where we put our plan into action," whispered Jorge to his pal. "Dig them graves three feet deeper like we agreed, then wait for my next move... Got it?" he said quietly to Paddy.

Following his mate's advice, Paddy went about deepening the grave another three feet... Or thereabouts.

The bodies of those who died in the night were now ready for burial. There were no coffins or even a shroud to cover them, but Jorge insisted they were interred with a covering of banana leaves. The two guards were smoking and chatting away to each other, oblivious to Jorge sharpening the edges of his entrenching spade with a stone. Spitting on it every now and then helped bring an even keener edge to its blade. Even as he ran his fingers along the edge, the guards were too busy to notice or even ask why.

His mind went back to the time in Korea, when his unit was ambushed by a sniper hiding in a haystack. A huge grin appeared on his face, remembering how he dispatched the sniper when he stuck his head out from the haystack after Jorge set fire to it. His smile developed into a chuckle when he relived the moment he put the assassin out of commission for good, sending him to eternity with a couple of swift strokes of his entrenching spade. *I wonder if I could do it again?* he asked himself. Then, answering his question, replied, *of course you can, Jorge, me boy... Of course you can.* To make any plan work well, one must have complete confidence in one's ability to carry it out successfully.

Five miles away, the other two members of the 'quartet' were engaged in planting rice outside a village used frequently to supply food for the armies of Ho Chi Minh and General Giap. It wasn't too bad a job, made favourable by the little perks bestowed upon them by the friendly and sympathetic farmers and villagers. Pieces of the locally baked bread – a type of flat pancake – were left out for the prisoners during one of the infrequent breaks, taken whilst waiting for more rice plants to arrive. During these breaks, the guards took the opportunity to avail themselves of the favours the local girls had to offer. In exchange for cigarettes or other forms of payment, these ladies could earn a reasonable little income from their various sexual favours. If these immoral escapades had been brought to the attention of their superiors, it was certain those guilty would have been punished most severely. For this reason, the guards turned a blind eye to the other goings-on in the village, regarding supplying the prisoners with food. In all, everything proceeded well in the village, provided the quotas were fulfilled.

There were many instances such as these where rules were broken, but, despite this, the end results were achieved to a reasonable satisfaction. Frank and Eddie realised whatever the future held for them; it was going to be grim. The war between the French and Vietminh was destined to carry on for many months, if not years. Considering this, how many years could they endure their present treatment. Living on starvation rations and being worked until they dropped was inevitable, unless they did something to prevent it – what, they had no idea. Apparently, the other two in their foursome had ideas of their own about how to make an escape and were currently in the process of putting their plan into operation... Or *execution*.

Jorge and Paddy had dug the graves which were ready to receive their occupants. The bodies of the two prisoners who'd died during the night were placed alongside their intended last resting place. Jorge, as usual, insisted on saying a little prayer for the departed, in which the two guards always participated. "Our Heavenly Father, please receive into your care, the remains of those recently departed, and give them eternal peace," lamented Jorge in his Sunday morning sermon's tone, whilst looking around a little nervously at his congregation of two. "They have sinned, but now seek repentance and forgiveness of your infinite mercy…" he continued, still droning on, but in reality, reading the last rites of the two guards deep in prayer. "For what they are about to receive… Please forgive me, Lord."

After this, he lifted his spade high above his head and, with one foul swoop, brought it down with such force on Brute, it split his head wide open, reaching where his neck joined the breastbone. The head had split in half, shattering the skull completely with bone fragments, blood, brains, and other bodily parts scattered all around. The other guard, Thug, on being covered with his comrade's brains, and scull fragments, was too stunned to react, before the spade, wielded by Jorge, took a huge side swipe at his neck, severing his head completely from his body. Paddy looked on at the spectacle in amazement and was too stunned to react immediately. Seeing the carnage on the ground his carefully sharpened spade had caused, he called out to Paddy, "For fuck's sake, 'urry up and get one of those bastards in a grave, and don't forget to bury his bleedin' head as well; I'll do the other one." Paddy swiftly went into action, dragging the headless body of the sadistic monster into one of the freshly dug graves, carefully placing the head in with it; then watched his comrade quickly inter the other.

Looking down at the body of Brute, lying in the grave, with its head split wide open, Paddy, in his laconic gallows humour, remarked to his comrade, "If ever the poor fucker wakes up, he'll have one hell of a splitting headache."

George afforded a little smile at his pal's remark, replying, "Yer correct, matey, and it'll take more than a couple of aspirins to fix the bleeder!" Both men looked at one another with huge grins on their faces, oblivious to the enormity of the grisly undertaking they'd just performed.

Once interred, the blood and gore-soaked earth was quickly shovelled on top of the corpses, leaving the ground relatively clear of the remnants of human remains. "Paddy," called out Jorge whilst nervously looking around, "shovel plenty of earth on his body and tread it down well; quickly now, for fuck's sake!" Jorge was beginning to lose his composure slightly now, realising if anyone should appear, he'd have one hell of a job explaining the situation and what had just occurred. After Paddy had covered the corpse with soil, Jorge suddenly remembered he hadn't searched them for anything which would help them whilst on the run; they quickly searched both bodies and found only cigarettes and matches, but nothing else, so they continued with their frantic shovelling.

Once the guards' bodies were covered over, it was now time to bury those of the prisoners who'd died in the night on top of them. Covered only in banana plant leaves, the men were laid to rest with slightly more reverence than the other grave's occupants. Both men even muttered a prayer before shovelling earth in to cover both bodies completely. With the four deceased well and truly interred and level with the ground, the extra soil was now piled up above them, forming a mound on each grave. Although Archimedes' principal referred to the buoyant force on an object being equal to the weight of the fluid it displaces, similarly, the extra soil dug out from the graves to accommodate those two guards recently dispatched, was equal to the volume and weight of their bodies. Unfortunately, Jorge and Paddy's education didn't include Archimedes' principal, or physics in general, which was about to cause a bit of a problem for the two gravediggers. This 'Eureka moment' became apparent when the graves were filled in, and they were left with a huge amount of extra soil; around three cubic meters. Not having time to address this unforeseen circumstance, they tried to hide the soil on other graves but not completely, leaving both fresh graves with an inordinate amount of soil covering them.

The operation both men performed with great expediency and proficiency left them with a clear run into the jungle, armed not only with a couple of spades and a meagre supply of food and water, but with two AK-47 semi-automatic rifles, compliments of the two departed guards. After crouching down and having one last look around, Jorge cast his eyes towards the sun to take a bearing and said to his mate Paddy, "Come on, pal, make 'aste and let's get the fuck outa 'ere!"

Chapter 37

Should We Stay or Should We Go?

There was much fervour and frenzied action inside the camp that evening. Two guards failed to show up for their evening briefing, and it was later discovered the prisoners they'd been guarding during the burial detail had disappeared along with them. The camp commandant, along with the political commissar, accompanied by half a dozen guards, burst into the prison compound, turning everything upside down. Pots of boiling water, along with rice meant for the evening meal, were kicked into the air just missing those who were attending them.

The guards herded all the prisoners onto the parade ground, where the roll call was held each morning. It was rare to have a roll call in the evening. One prisoner reacted to having his pan of boiling rice kicked into the air, and was rewarded with a whack on his head from a guard's rifle. Suddenly, the prisoners were held at gunpoint lest a riot broke out. All prisoners, including the sick, were ordered to attend the roll call; even the dying and dead were included in the evening count.

The result of this hurried parade revealed two prisoners were missing. After shouting out names from the register, the two who failed to answer were discovered to be Jorge and Paddy. Despite the camp being turned upside down whilst the prisoners were being counted, the search failed to discover the missing two.

There was much discussion between the commandant and the commissar as to where the missing pair spent the day. When it was discovered they were on the gravedigging detail, events moved outside to the makeshift cemetery, situated at the edge of the jungle. After having a look around and seeing two freshly dug graves, alongside two which had recently been filled in, two guards entered the prison compound and returned with Frank and Eddie.

"The reason why we are interested in you two," said the commissar, "is that you were acquaintances of the two missing prisoners. What do you know of their disappearance?"

Frank had to be very careful with his reply, knowing they'd both be punished severely if they were found to be lying. "I'm sorry Commissar, but although we did have a brief acquaintance with those two men, they never confided in us about anything such as a disappearance; unfortunately, we cannot help you."

The smartly dressed and well-manicured young commissar thought for a while, wondering if he was being told the truth. Usually, a whack across the head with a rifle butt followed such responses, but this young man was against brutality... Or so he maintained. His attention turned to the two recently filled-in graves, and the fresh soil on top. He asked the commandant who were in the graves, and after consulting with a guard, replied that two prisoners who died during the night were interred there.

"Well, let's dig them up to make sure!" he replied, beckoning the brothers to the graveside, whilst calling for two spades to be brought over.

The first impression the brothers had was that there seemed to be much more soil on the two recently filled-in graves, than on the others; quite an inordinate amount, thought Frank, who mentioned it quietly to his brother. After digging down about a couple of feet, the banana leaves covering the corpse on one body appeared. The same happened on the other grave. Lifting both bodies out of the graves and uncovering them, they were asked if they knew who they were. Eddie replied all he knew was they both died of cholera after suffering terribly due to its ghastly effects. The facial expressions on both corpses bore out the great suffering endured before death finally brought relief to the pair.

This description was a little distasteful for the fussy commissar, who, after peering into the empty graves, told Frank and Eddie to dig deeper. It had already crossed their minds that the bodies of the two guards could be underneath, and panic slowly set in. If the bodies of the two guards were discovered, there was a very good chance that retribution would be taken out on the prisoners, resulting in the slaughter of many.

Once more, fate played a hand in preventing this, when one of the watching guards fainted, after being confronted with the two dead bodies, and seeing the effect cholera had on their appearances. Feeling very queasy and finally dizzy, he passed out and fell headlong into the grave, where previously the cholera victim lay. Regaining consciousness only to find himself lying in the grave, he went berserk and had to be restrained. After pulling him out of the grave, Eddie asked if they should continue with the digging, hopeful they'd be told not to. "Just throw the bodies back inside and cover them... I've seen enough dead bodies today to last me; let's just get out of this place!" Fortunately, the commissar was feeling a little queasy too, and needed to be away from that place of death and dead bodies. This incident was too distasteful for his delicate disposition, leaving him feeling extremely sick.

Returning to the prison compound, the roll call was suspended until the following day, when the mysterious disappearances would be investigated once more. After being involved in the graveyard charade, between them, Frank and Eddie had worked out what transpired. "That soil underneath the dead man in the grave was loose, and I could have sworn I trod on something round in the centre, such as a football."

"Or even a head!" suggested Frank to his brother's remark.

"But how on earth could a head appear in the middle of a grave... Unless—" Without finishing his sentence, Eddie remembered Jorge telling his exploits of his term in Korea, where he decapitated a sniper with a shovel. Both men looked at one another, thinking the same thing, and realising the spades were missing as others had to be sent for. It didn't take much to piece together what had happened, and how close they all came to being executed in reprisal for two guards being killed... Had their bodies been discovered.

This incident brought home how close to death they all were. If they didn't succumb to one of the many prevalent diseases, or die of malnutrition, there was every chance a gun-happy guard could lay into them with a sub-machine gun in a fit of anger, for no apparent reason. They were, in fact, all under sentence of death, virtually living on 'death row'.

The following day, the roll call revealed nothing new about the disappearances, but left the atmosphere in the camp very hostile towards the prisoners, with frequent visits from the guards, behaving more aggressively than usual. The commissar spent more time in the compound interviewing men, one by one, hoping he'd learn something, but there was nothing to learn, as no one was privy to the intentions of the two missing inmates.

Food rations were held back or simply withheld completely, making what was a miserable existence, even more wretched as days and weeks passed. Beatings became more frequent, as the sadistic guards needed little or no reason to use their batons or rifle butts on the unsuspecting and innocent prisoners. Because of the reduction in an already meagre food allocation, men fell ill due to malnutrition and more died of starvation.

There were occasions when food was smuggled in by those able to procure it from a friendly villager, during an outside working detail's association with local farmers. These farmers received their foreign labour free of charge, but in return had quotas to fill to help feed the armies of Chairman Ho. If it wasn't for the extra food brought in by the outside working parties, many more men would have died of starvation.

Although many men died in the camp from hunger and related diseases, their places were filled by fresh prisoners who'd been captured during other battles fought between the French and Vietminh armies. It was from these newly captured men that news outside the prison filtered in, predominately on how the war was progressing... And it wasn't good. News such as this did much to depress the men even further, realising they would all die in the camp at some time or other. Little groups of men would meet in one of the huts to discuss escape, but Frank and Eddie had little to do with these meetings, knowing, if found out by the guards, it wouldn't take much to learn what had been discussed. If planning an escape was discovered, heads would roll... Quite literally.

An incident which occurred on a warm summer's evening was possibly the catalyst which helped bring about an escape attempt, which was known only to the brothers. Far from being ready, their plan needed more knowledge of the local area, as well as weapons... Or simply one weapon. The Vietnamese workers in the kitchens had a certain amount of sympathy with the prisoners. After seeing them in a state of semi-starvation on a regular basis, when they could, they emptied their garbage bins just outside the prison compound. They were safe in the knowledge it would quickly disappear, and before returning to their kitchens, it had been gathered up by the starving prisoners. On this occasion, a kitchen knife had inadvertently been thrown into one of the bins along with the food waste. It didn't take long to find this 8-inch knife and swiftly hide it away, believing the kitchen workers had done it purposely... But they hadn't.

Back in the kitchen, the head cook – who *wasn't* sympathetic to the prisoners – discovered his best knife was missing, and, realising it had been thrown out with the garbage and could be in the hands of the prisoners, alerted the guards. After turning the kitchen upside down, and beating the kitchen helpers mercilessly for effectively giving the food leftovers to the prisoners, they stormed over to the prison compound. All prisoners were made to form a line and stand to attention whilst the guards went about their search.

"If that bloody knife's discovered, some poor bastard will be for it!" said Eddie to his brother.

"Don't worry, kid... They won't find it!" replied Frank.

Eddie turned to him and asked, "Don't tell me you've learnt how to do a sword swallowing trick, and have it sticking down your gizzard?"

"Better than that," replied his brother, tapping the side of his nose.

The search finally ended, with a few of the men receiving beatings, presumably not for *not* knowing the whereabouts of the missing knife, but for satisfying the exasperation and failure of the guards to find it. When the heat died down and it became dark, Frank took his brother to where he'd hidden the offending kitchen utensil. Entering the hut where a man was dying of cholera, he gently rolled him over to reveal the top of the of the knife handle. After being given it by an excited prisoner, who didn't know what to do with it, Frank sauntered into the 'hospital' hut, and after rolling the sole occupant over, plunged the knife into the earth up to its handle. He pressed the protruding handle down with his boot, and before rolling the cholera victim back over, covered it over with earth. "That's where it stays until we need it; or until this poor bastard dies," whispered Frank whilst looking at the dying man, and thanking him for his help.

The knife incident gave Frank the weapon he'd need to get his escape plan into action. He knew when it was to be activated – up to a point – but needed the help of the other men, but was reticent to reveal it to them. Naturally, Eddie was fully briefed, and his input was invaluable to his brother, as he'd suggested items Frank overlooked. It was to be a do or die attempt, and many men, especially the new intake, would not be ready to make that decision at this early phase of their incarceration. On the other hand, most prisoners would jump at the chance to escape, whether or not they died in the attempt, which possibly they would.

"Okay, brother, now you've been filled in on all the details, what do you think; should we stay, or should we go?"

After hearing his brother's suggestion, Eddie replied, "If Jorge and Paddy can do it, so can we; let's get planning!"

Chapter 38

"Raise High the Black Flags, My Children!"

As the days and weeks passed inside the prison compound, there were no signs of the situation improving; in fact, they had worsened since the disappearance of two guards and the prisoners they were supervising. Had it not been for the queasiness of another guard and the delicate stomach of the political officer, it was certain the bodies of the missing Vietminh guards would have been discovered – one without his head. This discovery could have led to the deaths of many prisoners; reprisals would surely have been carried out by the vengeful Vietminh administrators, and their barbaric guards. Frank and Eddie realised their lives were hanging by a thread, as possibly, should an investigation be ordered by an official higher up in the command chain, it was certain the graves containing the missing guards would be exhumed, and their bodies discovered.

Prisoners fell ill with malaria, typhus and other diseases brought on by malnutrition; dengue and scrub typhus, along with weeping skin disorders, were other illnesses caused by insect bites, in particular, certain types of mosquitoes. There were no treatments for any of these illnesses, and the situation was compounded by the refusal to give sick men, who couldn't work, any food rations. The outstanding feature of all prisoners was their outward appearance; all had beards and scruffy, long hair. There were no washing or bathing facilities, and soap was unknown. Because of this, the men stunk profusely, and lice infested their clothes, making their bodies breeding grounds for disease.

More regularly than previously, prisoners would be taken from the compound and never seen again, when the sadistic guards played their deadly game of 'cat and mouse'. They were released into the jungle, one by one, only to be hunted down and slaughtered by their brutal tormentors. As previously, it was believed this barbaric act was to reduce the population of all sick prisoners, having no value to their captors and oppressors.

"We have to do something quite spectacular and do it very soon, before one of us takes ill and is used as sport by these savages," warned Frank as they toiled away in a paddy field far from the camp.

"Perhaps we should take some of the new guys into our confidence; we'll need some fit blokes to help get us out of there," suggested Eddie. The brothers spent most of their days planning an escape, or even a mass breakout, but needed weapons and the men to use them to achieve it... All they had so far was a discarded kitchen knife.

During the night of a heavy rainfall, Frank became ill. The heat of the day, along with the cold rain at night, caused him to develop a chill. Eddie was up all night keeping him warm, but to of no avail. "You'll have to do without me today bruv; I just don't feel well enough, I reckon I'm coming down with something." This caused much concern for his brother, as he didn't wish for him to be left in the camp at the mercy of the guards, who might use him for a deadly game of 'catch me if you can'.

Toiling away in the fields all day was bad enough, but the worry of his brother's welfare caused him much distress and concern. The march back to camp was followed by queueing for the measly rice ration distribution, which he'd have to split in half with his sick brother. Eddie was most downhearted as he waited his turn in the file of worn-out men, but his spirits were raised when he spotted his brother, walking around, helping others in the compound. He threw his arms around him as if greeting a long-lost friend, and Frank gave him a hug in return. "Thank the Lord, our kid, how are you feeling now?"

"Still a little weak, but hopefully what I had was just a chill, and with any luck I'll be okay in the morning, ready to do my share of the work." The brothers were overjoyed at the sudden turnaround in health of one of them, but once more, it brought home how vulnerable their situation was. "Whilst I've been wandering around the compound for most of the day, a foolhardy but risky plan formed in my head. It's most audacious, but realising how vulnerable we are, something drastic has to be done." Frank went on to acquaint his brother with the details of this 'most audacious plan', leaving him excited, and not at all concerned with the gravity of the consequences, should it go wrong. "Look, brother, it won't go wrong. If you think along those lines, worrying whether the plan will work or not, you are halfway to making it a failure. Be positive; we're getting out of here!"

"What, with just a fucking kitchen knife against a whole company of armed guards! Brother, I admire your courage and I'm completely in favour of anything that'll get us out o' this bleeding shithole. I for one, have had enough, and if I die trying, then so be it!"

"That's the spirit, my little brother, remember, if faith can move a mountain, having plenty of it will get us far away from here." The brothers' spirits had swiftly escalated from despair to optimism verging on exhilaration. They now had to enlist the aid of others in the compound with the same attitude they possessed… Which wasn't going to be easy.

Whilst this planning and high expectation was afoot, away from the attention of the unceasingly suspicious guards, an official enquiry was in progress at the headquarters of the Vietminh, concerning the whereabouts of the missing guards. It was suggested they could have deserted along with the two prisoners they were supervising. A delegation was assigned to investigate this strange disappearance, and many questions were left unanswered; especially the occupants of the last two graves which were being supervised by the missing guards. Some highly suspicious official was not convinced of the explanation he was given, and there was talk of him ordering the exhumation of all the recently dug graves, which numbered a good few. However, at that present time, as with all decisions made by committees, much agreement and discussion had to take place before the order was implemented.

In the prison compound, there was also a discussion in progress, where decisions had to be made concerning action needed regarding a breakout. There were altogether ten on the committee who were privy to the plan, but each knew if it was discovered, heads would roll once more. Time was running out and there was no 'Plan B' if 'Plan A' failed. "It's Saturday night or never, guys, if we do nothing by then, we are finished; but it will succeed as we are all of the same mind. We'll get away from this shithole, and kill as many of these murdering bastards as we can, in fact, we need to kill the lot of em!" Those listening to Frank's plan thought he'd gone a little crazy, but after giving it some thought, were in full agreement with what he suggested.

Reluctantly, because of his and his brother's weakness and failing health, Frank decided to hand the reins over to a recent American arrival named Mitch, who'd only been in the camp for a couple of weeks. He hated the Vietminh with a vengeance, and given the chance, he'd kill as many of them as he could.

Ephraim Mitchell was an American of Scottish ancestry. Hating his first name, he insisted on being called Mitch for short; a name that stuck with him. He fought during

WWII in the American army and reached the rank of sergeant first class. He distinguished himself in battle and was recommended for more than one medal for his bravery. His unfortunate demise occurred when, after battling through Germany towards the end of the conflict, his company came upon a Nazi concentration camp. What he and his men witnessed was unimaginable to fighting men. Entering the camp, they encountered dead bodies of inmates who'd been starved and tortured, then left to die where they dropped.

Not only did they encounter the emaciated bodies of men and women, but children too, dressed in rags, filthy and skeletal as if they hadn't eaten for weeks... Which, in fact, was the case. Mitch and his squad were put in charge of a group of SS camp guards, who tried to pass themselves off as inmates by dressing in the clothes of some of those who'd died. Obviously, they were soon found out as all of them were well fed and looked nothing like a concentration camp inmate. Whilst awaiting transportation to a POW camp, Mitch was guarding his prisoners when they began laughing and joking together. This incensed him so much that, after ignoring his warning to be quiet – which enraged him even more – he opened fire on them with his machine gun, killing two, and wounding the others. "That'll teach you, you evil bastards. Anyone else want to have another good laugh?" he called out to those who were still alive, but in a very bad way. He'd lowered his gun before opening fire on the crowd of prisoners, leaving them with injuries to their lower quarters, which were very painful indeed... As he'd intended.

For this instant but provoked act of retribution, brought on by the sight of so many dead bodies, starved to death by the SS guards, Mitch was immediately arrested and made a prisoner himself. He was given a military lawyer to defend him, who also informed his client he would serve time in Fort Leavenworth Correctional Facility in Kansas. When asked how long for, his lawyer mentioned five to ten years, as an example to any other servicemen who mistreated their prisoners. Mitch was aghast at this, and although he shot the prisoners on the spur of the moment, he and many others believed the punishment too severe.

Before being shipped back to the States, where he was to be court-martialled, some sympathisers – of whom there were many – helped him escape, and suggested he join the Foreign Legion. Mitch had plenty of help doing this, but was despaired to be in the company of SS soldiers also on the run, escaping justice as he was doing. He'd now learnt to control his hot temper and accepted the situation, realising it was better than serving time in an American military prison.

After serving five years in the Legion, which his contract required, he enjoyed it so much he signed up for another five. He'd been in many conflicts, finally being posted to French Indochina. It was whilst serving in Vietnam that he was captured by the Vietminh, and during the long march to the prison camp, he fell foul of the guards, suffering terribly after he'd punched one of them. Normally for attacking a guard, the punishment was death, but in Mitch's case, he got off lightly with a good beating and the confiscation of his boots.

The remainder of the march was endured barefoot, or with the occasional rag wrapped around his blistered feet. The rage boiled up inside him, realising he was now powerless, but swore terrible revenge on his tormentors when the time was right. Unknown to Mitch then, the time for retribution was fast approaching.

Looking for someone to take charge of the escape, Frank found the ideal candidate with Mitch. He was well built, not tall but stocky. Ginger-haired, with a beard to match now; he cut a fearless figure, capable of inflicting great harm on his enemies. After hearing Frank's plan, at first, he believed it unworkable, crazy, in fact, but the more he thought about it, the more it appealed to him. It would give him the opportunity to get his revenge on those who made him suffer during the long march to the prison camp after his capture; besides, he was a soldier, and a soldier's duty is to kill as many of the enemy as possible... Unless they are your prisoners. After going through the escape plan with Frank and some of the others, he asked specifically why it was necessary to carry out the escape on a Saturday, and why the Saturday approaching.

"Saturday night is when these over-sexed vermin search out the local womenfolk in the village of Cay Hoa. I've watched them previously getting tidied up and climbing into the Molotov trucks they keep just outside the camp perimeter. In all, around twenty of them pile in, leaving here before dusk and returning in the morning, mostly drunk and the worse for wear."

Mitch listened intently as Frank explained it all to him. "And how many guards are left in the camp to watch over us guys?" asked Mitch.

"I can't say exactly, but I reckon no more than ten. Of these, half a dozen will be in the guardroom where they eat, sleep, drink and play cards; so our old mate Jorge told us. He got a little pally with a couple of 'em, and in payment for their friendship, old Jorge bumped 'em off! But that's another story." Mitch was a little confused when he heard this, but Frank filled him in with the details, stressing why it was absolutely vital to make the break as soon as possible, with the likelihood that the graves could be exhumed.

"So, there's a possibility half of them will be in their guardroom, leaving the others patrolling the camp and keeping their eyes on us... Correct?"

"Correct!" replied Frank.

"So, we must take out all of these guys before their buddies return from their night on the town... Correct?"

"Dead on, my friend!" agreed Frank once more.

"All we need to do is knock off the guards who are patrolling our compound; take their weapons, boogie on down to the guardroom, kill the guys in there and steal *their* weapons, which we'll use to kill the rest of the bastards, and that's it! A cinch, and all we have is a fucking bread knife! You guys must be fucking nuts!" Mitch's response wasn't surprising to the brothers, but after going over it again with their new American friend, he told them, "Guys, your plan is that audacious and plain crazy... But I reckon it'll work!"

A new fervour sprang up in the camp with the decision to stage a full breakout. Not everyone was informed of the plan, but it was agreed by Mitch, who'd taken charge of the operation, that everyone must know the day before the actual plan was activated, which would be on a Saturday evening in just three days' time. Rehearsals of a kind were gone over, with Mitch choosing a team of six who'd mount the assault on the guardroom, after a suitable weapon was taken by force off whoever was guarding the compound.

Although the plan was simple, it relied upon circumstances beyond their control. They had to secure a weapon from a guard, which wouldn't be easy. Mitch volunteered for this task as his hate was still seething, remembering the beating he'd taken from them, along with the confiscation of his boots; the replacement of which came from the body of a dead comrade awaiting burial. The team of six who'd mount the initial action were from the recent arrivals who came in with Mitch a couple of weeks previously; these men were relatively healthy, compared to the long-term captives such as Frank and Eddie. A little strong-arm action would be needed, so Mitch gave his team plenty of coaching as well as encouragement. "Remember, you guys, we're at war with these bastards, so no going soft on anyone. Kill the fucking lot if you have to!"

It was decided, after surprising and killing those who'd returned from their Saturday soiree, the trucks they arrived in should not be damaged, as they were crucial to the escape plan. The whole camp would escape once it was secured. Those too ill to make it through the jungle would have a place in the trucks; around thirty inmates would benefit from this. The remainder would take to the jungle where they'd be guided by one of the Meo captives. Another Meo would guide the trucks far away from the camp and take the road towards Laos. Drivers and guides were appointed along with some of the men who were able to use a rifle, should they encounter resistance whilst on the escape road.

Mitch was in his element, and full of fire for the impending escape. His enthusiasm and drive were the forces needed to make this hare-brained plan work. He had the confidence and the vivacity to carry it out... Vengeance was his driving force, along with fortitude and determination.

The day of the breakout arrived; men were still having to work, but only in the morning as the lucky guards who'd been allotted places on the trucks to go into the village, needed time for preparation. These weekly outings had to be earned by a points system. Good performance warranted rewards, whereas bad performance at work earned nothing. It was a huge ploy by the Communist regime to keep their soldiers on their toes, by rewarding them for good conduct and devotion to duty, a type of competitive approach to their soldiering. They were paid starvation wages, but earned more if they showed promise and toed the line; and where would they spend their wages, why, in the village on a Saturday night's fling!

The village of Cay Hoa was in fact too small to be called a town, and too big to be classed as a village. Most residents were farmers growing mainly rice. There was a community of artisans who made shoes for the Vietminh army from old vehicle tyres. They were most durable for the long marches their wearers undertook, but very uncomfortable to wear. Old rubber tyres were very cheap to use as basic material, and required much skill in fashioning footwear from them.

Other manufacturers made the conically-shaped sedge or coolie hats out of straw. These too were sold to the VM army, but the payment given was most derisory, indeed no one dared question the price paid or indeed barter for a better payment... Especially in a Communist-administrated part of the country. The local girls earned their money from the prison camp guards, who came to town to spend their meagre wages on a Saturday night. There was even a local brothel sanctioned by the local council of the village. The economy ran quite well, considering the small amounts of money involved, but, after all, with a Communist-inspired authority, making a profit from one's neighbours was frowned upon, and those found guilty of profiteering faced a terrible punishment. Although the village had water and drainage, it lacked any communication such as telephones. Runners and passing peddlers were relied upon for news and deliveries of merchandise from outside the area. This village, or small township, was where the lucky guards would sample the delights of the local girls... And boys, on Saturday nights in the local bordello and at the late-night bars.

All was tense in the prisoners' compound, with every man aware of what was about to happen later. Naturally, there were those prisoners who didn't wish to escape, and participate in a forced march through the jungle to freedom! With a little cajoling and friendly threats from Mitch, they changed their minds... Grudgingly. "Okay, guys, zero hour is approaching; in a few hours' time, you'll either be free and escaping through the jungle, or dead! It's my intention to get us all out of here without any casualties, but I have a warning," continued Mitch with his pep talk and pre-battle instructions. "An old Legion officer told our squad, just before we went into battle with the fellagha, of something he'd read at school. 'No prisoners, no mercy, I'll shoot any man I see with pity in him.' These words were spoken by Prussian officer, Marshal Blucher, before leading his men into battle at Waterloo. I'm telling you guys now, if you get the chance, kill the bastards, all of 'em... Savvy?" Possibly this realistic no-nonsense approach to the forthcoming melee was what these men needed, and they couldn't have wished for a better commander to help them achieve it.

Darkness began to fall, and the two truckloads of merrymakers were well on their way to the village, where many pleasures awaited them. Their mood was buoyant, which prompted them to sing out loud; Communist songs of victory and defeating the wicked French in battle were the most popular. Once in the village centre, they dismounted the trucks and were given orders to be back at 6am for the return journey to camp; this would give them about 10 hours on the loose.

In the compound, all was prepared to implement the first and most important part of the escape plan, which entailed overpowering the guard and procuring his rifle.

The lookouts confirmed the departure of the trucks, and were eagerly looking out for the guard who'd spend most of his time patrolling the compound perimeter. "He's coming around to the front gate!" called out a watcher. "He'll stop for a smoke here, then throw his butt inside to watch us fight over it." This was how the repulsive guards got their entertainment, by throwing cigarette butts or pieces of food over the wire, whilst enjoying the havoc it caused between the prisoners.

Whilst the guard was having a smoke, Mitch was clambering through a gap in the bamboo fence they'd made earlier. He was outside now and could just about spot his prey. With the kitchen knife in his hand, and murder in his heart, he crept stealthily towards the guard who'd almost finished his smoke. Nearer and nearer he moved, until he was just feet away from him. The unsuspecting guard was about to flick his cigarette butt over the wire, when a slight movement from Mitch caused him to turn around. Seeing him approaching, holding out a huge knife, caused the guard to grab a hold of his rifle, which he'd leant against the gate of the compound. As he reached down to take hold, a prisoner inside the compound grabbed it through the wire, preventing him from snatching the rifle to defend himself. This split-second allowed Mitch to lunge forward with the knife, thrusting it directly into his heart. Grabbing him by the throat before he screamed, Mitch dragged him to the ground, withdrew the knife and stabbed his victim repeatedly in anger.

There was exhilaration at seeing this from those inside the camp, and it was soon suppressed by Frank and the others who now had to help Mitch drag the body of the dead guard inside the compound, lest one of his chums came looking for him. Once inside, the others asked Mitch where to hide the body. "In the shit pit... Head first!" called out Mitch as he wiped the blood from his hands and face. "Check his pockets first for cigarettes and the key to the gate."

With that done, they secured the rifle which an inmate cleverly grabbed a hold of and dragged under the fence. Finding the gate key before disposing of the body, they were now able to put part two of the plan into operation, which was for six of them to overpower the unsuspecting men in the guardroom. "Okay, guys, you know what I told you before, keep to the compound perimeter and follow me to the guardroom where we'll grab us a few rifles. I'll kick the door open and spray whoever's in there with a couple of short bursts, then you guys come in and grab a couple of their rifles. Huey, you wait outside and keep watch for anyone patrolling the perimeter, and keep it quiet! You ready, men... Let's go!"

Chapter 39

Breakout!

Back inside the compound, the prisoners were furtively carrying out Mitch's last orders before the assault on the guardroom. There was little they could do without weapons, and few would be able to use them even if given. Frank and Eddie were full of excitement, knowing the plan was in operation, but had to wait until they received guns, which Mitch and his assault team were about to acquire.

Now just outside the guardroom, with his lookout placed and the other men close behind, Mitch signalled his intention to spring open the door and burst in, whist checking the safety catch on his rifle was off. Taking a long deep breath, he leant back, bringing his right foot with him, then lunged forward giving the door such an enormous kick, it almost came off its hinges. Before the guards inside the hut realised what was happening, a hail of bullets accompanied the frenzied American's entry through the shattered door. Squeezing the trigger as he did so, Mitch fanned his rifle around, aiming at anything that moved. Four of the terrified guards died where they sat, as the deadly bullets from the

Kalashnikov tore into them. There were three others inside who had just enough time to jump away from the table, diving for cover under a bunk. Not wishing them to escape his wrath, Mitch fired again and again until his gun was empty. This gave the only guard who escaped the volley of gunfire a chance to reach for *his* gun. Before he could grab it from a rack on the wall, 'Mad Mitch' leapt at him, smashing his head with the rifle butt repeatedly until it resembled a crushed watermelon. Panting and almost out of breath, Mitch took another rifle off the rack, and emptied its magazine into those he'd already shot, just to make sure they were dead. There was no pity in this man's eyes, just anger and revenge. "Grab a fuckin' rifle quickly now, before any more o' them guards appear!" he called out to the men who followed him in.

"My God, look at all this blood and gore, it looks like a slaughterhouse in here!" said one of the men, staring in revulsion.

"You ain't seen nothin' yet, buddy, just let me loose on the rest o' them bastards, Old Mitch'll give the fuckers what for. Now grab a fuckin' gun and pass 'em out to the others!"

Each man had a gun now, and following their leader, went off in search of the remaining guards, who, for some reason, didn't respond to the previous gunfire. Not forgetting those left in the compound, the now fully-armed prisoners searched for more rifles, but had no luck finding any. Returning to the guardroom, Jacko, a young American, stepped over the bodies of the dead guards, and came across a door leading to a small room, which, in fact, was the camp arsenal. Apart from rifles and ammunition, Jacko discovered a rocket-propelled grenade launcher (RPG) with half a dozen rockets. Whilst looking around the room, he came upon a huge map of the area pinned to the wall above a radio transmitter (RT). Deciding to smash this radio would cut all communications with the Vietminh HQ, and prevent help being summoned during their escape. After using his rifle butt to destroy the transmitter, he carefully removed the map and slipped it inside his trousers. He was about to leave when he heard gunfire; Mitch and the others met with the other guards, and after a short gunfight, they emerged unscathed. Until now, all had gone well... Too well!

Now well-armed, the inmates did a circuit of the camp's inner and outer perimeters, making sure none of the guards had escaped the gunfight. Mitch, a master of organising and deployment, ensured any prisoner who could use a gun had one at his disposal. Whilst giving orders on what positions his men should adopt, one of them emerged from the cookhouse with two kitchen personnel, hands in the air, looking extremely frightened... They had cause to be. "I found these two in the cookhouse, hiding out of sight to avoid the fighting," called out their captor. "Both scared to death, they were trembling with fear, pleading with me not to shoot them," he continued whilst laughing out loud.

Mitch was furious. "I thought I ordered you guys to leave no one alive and kill anyone that moved. Now you bring me two prisoners that we'll have to deal with.

You found 'em, you fuckin kill 'em... NOW!" he bellowed angrily.

"Hang on, Mitch!" called out Frank, who'd been standing nearby. "These are the men from the kitchen who've been leaving us their garbage, and kept us going for all these months; we can't shoot the poor fuckers."

"What do you suggest?" replied Mitch, a little calmer now.

"Unless I'm wrong, these guys aren't Vietnamese, in fact, I believe they are Laotian, and no friends of the Vietminh!"

It later transpired, under interrogation, the two kitchen hands were in fact from Laos, and were pressed into service by the Viets under threats of death to their families if they refused. The Vietminh recruited many of their soldiers this way, which helped build up a sizeable army of men pressed into service, by threatening to kill their families if they refused. The two frightened kitchen hands told Frank and Mitch they hated the Communists, and volunteered to guide them through the jungle to safety if they spared their lives. After much discussion, Mitch agreed to this, but warned them they'd be shot if they tried any funny business. The escapers now had two qualified guides to lead them through the jungle, as well as the Meo prisoners from their compound.

At the Vietminh headquarters, the officials who'd intended to pay a visit to the camp regarding the missing guards and prisoners, were having difficulty contacting anyone. They tried to reach them by radio to inform them of their intended visit the following day, but to of no avail. Suspicions were aroused as there was absolutely no contact at all by radio and, as there was no other way to get in touch with the camp, it was decided to send a contingent of around a dozen men to discover the problem. They had no difficulty making contact previously, and combined with the suspicious disappearance of the guards, and now a complete radio malfunction, an earlier than planned visit to the camp was decided upon. It was late evening and getting close to midnight. If a truckload of men could be organised, they would reach the camp by early morning. It was close to eighty miles between both camps, but road conditions left much to be desired, and it wasn't easy to plan an estimated time of arrival.

Mitch, along with Frank and Eddie, were busy planning a 'surprise welcome' for the camp guards as they arrived back from an evening of debauchery in the local village. Knowing they'd possibly be the worst for drink when they arrived, was taken into consideration by 'master strategist', Mitch. Not wishing to have his 'ambush team' on permanent standby, he rehearsed the 'stake out' first to ensure all went to plan. His strategy was to wait until the headlights of the trucks could be seen far away in the distance, and then quickly take up battle stations. He had to consider most of his men were undernourished, suffering from malnutrition, and couldn't be on the alert for an undetermined amount of time.

Plans were afoot to stock up on food and water, along with any medical supplies they'd need for the two escape plans – one through the jungle and the other by road. Men were each given a task, as well as being allocated places on the two vehicles, which were yet to come into their possession – hopefully unscathed in the impending shoot-out.

Four men were stationed outside the camp, with orders to shoot any of the returning guards, should they decide not to stay and fight. Of these four, two would hide close to the main gate, and the other pair placed themselves on the perimeter. Mitch gave the men another of his pep talks before final battle positions were taken up, as there was no margin for error. "Make sure you've got plenty of ammo in them there guns, and, like I said before, shoot to kill, and give the bastards no mercy. I want to see everyone of them fuckers lying dead before we load up and git the fuck outa' here. Remember… No prisoners!"

The message had certainly got through to the little band of armed inmates, and with the constant geeing-up by Mitch, they were all out for blood and revenge. Remembering the friends and comrades who'd been murdered and tortured at the hands of these butchers, made them more determined to get their revenge. Men had their orders, and everyone was at the ready, waiting for the guards to return, which would be early morning. One of the inmates, after okaying it with Mitch, distributed food amongst their half-starved comrades, to fortify them for the coming battle.

The truck carrying twelve men, a driver and officer, left the Vietminh HQ around midnight, heading for the camp. They knew they'd have to pass through the village of Cay Hoa *en route* and would possibly make contact with some of the camp guards, who they knew would be engaged in rest and recouperation – of the horizontal kind. It was well known what went on at the weekends in these villages, and there was no intention of the top brass to end it. Now and again, a superior officer would visit the village, not only to inspect it to ensure rules were not being broken, but to participate in the activities as well. It was unlikely the contingent who arrived in the village would contact any guards, as they were preoccupied with other things.

When the truckload of VM soldiers arrived at the village at 4am, it was expected no one would be around to warn of the strange goings on at their camp. The officer in command left two of his men to warn them, as soon as any guards showed up. He then pressed on with the remainder of his troop, hoping to arrive at his destination around a half hour later.

Mitch had just about everything organised for his planned ambush and, after hearing a shout from his lookout perched high on the roof, called the men to take their action stations. "How far away are they?" he called to the lookout.

"About a half mile, but I can only see one truck," he shouted back.

This wasn't the news Mitch was hoping for, so he'd need to alter his plans. The truck neared the camp and pulled up; still being dark, the VM officer and ten men dismounted from it to investigate. They could see no guards about, and inside the camp one huge overhead light was shining down on the courtyard. The gates were open, so the men entered inside, their guns at the ready. Mitch and the others hadn't reckoned on this, assuming their intended victims would be unarmed and the worse for wear, arriving an hour or two later.

"Something's wrong here," said Frank, "it doesn't seem right."

"That don't matter, buddy, we're still gonna shoot the bastards anyhow!" he whispered back. With that, he waited until the officer and his men made an easy target of themselves, and opened fire, killing six but missing the others. These, along with the officer, were soon dispatched by two inmates up on the roof. Hearing the gunfire and seeing none of his comrades appear from the ambush, put the driver in a blind panic. He attempted to turn the truck around on the narrow track to escape, but this six-wheeled Russian-built juggernaut didn't respond to his efforts to make a three-point- turn. By doing so, it hit a tree and ended up in patch of soft ground, where his wheels just spun around, losing all traction. Now in an even bigger frenzy, he leapt out of the truck and ran down the road to escape, hopeful of meeting camp guards returning from their night out in the village.

Feeling very pleased with the result of his unplanned ambush, Mitch told his men to make sure all the enemy soldiers were dead. He took a group to search the truck to see if it was still serviceable, but discovered it needed to be pulled out of the soft ground where its wheels were stuck. Gathering branches and twigs from the jungle floor, and placing them under the wheels to enable traction, it wasn't long before it was back on hard ground, and completely serviceable once more. Had the panicking VM driver reversed the vehicle along the track to meet the wider road, he'd have been able to turn around. By panicking, he caused the Molotov truck to be completely unserviceable... To the delight of Mitch and his band. With the truck successfully removed from the soft ground, it was checked over and refuelled. This would carry half of the invalids and disabled to the border of Laos.

Some of the lesser bloodstained tunics, taken from the bodies of the VM soldiers, would be worn by the Meos. These men spoke Vietnamese, and would pose as Vietminh taking prisoners to a work camp, should they be stopped and questioned. All was arranged with food, water and medical supplies, plus guns and ammo, should they run into a fight. It was getting light now, and the sun was just climbing above the tree-covered mountain range... That which they needed to cross to enter Laos. The whole camp turned out to wish them God speed, realising they were heading for a perilous journey indeed, taking them out of Vietnam to the safety of Laos.

"Well, you guys, that's those poor unfortunates out of the way and on the road to freedom. God only knows what's waiting for us, as it's for certain those bastards back in that village have been put on full alert by now!" Unlike his usual optimistic attitude, he foresaw a gun battle looming, with half of his men unfit to fight a superior force.

Knowing what awaited them, some of the men approached Mitch, suggesting, as all was clear for the escape through the jungle, they should take the opportunity to breakout right away. Waiting for the guards to return and face a gunfight with them, would be taking too much of a chance. Apart from that, word would soon reach the Vietminh HQ concerning the massacre of their men by escaped prisoners, where they'd move heaven and earth to bring the killers to justice, and spare them no mercy when apprehended.

Mitch's concern was for those who he'd planned to evacuate by truck, which was still in the possession of the camp guards. If they decided to escape through the jungle without fighting for a truck, those disabled and sick men wouldn't make it.

"I'm sorry, Mitch, but those guys are in the minority, and half dead already; why should we stay here with the chance of getting killed, or worse still, recaptured and face God knows what sort of a death they'll have planned for us in revenge." It was one of the abler men, who had a lot of support from the others, who made this suggestion. This, to Mitch, seemed the most logical and obvious action to take; sacrificing those who wouldn't survive the jungle march, for the most able men, who had a very good chance of making it to freedom... If they left immediately. It was a difficult decision to make, as he didn't fancy the chances of survival for those unfortunates who'd stay behind, left to face the wrath of a very angry enemy.

"Okay, you guys, what you're suggesting makes sense; go now with my blessing and possibly the blessing of the poor bastards you've condemned to death!" responded Mitch, feeling very helpless indeed. "I will remain here with 'those poor bastards' and do the best I can for them, after all, it was me who promised they'd leave here in a truck. If they must die, I'll die with 'em." This dramatic and guilt-inducing retort from the self-appointed commander of the escapees brought dissent in the ranks, with arguments beginning to surface.

"Look, guys, whilst we are arguing whether to stay or go, those returning guards could arrive any minute now. Let's all fuck off while we have the chance!" The words spoken by the leader of the dissenters had hardly left his lips when a shout from the lookout still on the roof was about to put everyone in a turmoil.

"Trucks approaching... Two of 'em, and from the dust cloud they're making, they're coming at great speed!"

Chapter 40

Remember the Alamo!

Hearing the shout from the lookout, perched high on the roof of the commandant's quarters, sent a shiver down Mitch's spine at the thought of facing two truckloads of returning camp guards, in the knowledge they'd be well informed of the situation at the camp. Planning a surprise ambush to annihilate them, when returning the worse for wear after a night of sex and heavy drinking was one thing, confronting them when they had obviously been alerted as to the situation back at camp was something else.

Half the men hadn't the appetite for a straight gun battle, and the others were incapable of shooting a gun, or any other weapon. This was a situation he hadn't planned for. "Okay, Mitch, it's now or never. If we don't get a move on, we'll have lost the advantage!" called out Huey, one of those who suggested making their escape through the jungle before the guards returned.

"If you don't wanna stay and fight, just fuck off and take your buddies with you; we don't need you. NOW FUCK OFF!" called out Mitch, who was not only becoming very despondent, but angry too.

444

Whilst this exchange of angry words was underway, the two trucks had slowed down and came to a halt about 100 yards from the camp. An officer climbed out from the lead truck, accompanied by half a dozen weary-looking guards. Watching this, Mitch mused, "Here we go again; I feel that old *déjà vu* coming on."

Marching up to the gates – which were now shut – the officer called on the escapees to surrender and hand over their weapons. They'd not only been alerted from VM soldiers posted at the village, but received confirmation from the frightened truck driver who they met on the road, hurrying back to the village after seeing his comrades wiped out by the escapees. "Hand over your weapons now and surrender, or you'll all be executed immediately when reinforcements arrive from headquarters; they are on their way and will be here in a couple of hours." The officer was bluffing, as he had no means of contacting the HQ. "I will give you 15 minutes to make up your mind, after which we'll storm the gates and clamber over the walls. We will show no mercy!" With that, the officer turned around and marched his men back to their vehicle, awaiting an answer from the beleaguered prisoners.

To withstand a siege of the camp would be no easy feat. The entrance gates were high and could easily be defended. The surrounding perimeter was a mishmash of barbed wire, bamboo fencing, with trees and bushes. Mitch, being a lover of American history, compared his precarious position with that of the defenders of the Alamo in Texas, during the war with Mexico. In that siege, 200 Texian soldiers faced an army of almost 2000 well-armed and disciplined Mexican soldiers. The sixteen-day siege ended badly for the Texians, who were annihilated except for two men; one a black slave, the other a non-combatant.

Around a month later, at the battle of San Jacinto, General Sam Houston, commander of the Texian Army, rallied his men together while facing the Mexicans with the battle cry, 'Remember the Alamo', referring to how badly the Mexican Army treated their comrades.

"It ain't gonna go as badly for us as it went for them thar brave Texians!" vowed Mitch; although looking around at the sorry-looking bunch of defenders, he had second thoughts. He asked the man who found the camp arsenal about the armament's position, and how many guns and ammunitions could they depend on. "Jacko, what's the position with the guns in that arms stash you came upon?"

Jacko stroked his bearded chin and looking upwards, replied, "It looked pretty good, boss... Oh, and I came upon an RPG launcher with six rockets!"

"YOU FUCKIN' WELL WHAT?!" he shouted in exasperation. "YOU FOUND A BLOODY BAZOOKA AND YOU NEVER LET US KNOW?"

Poor Jacko felt a little disconcerted at Mitch's response and simply replied, "I didn't think we'd need it."

A little calmer now, the red-faced American spoke softly to the obviously upset and dejected Jacko, saying,

"Take someone with you, and bring the RPG launcher and whatever ammo you can find for it, and bring it out here... Savvy?" Jacko nodded his head, calling for one of his pals to help, returning a few minutes later with an RPG-7 rocket launcher and six rockets. Checking the ammo was correct for the launcher, Mitch told the men this was a game-changer. "We're in with a chance now," he told his little band of defenders.

Climbing up on the roof next to the lookout, the ex-GI sergeant sized up the situation. He had the weapons to destroy both vehicles, but needed one left intact to get his disabled and sick men to safety across the border – preferably the lead truck. These men could hardly walk, and Mitch felt it his duty to give them the best chance available to get them to safety. He could destroy one of the trucks, but must save the other at all costs.

Looking to where the vehicles had been parked up, Mitch calculated the distance as well as the trajectory needed to destroy one with a single shot. The lead truck was about 20 yards ahead of the other, carrying half of the returning guards, all looking very tired and in no fit state to fight. "Okay," whispered Mitch to himself, "imagine that's an SS Tiger tank out there, and you're resting a bazooka on your shoulder; your buddy has just rammed a rocket grenade up the spout, and you're ready to fire." Slowly going over the procedure he'd done so many times in Germany during the war, Mitch aimed the RPG directly at the rear vehicle, allowing for the angle. Then, slowly taking a deep breath and exhaling slowly, he squeezed the trigger, sending a rocket grenade directly to his target, where a direct hit blew it to pieces along with the unfortunate men inside.

The shock of this complete destruction of the Russian-built Molotov, along with the sight of men's bodies and body parts being propelled into the air, landing close to where they sat, sent complete panic amongst those in the lead truck; they feared the next round fired would be aimed at them. Leaping out of the truck in such a hysteria caused them to leave their weapons behind in the scramble to get away from that scene of horror as swiftly as they could.

"BULLSEYE!" called out Mitch, seeing the truck in flames, with the occupants of the one left intact scampering away down the track as quickly as they could, in absolute terror. "That'll teach you bastards to mess with Old Mitch; just look at ya scampering away like the cowards y'are!" Completely exhilarated by the experience, he decided to send another RPG after them, which he did, but aimed well ahead of the panic-stricken guards. Hearing the rocket whistling above their heads, sent the fleeing guards into greater hysteria, as they changed direction and headed into the jungle and safety.

Feeling most exhilarated, Mitch turned to the lookout who was enjoying the spectacle, saying, "I doubt very much we'll be seeing those guys any time soon; in fact, the speed they're running, I doubt we'll see them again… With any luck." Climbing down from the roof with the launcher across his shoulder and a rocket in his hand, he told his waiting men to bring the undamaged truck up to the entrance, and load those men who'd been allotted a seat on it to get aboard. Once more, the men chosen to 'ride shotgun' had a VM uniform and cap to help them through any checkpoints.

"Well done, Mitch, you played a blinder," said Frank, accompanied by the other men. "That really was a game-changer; with any luck we can all get going now lest any more VM arrive on the scene."

"If Messers Bowie, Crocket and Travis had one of them there RPGs at the Alamo, they'd as sure as hell given them there Mexican bastards a run for their money; in fact, they'd have wiped the bastards out to a man!" Everyone agreed to their leader's supposition, although many had no idea of what it was all about, but went along with it anyway, giving Mitch another big cheer.

"Okay, guys, no more moaning, groaning and messing around, we're all gonna get out o' this shithole and make it through to Laos. I don't wanna hear any more complaints, let's just do it... Savvy?" Their route would be through the jungle, however, having Meo guides would see them through the dense pathways. Having ample food, water and guns would make their journey away from the camp much easier and safer than the previous trip, when some had to march without boots, water, food or rest; not to mention the complete absence of medical supplies. With a map and half a dozen machetes, negotiating through the dense undergrowth would be much easier.

The ragged and sorry-looking band of escapees had a bigger task ahead of them than they realised. They numbered around forty, and none were up to this ordeal... Although their self-appointed leader vowed to get them to safety. They were told to exchange the filthy lice-ridden rags they'd been wearing for months on end, and after stripping the dead bodies scattered around them, find suitable VM uniforms, and wear those. Despite this, many men still had the lice clinging to them and couldn't shake the annoying parasites off. Each man had to carry his own water, food, guns and ammunition, but travel as lightly as he could. The fugitives were told the water would have to last until they found a clean source en route, which the Meo guide assured them they would.

They were warned by the guide of what perils awaited them in the jungle, apart from the obvious wild animals and snakes. Poisonous insects and types of mosquitos were prevalent, and all snakes should be treated as poisonous... As they were. The men were warned to beware of boa constrictors, which could creep up whilst one slept, and almost swallow a man whole. Wild animals which they may encounter were tigers, leopards and even bears. Giant scorpions and centipedes were to be looked out for and avoided as, if stung by one, their stings could prove fatal.

"Don't let this guy put the shits up you, fellas, he's only warning you about what you *may* come across, and not what you *will* encounter," interrupted their leader. If the men didn't have doubts about making it safely through the jungle before, they sure as hell did after hearing the warnings from the Meo guide.

"Okay, gentlemen," said Frank, after taking over from Mitch, "we have a journey of around 50 miles ahead of us. We need to average around five to eight miles a day to reach safety in approximately seven days. It'll be hard-going, and we need to keep pace with each other to make it through." He then spoke seriously, warning them, "If any man falls ill, he cannot depend on anyone to carry him, as we'll all have to look after ourselves. So good luck, fellas, and may God be with us all."

Mitch took over the lead now, with Frank and Eddie at the rear. His imaginative role of defender of the Alamo changed dramatically to that of Moses leading the Israelites out of Egypt. "Let's hope the Egyptian Army ain't hot on our heels like they were chasing old Moses and his band," he muttered to himself. His supposition could not have been more accurate.

Upon eventually hearing the news of the slaughter of so many of their men, enabling the prisoners to escape, the top brass at Vietminh HQ were absolutely livid... To put it mildly. Two truckloads of their crack soldiers, forty men and two officers, along with two expert trackers, were dispatched to the scene of the slaughter, with orders to capture and bring the perpetrators back for execution – after being tortured – or not to return at all. If they failed it, would be the pursuers facing execution instead.

Arriving at the scene of the slaughter, and seeing the dead bodies stripped of their clothes, made the officers determined to apprehend those responsible. The remains of the truck which suffered destruction from an RPG, along with the remains of the men inside, completely sickened everyone witnessing the devastation. After mustering up the people from the village to clear up the mess and bury the human remains, the two officers calculated how far ahead their prey would be. Seeing the remains of only one truck, they surmised the other two were used in the escape, which, by now, would see them safely across the border into Laos. However, despite this, they dispatched half of the men to go after them in one of the trucks. Possibly the escapers could have run out of fuel or had other mechanical problems, so there was a chance of catching up with them. When the trackers returned from searching the jungle, they affirmed a large party of men had chosen to take the jungle path and were about a day ahead of them. Calculations were made by the two VM officers, who believed the escapees would not be traveling at a swift pace because of their weak condition. If *their* men could travel twice as fast, there was a good chance of catching them up. Twenty of the best men, familiar with the jungle and its hazards, were kitted out and dispatched along with the two trackers travelling ahead. With Mitch and the band averaging five to eight miles daily, and their VM pursuers marching at twice their speed, there was a chance of catching them up in about four days... Or even sooner.

The hunted were now in a precarious position; their pursuers had a very good chance of catching them up, simply because of the speed they could travel through the jungle. Although they had a day's lead, this would soon be lost by their slow pace and weakened state, caused by their terrible time spent in the prison camp.

Those chasing them were crack soldiers, well fed, fit and healthy.

At first, the morale of the escapers was very good; they had food and water, as well as comradeship, with the possibility of being free men once they'd cleared the jungle. Their Meo guide was familiar with the pathways, but many were overgrown and had to be hacked away to clear them of the undergrowth. This was a benefit for the VMs, as they had a clear pathway courtesy of those they were hunting.

After the first day on the run, Mitch was pleased with the result. His men were making good progress but needed more rest breaks than he'd anticipated. Travelling through the jungle was a hot and sweaty experience for the men. The noises of birds chirping, with the buzzing of insects, along with the grunting and incessant squeaking of the monkeys took some getting used to. Being bitten by insects was most painful and unavoidable. The smell of rotting vegetation, fallen trees with brambles, rocks and dead undergrowth, slowed down the progress of the band of escapers.

Streams had to be crossed using rocks as stepping stones; these were most precarious for men who'd been deprived of food, whilst being worked half to death during long hours of captivity. Water was plentiful but food was running low. There were mangos and other exotic fruits, but eating too many of these caused diarrhoea, slowing the men down even more.

After about three days, Mitch made a calculation of how far they'd travelled, and was a little concerned.

He realised the Vietminh must have discovered the situation at the prison camp, and possibly were taking some form of action... What, he wasn't sure of. In three days, they'd travelled about 25 miles, which was reasonable, but the men were tiring and slowing down. If the 'Egyptian Army' was on their tail, there was no sign of them yet. If they did happen to catch up, would there be a 'parting of the Red Sea' to save them, as there was with Moses and the Israelites? This was only conjecture at present, but the possibility was likely. Those tired and weary men in the group were very much mistaken if they believed they were not being pursued.

Chapter 41

In Sight of the Promised Land

Halfway through their fourth day in the jungle, although relatively unscathed as far as injury was concerned – apart from various insect bites and bouts of diarrhoea – the band of escapers were becoming exhausted. Their Meo guide brought them to a clearing where they could be free of insects, with space to spread out and take a long rest. The thought of freshly brewed tea appealed to them immensely; a fire was soon burning with a pot of water at the ready.

As the men gathered round with their metal mugs, waiting to enjoy some of the stolen supplies from the camp kitchen, a familiar voice was heard coming from the perimeter of the clearing. "Milk and two sugars for us, me babbies, and a rich tea biscuit, if you 'ave one."

"My God… I know that bloody voice… It can't be!" called out Eddie in surprise. He suddenly leapt up to see his old comrade, followed by a group of men, emerging from the undergrowth.

"What the fuck are you lot doin' 'ere? You aughta be dead by now!" called out Jorge, who was leading the group.

"Well, thanks to you and Paddy, we nearly were!" replied the startled Eddie. He rushed over to his old comrade Jorge, and threw his arms around him, squeezing him tightly. Both men had tears in their eyes as they were joined by Frank, along with Paddy, who emerged from the group of men standing at the perimeter. Back-slapping and friendly punching took place as the old comrades celebrated their reunion.

"Well, you old bastard," said Frank, "are you gonna tell us what happened since you disappeared, along with those two guards?"

"All in good time, me old pal... At present, we've got bigger fish to fry," replied Jorge seriously. At that precise moment, two men from Jorge's group entered the clearing with a prisoner who they'd bound and gagged; he was a Vietminh tracker who'd been following Mitch's group for the last few miles. Under intense and painful interrogation with the threat of castration, the tracker revealed the main party of VM pursuers were only a couple of hours behind and were preparing a surprise attack on the group once he returned with Mitch's group's location.

"Well, we'll 'ave a surprise for them bastards instead," murmured Jorge, "now kill the little bastard!" The tracker was dragged away and swiftly 'dispatched'. "We don't take prisoners 'ere," he told Frank and the others, "they kill us, so we do the same to them!" Jorge, along with Paddy, were giving out the orders which were carried out unquestionably by the mixed band of followers he was leading.

A half-dozen of Jorge's men dragged along some huge nets and hauled them up the trees at the entrance to the clearing. After doing this, they sat up there and waited. Mitch and his men just stood and watched, completely bemused. Jorge told them all to get out of the way and sit to await instruction.

About an hour later, a couple more of Jorge's men scurried up with news that their enemy was nearby. Everything was set for the ambush, with orders to stand by for an attack, including Frank and the others. All was quiet, then, suddenly, around a dozen men appeared at the entrance of the clearing. They waited for the rest of their group to catch up and advanced with guns at the ready. Suddenly, out of the blue, the huge nets were released by the men in the treetops, completely surprising those below. As the nets landed on them, they became tangled up, struggling to get free but becoming more entangled in the process. Some managed not to be caught up in the trap but were gunned down by Jorge's men waiting in the undergrowth. Seeing the remainder of the trapped men completely tangled and unable to resist, the ambushers moved in and sprayed them with bullets, until there was no movement at all under the nets. The 'tree men' clambered down from their lofty perches and proceeded to drag the nets off the trapped bodies. There were no survivors, except a couple of badly wounded men who were immediately put out of their misery.

This wasn't the end of the episode. Immediately after it was confirmed all the trapped men were dead, a little army of old men, women and children appeared from out of the jungle, and descended upon the freshly killed bodies, proceeding to strip them bare of everything. Guns, uniforms, boots, underclothes and socks, in fact everything they wore and carried with them. It was a mind-boggling scene, equivalent to a shoal of hungry piranhas stripping to the bone the carcass of an animal who'd been unfortunate enough to fall into an Amazonian river, infested with these flesh-eating fish.

The dead bodies of Vietminh soldiers were dragged naked into the jungle to await being eaten by wild animals. Mitch, along with the rest of the group, couldn't believe their eyes. They were astounded, witnessing this macabre and well organised operation. The loot taken from the dead bodies, including arms, clothing and food items, were swiftly spirited away to await distribution to others who had need of them.

Seeing the bemused look on his guests' faces prompted Jorge to give an explanation. "You guys don't realise how lucky you are; this reception was meant for you, fellas!"

"How d'ya mean?" enquired Mitch.

"You lot were spotted a couple of days ago heading this way, wearing Vietminh uniforms, and carrying the weapons they use. We thought you were a troop of VM planning to raid one of the Meo villages, so we thought we'd plan a little surprise for you as the Meos have done many times before. Fortunately, one of our spotters noticed you were nearly all Europeans and believed you to be a partisan group. Our spotter noticed you being followed by VM and guessed you were escapees or summat like that." Jorge went on to explain his and Paddy's involvement in the group who planned the ambush. "Some of these men are partisans and villagers who we teamed up with," he went on. "After we went on the run, we came across these local natives who gave us food and shelter."

He described how the Meo villagers made them welcome, especially the womenfolk. There was a shortage of men in the village, as many had been killed by the VM, and others forced to join them, later to desert and join the partisans. It wasn't long before the partisans were contacted and asked the pair to join them in their guerrilla fight against the Communists. Jorge told of the attacks they'd made against their old enemy, and the fact prisoners weren't taken as they had no facilities to guard or feed them... So, they were simply killed; some were beheaded, others shot or bayonetted.

Jorge and Paddy frequently visited the village, where they had relationships with many of local womenfolk. "There'll be quite a few babbies born 'ere lookin' like me and Paddy," bragged Jorge, "we're in no hurry to leave this place; we both like it 'ere; love it, in fact!"

With the pleasantries done, the two groups – partisans and evaders – trekked to the local village, about a half hour's march away. After availing themselves of the villagers' hospitality, Jorge took Mitch, along with Frank and Eddie, to meet the local partisan commander who happened to be a corporal in the Foreign Legion.

He agreed to contact the airbase at Muong Sa where they had helicopters, as well as planes, and inform them of the situation. Once in Laos it would be another 60 miles before they reached the base, but a helicopter airlift could be a possibility. This was fantastic news for the sorry band of escapers, who were becoming wearier by the mile. There was a good way to go before they cleared danger in Vietnam and reached the relative safety of Laos. With the company of Jorge and Paddy, along with their troop of partisans, this journey wasn't as bad as expected. One or two incidents with wild creatures occurred en route, but nothing too bad to impede their progress. Whilst in contact with the commander of Muong Sa airbase, it was discovered the two truckloads of sick and disabled prisoners had arrived safely in Laos, and were met by members of the Legion, who escorted them to the airbase. There were confrontations at checkpoints out of Vietnam, but as the drivers and some others were dressed as Vietminh soldiers, as well as speaking Vietnamese, they managed to pull off the deception without any adverse incidents.

The problem arose as they were safely out of Vietnam, when they were seen by a French spotter aircraft, whose pilot, after seeing a Russian Molotov truck being driven by a soldier in VM uniform, believed the Vietminh were invading Laos. Luckily, the time taken for the fighter plane to arrive on the scene from the local airbase gave the escapers time to erect a white flag, made from a sheet covering one of the sick prisoners. Hearing the aircraft in the distance from the now parked up truck, the driver – minus his uniform – climbed on the truck roof and waved the banner furiously in the air.

The fighter pilot now believed it could be a truckload of Vietminh soldiers wishing to desert, so he held his fire and radioed for a reception party to come out to escort them in, whilst circling the truck to make sure. It was a happy ending when they were met and escorted to base by French soldiers.

Hearing these reports put the men's minds at rest. The occupants of the trucks, after arriving at the airbase, informed the authorities of other escapees travelling through the jungle. With this information, the French were alerted to the possibility of Mitch and his band arriving by foot and were able to meet up. The message from the partisan corporal confirmed this, so it wasn't long before the weary band were on their way to freedom.

There was another tearful parting between the 'famous four', with the vow to meet up again one day in the future. Jorge and Paddy were told to remain fighting with the partisans, which suited them perfectly. After arriving safely at Muong Sa, the escapees were flown to Hanoi for check-ups, and later to Sidi Bel Abbès, and finally to a military hospital in Paris, where they were given time to recuperate from their terrifying experiences.

Whilst in convalescence near Paris, Frank asked his brother what he thought would happen next. Would they have to serve the remainder of the five years they'd signed up for, with the possibility of being posted to Indochina again? His brother's succinct reply was the same as that spoken by Pygmalion's Eliza Doolittle, "Not bloody likely!"

Chapter 42

An Unexpected Confrontation

Many years later, after their amazing escape from the Vietnamese prison camp, whilst pursuing a career of professional hit men and botching up an assignment ordered by the Mafia, they were on the run once more. Whilst fleeing the scene, and taking a flight piloted by an aging and incompetent pilot, the brothers were recovering from this frightening and near fatal experience.

Arriving safely – but very distraught – at Luanda Airport, their main concern was to get away from reporters and TV crews, anxious to hear their version of what happened on the near disastrous flight. Unwilling to answer any questions, they took a conventional flight to Frankfurt, by way of Lufthansa Airways – much safer and less stressful than their previous journey.

They'd decided during the journey to fly to Geneva, where they would get a connection to the upmarket ski resort of Verbier. Here they'd lie low and take time out to plan their future; assuming they still had one, with so many nasty people after their blood. They had

a bank account in Zurich, so money wasn't a problem...
As yet!

When the skiing season came to an end, it was decided
that each should go their separate ways – to avoid being
recognised as a pair – and do whatever they'd always
fancied on retirement. Frank, who was very much into
art and paintings, decided to lease a shop in Geneva.
Not wishing to be far from each other, lest either's help
was needed. Eddie decided to rent a cottage over the
border in France. The village he chose was Saint-Pierre-
le-Chateau, situated up in the hills near to Annecy and
Bonneville, with lovely views of Mont Blanc, and
overlooked by a magnificent chateau. The village had a
beautiful, cobbled square, with a constant trickle of
water from a centrally situated fountain, surrounded by
red geraniums. Around this square, situated at intervals,
were a half-dozen cafes and restaurants, frequented by
the locals and tourists alike, who'd visit this little village
to avail themselves of its charm and magnificent views.

Eddie stumbled upon this hidden gem many years
previously, whilst tracking down a 'subject' he was
contracted to eliminate. Spending just one night there
was enough for him to fall in love with this pretty
village, and its rarefied atmosphere.

He soon adopted the regime peculiar to the village
regulars, namely, reading the newspaper whilst eating
freshly baked bread with butter and cherry jam; or,
occasionally, for breakfast he'd have croissants instead,
bought from the local boulangerie. After breakfast, he'd
challenge a local to a game of chess, or even dominoes,

if there were enough of them to engage in this typical English pub game. A little dog he'd adopted, named Scottie, was his constant companion, and followed his master everywhere. Walks in the forest behind his cottage in the morning were enchanting, especially in the early morning watching the mist rise from the valley below and evaporate as it reached higher ground.

This was all the retired assassin wished for, to live out the remainder of his life peacefully and without stress. To make things even better, he became friendly with the widowed owner of one of the restaurants. She had two children who'd left school and helped with their mum's business. They wished only for their mother's happiness, and were hopeful of her meeting someone to be more than a companion, perhaps a husband, possibly a man like Eddie!

After deserting from the Legion many years previously, the brothers made their way to Sicily, where they took refuge in their aunt's house. It wasn't long before the local Mafia became interested in the pair, and after discovering their father's connection with the Cosa Nostra, they were invited to join. Not wishing to seem ungrateful, the brothers graciously declined their offer, wishing only to operate on their own; but carefully added their intention to pay tribute to the organisation... Financially. There exists a special dispensation in Mafia circles, whereby, in certain cases, people wishing to work for them and not necessarily wishing to *join* the organisation, take the title of '*giovane de'honor*', or 'man of honour'. In effect, these men are simply associates and not 'soldiers' – the term used for Mafia killers and criminals.

A special meeting was held by Mafia hierarchy regarding the suggestion made by the brothers. Considering the work their father had done for the organisation during the war, the fact their grandfather was a born and raised Sicilian, and they went on the run after an honour killing of their father's murderers, it was decided to agree to their wishes, with the proviso they did 'work' for them when the occasion arose. This agreement suited the boys, as they were not constrained by Mafia rules – merely associate members – and were able to secure 'work' from them and pay tribute as agreed. This arrangement worked for many years, until they became involved with Diego Delgado, and the disastrous fiasco in Southern Africa.

This brought them up to present day, where they were still on the run and in hiding from the Mafia, with its deadly, far-reaching tentacles. All the brothers wished for was to be left alone to enjoy life, and spend what money they had – earnings from their murderous profession.

During breakfast one morning, Alain, who'd befriended Eddie, and knowing his brother had connections in the art world, asked a favour of him. It was a privilege to be accepted by the suspicious villagers, especially as Eddie's French had a strange accent, and they were not sure of his nationality. Giving them a breakdown of his travels – fictionally, of course – he managed to convince those who asked, that he was Swiss Italian, with English connections. Being baffled by the answer, his explanation was accepted, and nothing more was asked of his past. All that mattered was him being a thoroughly nice chap, and, seemingly, most trustworthy.

After breakfast, Alain asked Eddie to his cottage, where he had something interesting to show him. Climbing a ladder to the loft, they came across two old oil paintings covered in dust. After bringing them downstairs, Eddie was surprised at the signature on one of them and suggested to Alain he'd show them to his brother, based in Geneva.

Frank was extremely interested in the phone call he received from Eddie, and invited him to bring the paintings to his studio, where he'd arrange for an art expert to inspect them and verify the signature. After a couple of days, Eddie and Alain took the hazardous drive to Geneva, about 20 miles away. Driving carefully in his Fiat 500 motor car, with the paintings carefully placed on the rear seats, they arrived at Frank's studio 50 minutes later.

Frank welcomed them inside and introduced the pair to his colleague and art expert, Didier. Carefully unwrapping both paintings in a back room, Didier was surprised at their condition, but impressed by the signature on one; that of the village square with its fountain. The other of the chateau, bore no signature, but judging from the brushstrokes, pigment and general style, he deduced it was painted by the same artist, Claude Monet. Monet sometimes signed his work in pen or with a dry brush in legible cursive handwriting. The date usually followed the signature, and in this instance, it bore the year 1885. The great man painted hundreds, if not thousands, of pictures in his lifetime, and if he wasn't satisfied with the result, he'd destroy, or not bother to sign them. Didier assumed the painting of the chateau wasn't good enough to bear his signature but managed to escape destruction... Luckily.

After overcoming his shock and excitement, Didier affirmed both works of art were by the same artist, but in the art world, provenance was everything. He did, however, tell the three excited men that the signed painting could fetch up to three or four million dollars. He went on to inform them of clients who'd be willing to pay that much without the paintings going to auction, where a 25% commission charge would be levied. He and Frank agreed their commission on the private sale would amount to 10% each, being 20% in total. The remainder would go to the owner of the paintings. Alain agreed to this settlement and instructed Frank to go ahead with the sale. On hearing this, Didier was on the phone to America with the intention of lining up a private cash buyer and arrange for him to view the paintings in Geneva.

About a fortnight later, Eddie received a phone call from his brother, informing him the paintings had been sold for an amazing six million dollars; their share would be a tenth of this after Didier received his cut also. Rushing over to Alain's cottage, Eddie couldn't wait to give him the good news; he had quite a huge amount of money awaiting him in Geneva. Before making the trip to Frank's art studio, Alain was that pleased with the result, he told Eddie to take the other artists' sketches, paints, and easel with them, to give Frank as a token of his gratitude.

With a sizeable amount of cash now, along with the money they had already deposited in a Swiss bank, the brothers were financially secure, having no apparent money worries. All was going well, which motivated Eddie to propose to his lady friend, Louise, suggesting they waste no time in getting married, and spend their honeymoon on an island somewhere in the Caribbean. Louise was overjoyed with this suggestion, as were her two children, who urged her to accept the proposal, and be well taken care of in her twilight years. Naturally, Eddie was delighted when his proposal was accepted, and plans for a wedding were underway. He realised how lucky he was to be in such a fortunate position, and was looking forward to spending the future with the woman he'd fallen in love with.

Word got around the village of the difficulties the owner of the chateau and landlord of the village was having financially. He hadn't increased rents in his village properties for many years, and the elderly count was finding things difficult, especially as his chateau needed a huge amount of money to maintain it in good repair. He could see no way of raising the cash needed, so, reluctantly, he put the chateau, its estate and properties – including the village – up for sale. There didn't seem much chance of a purchaser coming forward soon, because of the liabilities a new buyer would have to contend with. The amount of money needed to repair and maintain the buildings in the village, as well as the chateau, was enormous. Believing no changes would occur immediately, the villagers relaxed, and weren't too concerned. Unfortunately, everything was to change, and the rent-paying villagers' fears were about to materialise... Very soon.

It was a pleasant autumn morning, which brought a slight chill to the village... In more ways than one! Eddie was engaged in a game of chess outside the restaurant, carefully planning his next move, when a bright red Ferrari sports car sped up to the square, screeching to a halt beside the fountain. Two well-dressed men got out, having a good look around as they did so. Shortly afterwards, a huge black limousine slowly rolled up, and parked behind the Ferrari. The two men walked up to the limousine, opened its rear passenger door, and helped an immaculately dressed, grey-haired gentleman out of the vehicle. Thanking his two aides whilst straightening himself up, he made his way to the restaurant, helped by the two assistants.

Those sitting outside the restaurant were extremely impressed at the entrance these men made, wondering who they could be – they were about to find out. Still pondering over his chess game, Eddie took no notice of what was going on, until his partner nudged him over the chess board. "Who do you think they can be?" he asked, nodding his head towards the three men walking towards them. Looking up from the chess board, Eddie's face changed suddenly, as he recognised the elderly gentleman to be Don Alfredo Martuccio – 'capo dei capi' – otherwise known as the godfather of the Cosa Nostra.

Walking towards where Eddie sat, he at first ignored the two men playing chess, but sensing one of them was staring at him, turned around to notice the pale face of Eddie, known to him as Eduardo. Both men's eyes met for a moment, bringing a wry smile to the face of the stranger. Eddie made no effort to acknowledge the man, but recognised the smile as the same one given to men who received the kiss of death shortly after.

It was obvious the don had recognised him, but not knowing what to do, remained at the chess board to hear an announcement made by one of his aides. He introduced the Mafia boss as Carlo Emanuele, Duke of Montebello, or simply Duke Carlo for short. This title had obviously died out many years ago, but revitalised and purchased with a piece of land for a substantial amount of money.

The villagers were all impressed with this 'aristocrat' and even more so when they learned he was to be their new lord of the manor... Or chateau, in this case. Their main concern was rent increases to be levied by the new landlord. These anxieties were put to rest when they were informed by an aide that there would be no increases in rent for the near future. To celebrate the appointment of their new lord and master, they were all invited to drink to his health with the best champagne the house could offer.

Chilled bottles of champagne were brought out to the terrace, where everyone around was invited to toast Carlo Emanuele, and wish him health, happiness and a long life. Everyone seemed overjoyed with this change of landowner, and celebrated his generosity with the wine; except for Eddie, who thought his run of good luck had suddenly ended. Now, perhaps, he and Frank would be going on the run once more. The introduction, along with the free champagne and promise of no rent increases, gave way to a cheer, which was followed by another announcement of a huge party to be thrown by Duke Carlo, as soon as they were settled in. A calling card was posted at the restaurant, with a phone number for anyone who had queries or concerns regarding the change of landlord.

It had worked for the Mafia boss; everyone was on his side, and all were content... For the present. The duke took only a few sips of his wine, then bid farewell to his tenants until the grand party was held. With the help of his aides, he got back into his limousine, and amid the cheers and waving from his grateful tenants, was driven back to his new headquarters, the chateau.

Eddie couldn't wait to get to his cottage and make a phone call to his brother, giving him the bad news. As he stroked his little white Scottie, he wondered if they'd be parted from each other, as well as his new love, Louise.

There was a long pause after Eddie delivered news of the terrible events which had just occurred, and Frank's reply came in a very dry and croaky voice. "I thought it was too good to be true, and everything was going *so* well," whined Frank. "It looks as if we're going to hit the road very quickly, especially as the don has recognised you!"

"Not so fast, big brother," interrupted Eddie, "before we do anything rash, I suggest we go to the chateau and meet up with the don, face to face; throw ourselves at his mercy and ask what we can to put matters right with him and the American Mob. What do you think of *that*?"

"It's too big a decision to make right away, give me a few minutes and I'll ring you back later," suggested Frank. After five minutes, he rang back, agreeing to the proposition, adding he would accompany Eddie to see the Mafia boss, and try to reach a reasonable settlement. It was a big chance they were taking, as the crimes they'd help commit against the Mafia were unforgivable in their circles; extortion and deception just two of them.

A half hour later, after giving it much thought, Eddie rang the chateau, reading the number from the calling card left at the restaurant. He asked to make an appointment with Don Alfredo. "You'll have to be quick, as he'll be returning to Italy this evening," replied the voice on the other end.

"As soon as you can then... Please," said Eddie, wondering when his brother would arrive.

"Within the hour, then, but don't be late; the boss hates being kept waiting," came the response. Eddie put the phone down, believing he'd have to attend the meeting, on his own, but just as he was about to leave, Frank appeared outside the cottage in his Mercedes. He'd driven from Geneva straight away to be at his brother's side, when they'd face their nemesis, Don Alfredo.

"My God... I never expected to see you here this soon!" called out a surprised Eddie.

"As soon as I put the phone down, I decided to come up here to have a chat, face to face. I put my foot down and managed to do the journey in record time; around 35 minutes, allowing for traffic. I instructed my manageress to lock the salon up whenever she wished, so I'm all yours, kid brother."

Arriving at the chateau, two men were waiting at the huge iron gates, signalling them to stop and get out the car. Immediately, a long rod with mirrors attached was shoved under the car by one man, and the interior was searched by the other... Even under the bonnet. "Okay, you guys, follow me," instructed one of the guards after patting them down, looking for hidden guns.

Taking the long walk to the huge, impressive entrance of the chateau residence, stepping over building materials and paint tins, they once more underwent a search for guns. Ushered inside a reception area, they were told to wait until the don was ready to see them... They didn't have to wait long.

The large room they were finally led to was like nothing the brothers had seen before. Huge tapestries covered most of the walls, and enormous oil paintings of previous owners of the chateau covered those which didn't. Figurines and suits of armour were dotted around the corners of the room, and an enormous oak table was the centrepiece.

"Gentlemen, good to have your company once more, how do you like my latest acquisition?" The brothers registered their approval and were asked to sit down at the table. Whilst seated, a half-dozen armed guards entered the room and took their places, standing by the doors and windows. "Now, down to business. *I* know why you're here, *you* know why you're here, so let's not have any more small talk. You guys are in big trouble with our friends Stateside." The don then went on to say he'd been advised by his associates in the States to apprehend them both if ever they came his way, and deal with them as he wished. "At present, I'm not sure what to do with you," he said ominously whilst gazing over at the sinister-looking men standing by the door.

"But Padrino," pleaded Frank, addressing the Mafia boss by calling him 'godfather', "we were nothing to do with the failed attempt on that dictator's assassination, it was something we never planned on."

"I know all about the mess you made over there, and I'm fully acquainted with the details; I also know you pair never received any of the money your agent Delgado stole from the cartel in New York. Delgado told us of your innocence in the matter, and that you were not to blame. He confessed to us under 'persuasion' just before he *died*. What *we* must decide now is what to do with you two." The brothers began to feel a little queasy when they heard of DD's death, wondering if they'd meet the same fate. "I like and respect you two. I respect that the assassination of your papa's killer made you go on the run, but I don't agree with what you did in Africa... Going on the run, I mean."

For a man not known for wasting words, the don was really overdoing it on this occasion. The brothers wondered what punishment he had in store for them, and readied themselves for what was about to come. They knew about Mafia punishments and trembled at the thought.

Standing up from the table, and motioning the brothers to remain seated, a guard entered the room with a huge waterproof sheet, and proceeded to lay it across the floor. "That's it, bruv, we're well and truly fucked now, that sheet is to stop our blood making a mess on this expensive carpet."

The don gave them a strange look, realising the thoughts going through their heads. "No, no, you guys, that sheet ain't for you, we're having the decorators in and that's to prevent this irreplaceable carpet from being soiled. If we were going to shoot you guys, we'd take you down to the dungeon and do it there; or simply take you to the dungeon and leave you there... Forever."

Feeling sudden relief, but a little fear regarding the dungeon, the boys sighed. "*Grazie, mio padrino, grazie mille*," uttered a much relieved Eddie.

"As I said before, I like you guys and have a suggestion to make that will make everyone happy."

Oh my God, what's the old bastard gonna suggest? thought Frank.

"I'm gonna call our friends in the States and see if they'll agree to the proposal I'll make regarding your punishment. Now, what time is it in New York City?"

He left the room to make the call in private. The brothers were still a little apprehensive, wondering if the American Mafia would agree to whatever the don asked, and what he was going to suggest.

Half an hour later, their host reappeared with a huge smile on his sun-tanned face. "Guys, guess what, our Stateside buddies have just agreed to my suggestion, giving me *carte blanche* to do what I suggested." He looked toward the men standing by the doors and windows, beckoning them to leave, by a simple movement of his eyes. "Okay, fellas, here is the lowdown; they wanted me to rub the pair of you out for what you cost them over that Africa fuck up, but when they heard my suggestion, they went along with it. I got my men to clear out of the room cos I don't like 'em knowing too much, so listen carefully to my suggestion; remember your lives and future depend on it."

The brothers wondered if they'd ever know what was suggested, as he kept talking, but said nothing. "Please, Padrino, please tell us what we must do to settle this unfortunate rift we have with those who have been so good and kind with us in the past!" urged a patronising Frank, who was wondering where his guards had gone, and what they would return with. The boys were becoming more nervous than before.

"Right, you guys, this is the lowdown, you must pay back the two hundred and fifty grand your agent robbed from my associates." The brothers sat back in amazement, hearing this huge amount, knowing they could access it, but it would leave them very short of money.

"Okay, Padrino, how will we pay it to you?" asked Frank.

"Cash, of course, my boy, cash!" replied the don emphatically.

The pair had a whispered conversation about their financial status, finally agreeing to pay the cash from their Swiss account. "Please, *Capo dei Capi*," asked Frank in an even more patronising voice, but feeling relieved they'd both be off the hook, "will this be the final settlement, and will we cease to be enemies and become friends?"

"*Mio Dio*, that's just part of it. To be completely free, you'll have to pay interest on the money stolen, which is another two hundred and fifty grand; making a total of half a million dollars... To be paid by the end of the week," he replied in a more serious tone.

Hearing this, the boys almost fell off their chairs, realising they would be ruined if they had to pay the amount demanded. They had the first payment in their bank, but suddenly remembered the money earned from Frank's commission selling the two Monet paintings.

On the journey back to the cottage in the village, the brothers discussed their options. Arriving at the cottage, the pair went into more detail of what lay ahead, giving serious thought to how the settlement would change their lives. "If we pay the old bastard what he's asking, we'll be just about penniless," complained Eddie.

"But still alive and not looking over our shoulders for the rest of our lives," replied his brother, more upbeat.

"But what's to stop the murdering old bastard from taking the cash off us, and then dumping us both in one of the dungeons he'd mentioned! No one would really miss us, and if they did, they'd be too scared to mess with the Mafia!" cautioned Eddie.

"It's a chance we'll have to take. Although," Frank suggested, "what if we take a passenger with us; he won't be there for the handover but waiting in the car for our safe return."

Eddie thought for a while and once more cautioned Frank. "Look, our kid, if those Mafia bastards thought they had a witness, they'd bump off whoever it was without a second thought. No, we must see this through ourselves with no one else involved."

So, it was decided to go ahead with what the godfather suggested, praying he was a man of his word and respect their full cooperation. After making arrangements with the bank in Zurich a few days later, the brothers drove back to the chateau with the money. They'd already made an appointment with the don, who expected them at the time arranged. The routine was the same as on the previous visit, with mirrors placed under their car, as well as a thorough search of themselves and the huge briefcase they carried which held the money. They were accompanied once more to the great hall, where they didn't have long to wait until the man himself came to meet them with a huge smile, and both hands outstretched in a friendly greeting.

Seeing the huge briefcase strapped to Frank's wrist, the don gave an even bigger smile. "I see you have the money, fellas, is it all in order?" he spoke in a friendly but business-like manner.

"Of course, Padrino, exactly what we agreed on, a half a million US dollars. Is that correct?" replied Frank, lifting his arm and showing the briefcase.

"Of course, I trust you guys, but I must count it first before we conclude our deal." Frank agreed and took out the key, removed the briefcase from his wrist, then handed it to the godfather after unlocking it. It was taken from the room by an aide to be counted. "Time for a drink, fellas, or are you in a rush to get away from here?" asked the don sarcastically.

"Thank you, Padrino, but we had a long drive from Zurich, and are anxious to get back; that is, of course, if you don't mind," said Eddie, wondering how his refusal would be taken.

"No, no, not at all, guys, as soon as I get the okay the money's all there, you can be on your way." Then, sinisterly, he added, "I can understand you not wanting to wait around, especially under these circumstances, but you will always be welcome here, and should you need help of any kind, please do not hesitate to call us" The last thing the brothers wanted was to have a social gathering there, but thanked their host anyway, for being so kind.

A man looking like an accountant entered the room. He walked up to the don and nodded that all was in order;

the money was correct. At this stage, the brothers' heartbeats reached an alarming rate, waiting for what was about to happen next, but when the don ushered them to a waiting aide beside the doorway, he bid them goodbye. The brothers still held their breaths with freedom and deliverance in site, when the don gave them an ominous reminder. "Just because you have paid the money back with interest, doesn't completely free you from our organisation. You are both a *giovane d'onore*, and can never be free from the Cosa Nostra. You have responsibilities to honour and must be free to be called upon to perform certain services for us when the occasion arises." This news shocked the brothers, realising they would never be free of the Mafia; but the caveat from the don was accompanied by a slightly happier adjunct. "We are a caring organisation and realise the hell you have gone through with that Foreign Legion thing, so don't worry too much about what I just said. Go ahead and enjoy your lives and remember the harsh lessons you have learned." The godfather closed the huge door behind him after waving the brothers off; he'd taken a liking to them... But not enough to release them from the financial debt.

The brothers were now free from the fear of being caught by the Mafia, and undergoing the torture prescribed to those who swindled and deceived them. They could get on with their lives now, hopefully unhindered, and able to settle down to their chosen retirements. Frank with his beloved art studio, and Eddie to married life and a well-earned honeymoon somewhere in the Caribbean; where, was yet to be decided.

Chapter 43

Back on the Run

With the surrender of the French garrison at Dien Bien Phu on May 4th 1954, after a four-month siege, the northern area of Vietnam was not a safe place to be. During the long hard and brutal siege, the French forces lost 2900 men killed, 5000 wounded, and 10998 captured and taken prisoner. It was a harsh and bloody conflict, and, although the Vietminh forces of General Vo Nguyen Giap suffered 23000 casualties, they went on to win the battle *and* the war.

The problem at the time was how the bulk of French forces in the north could withdraw from that area – based in the South Delta, which included their airbase in Hanoi – and avoid being captured by the victorious and bloodthirsty Vietminh. They not only had to plan a successful retreat, but had to do so with the minimum of losses to men and equipment.

A plan code-named 'Auverge' was drawn up and put into operation on Jun 15th. Most of the equipment and personnel travelled by boat along the waterways, ending up at the port of Haiphong, where ships were waiting to evacuate them to safety. It was an arduous task to perform, with Vietminh constantly attacking their rear as they made their way to the coast.

The whole exercise was over by the night of July 4th, when the entire force of 68000 men and civilians reached safety, with the loss of 38 dead and 129 wounded. The French forces saved most of the equipment they were forced to carry with them, preventing it from falling into the hands of the enemy.

The evacuation of regular forces was almost complete, but the 'forgotten army' of partisans, which included Jorge and Paddy, had to fend for themselves. The area where they were based could not have been more dangerous, as not only were the Vietminh scouring the area for them, but Chinese forces from just across the border joined in the search for the soldiers of the stranded army. Many encounters were met in the process, where the two pals strove to fend off both Chinese and Vietnamese pursuers. They'd already said farewell to their hosts, the Meos, who they lived, fought, slept and drank with, leaving them with as much of their equipment and money as they could. More than one or two young Meo ladies were most sad to watch their lovers depart, but both men left them with a 'reminder' of the romantic nights they had spent together... Especially Jorge.

Both men found travelling as a pair easier than being with a group of fleeing partisans, enabling them to hide and dodge their hunters. The whole place was scattered with Vietminh, who were engaged in mopping up pockets of fleeing French forces, or civilians who'd supported them.

Jorge and Paddy had maps, and could make out their position to a reasonable degree without being detected. They were heading southeast to the port of Da Nang, about a 300-mile march from where they were based. Having been trained by some of the best NCOs in the Legion, they were able to endure such a trek, which wasn't easy, even without being pursued by a vengeful enemy.

Jorge estimated the march would take them three weeks to arrive at the port where they were heading for, if they could average 20 miles a day. "That's what Napoleon's armies used to average," said Jorge with an air of knowledge, "and them blokes had to march to Russia and back!"

"How many miles was that then, old buddy?" asked his companion.

Jorge just shrugged his shoulders, saying, "Quite a bloody lot, I can tell you!"

They agreed not to return to the Legion, as they'd had enough killing and fighting, as well as dodging bullets constantly. It was certain they'd be called upon again to do some more dirty work for the French government if they *did* return, so they decided to desert. "Fuck the Foreign Legion, they've had enough out of me and I ain't goin' back. What about you me, old mate?" he asked Paddy.

"Whatever you do, I'll go along with," he answered. The two men had been through so much together that they became inseparable, and would do anything for each other, although Paddy had yet to tell his best pal the reason for joining the Legion. Jorge, on the other hand, always went on about his affair with the CO's wife, his trial, and his subsequent absconding after shackling two redcaps to a tree with their own handcuffs. The nights they spent on the march were always filled recalling events occurred in the past, but Paddy was always too reticent to make much of a contribution to their reminiscences.

After an exhausting three-week march, the intrepid two finally arrived at the port of Da Nang. By July 1954, it was decided by the UN that a demarcation line should be drawn across Vietnam, separating the north from the south. This line was known as the 17th parallel, which dissected the country; the north would be known as North Vietnam, with its capital of Hanoi, and South Vietnam, with its capital of Saigon. Later, other names were given to the two countries, but at the time, those given were accepted and referred to. Fortunately for our two absconders, Da Nang fell in the southern zone, and was a good way from the border with the north.

Jorge suggested to Paddy they get a passage to Hong Kong, which was not too far away, and a friendly British colony. He'd spent time there during his army days and had fond memories of the place. At the port, they told the authorities they were businessmen fleeing from the Communists in the north, and only managed to escape with the clothes they came in... Jungle camouflage combat kit. They claimed they were advised to wear these clothes to blend in with the jungle and would avoid being seen by their pursuers. Whether the man with the authorising stamp was ready to give them refugee status and believe their story didn't matter much. He had a long queue to attend to, with hundreds of people claiming asylum. The official merely stamped the papers, giving the intrepid pair free passage to the port of Kowloon in Hong Kong. "Paddy, me boy, I reckon we're on our way to freedom at last!"

The pair managed to get somewhere to settle down for the 500-sea mile journey, which would take the old steamer two and a half days to complete. There were plenty of people suffering seasickness on board, which didn't help, but the journey was nothing like the crossing they experienced sailing from Marseille to Oran, some months previously. "We're getting to be seasoned seagoers, Paddy, me boy," remarked Jorge. "If I had the money, I'd buy us a boat and we'd sail the world together... What do you say, me old mate?" Paddy never replied, he was fast asleep.

After a reasonably comfortable crossing of the South China Sea, the tired and weary passengers disembarked from the ferry in Kowloon and were met by immigration officials. Some passengers had papers and were sent on their way, many others did not, and were told to queue until an official could deal with them. Jorge pushed to the front of the line of forlorn passengers, as he and Paddy didn't fancy a long wait with screaming children and visibly upset adults, crying about losing everything to the Communists.

Amid the protests at their queue-jumping, which were ignored, they soon had the attention of an immigration official. Jorge once more went into his story of them being businessmen who were fleeing oppression and persecution from the Communist invaders, claiming asylum, and asking for financial help. After filling in several forms and asked many questions, the pair were driven in a bus, along with other British nationals, to the British embassy.

Here, once again, they were subjected to more questioning and form-filling, until at last they were given a six-month temporary passport, and an introduction to a bank where they eventually took out a loan – secured and guaranteed by the British embassy – to purchase a business in Kowloon. "By the way, gentlemen," asked the official as he handed them their passports, "how on earth did you come to be wearing those jungle clothes... With your beards you look as if you've been living in the jungle for a few months!" He gave a hearty laugh as he finally stamped their papers.

"That's quite funny, sir... Quite funny indeed... We'll have to visit a barber shop and a tailor before going to the bank. They'll think we're a couple of escaped convicts who've been living in the jungle. Thank you for your help, sir, especially the $100 you've advanced us; I'll make sure you are repaid," replied Jorge in his posh officer's voice.

After they'd visited a barber shop, as well as a bath house and tailor shop, the pair went off in search of the bank they'd been recommended. As previously, there were many questions asked, and more notice was taken of the answers, as the bank official didn't have a huge queue of applicants to attend to... So, Jorge had to be selective with his answers.

"You say you wish to open a bar here in Kowloon?"

"Yes, sir, correct," answered Jorge in his posh voice once more. They'd already decided upon opening a bar, as, during his time spent previously in Kowloon, Jorge and his pals always had difficulty getting a drink, as the bars were constantly full of tourists, sailors, and other service people.

Anxious to help this dispossessed pair of businessmen, who wished to begin again after being so cruelly robbed of everything they had, the bank official gave them the loan they'd asked for. With the loan guaranteed by the British embassy, there was no question of asking for security, as the applicants had been stripped of it by the insurgent Communists. Shaking their hands whilst handing them their bank book, chequebook and other documents, the jolly official wished them well, adding if there was more he could do for them, he was at their disposal.

Leaving the bank, Paddy asked his chum, "How the fuck did you get away with that, you old bastard? I've never known anyone who could spin a yarn as good as you can; you must have kissed the Blarney Stone sometime or other, you old blagger!"

"Paddy, me boy," replied Jorge, "we 'ave a sayin' in our neck o' the woods."

"And what would that be, me ald English pal?"

"If you can't blind 'em with brilliance, baffle 'em wi' bullshit... It never fails!" However, there were times in Jorge's eventful life when it did fail, but being a fighter, Jorge never gave up.

Strolling along by the harbour, the two pals paid special attention to the bars along the waterfront. "Bloody gold mines, Paddy, just look at 'em!" pointed out Jorge. Visiting not one, but two or three, Paddy asked an Irish bar owner how they could get into the trade. Being a little suspicious, and not wishing to ruin his own business, he suggested they pay a visit to an estate agent around the corner.

"Look out for yourself, me ald mate," called out the bar owner in a broad Dublin dialect, "there's empty premises along the front, where the proprietor went bust, thinking this trade was an easy one to make money. He soon found out otherwise, and did a moonlight flit owing money to everyone."

"Take no notice, Paddy, he's just trying to put us off, scared of the competition!" retorted Jorge. "Ignore the miserable bastard." Paddy wasn't so sure and let his pal know, but it wasn't long before he was on side again, listening to his pal's ideas.

Taking note of the bar owner's advice, they paid a visit to the letting agent whose office wasn't far from where they'd been looking. There were no bars or other food and drink premises for sale, or to let, the agent informed them, and was sorry he couldn't help. "What about the bar along the front where the owner did a runner, owing everyone money?" asked Jorge. Once more, he was dissuaded from renting those premises, as it had already failed and went into liquidation. Not allowing the agent to put him off, Jorge asked for a viewing. Picking up the keys and locking his premises, he took the pair of potential bar owners to view the deserted premises. The pair were most impressed, especially as it had been fitted out, and had a cellar as well as everything needed to make it a going concern. All it needed now was Jorge's unique magic touch... And a good supply of drinks.

The excited couple had a quick conversation with each other, finally and triumphantly saying, "We'll take it... As it is... Lock, stock and barrel... *Especially* the barrels!"

"You haven't even asked me how much the rent is!" stressed the agent.

Jorge replied with an almost threatening tone, "Well, you ain't exactly in a position to rob us, are you now?"

"Okay, I'll give you a fair price, and won't even charge extra for the living premises upstairs."

"What!" called out Jorge enthusiastically. "It comes with an apartment too?"

"Only a small one, but it has a couple of beds, as well as a kitchen," explained the agent.

"Let's get back and sign the papers, we want to get started right away," called out Paddy. They couldn't believe their luck, and the agent was true to his word, giving them a low rent, and overlooking the lease-signing fee, assuming it wouldn't be long before the business failed. He had no wish to go through a lengthy legal procedure once more, as the previous owner had left him with many problems. All he asked was a month's rent in advance, paid promptly on the first day of each month. The two pals couldn't wait to get started and immediately set about ordering beer, spirits and wine from local wholesalers, who were strongly advised by Jorge not to overcharge them, simply to appease their other customers.

Within a week, the bar had opened, well stocked, well fitted out and ready to go… All it needed were customers, who were very few in coming. Two weeks went by, and it became the same story, repeatedly. Whether the other bar owners had done something to put potential customers off, as possibly happened with the previous owner, no one knew. What Jorge did know was nobody would be allowed to interfere with their trade under any circumstances. "We need a plan, Paddy, me boy… A gimmick… And I reckon I might have just thought of one," declared the canny Englishman triumphantly.

He immediately got to work at the printers after paying a visit to the local entertainment agency. A couple of nights later, Jorge stood outside the bar, waving a wad of tickets, inviting passers-by to accept one, and have the first drink on the house. Entering the bar, customers were overcome with surprise to see a scantily clad female dancer, singing, dancing and performing on a hastily erected stage – built by Paddy – to the sounds of a trio of musicians, positioned behind her. Within an hour, the place was heaving with customers, queuing up outside to get in. The place was well and truly going at full pace, and the police were called to control the revellers.

After the first week, they did away with the free drinks token, as no inducement was needed to enter the bar. Revellers only wanted to enjoy the live music, *and* the exotic dancer. The young dancer asked Paddy to give her friend a job at the bar, to which he replied, "If she's half as good as you, sweetheart, she's got the job." And so it was, another gorgeous beauty joined the entertainment group, making it twice as good as before.

There were the usual complaints from the jealous competition, as well as objections from the police. However, Jorge, with his gift of calming things down, and promise of keep a lid on the revelries, managed to placate both parties by agreeing to recommend his customers visit the other bars, after they'd spent enough time – and money – in his and Paddy's.

Many servicemen frequented the bar – which they named simply as 'Paddy's Bar' – and enjoyed having a chat with its owners. Jorge too, loved the banter and joined in, telling of his exploits in Korea and Vietnam; careful not to reveal too much. During one particularly pleasant evening, a couple of squaddies asked Jorge if he missed the adventure of life in the services. Stroking his chin and thinking deeply, he told them he did. They, in turn, told of their plans after finishing their time in the British Army. Rather than sign on for another number of years on paltry service pay, they'd decided to serve as mercenaries to a foreign country. Apparently, good money could be earned in certain African countries, who needed well trained and experienced European ex-soldiers.

Jorge told them he wasn't interested, but they gave him the phone number of an agent based in Hong Kong, in case he changed his mind. He thanked them, and placed the piece of paper with the number on in his wallet, but never intended to use it; they were doing too well, and the last thing he needed was to don a uniform and take up arms once more.

After an unbelievable busy and profitable six months, the two bar owners had enough money to pay off their debt to the bank – which they did as soon as a meeting could be arranged. Whilst doing this, they paid a visit to the embassy, to thank them for their help and give them the good news of their whirlwind success. The embassy official was most pleased to hear this news from the two entrepreneurs, who, in return, had some good news for them... Their full-term passports had arrived, they were now *almost* citizens of Hong Kong.

Arriving back the bar, they popped open a bottle of their best champagne and celebrated with their staff of four, and the entertainers. Later, whilst on their own,

Jorge told Paddy they were going places, and wanted to open another bar. His partner agreed with him, they *were* going places.

One particularly busy evening in the bar, Jorge thought he recognised two British soldiers. Not wishing to be seen by them until he ascertained their identities, he slid into the backroom behind the bar and carefully scrutinised the pair. After suddenly recognising them, his heart began beating faster and he felt a numbness in his legs. *It can't be… It just can't fucking well be… No, it's not them!* he told himself. But after giving the pair a long look, he realised it *was* who he thought they were. They were dressed differently now, as last time he had dealings with them, they wore the uniform of those most hated of servicemen, the Redcaps! Jorge experienced a shudder in his body and a dryness in his throat. These were the men who'd tried, but failed, to take him to the army prison at Colchester to serve ten years hard labour for attacking a senior officer. When last he saw them, they were chained to a tree by their own handcuffs. Jorge outwitted them and stole their truck to make his getaway.

Here they were now, all these months later, in his bar. They had no stripes on their uniforms and weren't wearing red caps. They'd obviously been reduced to the ranks for failing to deliver their prisoner to serve his sentence, as well as losing equipment belonging to the Ministry of Defence.

Calling Paddy into the backroom, he quickly informed him of his fears, emphasising the two squaddies must not see him under any circumstances. Paddy agreed and told Jorge to make himself scarce. In conversation with the two ex-redcaps, Paddy managed to find out how long they would be in Kowloon. When he was told around a month or more, Paddy's heart sank too. After being informed by the pair they liked his bar, and intended spending lots of time there, poor Paddy despaired further.

"I knew this would fucking well happen one day, if it weren't these bastards, it'd be some other fuckers. We're well and truly shagged now; that's it, finished!" Jorge was certainly at no loss for expletives in expressing his feelings on this disastrous and most unhappy occasion. He told his partner he'd compromise his position, as well as his business, if he remained, with the chance of being recognised. Jorge must now leave his old friend and comrade, and disappear, before he was spotted and compelled to return to England to serve his time in prison. Paddy was having none of this, and reminded his pal that wherever he went, Paddy would follow. So that was the end of it; no discussion, no debate.

Their decision was unanimous; the bar would be sold – there would be no problem here as it was doing well, and other bar owners registered their interest to the partners when they saw how busy they were each night. So, after making approaches to one or two of them, a price was agreed, and the bank took care of the transaction. The bank manager was most surprised at the decision to sell but, agreed to see it through in their absence.

Remembering the discussion he'd had previously about being mercenaries, and locating the phone number that had been jotted down on a scrap of paper, Jorge gave the agent a ring and arranged an interview. There were vacancies for ex-soldiers, but only ex-NCOs were required for the latest assignment. Jorge managed to convince the agent they had both served as NCOs in the British and Irish Armies, and had lots of experience being in charge of men, as well as seeing plenty of action. Paddy told the agent he was an explosives expert, and with a little patter he'd learnt from his pal, managed to satisfy what the agent needed.

Not wishing to be too fussy, they were both accepted onto his books, but their positions had to be ratified by a representative of the employer, who happened to be the president of a small republic in Southern Africa. This distant country was in a poor state, and the standing army lacked training and discipline. Skills and expert training were needed, and the agent convinced the representative that Jorge and Paddy were the right men to instil discipline, as well as drill and train the reluctant soldiers.

Karanga was situated between Botswana and South Africa, with Namibia and Zimbabwe on either side. It was a republic ruled by an unelected president, who was more or less a dictator. The almost destitute country was propped up by donations from European countries, as well as other African neighbours. It was rich in minerals and had several of its copper and zinc mines in operation, but nowhere near the capacity to make it viable, or indeed profitable. Located near to the border with Botswana, was its only real *jewel* in the crown, namely a small diamond mine. Once more, this facility was under-exploited but did make profits – most of which were never used to improve the lives of its indigenous population.

The president of this impoverished country, or kingdom, as its president insisted on calling it, had several African wives, but none of them produced a male heir to the throne. Visiting England as a guest of the British government, the president fell in love and married a wealthy heiress, who insisted she was of royal blood, as her father was a count. The thought of gracing a throne in an African kingdom appealed to her, and she willingly accompanied her new husband back to Africa.

The countess – as she liked to be called – was not a woman of beauty – in fact, she was downright ugly. Her son, however, who was born about a year later, turned out to be a very handsome little child. He was sent to England and educated at Eton; later he took a place at Oxford University to read economics. The child was named by his mother as Prince Rufus, although the 'Prince' was a forename and not a title. During his time in England, he was known by friends and girlfriends alike as a prince, heir to a small African kingdom.

Being dark skinned – but not Black like his father – he grew up to be a swarthy-looking, handsome fellow; a hit with the ladies and a 'thoroughly decent chap' to his male friends. Prince Rufus did return home on occasions, but only when summoned by his father, who'd spent a lot of money on his education and living accommodation, and wished to see how his money had been spent. Rufus rented an apartment overlooking the River Thames near to the City, where he was offered an appointment as a merchant banker. The rent for this accommodation, as well as a generous monthly allowance, was paid by his father, who, in turn, received it from the British government as foreign aid.

All was going well for this dashing young man, who had everything most men could only dream of. The associations he'd made at Eton and Oxford developed into great friendships with people of class and money, who, in turn, loved the company of this 'Prince' and invited him to balls, garden parties and other upper crust gatherings.

Unfortunately, as with most things, a change was about to occur... A most dramatic change. He received a message from government officials, no less, that his mother and father had been assassinated during an uprising. Rufus was desperately urged to return to Africa and take over as head of state, and so restore normality. The British government did all they could to assist Rufus, as they feared his country could be taken over by Communist insurgents, as happened in other countries of that region.

Rufus was flown to Karanga by an RAF aircraft, but was advised that was as much as they could do, as the British government had no wish to get too involved with civil conflicts, and would only give verbal advice... And cash. Arriving at the airport, he was met by his father's military advisers, and shown to where his parents were lying in state, ready for their funerals, which needed to be implemented without too much delay, because of the oppressive heat at that time of year.

With his parents' funeral out of the way, Rufus was declared President of Karanga... But not King, as he'd imagined. Now the reprisals would begin. His army officers had imprisoned those believed to be responsible for the uprising, and under harsh interrogation and torture, they, in turn, revealed names of others in the revolt. These named by the informers were, in turn, interrogated, only to reveal more names. After questioning these suspects, a list of over two hundred names was compiled, all of whom were put on trial, and convicted of treason, along with murder and sedition, then sentenced to death. The manner in which the sentences were carried out was particularly gruesome, as instead of using a firing squad, half the condemned were hanged from trees, because gallows would take too long to erect. The deaths of the remaining unfortunates were beheadings, all carried out in public. The town square was packed, as spectators came from miles around to watch this gruesome and distasteful spectacle. Over two hundred executions took place that day, and the president and his military advisers hoped this would set an example to any who even thought of committing treason or insurrection.

With these executions out of the way – with many of those executed from his army – Rufus needed to overhaul his military, for fear of a reoccurrence. Into this bubbling cauldron of death, rebellion and conspiracy, entered Jorge and Paddy, ignorant of what had transpired previously, and clueless of what awaited them.

Chapter 44

The Diamond Mine

After being met at the airport and driven to the army barracks, both comrades were disturbed at the sight of dead bodies hanging from trees, as well as heads on spikes, placed at intervals leading to the main town of Barutu. The two pals just looked aghast, with Jorge uttering beneath his breath, "What the fuck's gone on, and what in God's name are we doing here?"

"I don't like it one bit, me ald mate, and if we had any sense at all, we'd get ourselves back to the airport and out of this godforsaken place, back to civilisation!" replied Paddy. However, it was too late, as the tiny aircraft which brought them from Botswana had just taken off. Finally arriving at the barracks, they were introduced to the other mercenaries responsible for training the standing army. They were a mixture of nationalities, and the senior of the group introduced himself, saying, "You guys must need the money pretty bad to come and work over here, it's an absolute shithole, with no one knowing who's who, and whether or not you're gonna get a bullet in the back any moment."

"If it's that bad, why the fuck are *you* here?" asked Jorge. "Our plane's just taken off for Botswana; you could have been on it if you wanted to!"

"I tell you what's keeping us here... $500 a month... That's why we are here!" answered the officer.

"Well stop your fucking moaning then and show us to our quarters... Sir!" replied Jorge sarcastically.

The mercenary officer showed the two pals to the bunkhouse, informing them the president would wish to see them immediately after they'd settled in. He then went on to inform the two of what had been going on, and why the bodies of the freshly hanged men were still dangling from the trees. "It's to show the peasants here what happens to anyone guilty of treason or murder... If the sight of those dead bodies doesn't put them off, then nothing will," said the officer.

After settling in, the two new recruits were summoned to the palace to meet their new employer, President Prince Rufus. Paddy's first impression of him was of a very dark Errol Flynn, with the manners and voice of David Niven... A veritable film star president. "Gentlemen, welcome to our humble little country, I trust you have made acquaintances with those other chappies down at the barracks?"

Not knowing how to address this imposing and remarkable-looking man, Jorge answered, "Yes, Your Highness." The president laughed at this and informed the pair they should address him as sir or President

Rufus and forget the prince for now. "Thank you, sir, we'll remember that." Rufus then went on to inform them of what had been going, on and why so many men had been hanged and decapitated after being tortured brutally. The sight of the bodies was, as the president explained in a well-known French phrase, *pour encourager les autres* – to encourage the others; or in this case, 'dis-encourage'.

He went on to tell them why he was at the palace, and not at his luxury apartment in London. The atmosphere in Karanga was very tense and he was relying on his army to maintain order, so guaranteeing his safety. He further went on – in confidence – to enlighten them of many serving officers in his army who were behind the plot, which resulted in his mother and father being assassinated. "After discovering many soldiers serving in the army were involved in the conspiracy, I am now suspicious of the lot of 'em. I just cannot trust anyone." He went on to give the reason for Jorge and Paddy being there. "I want you two to be my personal bodyguards... Day and night. You will be well paid with a bonus for discovering any attempt on my life. You will be provided with uniforms, and hold the rank of... Er, let me see... How about captain, or even major... That's it, you will both become majors, and therefore not overruled by anyone beneath that rank. How about that, superb or what?"

Both men agreed and, referring to being given such extremely high ranks, Jorge said, "This must be the fastest promotion ever given to anyone, living or dead.

Thank you very much, sir, from a sergeant to a major in one day must indeed be a record."

"Not at all, gentlemen, just to inform you, you'll be given quarters in the palace near to me as you are my bodyguards. To further celebrate your promotions, I wish for you to dine with me this evening amongst my other guests. Just be sure to change out of those scruffy civilian clothes and get your new uniforms from the quartermaster. He should have one or two spare major's uniforms, as we executed a couple just last week." He waited for the looks of shock on the men's faces to disappear and added, "Just joking, my friends, just joking."

The two men couldn't believe their luck, landing such a cushy job with good pay, excellent food and positions of high-ranking officers. They were, in the course of their duties, invited to many events, where outstanding food and drink were served, and they took it in turns abstaining from the overabundance of drink, as one of them had to be sober whilst on duty... Which was all day, every day. This arrangement was approved by the man they were guarding, and whilst serving the president, they encountered no hints of civil disobedience.

At his dinner parties, the president was always happy reciting quotes from famous people. '*Panem et circenses*' was one of his favourite Latin phrases – 'give them bread and circuses and they will never revolt'. He was referring to the second century Roman poet, Juvenal, who coined the phrase, implying that if the populace was entertained and well fed, they would have no wish to lose these two important base requirements, by entering into civil unrest. President Rufus took note of this, and ensured his populace had free bread, beer and tobacco. These commodities were supplied by his neighbours, who wished to remain on good terms with Karanga by ensuring the population was reasonably fed.

Since taking over the country, his father behaved tyrannically to the people, in particular the colonists from Europe who'd been there many years and ran most of the industries. They were made to quit their farms, and relinquish positions held in the mining industries. These were handed over to the indigenous population, who had no idea of how to operate the farms and mines, resulting in their decay. The country was blessed with copper, zinc, and tin mines, with the occasional gold or diamond mine. The countryside was perfect agricultural land for growing corn, wheat, tobacco, and other cereals. Unfortunately, as these were not operated in a profitable and professional manner, they simply stagnated beyond restoration.

As Rufus' father received much outside help from other countries, including many from Europe, he had no interest in taking advantage his own country's assets, and was happy with the *status quo*. Many banquets and feasts were held during the few months the two comrades spent there, and they were always invited in one capacity or another. President Rufus invited guests from other countries to attend, as it was a profitable way to remain friends with one's neighbours. The pair were not the only officers to attend these feasts, but other military officials were there frequently, availing themselves of the luxurious food and drink being served most lavishly.

One particularly cool afternoon, Jorge took the opportunity to have a walk around the town on his own for a change, without escorts. He changed into his civilian clothes as, for some reason, the sight of men in uniform tended to make the population a little uneasy. He'd been warned it was dangerous for soldiers to wander around the town unaccompanied, as there was always the possibility of being robbed, attacked, or even murdered. However, Jorge being Jorge, he decided to go alone and unarmed, except for packets of cigarettes, with sweets and chocolate for the kids.

Venturing through the backstreets, he was shocked and disgusted to see the conditions the ordinary folk had to endure on a day-to-day basis. Their living accommodation comprised of corrugated steel and tin-roofed shacks, perilously erected side by side to prop themselves up. In the centre of the dirt tracks between these hovels, flowed an open sewer. The stench was unbearable. Faeces, urine, sputum, dirty washing water and other disgusting liquids flowed side by side, becoming jammed together because of the unevenness of the track. At these points, it was impossible to remain for long, as the stink caused by the combined filthy mixture of these effluents, made it impossible to bear.

Pulling out his handkerchief whilst coughing and retching, Jorge couldn't get away fast enough, but the terrible smells lingered on his clothes a good while afterwards. Seeing a group of local kids – all dressed in rags – he pulled out the sweets and chocolate he'd brought with him and passed them around. He managed to attract an audience of similarly dressed adults, all giving him suspicious looks. These unfriendly stares soon melted away when he handed round the cigarettes. Leaving these wretched and dispossessed people to enjoy their sudden windfall, Jorge could venture no further. He returned to the palace a changed man. To think human beings had to survive in such appalling conditions whilst, nearby, the well-to-do of the townspeople lived in luxurious conditions. This was beyond all decency, and a crime against humanity. *Something has to change*, he told himself.

Whilst walking through the army barracks on his way to the palace, he was approached by the mercenary officer he met on his first day there. "A quick word with you, my brother, if I may," he said in a muffled voice. Leading Jorge to a quiet spot away from everyone, the visibly disturbed mercenary gave him some shocking news. The officer had been informed of an impending uprising about to occur within a couple of days. The revolt would be led by outside factions of well-armed and well-equipped soldiers, ready to take over this badly run country. By doing so, they would rid it of its incompetent president, and all his crooked followers. He went on to warn Jorge that all mercenaries and outside hangers-on were on the hit list, along with him and his buddy, Paddy. By being the president's bodyguard, they were lined up for execution. "So, my friend, you are welcome to join us within the hour as we have a plane lined up to fly us out of here. You'd be a fool to refuse!" warned the mercenary.

Not knowing whether to believe this alarming news or not, Jorge hurriedly made his way to the palace to inform his pal. After hearing his friend's account of the impending uprising, Paddy said to his pal, "It's sound like a load of bollocks to me; I reckon they just want us out of the way to steal our cushy jobs. Forget it, pal, it's all a load of crap." After hearing his chum's reaction and having further deliberation on the subject, Jorge was left believing it might *well* be a ruse to get them out of the way swiftly, perhaps even to make an attempt on the president's life. No, he was not going to be fooled by this preposterous supposition, and decided to ignore it, so he went in search of the president for further orders. It did occur to him he should inform the president of the rumour but thought better of it.

"Where have you been, I've been looking everywhere for you!" called out the president upon seeing Jorge.

"Sorry, President, but I went for a walk, and was waylaid on my way back by a colleague."

The president was very agitated and remonstrated with his bodyguard for not being available when his services were needed. "Close that bloody door, and make sure your firearm is handy!" he advised Jorge, in a quieter voice. "I've just heard a most disconcerting rumour which I cannot ignore." Checking the door and making sure no one was behind it, the president went on to inform Jorge of more or less the same story he'd been told by the mercenary officer. "These bastards want to do to me what they did to my parents, but the scum won't get the chance. There is something important I wish you and your colleague to do for me." Still a little nervous, the president continued to tell Jorge his plan, and the part he and Paddy would play in it. Noticing the civilian clothes his bodyguard was wearing, Rufus went on to say, "Perfect camouflage, your attire is ideal for the task I wish you to perform. Ask your colleague to do the same. Anyone in an officer's uniform is in great danger, so maintain those scruffy, dirty... And smelly clothes as a disguise."

Jorge was a little put out to hear his best 'civvies' described by the president as 'dirty and scruffy' once again but chose to ignore the remark. "Who'll guard you while we're away?" asked a concerned Jorge. The president answered, stating he had two trusted officers to take over as bodyguards in their absence.

He then buckled down to listen intently to what the president had to say. Nervously twitching and constantly looking around him, President Rufus continued. "I want you to listen most carefully to what I am about to discuss with you and say nothing to anyone except your colleague," he told Jorge, who was listening intently. The plan was for the two pals to load up a Land Rover 4x4 and drive 100 miles north to a village called Tanguto. Around five miles from there was located a small diamond mine, worked by local villagers and their children.

Of the three methods of mining in operation around that area, 'pipe mining' was used to extract the precious stones from the kimberlite, a diamond-bearing rock. Underground, two tunnels were dug horizontally, and parallel to each other. Connecting these tunnels, were vertically dug funnels, down which the mined rock was dropped from the top tunnel, into the one below, then carted along to be unloaded above ground. Here the rock was 'tumbled' in a type of rotating cement mixer and shovelled onto a huge flat iron table about a meter square, located just above the ground. To call the methods used here outdated would be an understatement, they were downright archaic.

Once the flat-bedded cast-iron table had its surface scattered with the spoil, an enormous flat hammer, fixed to a triangular support and dangling from a rope was dropped from a height of around 40 feet onto the table, crushing everything beneath it into small pieces. The huge 'drop hammer' was then raised to its full height, and its rope secured around a huge peg driven into the ground at an angle.

After this procedure, all the crushed rock was carted away, to be chipped individually with a hammer and chisel. The finished result of his operation was sometimes a quantity of various sized diamonds, but often, simply well-crushed pieces of rock.

This technique hadn't changed for decades, simply because it produced results. The daily or weekly yield of diamonds was locked away in a huge man-sized safe, where a key and combination – known only to the manager – was used to secure it. Each fortnight or so, a private plane arrived from Amsterdam with a diamond expert acting as agent for the president, who roughly graded the stones to industrial and gemstone grade. The ratio between the grades was always much higher for the industrial diamonds than that of the gemstones. A receipt was given to the mine manager, who in turn passed it on to the president... Secretly.

Of course, there was much pilfering at the mine, with the workers – mainly children because of the small size of the tunnels – using many ingenious methods of smuggling the diamonds out of the fenced and patrolled perimeter of the mine. The most common method of smuggling was to simply swallow a stone and wait for it to be passed through the smuggler's body – hopefully whilst he was at home. Another method was to insert the rough stone into the anus cavity and hope not to be searched there by the guards. Some boys cut themselves purposely and hid stones in the actual cut or bandage, depending upon size of the smuggled stone.

It was because of a disastrous smuggling operation our two comrades were sent to the mine. One little boy worker decided to insert a large diamond into his back passage before leaving for home. As the stone was large and hurt his little bottom badly, his itching and scratching of that area drew the attention of a watchful guard. He called the manager, who after inspection of the lad's rear passage, discovered the diamond, and proceeded to beat him mercilessly in front of the other workers. He did this to deter anyone caught smuggling, demonstrating the punishment they'd receive if caught. Unfortunately, the mine manager, a brute of a man, went too far; he lost control and beat the poor child to death.

The boy's body was carried to the village by his co-workers, where, upon seeing it, his parents and family went into a frenzy, vowing revenge. After becoming fired up on the local spirit brewed out there, they marched to the mine, ransacked it, and beat the mine manager to death with clubs and cudgels. Whilst this was occurring, the guards took shelter in their barricaded brick blockhouse, threatening to shoot anyone who came near.

Eventually, the riot quietened down as the villagers returned home with anything of value they could carry, including cigarettes and food taken from the frightened guards. It was a couple of weeks before everything began to return to normality, with President Rufus taking no action, preferring the mine to remain secret and avoiding all publicity of the beating to death of one of his key workers. Into this viper's nest of intrigue and mayhem once more, entered our two intrepid adventurers, Jorge and Paddy.

Chapter 45

Yet More Surprises

President Rufus was in a fluster as he gave Jorge his instructions for what he knew would be his last order as a president. Nervously looking out of the window, and pacing up and down with a pistol in his hand, gave the impression his days were numbered. Since he took over the role of president from his murdered father, he'd done nothing to improve the lives of the people, and continued to live the life of a Roman emperor, completely out of touch with the needs of the populace. It was because of this that another uprising was planned by the underprivileged, who sought and found outside help to overthrow the president, and install one who'd improve their lives.

President Rufus could see the writing on the wall and decided to make a run for it before he suffered the same fate as his parents. Hurriedly putting a finishing touch to some documents he'd drafted beforehand, he gave them to his most trusted bodyguard with instructions for their use.

He instructed Jorge and Paddy to go directly to the diamond mine and secure the stones which were safely locked away in the safe inside the blockhouse. With the safe combination and key given to them, they were instructed to ensure the stones were delivered to the agent, due to arrive in two days' time. He and Paddy would fly back to Amsterdam with the agent, who would then sell the stones on the Diamond Exchange. The money raised would be paid into a Swiss-numbered account in Zurich.

President Rufus would arrange a meeting with the pair at the Hotel Schweizerhof in Zurich, where they'd be paid off with an enormous bonus. "Oh yes, Major, before you leave the mine... I want you to blow it up, especially the entrance. If I am denied the diamonds inside, I'll make sure no one else can dig them out," said Rufus spitefully.

"What about the workers?" asked Jorge.

"Those thieving bastards... Fuck 'em!" he replied again spitefully. "Let the bastards starve!"

Jorge was taken aback with this attitude, but being a professional, went about doing as ordered by the man who was paying the wages. Shaking hands and giving him a strong hug, the president finished by saying, "I know I can rely on you two to ensure this task goes smoothly, and I'll make sure you are well looked after when we meet in Zurich. So, goodbye, my friend, and good luck." With that, Jorge scurried back to look for his chum, and make arrangements to drive to the diamond mine.

Following orders, a Land Rover had been loaded with supplies, as well as explosives to destroy the mine, making it impossible for anyone to dig the diamonds out. The appropriate machinery and equipment needed to do this was beyond the reach of anyone in the vicinity, except for a large organisation such as De Beers, who ran most of the diamond mining operations in the area.

After a hot and dusty drive on roads strewn with rocks, and pitted with potholes, as well as having to avoid wild animals roaming the plains, the two pals eventually arrived at Tangutu, a small village which hadn't changed in over a century. It wasn't as bad as the slums in the capital, but conditions were very basic, with a noticeable lack of rudimentary facilities. Most of their food was grown on plots of land just away from the village, and water was drawn from a centrally situated well. There were no visible signs of improvements made from the money earned from pilfered stones. In fact, the diamonds smuggled from the mine, fetched nothing like the price one would pay for an expertly cut and polished stone one could find in a high street store in New York or London. For example, a four-carat diamond priced at say $4,000, could be purchased from a smuggler for as little as $10, perhaps even less.

After asking directions to the mine, the pair arrived there just fifteen minutes later, only to be met by uncooperative attitudes, and suspicious stares from the guards and workers. It was futile showing the president's document giving them full power and authority over the mine's workings, as none of them could read. What

Paddy *did* was make friends with the child workers, by giving them sweets and biscuits, which the half-starved waifs gobbled down with great delight, having never eaten anything like them before in their short lives.

Jorge asked to see the safe in the blockhouse, and was grudgingly led there by a senior guard acting as deputy. The guard was told to wait outside, whilst Jorge opened the safe with the huge key, and combination given to him by the president. The strongbox inside the safe was filled with the rough, uncut stones, and Jorge had no idea of their value, but he guessed it must have been in the region of a million dollars... Perhaps more.

There were some which needed to be added to this treasure chest, as the safe hadn't been opened since the mine manager was murdered. Before closing the huge door, he noticed a pistol tucked behind the strongbox. Gently running his hands across its smooth features, he identified it as a Walther PPK, used by the German police. Finding its magazine to be full, he replaced it behind the strongbox. He now had to sort things out with the belligerent deputy, and the other guards who were anything but cooperative.

Paddy, being an explosives expert, was having a good look around the mine, deciding where to place the charges needed to seal the entrance. He still hadn't told his friend the reason he joined the Legion, for fear of ruining the excellent friendship they'd enjoyed together. As he was inspecting the mine workings, a shout rang out from a guard who was pointing to a cloud of dust, gradually increasing as it came nearer. Paddy strained his eyes in the direction of the dust cloud, and identified it as a vehicle racing towards them. He gave Jorge a shout as he'd just returned from the blockhouse, asking who he thought was in the vehicle. He didn't have long to wait. Before his pal could make out the occupants of the pickup truck, it pulled up just a few yards from the perimeter fence.

Gorgo, a giant of a man, leapt out from the passenger seat, followed by six others who were in the back; only the driver remained behind the wheel. "Who's in charge here?" he bellowed. "Where's the boss?" Just as Jorge stepped forward to ask him his business, two of the accompanying men leapt forward and grabbed him, forcing him to the ground. Paddy remained still; he could see they were outnumbered and outgunned.

Protesting loudly, poor Jorge was almost strangled by the thugs as Gorgo sauntered over and stamped a heavy boot on his neck, asking, "Who the fuck are you, white man? What are you doin' here?" He pressed his boot harder on his victim's neck.

"If you tell your goons to release me, I'll tell ya'. I can't do 'owt with you pressin' me bleedin' neck down, can I!" protested Jorge. Realising he wasn't going to get an answer with his victim pinned to the ground, Gorgo lifted his boot slightly and ordered his men to slacken their grip. Rubbing his sore neck and throat, Jorge went on to tell the intruders he and Paddy were working for the president as mine supervisors.

"That bastard's dead, so now you work for me... Get it, white man?" growled the giant as he informed Jorge he'd come to take charge of the diamonds, and wanted him to open the safe and hand them over.

How on earth did he know about the safe and the diamonds inside; more importantly, how did he know of the president's death? he thought to himself.

"I'll tell ya now, white man, if you don't hand 'em over pretty double quick," he said whilst looking around at Paddy, "I'll chop your fuckin' mate's head off. After that, I'll start on these little bastard kids here. You understand?"

Jorge understood all right, as this unwelcome and uninvited guest had all the information and was holding all the cards. Looking over at Paddy being restrained by two of the accompanying goons, he decided to acquiesce to the giant's request and open the safe, then perhaps do some sort of deal with him over his and Paddy's fate. "Okay, big man, guarantee our safety, and I'll open up for ya. How's that, big fella?"

"You ain't in no position to make deals, blondie," he replied, eyeing Jorge's long hair, almost resembling Tarzan. "Open up and I *may* let you go."

"Okay, if you put it like that, how can I refuse such a request?" replied 'Tarzan' as he led the way to the blockhouse, looking over towards his pal and giving him a huge wink along with a beaming smile. "Remember the gravediggers!" he shouted across, hoping Paddy understood. His long-time pal *did* understand, and wondered what old Jorge had up his sleeve, especially as he wasn't carrying a spade with him.

With a pistol in his hand, Gorgo and four of his men followed Jorge to the blockhouse, leaving two others and the driver at the mouth of the mine. Ordering two men to wait outside on guard, he entered inside with the others. Jorge faltered for a while pretending not to know the combination, but this tactic only annoyed the huge gang leader more. "Just get on with it, or I'll get the lads to give you a good punching!" he threatened. Having riled his oppressor up a little, Jorge dialled the combination number into the safe's control panel, turned the huge key, and opened it very slowly. No sooner had he opened the door and fetched out the strongbox, the huge brute grabbed it from Jorge's hands, giving him the chance to drop it to the ground, scattering the whole floor with diamonds of every shape and size as he did so.

Immediately, all three men dropped to their knees and began picking them up, leaving Jorge free to enter into his 'gravedigger routine', though instead of using a spade, he grabbed the pistol from the safe, clicked off the safety catch and fired two bullets each into the heads of the men scavenging on the floor. Their deaths were instantaneous, with the shots bringing in the others from outside to see what the commotion was. Being at the ready, Jorge waited for the two men to enter, and as soon as their attention turned to their comrades lying on the floor in pools of blood, they joined them, courtesy of the Walther PPK and the expert marksman firing it.

The shooting soon brought the remaining two ruffians scurrying up to the blockhouse to see what the commotion was about. Looking out of the window and checking his gun's magazine, Jorge was alarmed to discover there was only one bullet left. With the remaining two thugs almost at the door, he picked up Gorgo's pistol just as they entered. From a squatting position, he was able to open fire on them just before they levelled their guns at him, sending two more vicious thugs to their deaths. There remained just one left in the driving seat of the pickup. Fearing for their lives at the hands of the thugs, the mine guards decided to wade in and help, grabbing the driver from his cab, and savagely beat the poor fellow to death, with whatever they had at hand... Shovels and rocks.

Amidst all this carnage, with the floor covered in blood, and more oozing from the warm, but dead, bodies of the thugs lying on the floor, Jorge had to somehow scoop up the diamonds. With almost all soaked in blood, he struggled to replace them in the strongbox. The scene resembled that of a slaughterhouse, only instead of dead animals, there were dead humans scattered everywhere. Jorge was not at all affected; he'd witnessed death and destruction many times, and carried on with his task unperturbed.

After gathering up the diamonds and checking to make sure the bodies lying on the floor were dead – as indeed they were – he made his way back to the mine, amidst cheers from the guards and child workers. He dropped the strongbox onto the ground, and told the youngsters standing around, to fetch water and wash the fresh blood off the diamonds.

The president's death came as a shock, but he and Paddy had to finish the job in hand. They had a meeting with the guards and workers, informing them of a change in leader, and possibly working procedure. The acting manager had his position confirmed, and after getting rid of the bodies in the blockhouse as well as cleaning up the mess, he continued with the mining operations. Jorge instructed him to lock each day's production in the safe, after giving him the combination. "Do not pilfer any stones for yourselves, as the price you'll get will only be a fraction of their true worth. Wait for news of the change of leadership and follow their orders." He was determined to allow the mine to continue operating, despite the president's spiteful order to blow it up. He was more resolved to ensure the money earned from the stones went towards the welfare of the ordinary people, and not the high-ups.

Whatever it took, the people of Karanga would receive what was rightfully theirs; if Jorge had anything at all to do with it. A tall order, as there were many greedy, scheming people in that country, who'd stop at nothing to achieve their underhanded ambitions. Paddy, as usual, went along with Jorge's proposals, and offered to do whatever he could to ensure his pal would succeed in his tough undertaking. All they had to do was be ready to meet the plane due in from Amsterdam, and get the strongbox, along with themselves, on board, before more nasty incidents manifested themselves. If Gorgo and his brutes were fully aware of the diamond mine, and where the stones were kept, it was highly likely others did too. The safest thing now was to get out of the country as quickly as possible. Being the late president's bodyguards and emissaries would automatically qualify them to be on the hit list, possibly with prices on their heads.

All eyes were looking skywards for the sight of the aircraft which would take the pair to safety, along with a highly valuable cargo. The president's last words to them were to meet him at a hotel in Zurich. However, it was later discovered the president's last words on earth, as he was led away to face a firing squad, dramatically to the end, were from Dickens' novel, *A Tale of Two Cities*. As the young hero was led to the scaffold, he spoke these words most softly to himself, "It is a far, far better thing that I do, than I have ever done; it is a far, far better rest I go to than I have ever known." After being allowed to say his last words, President Rufus died ignominiously in a hail of bullets.

Back at the mine, the whirring sound of an aeroplane was heard; looking up, Jorge and Paddy recognised it to be the private plane from Amsterdam. After refuelling en route, the pilot and his crew wasted no time in turning the plane around to make their way back, after its two passengers were safely on board. They'd heard on their radio of another uprising, resulting in the president's death, and wasted no time in getting back into the air. Amid cheers from those below, the plane quickly disappeared into the distance, bound for Amsterdam and safety.

Those left below at the diamond mine not only had the pickup truck belonging to Gorgo and his thugs – whose bodies were dumped unceremoniously at the bottom of an old tunnel – but inherited the Land Rover and its contents, passed on to them by Jorge and Paddy.

Making themselves comfortable for the 5000-mile journey to Amsterdam, the intrepid pair acquainted themselves with their host, Jan Van Kloppen. After reading the letters of authority from the deceased president, giving the pair full power over his assets, including the bank in Zurich, Van Kloppen decided to get down to business. Opening the strongbox and examining its contents, he noticed some of the stones had blood on them. "How on earth did that get there?" remarked Jorge, sounding surprised. The agent simply carried on with his inspection of the stones, separating the industrial grades from the more valuable gemstones.

Explaining to Paddy, who asked the difference between the two, Van Kloppen told him gemstones had to be clear with no inclusions, and were to be cut and polished, to make them sparkle and shine. Coloured and opaque stones would not sparkle as the clear ones, and were only good for industrial uses, such as drills and saws which had to cut through stone or very hard surfaces.

Picking a couple of stones from the industrial pile, Jorge questioned the agent on why they were not good enough for gemstones. "Because they are coloured; pink, blue and yellow are unsuitable for cutting and polishing into gemstones."

When Jorge was a teenager back in his hometown of Bedworth, whilst sitting in the dentist's reception room waiting for a tooth to be removed, he flicked through a magazine which carried an article about diamond mining. Being unable to finish the article, he ripped the pages from the magazine and read them at home. Being a young miner, he was very interested in the article's content regarding diamonds and their true worth. "I reckon you're taking the piss out of us, mate!" exclaimed Jorge.

"Why on earth would I do that?" replied the agent, a little surprised.

"Cos these 'ere coloured stones are more valuable than them clear ones. I know because I've studied the subject and know all about the 'Cs'."

"What on earth do you mean by the, er, 'Cs'?" he replied haughtily.

"Cut, clarity, cracks, carbon, carats clearness and, of course, COLOUR! Especially canary yellow. One of the most sought-after colours, which command a very high price indeed." The agent knew the game was up, as there was no fooling old Jorge, so he'd have to admit what he was up to. "There's a sayin' where I come from, matey," said Jorge.

"And what, may I ask, would that be?" replied Van Kloppen again condescendingly.

"You can't kid a kidder!" replied Jorge triumphantly. "And don't you ever try to kid me, matey, cos I know what your little game is. You've been robbin' the people of Karanga for too long now, and the game is up! Get it?"

The gloves were off now, as Jorge and the Dutchman bargained and bartered over the value of the diamonds, past and present. To protect his good name and keep his reputation as an honourable diamond merchant and expert, he gave way to Jorge's demands, which included sharing some of the spoils with him, and keeping quiet about the Swiss bank account, its contents and who they belonged to. By the time the crew had refuelled four times, and landed at Schiphol Airport, Jorge and Paddy were very rich men. Parting company with his host and travelling companion, Jorge reminded him of their deal, and his expectation for Van Kloppen to honour it... Which he did.

After refreshing themselves at a hotel – with money advanced to them by Van Kloppen, they planned to fly to Zurich, where they discussed the numbered account with the bank president. Checking the letters of authorisation to be valid and proof enough of accessing the account, the boys were flabbergasted to discover how much was in there... Millions of dollars. Informing the bank of their intention to use most of this money to improve the lives of the people of Karanga, the bank's president informed them he'd do everything he could to assist them.

Jorge's plan was to wait until the situation in Karanga had improved, and things had settled down, before using some of the money to build social housing, schools, surgeries and improve sanitation. The new democratic government of the country lost no time in opening it up, with investments from outside to run the mines, and make the farmland suitable for crop growing once more. It seemed the socialist government really did have the welfare of its citizens at heart, which gave Jorge and Paddy the opportunity to provide the cash for much-needed infrastructure.

After a few years supervising the use of money to erect buildings, and not hand it out in cash, the two pals – even richer now, with interest earned from the money – decided to settle down somewhere they'd always dreamed of... The Caribbean. They chose Bermuda. They bought a house and lived together, but later noticed an opportunity to buy a run-down hotel and plough money into it.

They called it The Paradise Beach Hotel, and it soon built up a magnificent reputation for its luxurious rooms and suites. The pair loved running a hotel between them, and situated where it was, close to the pink sand beaches in Hamilton, the capital, it was given a five-star rating. Their hotel was now amongst other five-star hotels in the area, such as the Rosewood Bermuda and Hamilton Princess. Life, and position in life, could not have been better. Their philanthropic deeds and accomplishments in Africa not only improved the lives and living conditions for much of Karanga's population, but in doing so, gave the pair a great sense of achievement. Instead of simply handing huge amounts of money over, not knowing what use it would be put to – as other countries did – Jorge and Paddy were on site to organise matters, and insist upon having receipts to see how the money was spent.

One warm and sultry evening on the veranda of their house overlooking the ocean, the two friends sat there watching the sun disappear over a gold and orange sea, until it turned a dark blue, and finally black. Reflecting on their past, they realised how very lucky they were to have survived some of the near-death situations they'd found themselves in. How lucky, also, to have made this great, unbreakable friendship that withstood many ordeals.

In this reflective atmosphere, Paddy knew he had to tell his friend what provoked him to join the Legion. Jorge had already given his reasons – on many occasions – but Paddy's previous actions were not at all noble or praiseworthy. By confessing to his friend, he risked destroying their friendship, but honesty and decency had to prevail to sustain it.

As they sat together, drinking rum and cola, becoming slightly inebriated, Paddy began disclosing his sordid past and the crimes he'd committed. He was a member of a nationalist group in Northern Ireland... A terrorist, in fact. Jorge wasn't too happy hearing this, but urged Paddy to continue. He was in fact the bombmaker for the group, but never actually laid them in situ or held a rifle... He simply made bombs. An atrocity was planned to make a statement by the group, showing what they were capable of if their demands were not met by the government. A huge bomb was needed to make this 'statement' and Paddy had the task of assembling it. After discovering the bomb was to be placed under the stage of the assembly hall at a local school, and set to explode whilst the kids were singing hymns and saying prayers, sent shudders down Paddy's spine. Realising how much devastation and carnage it would cause, made him think again. He knew, if he refused, he would most likely be shot, and someone else would do the job, so he devised a plan. Because this bomb was bigger and more complicated than those used before, he insisted he should be the one to install and set the detonator.

The night before the planned atrocity, three men broke into the school, leaving Paddy to position the bomb and set its detonator. Everything done, the group of men returned to their normal activities and waited until morning. Paddy, however, was packing his suitcase and making plans to leave the country, and take shelter with family in France.

The bomb never did detonate, because the only man in the terrorist group with a conscience failed to set the detonator. Apart from that, Paddy phoned the police, who, in turn, closed the school and called the bomb squad to remove the device and make it safe. This action of the brave Irishman was considered treachery by his comrades, who ordered his immediate execution. It was this which motivated Paddy's move to join the Legion, to escape the wrath of the terrorist group, and in doing so, he met up with his bosom pal... Jorge.

"Well, matey, it's all in the open now, and you know what I've done in the past, so I don't blame you if you want to end our friendship," uttered a devastated Paddy, after confessing to his murderous activities.

Jorge was silent. He picked his glass up and walked away from his pal to the other end of the veranda and thought, whilst downing his drink. Finally, after being in deep thought for a short while, he walked up to Paddy, saying, "Those men and women in armaments factories build the guns and other killing apparatus, but don't necessarily use them to kill anyone; some other bugger has to do that! As far as I'm concerned, you ain't directly killed anyone – before you joined the Legion – so in my eyes you weren't a killer. Thanks for telling me all this, mate… it must have taken some courage."

"So, we are still mates then?" replied Paddy, his voice all a whimper.

"Of course we fucking well are, nawt will change that. We are mates to the end; 'til death us do part!" Jorge put his arms around his pal, gave him a big hug and began to weep, sobbing like a baby. Both men hugged and squeezed one another, with huge tears running down their craggy faces, with Jorge quipping, "We must stop doing this… If we don't watch out, we'll end up in bed together."

"As much as I like you, pal," replied Paddy seriously, "I hate to disappoint you, but you simply' ain't my type!"

With that, the crying suddenly changed to laughter, as both men realised the implications of their behaviour. The evening ended with both men reaffirming their friendship, and not ending it as one of them thought.

The following morning, Jorge and Paddy drove along the scenic coast road to the hotel, where they'd check on the following week's menus and guest list. What a lovely evening they both had, being so happy, now believing nothing could ever to spoil it. Paddy was busily looking through the lunch menu posted in reception, whilst Jorge was looking through the register at the new arrivals. He always anticipated seeing a famous person's name there, such as a film star, sports personality or even nobility. Looking down the list of names, he stopped suddenly feeling a huge shudder run down his spine. It was as if he'd just been hit by a thunderbolt. Reading the guests names once more, believing he was mistaken, it turned out to be the one he was dreading most.

Pulling his Panama hat down over his face, and looking carefully around, he called to his pal, "Hey, Paddy... Get your fuckin' suitcase packed... We're going away for a few weeks!"

"Where to, matey?" replied Paddy.

"I ain't decided yet, but I hear Africa calling... Come on, mate, we've no time to waste!" A most puzzled Paddy walked to the reception desk to see what had spooked poor Jorge. Seeing the hotel register open at the new arrivals page, he ran his fingers down it, looking for anyone of interest. Recalling one of the many stories his friend had told him, two names became apparent; they were Major and Mrs Tweedsmuir from Scotland.

Tired of having his wayward daughter living in his house after yet another messy divorce, her well-to-do father booked a two-week holiday at a five-star hotel in Bermuda... The Hotel Paradise Beach. Determined to get her back with the man he admired – Major

Tweedsmuir – he believed a two-week romantic holiday might hopefully do the trick, and repair their previous marriage. This, her father believed, might help dissipate the unpleasant memories of the brief affair she had with a certain soldier... Corporal George Stubbs.

Hurrying to find his pal, Paddy caught up with him in the kitchen, and told him he knew the reason for wanting to disappear for a while. They arranged for Paddy to remain at the hotel, whilst Jorge would get a flight to Africa, where he could be as far away as possible from the temptress and her ex-husband. He knew nothing of their divorce, or the fact he was found not guilty of the false charge made against him. What motivated Jorge to vanish for a while was the thought of ten years hard labour in an army military prison.

The story didn't end there; instead of the major and his ex-wife, Agnes, bonding together, it wasn't long before she went off with another man she met on the island... A Bermudian! He was older and richer than the major and lived in a beautiful house near Horseshoe Bay.

The hapless major returned home on his own to give the bad news to Agnes' father, who was secretly delighted to hear his daughter was to be married to a Bermudian, and would take up residence there. On his return to the island, Jorge knew nothing of this romance, nor did Paddy wish to tell him. However, being a small island, there was a good chance of the pair bumping into one another and, possibly, Jorge would discover he'd been on the run all those years... An innocent man. On the other hand, if an encounter between the two ex-lovers did occur, was there the slightest possibility of a continuance of their brief but eventful affair, so rudely interrupted, many years ago? No one could really guess the outcome of such a reunion but, knowing Jorge, who could say?

Bibliography

The Last Valley by Martin Windrow.

Legionnaire by Simon Murray.

Inside the Foreign Legion by John Parker.

The Making of a Legionnaire by Bill Paris.

Mafia Republic by John Dickie.

About the Author

Peter was born in Leamington Spa, Warwickshire, but spent his childhood in bomb damaged Coventry during the 1940s. His schooling was at The Coventry Technical School, and later Woodlands Comprehensive, where he studied foreign languages, including Latin. He also studied English literature and grammar, as his ambition was to be a journalist after leaving school. He never realised his ambition, as living in an engineering environment, he became a draughtsman instead.

He never lost his ambition to be a journalist, and later gained experience writing articles for the Coventry Telegraph, where many of his photographs were published; photography being his passion after writing.

Peter has also written many short stories, now awaiting publication. Depending upon the success of this, his second novel, he has two more in the pipeline, which he hopes to publish in the future. His advice to anyone is, *don't be afraid to take a gamble, especially if the odds are in your favour.*

Lightning Source UK Ltd.
Milton Keynes UK
UKHW040834250522
403501UK00003B/141